FAITH IN FLAMES

Book Two of The Dragons of Mother Stone

MELISSA MCSHANE

Cover design by MiblArt

Night Harbor Publishing

www.nightharborpublishing.com

For Aerin,
enthusiastic reader of other people's books
and beloved daughter

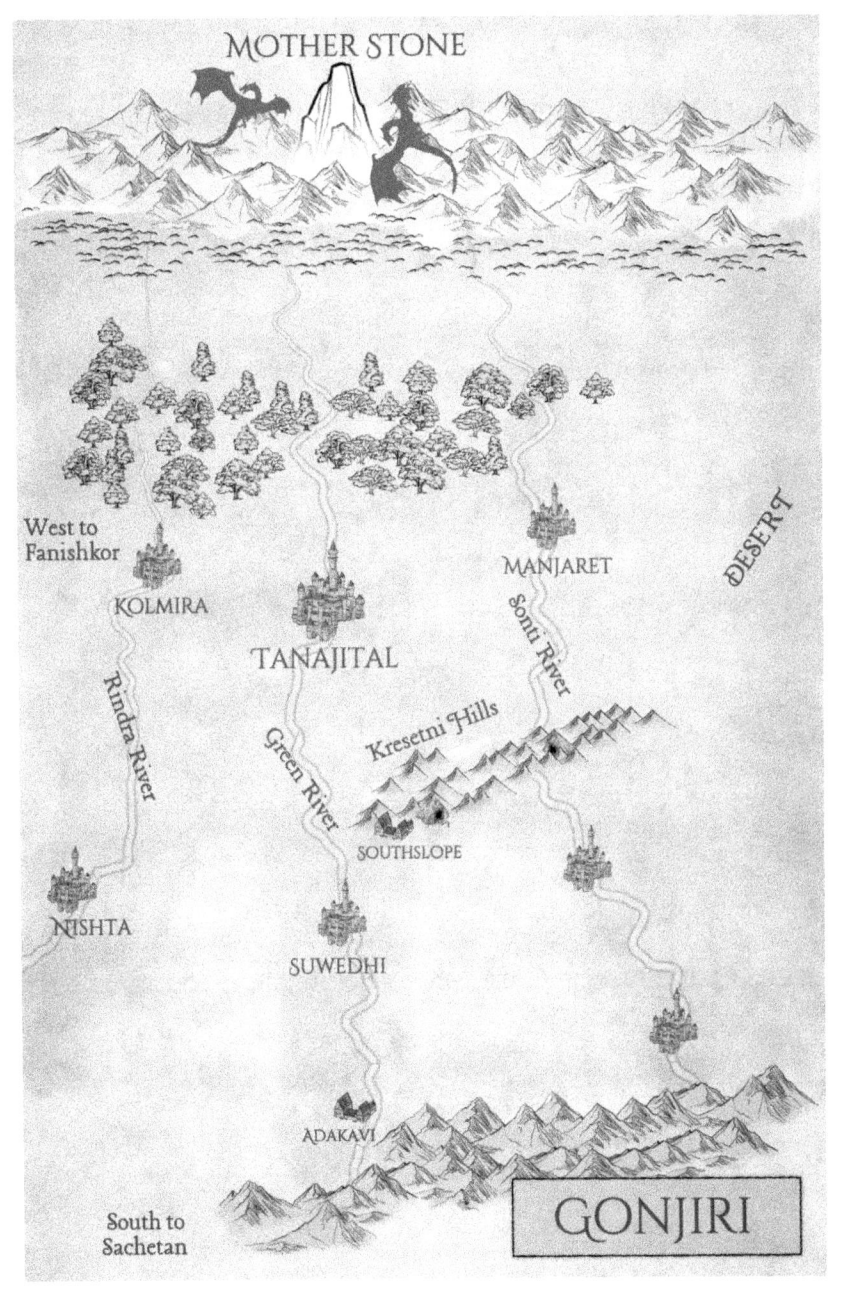

AUTHOR'S NOTE: ABOUT DRAGONS

Dragons have six fingers on each hand, and the number twelve has semi-religious meaning to them. They measure the passage of time in twelvedays as well as seasons and years, and frequently count by dozens as well as more conventional base ten numbers (thanks to having ten toes on their feet).

Dragons measure time of day by the position of the sun: dawn, morning, mid-morning, noon, mid-afternoon, late afternoon, dusk/sunset. Time of night is measured by relation to midnight: dusk/sunset, evening, late evening, midnight, the dreaming hours, pre-dawn, dawn.

Dragons take approximately thirty years to reach adolescence and are considered adults at age fifty-five, though it can take another ten to fifteen years for a dragon to achieve her full adult size.

Dragon time and distance measurements are inexact and based on the average dragon body. The basic unit of time is the heartbeat, or beat. A dragon's resting heart rate is about twenty-five beats per minute, so a single beat is the equivalent of two and a half seconds, a hundred beats is a little over four minutes, and a thousand beats is almost forty-two minutes.

An adult dragon is approximately the same length and height (not including wingspan) as a double-decker bus, but slimmer. Their basic unit of distance is the dragonlength, which is somewhere between twenty-five and thirty feet long (counting from tip of the nose to tip of the tail). For smaller distances, they use the handspan, which is approximately twelve inches long. For long distances, they are more likely to measure by the length of time it takes to fly somewhere rather than how far it is in dragonlengths. A dragon standing erect is sixteen to twenty feet tall.

Adult dragons weigh between 4000-5000 pounds. An active dragon will eat, on average, 250-300 pounds of meat per day, plus a quantity of stone equaling another 8-10 pounds (sometimes less depending on the "richness" of the stone). Dragons generally eat twice a day, though in lean times a dragon will gorge herself on available food and then not eat again for several days.

An adult dragon can fly up to 120 miles per hour.

CHAPTER ONE

The oncoming storm that blackened the western skies smelled of lightning and cut grass and fresh warm water, a lake's worth of it. The rainy season in the lowlands had proved to be more uncomfortable than the hot, drier spring had been. Lamprophyre had thought rain would keep the temperature low, but all it had done was saturate the air the sun heated to an unbearable level so it clung to her scales and wings like a caul. On the worst days, the ones where clouds didn't dim the sun and any movement felt like swimming in soup, she napped fitfully in her hall and dreamed of crisp, cold mountain air, of sleeping on chilled stone in a cave warmed by her body heat, and woke to the unpleasant reality of Gonjiri in summer.

Rokshan never seemed disturbed by the weather, but humans were acclimated to the lowlands in a way no dragon could ever be. He wore long-sleeved linen shirts regardless of how hot it was, which made Lamprophyre's heart ache for him because she knew his clothing choice had nothing to do with comfort and everything to do with the burn scars she still had never seen. It wasn't something she could task him with, not even on days like today when there was no one else around and he was perched comfortably in the notch behind her shoulders. Once again, she promised herself she'd find a time to discuss the forbidden subject, and once again she knew she was lying to herself.

Lamprophyre eyed the clouds and calculated how long it would take for the storm to arrive. More than a thousand beats, which was more than long enough for her purposes. The wind blowing those clouds in her direction buffeted her, prompting her to put her back to the wind so she didn't have to close the nictitating membranes over her eyes. She wanted to see this through to the end, even though it had been Rokshan's idea and she wasn't totally sure it was a good one.

"I'm not sure this was a good idea," Rokshan shouted. "The soldiers are all distracted." He shifted his weight so he was leaning over her left shoulder, putting more of her body between himself and the wind. Below them, the great granite wall of Tanajital loomed dully, its usual sparkle dimmed by the overcast. Soldiers thronged its wooden wall-walk, all of them intent not on potential enemies approaching from the north, but on the colorful specks speeding along the southern wall, on the far side of the city. Lamprophyre decided not to say she'd told him this might happen.

"Too late now," she said instead. The specks were moving fast enough around the curve of the wall that already they were visible as colored blotches, red and midnight blue and tarnished silver and, ugh, grass-green. In another beat or so, they were recognizable as dragons.

Despite herself, Lamprophyre's heart raced with excitement. Rokshan had been right about one thing for sure: there was nothing in the world to beat the sight of a magnificent, powerful creature in motion. She wasn't racing because she feared her rider losing his seat, and also because the dragon ambassador losing might look bad, but watching was almost as good. Now, if only Porphyry would pull ahead...

The dragons were headed directly for her. Lamprophyre resisted the urge to fly backward, out of their path. Dragons never collided with each other intentionally, and moving would just make her look stupid. Rokshan clutched her ruff more securely, but gave no other sign that he felt nervous in the face of four dragons barreling down upon them. Closer, closer...Porphyry was right on Coquina's flank—

—and the dragons swept past, four streaks of color that separated to fly in all directions as they shed momentum. Lamprophyre ground her back teeth together. She'd promised not to compare herself to Coquina anymore, not after the illuminating conversation she'd had with her mother Hyaloclast about Coquina's true merits or lack thereof, but old reactions died hard, and seeing Coquina fly past head and neck in front of Porphyry irritated her. She put on a pleasant smile and flew to where her clutchmates had gathered in the lee of the city wall, their eyes dilated and their breathing heavy from their exertions.

"Coquina wins again," she said. "That's three out of five."

"I'm just lucky," Coquina said with a laugh and a flutter of her wings that pretended to humility. Lamprophyre resisted the urge to grind her teeth again. Coquina was pretty and fast, both of which qualities Coquina had Mother Stone to thank for rather than her own perseverance in developing them, though Coquina persisted in acting as if possessing them made her superior.

"I don't know why we bother," Orthoclase said, flapping his wings in a leisurely fashion at odds with his breathless voice. "Only Chrysoprase can beat her every time, and she thinks it's beneath her dignity to race younglings."

"As if Chrysoprase weren't only twenty-seven years older than us," Flint said. He stretched, showing off his shapely, muscular torso, a move that on anyone else would have indicated vanity. "She thinks being a mother means she has to protect her dignity."

"What does a dragon mother do to raise her child?" Rokshan asked. "I thought dragons didn't care as much about parentage as they do about their clutch or their respect for Hyaloclast."

"That's when we're adults," Porphyry said. His scales, red as ripening cherries, were darker in the light from the oncoming storm and became even darker as he did a slow loop in midair. "Dragons can't fly until they're fifteen, so they need to be watched before that so they don't venture into places they can't get out of, or might fall off of."

"And they need feeding," Flint added, "particularly the males, who can't cook their own food. So mothers and fathers take care of their physical needs, and they also tell stories so the dragonets learn their history."

"Chrysoprase is overprotective," Coquina said. "Pyrope is eighteen, but her mother still keeps her close to the nest. It's ridiculous."

"There's nothing ridiculous about caring about your child's safety," Lamprophyre said. "And Pyrope is accident-prone. Remember when she climbed up to that ledge looking for garnet and got stuck? It was almost two thousand beats before anyone figured out where she'd gone."

"That was when she was ten, Lamprophyre," Coquina said. "And Chrysoprase has been overprotective ever since. I know if *I* had a child, I wouldn't want it to grow up frightened and stunted." She cast a quick glance at Flint, who was looking back at the city wall and missed her coquettish look. Lamprophyre, who hadn't missed it at all, wondered once more if Flint knew Coquina was pursuing him. He was too smart to be ignorant of her flirtation, but he'd never once acknowledged it, and Lamprophyre couldn't tell if maybe he really was ignorant, after all.

"We should go," Rokshan said. He pointed up. "The soldiers are still staring. They're supposed to be alert to threats, not watching dragons. Sorry. I didn't realize, when I suggested racing, that it would draw their attention so thoroughly."

"But it proves you were right, Rokshan," Orthoclase said, "about humans being interested in dragon races. I didn't hear a single frightened thought the whole time we were up there. Though I wasn't really listening. Too busy eating Coquina's dust."

Coquina laughed again. This time, it was a more brittle sound, and to her surprise Lamprophyre felt sorry for her clutchmate. She was almost certain Coquina had only set her sights on Flint because he was gorgeous, but if she felt genuine affection for him, how terrible if he really didn't care for her. Lamprophyre almost listened to Coquina's thoughts, but eavesdropping was bad manners, and she didn't want to fall into old habits of being obsessed with Coquina.

They flew lazily back to the warehouse district, not needing to race the storm, though Lamprophyre suspected she and Rokshan would get a little wet returning to the embassy after seeing the others to guest quarters. Humans thronged the streets below, heading for shelter. None of them looked up or pointed in amazement; none of them gave the dragons more than a passing thought. That was another thing Rokshan had been right about. Nine twelvedays before, when they'd arranged to rent these warehouses as temporary homes for dragons visiting Tanajital, he'd said, "Humans don't stay amazed at the extraordinary long. Soon enough, extraordinary becomes normal, and then normal becomes taken for granted. You'll see." Based on the thoughts she overheard from below, dragons—at least these dragons— were definitely taken for granted.

The streets surrounding the warehouses were wide enough for dragons to land on, and once humans had become accustomed to their draconic neighbors, they'd stopped using those streets entirely. Lamprophyre never feared stepping on humans here. Even so, today she hovered rather than landing, saying, "Are any of you going home this evening?"

"I have business with a stone supplier," Orthoclase said. "He has some stone I've never tasted. You'll all love it once I've worked out what else to pair it with."

His clutchmates laughed. "We eat better than anyone in the flight thanks to you," Porphyry said. "I'm staying the night. Don't feel like flying as late as that storm will require." Flint nodded agreement. Coquina just shrugged and walked into her warehouse.

"All right, then I'll see you in the morning," Lamprophyre said, flapping hard to propel herself skyward. She felt Rokshan wave at her clutchmates, and then the two of them were high over Tanajital and headed for the embassy.

Fat drops of rain had begun to fall when she descended to the courtyard in front of the embassy and hurried inside before crouching to let Rokshan climb down. She turned so she could watch the rain fall and settled herself comfortably on her stomach. "It's still pretty," she said, "even though I'm ready for the rainy season to be over."

"We have another couple of months before that happens," Rokshan said. He settled himself in the cross-legged position that always made Lamprophyre's hips ache just looking at it. "That's five twelvedays."

"I'm getting used to human time measurements, too," Lamprophyre said. "Though I still have to count it out in my head. Maybe someday it will be more natural."

Rokshan nodded. "Odd," he said. "I smell cooking. Isn't it a little early for Depik to make supper?"

"It's not supper, it's soup," Lamprophyre said. "It's for the beggars."

Rokshan's eyebrows rose in an expression of disbelief. "Soup for beggars? Why is Depik making soup for beggars?"

"He wanted to help our neighborhood," Lamprophyre explained. "Because he needed help for so long, and now he's in a position to help others. I don't always use all the meat from a cow or a pig, and he asked if I minded him using the scraps and the bones to feed the hungry. Though it's not always just the hungry. Anamika and Varnak sometimes get permission from their parents to eat here. But mostly it's beggars."

"Lamprophyre," Rokshan began, then fell silent. She recognized the expression he got when she came up with a question that had a complicated, human answer. "Lamprophyre," he went on, "you're an ambassador. I'm not sure you should be feeding beggars out of the embassy. No human ambassador would do such a thing."

"I'm not human," she pointed out, "and I don't see why not. Maybe Tanajital is welcoming of dragons now, but it can't hurt to build good-will, just in case. And Depik was so excited about his idea, I didn't want to turn him down. He's had fewer bad days in the last month, and while I don't think his illness is cured, this certainly seems to have made a difference."

Rokshan shook his head slowly. "I can't argue with your logic. It's just an unusual idea most humans wouldn't have—but you're not human, yes, I'm aware." He chuckled. "I don't know why I'm objecting. This plan of Depik's will probably end up having unexpected and posi-tive side effects, just like everything you do."

"I'm glad you can see sense." She settled herself more comfortably on the floor and closed her eyes. The rain rattled the roof tiles and occasionally blew through the window holes near the ceiling, spat-tering her hindquarters in a not-unpleasant way. Beside her, Rokshan leaned against her side, tucking himself into the crease of her shoulder. It was so restful, sitting and napping with a friend.

She'd almost drifted off to sleep when she heard Rokshan say,

"There's someone I want you to meet. A friend of mine. A, um, female friend."

She blinked and shifted a little, not enough to dislodge Rokshan. "A female friend? Or do you mean more than a friend?"

"I'm not sure yet." Rokshan laughed, a little self-consciously. "Nevrita's attractive, she's intelligent and funny, so I'm not sure what she sees in me—"

"Don't be derogatory of yourself. That makes you look weak and stupid, and you're neither of those things."

This time, his laugh was amused and unforced. "Sorry. I meant that as a joke, but—anyway. I met her at a concert hosted by Lady Tanura, where it turned out we both like the same composers, and then she was a guest at the reception for the new Rezmish ambassador, so we talked some more, and I've seen her several times since then. She's interesting, and I like her, and I think it might be more than just liking."

"I was at that reception, and I don't remember meeting anyone named Nevrita."

"You didn't. Remember, you left early? She arrived after that."

An unexpected pang of jealousy stabbed through Lamprophyre. "And you're just now telling me about her?"

"Why are you upset? I wasn't sure this was anything more than casual acquaintance, and I didn't see the point of doing something so dramatic as introducing her to my best friend until I knew she was someone I wanted you to meet."

"Best friend" comforted Lamprophyre and made her feel stupid about her reaction. "You're right. I'm sorry. I'd like to meet her, if she's as interesting as you make her sound."

"She is. She's never met a dragon before, and she seemed excited when I suggested I introduce you. Maybe in a few days?"

"I look forward to it." She closed her eyes again and felt Rokshan relax into her side. So. Rokshan hadn't had any romantic relationships since she'd met him last spring, and after he'd been burned badly by a Fanishkorite spy wielding a fire-blasting artifact, she'd wondered if he felt uncomfortable getting close to a female human. He'd said something along those lines that day, but they hadn't discussed it since. If he liked this Nevrita, and Nevrita liked him, Lamprophyre was happy for him. And she wasn't going to let a stupid irrational jealousy affect how she treated the female. It wasn't as if Rokshan would stop being her friend just because he started a new and different relationship.

She let the pounding of the rain lull her to sleep, and woke to find the noise had ceased and the air was cool and fresh. It was the only thing about lowland weather she enjoyed, the pause after the storm before the sun could once again heat the air hotter than dragon's breath. They didn't have anything like it in the mountains.

Beside her, Rokshan stretched and got to his feet. "That soup smells amazing," he said. "I'm almost tempted to become a beggar."

"You can have some without being a beggar," Lamprophyre said. "Though aren't you supposed to attend a banquet at the palace tonight?"

Rokshan groaned. "It's Khadar's birthday. I wish I could gracefully break my leg or something to get out of it. He's always so insufferable, as if birthdays were invented solely to benefit him."

"I'm too big to fit into the banquet hall," Lamprophyre said, not concealing her relief.

"I wish I could ask Nevrita to accompany me, but singling her out like that would have my parents all over me, wanting to know when we're getting married. So I'll have to suffer alone." Rokshan stretched, making his joints pop in a way Lamprophyre hated. Humans were so fragile, she always expected him to snap his bones or pop his arms from their sockets. "Have a nice meal, and I'll see you tomorrow."

Lamprophyre followed him out into the courtyard and watched until he disappeared up the street. The earth of the courtyard, hard-packed from generations of human feet, always had its top layer stirred up by heavy rains, and the mud clung unpleasantly to Lamprophyre's feet and tail when she incautiously let it sweep the ground. She tried wiping off the dirt, but it just clung to her hand instead. Irritated, she scooped water from the brim-full rain barrel and washed her hand, then entered the dining pavilion and settled herself in her accustomed place near the kitchen.

Depik came around the corner and bowed. "If you're ready, supper's near done," he said. "And the soup is ready."

"It really is a lot of work, making the soup and then washing all those bowls," Lamprophyre said, remembering Rokshan's dubiousness. "Are you sure this is a good idea?"

"My lady," Depik said with a frown, "you've never been hungry, truly hungry. I have. I remember how it feels. I'd wash a thousand bowls if it meant sending these people away full."

"I understand, a little," Lamprophyre said, feeling abashed. "And I agree that it's satisfying to help." She stood until she towered over the kitchen wall, which was taller than Depik but still only half as tall as she was at full height. "Let me handle the soup cauldron, and you can carry the bowls and spoons."

The cauldron wasn't very big, not nearly the size of the one Depik used to cook soup for her, and she lifted it easily and set it down near the entrance to the pavilion, opposite the rain barrel. Depik set down a stack of wooden bowls as the first of the evening's beggars approached. She and Depik had been providing soup for almost a twelveday, but those who came for a meal were still timid, even the ones Lamprophyre recognized as repeat visitors. She watched as they filled their bowls and retreated into the courtyard to eat. Some of them brought their own bowls, but even they stayed to eat, watching Lamprophyre as if they expected her to do something interesting.

Depik rolled out the trolley containing the evening's half a cow, expertly butchered and cooked to perfection, and Lamprophyre tore happily into the meat and idly listened to the thoughts of her "guests." The ones she saw regularly interested her, like the woman with two children in tow—all right, that was less interesting and more heart-breaking. The woman's thoughts were always focused on her children, but Lamprophyre wished she knew her story, why she had no mate—or maybe she did, and he wasn't capable of helping to provide for his family. It wasn't something Lamprophyre felt comfortable asking.

There was the young man with only one leg; Lamprophyre tried not to stare, but that wasn't something that ever happened to dragons and she almost couldn't help herself. There was the old man whose wispy white hair flew in all directions like one of those flowers that broke apart into a thousand fluffy seeds. His thoughts were chaotic, unintelligible except for the occasional snatch of coherent language,

9

can't find my way or *it speaks like thunder*, and his constant smile and vacant eyes reminded her of the dragon Gabbro, who'd needed help to find his way to Mother Stone when his madness took him completely.

And there was the odd woman who didn't look like a beggar at all. Her clothes were finely stitched and dyed a rich purple and blue, and she wore a faceted garnet the width of Lamprophyre's thumb in a setting of gold wire wrapped around her upper left arm. That alone told Lamprophyre she was wealthy, or had wealthy friends. Her thoughts were always amused, as if she were laughing at the people around her, and Lamprophyre couldn't decide if she disliked the woman or not.

Depik came to supervise serving the soup, and Lamprophyre ate and watched the humans. Dragons took care of each other, and this was a way in which humans did the same, but she knew it wasn't a universal trait. For every human they fed that night, a dozen or more elsewhere in Tanajital or in the other cities of Gonjiri would go hungry. She understood why Rokshan was so skeptical of Depik's efforts; when she thought about how many humans were in need, she knew it was impossible to help them all. And yet not helping when she was capable felt wrong. She could only do her best, and hope it made a difference to some.

She finished her meal before the last of the soup was served, so she sat and watched the beggars in silence until they'd all departed, the wealthy woman with a nod and a smile for Lamprophyre as if she knew what Lamprophyre thought of her. Then Lamprophyre lifted the cauldron into the kitchen to be washed, waved good night to Depik, and entered the embassy. Rokshan was probably still at supper, listening to Khadar talk about how wonderful he was. Much as she enjoyed being with Rokshan, she didn't envy him his supper companion tonight. Khadar, the Fifth Ecclesiast and a powerful religious figure, didn't like her any more than she liked him, and since he always found a way to steer conversations around to how she was a heretic for not believing in his religion, she was just as happy to have been excluded from the birthday celebration.

She settled in to sleep, watching the lazy evening sunlight slant across the courtyard and illuminate the end of the street that terminated there. Maybe she should make an effort to get to know the people they fed, now that they had regulars. She fell asleep imagining a conversation with the old man, whose thoughts floated as madly as his hair, and who told her a secret she couldn't remember come the morning.

CHAPTER TWO

"I'm sure this is all a terrible misunderstanding," Lamprophyre said, as patiently as she could manage. The day was hot and promised to become hotter, so she was already irritable even before this little man had intruded upon her day. That dealing with humans like him was part of her duties as ambassador didn't make her less cranky.

She shifted her weight, wishing she could sit up and stretch, but aware that such a move might seem like intimidation. "If your cart was trampled, it was surely by accident," she continued. "And if Bromargyrite were here, he would be very embarrassed and apologetic." No need to reveal that Bromargyrite's clumsiness was nearly legendary among the flight.

"That doesn't give me back my cart," the little man said. He was shorter even than most human females and had thin black strands of hair arranged across his bald scalp. The hairs fascinated Lamprophyre. They never moved no matter how agitatedly he twitched. "Nor my goods. The contents of that cart represented hours of labor. Keg stands don't build themselves."

"Keg stands?"

The man flapped his hands distractedly. "Keg stands. For holding

12

kegs of beer or ale. Very important to tavern owners and innkeepers. Now I'm out hundreds of rupyas and my business will suffer."

Lamprophyre began to feel she was drowning in words. This little man was one of those whose thoughts echoed his speech so closely it gave Lamprophyre a headache listening in, but even without the deluge of thought, his words were like tiny missiles plinking off her hide. "Of course we'll reimburse you for your losses," she said. Reimburse was a word she'd learned from her teacher Dharan and, thanks to Bromargyrite's frequent visits to Tanajital, had used far too often in the last several twelvedays. Months. "But surely keg stands don't represent your entire business? Because I can't imagine them being disposable. One sale would be good for years, yes?"

The little man gazed at her, his mouth open. "Well, I...naturally I make other wooden objects, but my competitors will move in on this part of my business! I demand recompense for that loss, too."

Purposeful movement in the street drew Lamprophyre's attention. To her relief, it was Rokshan, trotting toward the embassy heedless of the heat. "Rokshan can help us work those details out," she said. "I'm afraid I'm still not familiar with the relative value of human coin. Rokshan, this man has made a claim on the embassy. Will you determine a fair compensation—" another word from Dharan— "for his losses?"

"What? Oh. Yes." Rokshan came to a halt beside the man. He wasn't much taller than the average human male, but he still towered over the little man. "Where are your damaged goods?"

The little man stilled. "Well, I disposed of them already, naturally."

"I don't know how I can assess their value if I can't see them. Or did you think you'd be allowed to set a price? What goods were they?"

"Keg stands," Lamprophyre said. "For holding kegs of beer or ale."

"Keg stands?" Rokshan glanced quickly from Lamprophyre to the little man. "Those aren't worth much."

"But there was the cart, too," the man said, rallying.

"Which I notice you also didn't bring," Rokshan said. "What evidence do you have that there ever *was* a cart containing keg stands?"

The little man froze again. Now Lamprophyre stood, towering over both humans. "You weren't trying to cheat me, were you?" she said in her deepest voice, and listened closely. The little man's thoughts, previously a chattering torrent of words, had become incoherent and guilty, though guilty about what, she couldn't tell.

"I'll give you one chance to tell the truth," she intoned, lowering her head to be level with the little man's. "After that, Rokshan is going to boot you in your posterior and send you on your way." She caught the sound of drifting amusement from Rokshan before she focused once more on the little man.

The man swallowed. "The dragon did step on my cart," he said in a weak voice, "but it was because it had crashed into a house and the axles were broken. But it did have a few keg stands in the back. I didn't lie."

"Interesting," Lamprophyre said. "A dragon would definitely consider your original tale a lie. Rokshan?"

"Humans, too," Rokshan said. "What made you think you could cheat the ambassador?"

The little man said nothing. His guilty thoughts had become fearful. Lamprophyre's irritation mingled with sadness. Some people still feared she might hurt them, even though she had never hurt any human who wasn't trying to kill her.

"If your cart was damaged before Bromargyrite stepped on it, I shouldn't pay you anything," she said, "and you should be ashamed of yourself for trying to cheat me and make Bromargyrite feel bad. However, I'm sure your cart would have been repairable before it was smashed by a dragon, so we'll pay for that damage. But if you thought you could get more out of me by lying, you are very much mistaken. I think you have lied to more people than me in pursuit of coin, and I think you deserve for your business to suffer. Now, take your money, buy a new cart, and try honesty for a change."

The little man stared at her. Rokshan fished a small handful of silver out of his pouch, the one containing Lamprophyre's money, and pressed it into the man's hands. "I suggest you leave," he said, "before I remember that Lamprophyre wanted me to kick you in the ass to get you going."

The little man twitched, startled, then ran for the street. Rokshan watched him go. "You should have caught his deception yourself," he said.

"His thoughts made my head echo. I wasn't listening to them," Lamprophyre protested.

"It worked out in the end, so I suppose it doesn't matter." Rokshan entered the embassy and flapped the hem of his shirt to cool himself. Lamprophyre thought about suggesting he remove the long-sleeved garment, but that would have prompted one of those direct, challenging looks Lamprophyre found so uncomfortable.

She followed him inside and settled on the floor. "Did they let you into the Hall of Visions this time?" she asked.

Rokshan grimaced. "No, and I think someone may have interfered to prevent it," he said. "The first time, it was closed to the public. The second time, I didn't have the proper paperwork. This time, the excuse was flimsy—something about how I needed to prove I had good reason to be there. But the ecclesiast who told me that looked shifty, like she was lying. I wish you'd been there to confirm that."

"I wouldn't fit."

"I know. It still would have been nice to be able to task her with her falsehoods." He sighed. "Three guesses as to who's interfering, and the first two don't count."

"Khadar. But why would he care?"

Rokshan leaned against her side. "He's not stupid, for all he's venal and obnoxious. He knows if I'm interested in a prophecy or prophecies registered in the Hall of Visions, you're likely interested too. And you're a heretic as far as he's concerned. That's enough for him to want to keep us from learning whatever it is there is to learn. He doesn't even have to know what we're interested in."

Lamprophyre blew out an impatient cloud of smoke that drifted away through the window holes near the ceiling. "*We* barely know what we're interested in. 'The skies will burn' is such an oblique phrase, and if it's embedded in other prophecies, we might not be able to find more than just the two we know about. Assuming there's more to find."

"If not for what Hyaloclast said about those words being passed down from dragon queen to dragon queen, I would have put its appearance down to coincidence," Rokshan said. "At any rate, we're at an impasse for now. We may need to pay someone to do the digging for us. Someone not known to have a connection with us."

Lamprophyre made a face. "I can't think of anyone like that. Dharan would be perfect if he weren't our friend."

"He might still be perfect. He's good at charming women, and that ecclesiast struck me as the type who's readily charmed."

"I don't know what makes humans attractive to each other, so I'll take your word for it. Is Dharan handsome?"

Rokshan laughed. "He's handsome, yes, but he's also charming—not two things that have to go together. All his male friends wish he'd get married already and take himself off the market."

"What about you? Are you handsome?"

"Modesty prevents me answering that question, Lamprophyre."

All his amusement had vanished, and there was a dark undertone to his words Lamprophyre didn't like. She persisted anyway. "Your face isn't scarred much, and—"

"The scars aren't the issue." Now he sounded angry.

"It certainly sounds like they are. You won't take off your shirt even to go swimming."

"Because I don't like being stared at."

"I wouldn't stare at you. And we never swim where humans are."

"Could we not talk about this, please? It's not something you'll understand. Let's think about how to get into the Hall of Visions."

"I—" She couldn't help feeling he was never going to overcome his self-consciousness about his appearance if he wouldn't talk about what had happened to him. At the same time, she was uncomfortably sure that pushing him was the wrong way to go about it. It just made her so unhappy to see him afraid of his own body—but her happiness wasn't the issue here, was it? "All right," she said. "Who can we find to do the work? Someone who's intelligent enough to dig through the records and spot what we need?"

"If little Anamika were older—"

"Oh, yes, she would be perfect! But she's only eleven. Maybe her father? No, he's too devout. He'd be uncomfortable searching through prophecies for anything but divine insight."

"There's always Manishi." Rokshan scowled. "No one would believe she was doing it for anyone but herself. And she'd intimidate those ecclesiasts so much they wouldn't dare deny her access."

Lamprophyre scowled even more deeply. "She'd want to know why we wanted the information, and she'd want to be paid. Probably a lot. And while no one would make the connection to us, she'd certainly stand out in the Hall of Visions, given that she's as close to being a heathen as Dharan." Rokshan's sister Manishi, an adept skilled at working magic into stone, had helped them in the past—always for a price.

"We'll figure something out," Rokshan said. "Now, how about a story? It's too hot to do anything but sit in a shady spot and read or nap, and it's too early for a nap."

"I disagree. I can nap at any time."

"Well, you shouldn't. Civilized people nap after a midday meal, not before. And wasn't Porphyry coming this afternoon for reading lessons?"

"All the more reason to nap when I can. But I'd rather you read to me."

Rokshan got to his feet with a grunt and walked to where books lay piled on a cloth next to the slates Lamprophyre, and now Porphyry, practiced writing on. Dharan had insisted on the cloth to protect the books from the hard-packed earth floor, and since most of the books were his, Lamprophyre agreed. "What do you want to hear?" Rokshan asked. He knelt beside the stacks of books and ran his finger down the spines. "More of the history of Tanajital?"

"It's too hot for anything serious. What about more of the constellation stories?"

"That one's big enough for you to read it to yourself."

"I know, but you have a nice voice and I like listening, too."

"Flattery, flattery," Rokshan said. He extracted a very large book from the pile and returned to sit against Lamprophyre's flank. "Let's see. Ah, this is a good story, the Healer." He turned the book around so Lamprophyre could see the brilliantly colored illustration facing the first page of text. It depicted a human male lying on a pallet, reaching his hand toward another human male whose body was surrounded by a golden glow. Lamprophyre sniffed the page; real gilding.

"It's a good picture," she said. "Is that supposed to be Jiwanyil? The one surrounded by gold?"

"Right. Now, listen." He turned the book back toward himself and read:

"*Mandar was born to poor weavers who lived in Umrit, and had he been ordinary, he would have lived out his life in obscurity. But as a child, Mandar was blessed by Jiwanyil with the gift of healing others. His touch could heal a wound or cure illness, even of those close to death. Mandar's abilities made him famous, and as his fame spread, he was thronged by men and women wanting his healing touch.*'"

"That seems like a terrible way to live," Lamprophyre said. "All those people clamoring for attention. It's not as if he owed them anything. Or did he?"

"The story doesn't say," Rokshan said. "But—just listen. '*Mandar gave his gift freely, without charge and without regard to the status of the supplicant.*' That makes sense, if he felt it was something Jiwanyil expected of him."

"I think he should have charged them money. That would have cut down on the number of people bothering him."

"Dharan gave you that idea, didn't he?" Rokshan shook his head in mock sorrow. "That's true, but I'm not sure I could do that if I were Mandar."

"You're generous of spirit. Just like a dragon."

Rokshan laughed. "I'd like to think humans are capable of generosity, too. Let me continue. This is the important part, what comes next."

"*Over time, Mandar found himself growing weaker with every healing, as if vital force ebbed out of him to flow into the person he healed. Concerned, he sought the guidance of a reverend. 'I fear using my gift,' he said, 'and I fear the consequences of denying it. What should I do?'*

"*The reverend went away for three days and prayed for Jiwanyil's guidance. When she returned, she told Mandar that Jiwanyil had given him the healing power to bring Jiwanyil's light into dark places. 'You must have faith,' she told him, 'and follow Jiwanyil's path.'*

"'*But it may kill me,' Mandar said.*

"'*The reverend repeated, 'You must have faith.'*

"'*So Mandar went back among the people and continued to heal them. With every healing, he grew weaker. He gradually lost his strength until he was incapable of walking, then of standing, and finally all he could do was lie on his bed. And yet he continued to heal those who asked for his gift.'*"

Lamprophyre sat up. "That's so unfair," she said. "Why would Jiwanyil want him to die for the sake of healing others? He shouldn't have to sacrifice himself."

"Are you saying there aren't things you'd be willing to sacrifice yourself for?" Rokshan asked.

"Well, yes, but this is different! Mandar doesn't even know these people, and yet he's going to die for their sakes! I don't understand your religion at all."

Rokshan smiled. "The story's not over yet. '*There came a day when Mandar knew he only had one healing touch left in him, and it would mean his death.*'"

"I don't like this story, Rokshan."

"This is important if you want to understand humanity. '*As he lay on his bed, a blind man groped his way toward Mandar and stopped a short distance from him. 'Come closer, and let me heal you,' Mandar said.*

"'*The blind man did not move. He said, 'Why would you give your life to heal me?'*

"'*Mandar said, 'Because Jiwanyil told me to have faith, and I trust God's word.'*

"'*The blind man put his hand on Mandar's wrist. Mandar felt power rush through him, strengthening him. Suddenly it was Jiwanyil standing before him. 'Rise,' the God said, and Mandar rose from his bed as if he had never been ill. 'You had faith in me when the path seemed unclear, and you will be blessed above all men for my sake.'*

"'*Then Jiwanyil disappeared, and Mandar felt the God's love surge through him. From that day on, Mandar traveled the world, healing those he met and telling the story of Jiwanyil's grace. When Mandar died, Jiwanyil set him in the sky as the constellation The Healer, reminding all that faith in God is always repaid, no matter how confusing God's commandment seems.*"

Lamprophyre thought about the story for a few beats. "I'm not sure I agree with that," she said. "I don't think I could do something that hurt me and didn't make sense. Mandar didn't know he wasn't going to die."

"You don't have people you trust with your life?" Rokshan countered. "Suppose Hyaloclast told you to...to fly up the slopes of Mother Stone. Would you do it?"

"Well—but that's different. Hyaloclast wouldn't tell me to do something that foolish."

"Unless Hyaloclast understood something you didn't. Truthfully, Lamprophyre—you trust Hyaloclast never to lead you astray, right? Jiwanyil is the same. His instructions to us through his ecclesiasts are meant to bring us happiness. That's why Mandar obeyed even though he didn't understand the reason."

Lamprophyre shifted uncomfortably. "Our religion isn't like that. Mother Stone doesn't tell us how to behave. We simply try to follow her example. She is eternal and unchanging, so we are honest and consistent in our dealings with each other. She accepts us into her heart, so we are generous and forgiving of others' faults. She knows us, which lets her be perfectly just and perfectly merciful, so we are as just and merciful as our limited understanding allows."

"I see," said Rokshan. "That makes you not so different from humans, at least so far as our obedience to Jiwanyil's laws goes."

Lamprophyre shook her head. "From what I've seen of humans, though, that obedience isn't essential to being human. You've said humans can choose to obey Jiwanyil's laws, or not."

"That's right. And the fact that we can disobey makes our obedience more meaningful."

That didn't make sense to Lamprophyre, so she said, "Well, we consider all those behaviors as essential to being dragons. They're part of our identity. So, for example, when we're at odds with each other, we meet with the flight and talk about what's bothering us. And the flight helps the two who are fighting come to terms so they can be one with the flight again."

Rokshan tilted his head back. "What about you and Coquina? You never did that with her."

Lamprophyre flushed a delicate purple. "I was afraid of looking stupid in front of the flight, or maybe just in front of Hyaloclast. Jealousy is considered foolishness, among dragons, because we're supposed to celebrate our differences, and I was sure challenging Coquina would make me seem like a child. So I pretended it wasn't real and that Coquina and I were still getting along."

"But she still bothers you."

"Not as much as before. I've learned the truth of what our parents teach us—that we should honor and respect each other for the strengths we bring the flight. I have strengths I didn't realize back when I was jealous of Coquina. So any lingering bad feeling is just that —lingering from the way I used to be."

"That's very mature thinking," Rokshan said with a smile. "I'm afraid I'm not that well-adjusted, or I'd get along with Khadar."

Lamprophyre made a face. "I'm glad Khadar isn't a dragon, because I don't know if I could ever not be at odds with him. Though if he were a dragon, he wouldn't be an ecclesiast and wouldn't be so obnoxious."

"This is true." Rokshan sat up. "There's Dharan. He's early."

Lamprophyre extended her neck so she could see down the street. Dharan strode along confidently, with a couple of books in one arm and a crumpled piece of paper in his other hand. She stared at him, wishing she knew which of his features made him so handsome to humans. Or maybe it was how all of them were arranged. Dragons saw beauty in a symmetrical form, in well-shaped eye ridges and a smoothly muscled torso that curved to a narrow midsection, and in colors that complemented each other. Coquina's beauty, for example—Lamprophyre made herself think about Coquina rationally—was as much in how her rose-colored wing membranes suited her grass-green scales, like a flower, as in her symmetry. Humans all had more or less the same coloring, and if they were symmetrical, it was in a way Lamprophyre didn't yet understand. Maybe Dharan could tell her if Rokshan was handsome.

"Did you see this?" Dharan demanded when he was close enough for speech. He brandished the crumpled paper at them. Rokshan looked up at him, but didn't rise, so Lamprophyre had to stay lying down or knock her friend over.

She held out a hand for the paper. "Is it something bad?"

"Stupid and annoying, yes," Dharan said, handing the paper over. "It's certainly offensive to me."

Lamprophyre peered at the tiny writing. She had a lens for magnifying letters too small for her to easily perceive, but it was across the room and Rokshan was still reclining against her side. "It says something about the gods? That they demand devotion? That doesn't seem unusual."

"*Greater* devotion," Dharan said. "As in, the ecclesiasts have written this proclamation to call Gonjiri to repentance. But that's just the beginning." He accepted the paper back from Lamprophyre and read: "*Katayan, the Lonely God, is disappointed in his followers, who refuse to acknowledge him as their Lord. He calls on dragons everywhere to forsake their heretic religion and give their devotion to the True and Living God of the Dragons.*"

"Heretic religion?" Lamprophyre exclaimed.

"They've said as much before," Rokshan said.

"Not like this," Dharan said. "Not so publicly." He handed the paper absently to Rokshan, his attention all on Lamprophyre. "I think we've just seen the first moves in a religious war."

CHAPTER THREE

"Religious war?" Lamprophyre said. "But why would they do that? Gonjiri doesn't want any kind of war with dragons."

"Gonjiri doesn't," Dharan said. "But the ecclesiasts have different priorities. And topmost on that list is maintaining power. Dragons openly challenging the official doctrine are a threat to that power."

"That's an overly cynical way of looking at it," Rokshan said. He'd been reading the paper, and now he stood, dusting off his posterior. "Ecclesiasts have the ability to hear the mind of Jiwanyil. If God speaks to them, isn't it reasonable that they'd believe in the tenets of their faith as revealed by God? And that they'd want others to believe as well?"

"I'm willing to give most ecclesiasts the benefit of the doubt because of that," Dharan said. "But that language—" He flicked the paper with his finger— "is inflammatory and irresponsible. If they really were concerned about the state of dragons' souls, they wouldn't start by demanding they change their beliefs. Or claim to know the mind of Katayan."

"I agree," Rokshan said. "Whatever their motivations, this is a problem."

"How is it a problem?" Lamprophyre said. "I mean, yes, I see that there will be conflict, because the flight isn't going to bow to the eccle-siasts' demands, but I don't know what the ecclesiasts can do about it except make more demands we will also ignore."

"They can turn the people against you," Rokshan said. "Most humans in Tanajital believe in Jiwanyil and respect the reverends and ecclesiasts. And Katayan is sort of a romantic figure. So the people might be upset that you're not following the will of Jiwanyil the way they do."

"Why is Katayan a romantic figure?"

"He's called the Lonely God," Dharan said, "because it was believed all the dragons were dead and he didn't have any worshippers. Legends say he wanders the world, appearing to humans who have experienced a loss. The death of a loved one, for example, or a change in fortune. We're taught to respect Katayan and honor his grief."

"Oh." That did sound sad, and Lamprophyre could see how humans might find the concept appealing. Any dragon would feel the same. "That's a nice story, but dragons worship Mother Stone, and we have plenty of evidence that our faith is real."

"That's not something most humans will understand," Rokshan said. "They hold to their faith as strongly as you do to yours. And that faith has sustained humans for over a thousand years. Up until now, very few of them knew anything about dragon religion, but this procla-mation will change that."

"Unfortunately, I don't know what dragons can do about this," Dharan said. "Challenging the ecclesiasts will only give them more opportunities to spread their nonsense."

"I agree," Rokshan said. "Ignore it, and maybe it will go away."

"Do you think so?" Lamprophyre asked. "Because I'm not sure Khadar, for example, will let this go at one piece of paper."

Rokshan and Dharan looked at each other. Rokshan shrugged. "Then we see what comes next, and maybe that will give us some idea of how to proceed."

Lamprophyre didn't like that answer. Challenging the High Ecclesi-asts, starting with Khadar and working her way up to the Archprelate, felt like a better move. But as satisfying as that would be, it would also be aggressive, and that would only raise public sentiment against her.

"All right," she said, "but at some point, if they don't back down, there *will* be a fight."

"I'm looking forward to that day," Dharan said with a grin.

"You would," Rokshan said, but without malice. "Let's move the slates outside before Porphyry gets here. And then I'm going to see if I can hunt down someone who can do that research for us, Lamprophyre."

"What research?" Dharan asked. "I like researching things. What do you need researched?"

"See?" Lamprophyre said. "He's even eager about it. I think we should use him."

"And now I'm not so eager," Dharan said. "You make it sound like you want a Dharan-shaped weapon."

"We almost do," Rokshan said. "Lamprophyre and I need some information about certain prophecies from the Hall of Visions, but Khadar keeps interfering. So we have to get someone else to go instead."

Dharan made a face. "The Hall of Visions. I thought you were after something interesting."

"It *is* interesting," Lamprophyre said. "Khadar was possessed of a prophecy a few months ago, back when Hyaloclast came to meet with the king, that said 'the skies will burn.' And Hyaloclast told us that phrase has been passed on from dragon queen to dragon queen since the Great Cataclysm. *And* it's appeared in other prophecies. We want to know which prophecies."

"Not only that, but we'd like to find out the details," Rokshan added. "Who was possessed of them, what questions were they in response to—anything that might indicate what that phrase might mean."

"I take it back," Dharan said. "That's very interesting. So why don't you want me to do it? Because I'm an unbeliever?"

"We were actually thinking you might be known to be our associate," Rokshan said, "and you'd just get the same runaround we did."

"But Rokshan says you're good at charming women, so *I* think you should try," Lamprophyre said.

Dharan burst out laughing. "He does, does he?"

"You know you are," Rokshan said. "Remember Karana and the peaches?"

"I do, mainly because no one who knows that story will ever let me forget." Dharan made a face Lamprophyre had never seen before, his eyes half-lidded and his lips pursed. "'Mmm, just one bite...'"

It was Rokshan's turn to laugh. "And she still liked you after everything fell apart. You're definitely charming."

"So will you do it?" Lamprophyre asked, hoping to bring the conversation back to the important part and stop the two friends from reminiscing. "Because putting one over on Khadar would help me forget about the stupid proclamation."

"I can at least try," Dharan said. "But it will be a few days before I have time. I have lectures tomorrow and the day after."

"It's already waited a few months. It can wait a couple of days," Rokshan said.

Lamprophyre picked up the large rectangular slates, so unnaturally smooth, and set them in the courtyard, propped against the embassy walls. "I'll try not to be impatient," she said. "If you brought me new books, that will help."

"An illustrated codex of animals," Dharan said, "and a beginner's text on magic theory. It was hard to come by, too. Most adepts learn from other adepts rather than from books. This one was written by a non-adept who compiled knowledge from scholar-adepts. It's intended for people who don't intend to practice magic, so they can understand the principles of the artifacts they use."

"That sounds interesting." The human use of stone to channel magical energy fascinated Lamprophyre. To her, stone was mostly important as food, and the possibilities human adepts had seen in even such ordinary stones as feldspar and quartz intrigued her. "Though if there's a book that lists the different stones and what kind of magic they produce, that would be even better."

"I've looked, but there doesn't seem to be anything like that," Dharan said. "My instinct is that adepts don't want other adepts knowing about their discoveries, so they can monopolize their production, at least for a while. Why they don't like writing down the discoveries everyone knows about, I don't know, but secrecy seems paramount."

"Maybe that's something a non-adept could compile, like this book."

"Could be. It wouldn't be hard to make a start." Dharan handed the third book to Rokshan. "A history of the rulers of Gonjiri. Dry, I'm afraid, but it's organized in chapters by ruler, and some of them were interesting characters. I leave it to you to decide which ones."

Rokshan grimaced. "I feel as if I'm one of your students. Am I to write an essay?"

"Think of it as penance for all the reading you didn't do at the academy. Or as a privilege to instruct the first dragon student of Gonjirian history." Dharan clapped Rokshan on the shoulder. "So, tell me who the lady I saw you with at the paraveti two nights ago was. A new friend?"

Rokshan shrugged. "Her name is Nevrita, and we have a shared interest in the paraveti tangal. And she wasn't with me. We just happened to meet there." He wasn't meeting Dharan's eyes.

"I see," Dharan said. He sounded a little too casual. "I'm sorry I couldn't join you, but I had a rather importunate young lady with me and I didn't want her imposing on my friends. Besides, when I saw you, the two of you were having a very animated discussion, and I didn't like to intrude. She's an aficionado, you say?"

"We were arguing—not really arguing, discussing—the lead performer's interpretation of the role," Rokshan said. He seemed a little less stiff now, Lamprophyre thought, and she watched him in fascination. She was better at interpreting human body language now, or maybe it was just knowing Rokshan so well, and his demeanor struck her as either embarrassed or self-conscious. He must like this Nevrita more than he'd suggested to her the other day. "Nevrita's very knowledgeable about tangal recitation."

"So are you," Dharan said. "It's good to know you've made a friend who can match you in that." He turned to Lamprophyre. "It's too bad you're too big to fit in the paraveti, because the paraveti tangal and the paraveti huspeth are two of humanity's greatest artistic achievements.

And Rokshan is an expert on the tangal, and could give you a thorough grounding in the art."

"Dharan exaggerates," Rokshan assured her. "There are many interpreters more experienced than I."

"All of them professionals," Dharan said. "Don't be so modest."

"Yes, don't be so modest, Rokshan, you should be proud of your accomplishments." Lamprophyre leaned down to prop her head on her hands, putting her just below his eye level. "What's paraveti tangal? I don't know those words."

"Paraveti was a poet who lived about four hundred years ago, and Tangal was one of her students. The artistic form is named for both of them. It's a form of poetry recitation, but done on the spot," Rokshan said, "so it's composition as well. Though composing poetry in advance is also acceptable. Listeners know spontaneous composition is harder, so we tend to respect it more."

"I can't imagine it. New dragon poetry takes years to compose," Lamprophyre said.

Rokshan nodded. "It's a certain type of poetry, too. Performers take on roles, famous figures from history or living people or even mythological people, and create poems reflecting those people's personalities or passions, or their understanding of historical events or religion. It's a way of shaping our understanding of humanity, of seeing history and faith through a specific perspective and thus improving our own perceptions of events or beliefs."

"That's fascinating. Are you sure there's no way I can see it? You know I love poetry."

"I—actually, maybe," Rokshan said. "I know several of the paraveti tangal performers, and I might be able to arrange something. It would have to be in the coliseum, and I'm not sure how well sound travels there, but they could tell me if it's possible."

"I'd love that!"

Rokshan laughed. "I don't know why it didn't occur to me before. Give me a day or so, and I'll know if it's possible. It might still be impractical, so don't get too excited."

"Too late." Lamprophyre smiled. "And maybe Nevrita could come. If she's so knowledgeable, she could help explain the performance."

"Good idea," Rokshan said. He didn't look at all self-conscious now. "I'll talk to Pranesh tomorrow."

"I hope that invitation includes me," Dharan said. "I'm curious about what kind of performance a tangal reciter will put on for a dragon."

"Anything will do," Lamprophyre said. She was thinking, though, not of the human artistic performance, but of Nevrita. Once again she suppressed a twinge of jealousy. Rokshan could still be her friend if he had a romantic relationship. And she wanted him to be happy. Maybe Nevrita was the answer to that.

"No, P and H together make the F sound," Lamprophyre said. She tapped the slate where she'd written PORPHYRY in big letters. "And for some reason the two Y letters have different sounds in your name, 'ih' and 'ee'. Human spelling is so odd. I don't know why it can't be spelled P-O-R-F-I-R-E-E."

"That would make more sense," Porphyry said. "I know I have trouble remembering all the sounds made by putting two letters together. So much easier to memorize the words."

"Yes, but you still have to be able to sound out unfamiliar words so you know what you're memorizing." Lamprophyre turned to her own slate and wrote her name. Her handwriting had improved dramatically with practice. Below that, she wrote some of the other names she knew: ROKSHAN and ANCHALA, Rokshan's sister, and DHARAN and ANAMIKA.

"Psst! Lamprophyre!"

Lamprophyre turned and peered into the dimness of the embassy. As if writing her name had conjured her up, Anamika stood near the back door, jigging from one foot to the other in nervousness. "Anamika? Why did you come through the back door? I'm afraid I can't play right now. Lessons."

"I didn't come to play," Anamika said. She walked forward a few paces to where Lamprophyre could see her clearly, but Porphyry couldn't. Nor, Lamprophyre realized, could anyone else outside the embassy. "I'm not supposed to be here."

"You know I don't like you disobeying your parents—"

"This is *important*," Anamika whispered. "I'm not supposed to be here ever again."

"What?" Lamprophyre entered the embassy and crouched down to put herself on Anamika's eye level. "Why not?"

"Mam and papa say you don't believe in God and you've turned your back on Katayan." Anamika's restless jigging was starting to unsettle Lamprophyre. "They say we're not to play with you because you're wicked."

"I am not!" Lamprophyre controlled her next outburst. "I believe in a different religion, Anamika. It's not wrong for me not to believe in yours."

"But why don't you believe in Jiwanyil and Katayan?" Anamika cried out. "You have to believe in them or devils take your soul."

"They—Anamika, dragons worship Mother Stone. We have stone in our blood and bones, and when we die, we return to her. We've never heard of Katayan. That's something—" Lamprophyre closed her lips over the words *something humans made up*. Anamika was eleven, far too young by either human or dragon standards to be analytical about her religious faith and far too young for Lamprophyre to feel comfortable teaching her things at odds with her parents' teachings. "So your parents are afraid I'll corrupt you and Varnak?"

Anamika nodded.

"I promise I wouldn't do that, but I don't want your parents upset with you. They're just trying to protect you. So you and Varnak should stay away until your parents change their minds. I'll talk to them—maybe that will help."

That seemed unlikely, but it cleared the frown from Anamika's face. "Do you think you could talk to my parents soon? Varnak and I want to go swimming with you."

"I'll see what I can do. Now, get on back home before they guess where you've gone."

She stared at the back door, hanging slightly ajar from Anamika's exit, after the girl had gone, and wished she knew human curse words. The situation was too stupid for ordinary swearing. She'd almost forgotten that proclamation because nothing had seemed to come of it. It looked like she was wrong.

She stomped back out into the courtyard, prompting Porphyry to say, "Something wrong?"

She shook her head. "Nothing important." She hoped that was true. If she was wrong about that, as well, life for dragons in Tanajital was about to become extremely unpleasant.

CHAPTER FOUR

Lamprophyre coasted low over the river south of Tanajital, well beyond where the boats crossed from one bank to the other. The air coming off the river was marginally cooler, but still damp, and Lamprophyre dipped even lower and trailed her hands and feet in the water. Even at that slow speed, she sent up waves that sprayed her torso and belly and made her wish she could dive in—but that would soak her wing membranes and make flying extremely difficult. Dragons were creatures of air and fire, not water and earth. Even so, soaking in the river would be so comfortable on a day like this one, with the sun a white disc in the sky that broiled everything it touched.

"You're sure you don't want to go swimming?" she asked Rokshan. He'd been unusually quiet since they'd left Tanajital, but maybe it wasn't so unusual, given how the heat sapped her will to talk.

"I'm sure," Rokshan said. "Maybe tomorrow. I wish we didn't have to fly through the heat of the day."

"The alternative was staying in Umrit until evening, and they don't have accommodations for dragons. *I* wish we hadn't had to go there at all. They were all so afraid. Rokshan, is there ever going to be a time when humans don't fear me?"

"It's coming, Lamprophyre, I promise." Rokshan patted the side of her neck. "Most of the big cities are used to dragons now. It's just little towns like Umrit, and it's sort of Bromargyrite and Orthoclase's fault for racing so close to it."

"That's all it was. Racing. They didn't even enter Umrit."

"I'm sorry. That was more critical than I meant. I'm just saying we have to decide how dragons will approach these little towns, and it's clear now that sending out handbills in advance makes a difference because the townsfolk are prepared."

Lamprophyre sighed and banked to follow the curve of Tanajital's wall. "I wish you weren't right, but I know you are. I didn't realize how proud I am until I had to abase myself in front of that tiny little magistrate and apologize for my friends scaring his stupid fellow citizens."

"I was impressed at how civil you were. He was obnoxious about the whole thing. You're a far better diplomat than I am."

"Well, I feel more confident when you're with me, so thank you for coming along."

"My pleasure. Now, I'm going to eat something, and then I think a nap is in order."

Lamprophyre, descending toward the embassy courtyard, saw a familiar figure just inside the entrance, leaning against the wall so his face and body were half in shadow. "Dharan's here. Do you think he made it into the Hall of Visions?"

"I hope not," Rokshan said, "because I really want a meal and a nap."

Lamprophyre alit in the center of the courtyard and crouched for Rokshan to climb down. "You can wait inside where it's cooler, you know," she said.

"I know, but I like watching the people in your neighborhood." Dharan stood upright and stretched. "You're not going to believe what I learned at the Hall of Visions."

"Does it involve cold roast chicken and a large plate of saffron rice?" Rokshan asked.

"You're a slave to your stomach, you know that?" Dharan gestured for Lamprophyre to precede him into the embassy. "We'll eat after I tell you my story. I promise it's worth waiting dinner for."

Rokshan sighed and settled himself on the floor next to Lampro-phyre. "If it isn't, you're buying."

"Fair enough." Dharan sat cross-legged facing Lamprophyre, who settled onto the cool earth floor with a grunt of satisfaction. If she stayed in the lowlands long enough, she might end up so acclimated to the hot weather she'd find her mountain home too cold. Stones, but that would be awful!

"So I did some research before I went," Dharan said, "research as to who would be on duty at the Hall of Visions at which times. I may not actually be able to charm the birds from the trees, but I'll admit I've had success swaying ladies to my point of view. This morning, the ecclesiast supervising visitors was a young woman who was already inclined to be helpful, at least as far as assisting other visitors went. It's fortunate for the ecclesiasts I had no sinister motives, because she went out of her way to steer me in the right direction. I believe if I'd asked she might have shown me to the Archprelate's own chambers."

"I knew you were the right choice!" Lamprophyre exclaimed.

"We should have sent him to Umrit instead of us," muttered Rokshan.

"Are you finished, or do you want to natter on some more?" Dharan asked. Lamprophyre sat up and assumed her best attentive pose. Rokshan shrugged. "That was just the beginning. In fact, her helpful-ness almost worked against me, because she kept coming back to ask if I needed anything. It was distracting. But I managed to learn a few things regardless." He removed a folded sheet of paper from within his sleeveless shirt and passed it to Rokshan.

Lamprophyre peered at it over his shoulder. "I can't read it," she said. "Your handwriting is usually better than that."

"It's intentionally bad because I didn't want my so-helpful eccle-siast friend doing what you're trying to do now." Dharan flapped the hem of his shirt to cool himself. "The first thing I learned is that the Hall of Visions has the worst cataloguing system I've ever seen. I don't know how ordinary people manage to find anything. No index, no cross-referencing. It's as if they don't want people reading the prophe-cies, and I'd believe that if not for the ecclesiasts helping other visitors."

"What do you mean?"

"I mean, Lamprophyre, that I shamelessly eavesdropped on other people's conversations. The ecclesiasts do want people to be able to look up prophecies. They just want to control what people find. They have a system that's not obvious to laypersons, and using that system, the ecclesiasts can find just about any prophecy."

"But since you're a genius, you deduced the system from what you overheard," Rokshan said, rolling his eyes.

"Why, thank you, Rokshan, I was about to use those exact words," Dharan said with a grin. "It's a non-obvious system, but fairly simple once you know the rules. I've created far more complex organizational methods myself. So in between dodging the assistance of my besotted young ecclesiast, I located a number of prophecies containing the phrase you gave me."

Lamprophyre settled herself more comfortably, since Dharan had the look of someone about to tell a good story. "And?"

"And nothing," Dharan said. "That is, I couldn't see any commonalities between the prophecies except that the phrase 'the skies will burn' seems tossed in at random in almost all of them. The two non-random exceptions being the most recent prophecy, the one Khadar was possessed of, and a prophecy delivered seven years ago that refers to preparing for a great disaster. But I wrote summaries of each prophecy on that paper." He dropped the hem of his shirt and rested his hands loosely on his knees.

Rokshan was scanning the page with his eyes narrowed in thought. "What about the commentaries?"

"Also not helpful. Most of the relevant prophecies are unfulfilled, or partially fulfilled. Oh, and that was the other thing: I didn't see any ecclesiast's name represented more than once. That is, it seems any ecclesiast possessed of a prophecy containing those words only received one of them."

"That's unfortunate," Rokshan said. "If there were an ecclesiast who kept receiving those words, we might be able to confront him or her."

"What are commentaries?" Lamprophyre asked. "Commentaries on the prophecies?"

"Sort of," Rokshan said. "Ecclesiasts keep track of the prophecies they're possessed of and make notes on the written records of how and when they're fulfilled. And other ecclesiasts study the prophecies looking for correlations between them, and they write those down on the records, too. If the prophecies we're interested in were fulfilled, even in part, how they were fulfilled might give us hints to what 'the skies will burn' might mean." He folded the paper and handed it to Lamprophyre. "I'll make a fair copy later, so we can both read it instead of trying to decipher Dharan's chicken scratches."

"I love your expression of gratitude," Dharan said.

"He's kidding. We're both grateful to you," Lamprophyre said.

"Seriously, we are," Rokshan said. "Do you think you found all the relevant records?"

"All the ones it's possible to find with a superficial search. I'm sure there are more, but locating them might draw the kind of attention you want to avoid. But I'm willing to try again sometime if you feel it's necessary."

"That really is more than we asked," Lamprophyre said.

Dharan shrugged. "I'm curious now. And I don't like leaving a scholarly puzzle unsolved. Do you have any guesses about what you're looking for? What the phrase means?"

"Just that from what the dragon queen said, it might be tied to a future catastrophe." Rokshan stood and stretched. "Not necessarily as fatal as the last one, but if it is, wouldn't it make sense that Jiwanyil would warn us?"

"Better for us if Jiwanyil prevented it," Dharan said. "And I know what you're going to say. If God hovered over us all the time, humans would be stunted and never learn anything for themselves."

It was so like what Hyaloclast had once told her Lamprophyre blurted out, "But that's true, isn't it? Mother Stone never interferes in dragon lives because we would otherwise never do anything without her telling us to. We'd be children forever."

Dharan shrugged again. "Then what's the point of a god who only watches, if he or she is all-powerful?"

"This is too heavy a discussion to have on an empty stomach," Rokshan said, "but I think a god who creates rational creatures with free will expects them to act without his direction, and that kind of creation demands that a god be all-powerful. It doesn't dictate how else he uses that power. You may be a genius, but you don't use that genius directed by the preferences and demands of others. Now, food, Dharan, and then Lamprophyre and I will study what you've brought us."

Lamprophyre carefully unfolded the paper without tearing it. She could barely make out that there were words on the page and not, as Rokshan had joked, chicken scratches. Having taken such pains to improve her handwriting's legibility, it struck her as funny that anyone might deliberately make their handwriting worse. "Don't take too long," she said.

When the men were gone, Lamprophyre placed the paper between two books so it wouldn't get damaged or lost and settled in to read one of the books Dharan had brought the day before. The book she chose was a history of the Great Cataclysm, what humans referred to as the catastrophe, and it was extremely boring. How anyone could make a time that had probably been terrifying and full of danger boring was beyond her. She'd been skimming through the pages, though, trying to learn the basic facts without falling asleep on her magnifying lens.

What especially interested her was the human account of what had happened to the dragons. She'd heard the stories from Rokshan, about how the mountains had risen up and swallowed all dragons, but this book went into more detail. According to the writer, the dragons had tried to destroy human civilization, but the catastrophe, in which the earth had moved and cities had been sunken below ground or shattered by mountains rising in their place, had stopped their advance. That was where the legends of the mountains swallowing the dragons came from.

Lamprophyre swiveled the lens away and rested her chin on her folded arms. It was impossible. She'd lived in the mountains all her life, and there was no evidence anywhere that the mountains had been uprooted even as recently as a thousand years ago. But Dharan had taught her that these old stories, and even the modern explanations for the old stories, weren't necessarily false just because no one had proof they'd happened. "Kernels of truth," he'd said, and then had to explain what kernels were.

So what was the truth here? *Something* had happened to the dragons to make humans believe they were all destroyed. Her own people's history wasn't much more detailed than the human legends. Dragons told stories of how the humans had turned their backs on them, and the dragons had retreated to the mountains in response. But that didn't fit with how human legends said dragons had attacked them. Lamprophyre couldn't imagine that ever happening. Humans were too soft and fragile to be a threat to dragons, and dragons wouldn't attack anything that wasn't a threat. It was all too confusing.

She read a few more pages before her eyelids became heavy. This was all wrong. Reading should be fun, not sleep-inducing. Even so, a nap felt like a good idea. She slept, and dreamed of dragons raining fire and acid down on human cities until Mother Stone reached out her arms and gathered them to her, crushing them under her weight.

CHAPTER FIVE

Lamprophyre chewed a mouthful of roast pig and listened to Rokshan eating soup. He was usually a tidy eater, but either the soup was too hot, or he didn't feel a need to use his best human manners in front of her. She tore off another mouthful. She didn't use utensils when she ate the way humans did, so her manners from a human perspective were fairly messy. It wasn't important when they were in her dining pavilion, but it did make her feel self-conscious about eating in public places.

"Some of these people come often," she told Rokshan, speaking in a low voice even though none of the beggars were close enough to hear. "The man with only one leg, for one, and the woman with two children also."

"I wonder about that woman," Rokshan said, and slurped another mouthful of soup. "What she does with her children during the day. You don't often see beggars with children, and I'm not sure why not. There must be many parents in Tanajital who have to beg for their survival, and it's not as if there are places that will watch their children while they're out on the streets. Or maybe those beggars have relatives they're supporting as well, and they tend the children during the day."

"She's afraid of me hurting her children, or I'd ask her," Lamprophyre said. She only occasionally listened to the thoughts of the people who came for soup in the evening, because there were enough of them that their thoughts were a chaotic, echoing tangle, but she'd heard enough to know how her "regulars" felt about her. Lamprophyre felt only a dull ache at knowing some of them still feared her. Maybe that was how things would always be.

"The old madman comes sometimes, too," she said to distract herself. "The one with the flying white hair."

Rokshan studied the man, who stood off to one side and drank from his bowl rather than use a spoon. "Why is he a madman?"

"His thoughts are shattered like broken glass. I tried listening, but they didn't make any sense. All I know is that he goes between agitation and serenity in an instant, and I can't tell what he's agitated about. Sometimes he's afraid in flashes, and sometimes he clutches his head like it pains—there, like that."

The old man had dropped his half-full bowl on the packed earth, spilling soup everywhere. He put both hands over his ears and twisted his head back and forth as if his hands were turning it, and a high, shrill keening escaped his lips. No one else in the courtyard paid any attention to him.

Rokshan stood and walked to the old man's side. He picked up the bowl and brushed particles of dirt from it. "Let me get you some more," he said, as if the old man could hear him even though it was clear the man was past hearing anything. Rokshan refilled the bowl and returned to the old man's side. The man had sunk to his knees and was breathing great sobbing breaths as if he'd been in terrible pain. Rokshan waited for him to lower his hands, then gave the old man the bowl. The old man resumed drinking soup as if nothing had happened. He ignored Rokshan completely.

"Thank you," Lamprophyre said when Rokshan returned to her side. "I wish I could help him. I'm so big I'm afraid I'd accidentally crush him."

"That's not a life I'd wish on anyone," Rokshan said. There was still soup in his bowl, but he seemed not to notice. "Who knows what he was when he was young? And now he's old and mad and dependent on strangers."

Lamprophyre listened briefly before she had to block out all the other thoughts. "He's calm enough now. I don't think he remembers those episodes." She sat up. "Oh, and there's the strange rich woman. I ought to tell her to leave the soup for people who really need it, but for all I know she does need it. And we have plenty."

Rokshan looked where she was pointing. "Oh," he said.

"Oh?" He'd sounded uncomfortable, as if he recognized the woman. "Do you know her?"

"Not her personally."

"Who is she? I've been curious for a twelveday, but I have the feeling she'd laugh at me if I talked to her."

"She's no one, really. Or, well, she probably *doesn't* need a free meal, so I wonder what she's doing here."

Lamprophyre blew out a cloud of impatient smoke. "That's what I thought. How can she be no one and also be wealthy?"

"I don't know how wealthy she is." Rokshan shifted so his face was in profile to Lamprophyre. "She's a Sister of the Red. A, um, prostitute."

"I don't know what that means."

Rokshan sighed. "I suppose it was too much to hope Dharan had explained it. Prostitutes have sex with men for money. It's considered shameful for both the women and the men who, um, patronize them."

Lamprophyre mouthed the words *sex with men for money*, trying them out to see if they made any more sense on her lips. "I still don't understand. You mean, more than one man? How can they be pair-bonded so often? Or—the men don't die afterward, do they?"

"Of course not!"

"Then how do they manage it?" A horrified thought struck her. "You don't mean they have sex without being pair-bonded?"

"Um, yes. The prostitutes aren't married to the men they have sex with. The men give them money in exchange for sex. Do dragons not —well, all right, obviously you don't have money so you can't pay for sex, but it sounds like you only have sex with the one you're pair-bonded to."

"Of course we do! We're not animals!" Heads turned at the sound of her shrill exclamation, and she hunched her shoulders as if that would divert their attention.

Rokshan cleared his throat. "Lamprophyre," he said patiently, "humans aren't animals either, but we—Jiwanyil teaches us that we should keep sexual relations within marriage, but humans can choose whether or not to obey that rule."

Lamprophyre stared at him. He still wasn't looking at her. "Sexual intimacy is powerful for dragons," she said.

"Powerful for humans, too."

She shook her head. "I mean that we share thoughts with the one we're pair-bonded with. Far more intimately than just hearing them. If we did that with someone we're not pair-bonded with, especially if we went on to do it with someone else..." She shuddered. "Imagine knowing the innermost thoughts and secrets of someone who wasn't going to spend their life with you. It makes me embarrassed just thinking about it."

"But how do you know when you've found your true mate? Couldn't you make a mistake, and be pair-bonded with the wrong person, and later realize your destiny lay elsewhere?"

Lamprophyre shook her head. "Dragons spend years getting to know each other before deciding on a mate. It's why so many dragons mate within their clutch." Another horrible thought struck her, this one embarrassing. "Oh. Have you had sex? I know you're not pair-bonded. Married."

"I have."

The words struck her to the heart. She'd been so critical of human customs without realizing she was directly criticizing him. "I'm sorry. Humans do things so differently—I didn't think I might have been insulting you. I apologize."

"It's all right. I wasn't insulted. Much." He smiled, the corner of his mouth turning up though he still wasn't looking her way. "It's true, we believe in sex only between married people, but our desires are strong enough most of us are weak that way. Sometimes couples have sex and get married later. Sometimes men don't have partners and they patronize prostitutes. The reverends and ecclesiasts preach against it, but it's like I said—we humans have the choice to obey Jiwanyil's law or not."

"The ecclesiasts must really not like prostitutes, then. How could you tell that's what she is? Her clothing?" The woman had left already, or Lamprophyre would have stared at her more intently than usual.

"Her armband. Women who don't want to conceive children wear garnet artifacts to prevent conception. Prostitutes wear theirs openly, so people know they're available for sex, and that they won't present a customer with an unwanted child later."

She didn't understand why anyone might not want children, but that sounded like an even more complicated conversation. Something for another time. "But wouldn't that make them obvious to the ecclesiasts?"

"It does, but there's no law against prostitution, so all the ecclesiasts can do is chastise them and insist God-fearing folk shun them. Sort of like what they've done to dragons."

Lamprophyre's dislike of the woman evaporated in the knowledge of this shared experience. "So, when you had sex, was it with a prostitute?"

Rokshan burst out laughing, causing the few beggars still in the courtyard to look his way. "No, Lamprophyre, I did not pay a prostitute," he finally said, "and you should know it's insulting to suggest to a man that the only way he can get sex is to pay for it."

Lamprophyre blushed. "So who was it with?"

"That, I'm not going to discuss with you. It's ungentlemanly. I'll just say that in recent years I've come to see the wisdom in Jiwanyil's laws, and I've decided not to have sex again until I'm married."

That relieved Lamprophyre's mind, though she didn't know why. Possibly because it made him seem more dragon-like. "If it makes you happy, I'm glad of it," she said, refraining from asking him more detailed questions like *What changed your mind?* or *How does sex feel for humans?* which she was sure he wouldn't answer.

She settled in more comfortably and helped herself to the last swallow of Rokshan's soup. Humans were so strange. Once more she reflected on the males in her clutch. They were all friends, and they all had different things in common with her, but she didn't feel an urge to single one of them out as a potential mate. Maybe she needed to look at the clutch born just three years before hers, or the one five years younger—though the younger clutch members were only just fifty-five and not ready for pair-bonding at all.

She sighed. Or maybe she needed to stop worrying about it. She was young enough not to be expected to choose a mate any time soon. But with five males and two females in her clutch, she was always conscious of her friends watching her and Coquina, wondering which way they'd go. So long as none of her clutchmates was harboring a secret passion for her, she was comfortable letting things go on as they had.

Even so, as she watched the last beggars deposit bowls in the box near the soup cauldron, she couldn't help wishing one of her clutch-mates had captured her heart. How wonderful, to have someone to share such intimacy with! *Someday*, she thought, and crossed the court-yard to the embassy.

CHAPTER SIX

The following evening, the courtyard was more than usually full of beggars. Depik had told Lamprophyre, when they'd begun this practice, that there were holy days in which people were more generous in their giving than usual, and on those days they should expect to see fewer people coming for soup. He hadn't said if there was anything special about the days when they saw more people. Lamprophyre watched the crowd from the dining pavilion, searching out her regulars. She didn't see the old man or the prostitute, but there was the mother, gripping her children's hands as if she feared being separated from them. A reasonable fear, given how crowded the courtyard was.

She saw the young man with one leg, hobbling down the wide street that led only to her courtyard. He was usually earlier than this. Lamprophyre tossed a large steak into her mouth and chewed blissfully. It was too bad it was impractical to feed all her beggars steak, because steak was delicious and Depik was very good at cooking it.

The young man was halfway across the courtyard now. Three other men, all of them short but burly, with large arms bumpy with muscles, were crossing the courtyard toward him, bowls of soup in their hands. They had their backs to Lamprophyre, so she couldn't see if what happened next was accidental, but the three burly men made no attempt to get out of the way of the young man, and one of them kicked the wooden device Rokshan had called a crutch, knocking the young man down. Lamprophyre rose to her feet. The three men laughed and kept going as the young man fumbled with his crutch, his brown skin darker with humiliation.

"Hey!" Lamprophyre shouted. "You three!"

The three men took a few more steps before turning around hesitantly, as if they weren't sure she was addressing them. "Yes, you," Lamprophyre said, stepping away from the dining pavilion and then stopping to avoid crushing anyone. It probably wasn't an issue, because everyone in the courtyard had backed away from her when she emerged. "Help him up."

The men exchanged glances. "What?" said the one in the middle. "Who?"

"Oh, spare me," Lamprophyre said. "You know who and you know what. How dare you come here and take my food and think you're somehow entitled to treat other people like dirt? I don't think you're even beggars. You're far too well fed."

The burly man on the left took a step backward. "Don't you dare," Lamprophyre said. "You put those bowls down and get out of here. And I don't want to see you again. Dragons have *very* good memories, and I assure you I won't forget your faces. And if I'm wrong, and you are in need of a meal because you're poor, you should remember that you lost your chance here because you were selfish and cruel to someone even worse off than you. Get out."

Slowly, the men placed their bowls on the ground and backed away, not turning around until they'd reached the street. Then they ran.

Lamprophyre blew out a cloud of smoke. That had felt good. Then she caught sight of the young man, who'd managed to get his crutch under him and stand up. She was better at reading expressions than she had been when she first came to Tanajital, and his flushed face and refusal to meet anyone's eyes, the way he hunched in on himself, told her clearly he felt humiliated. Guilt surged over her. She hadn't even considered the young man's pride, or that he might not want to be rescued.

"I'm sorry about that," she told him. "What's your name?"

His eyes widened. Clearly he'd never expected a dragon to speak to him. "Sumaan," he said in a voice almost too low for Lamprophyre to hear.

"Sumaan, my name is Lamprophyre, and I welcome you to my home," Lamprophyre said, falling back on words she'd heard Anamika's father using with guests. "I wish I could limit my hospitality to those who really need a good meal, but I'd rather not question people to have them prove their need. Please have something to eat, and the rest of you—" She raised her voice. "If you're here because you heard there was free food, there is. But I hope those of you who can afford to feed yourselves won't take the place of someone who can't."

She walked back into the dining pavilion and gulped down more steak. To her surprise, people were leaving without eating. She hadn't actually thought anyone would care about her appeal to their consciences. Something humans and dragons had in common was a love of getting something for free, though in dragons' case that meant being given something with no obligation to respond in kind. She and Depik had been lucky not to encounter this problem, this arrival of those not in desperate need, until now.

She finished eating and surveyed the courtyard again. There were still a lot of beggars, though she still didn't see the prostitute or the old man. Sumaan stood leaning against the embassy wall, his crutch propped beside him. It was growing near to sunset, and Lamprophyre needed to leave, but she didn't dare take off from the courtyard full of fragile humans who she might trample or knock over with her wings.

She left by the back way, past Depik cleaning up in the kitchen, and stood behind the embassy, looking up at its steeply slanted blue roof nearly as vibrant as she was. It had a narrow beam running the length of it, giving the roof the appearance of a book laid face down with its spine pointed up, something Dharan had yelled at her for doing once. Lamprophyre crouched, folded her wings back, and leaped for the roof, grabbing hold of the eaves and hauling herself up to the beam. Probably it wasn't that narrow for a human, but for her, balancing required her to spread her wings wide and extend her arms.

She wobbled once, got her balance, and leaped into the sky before she lost her grip on the roof beam.

Flapping awkwardly and hoping no one who mattered had seen her graceless ascent, she winged her way south and east, toward the coliseum. The towers of Tanajital cast long shadows pointing her way, some of them oddly shaped by the bulbous gilded tops that looked like turnips dipped in gold. To the west, the Green River was already fully in shadow, and lights had begun to come on in the little boats making one last quick dash from one shore to the other before darkness made sailing dangerous. The sun, halfway below the horizon already, looked like a blob of molten glass, dark yellow shading to orange where it touched the land. Lamprophyre admired it for a few beats before turning her back on it.

The coliseum was a large structure of red sandstone, with tall arches circling its outer wall. The arches fascinated Lamprophyre, the more so because neither Rokshan nor Dharan knew how they stayed up. Dharan had said only that it had to do with engineering, not his field of expertise, and Rokshan had said, "I was told the stones of the arches fit so closely together they might have gotten away with using no mortar. That terrified me as a child, the thought that those stones might come tumbling down and crush me if someone kicked them. It's not possible, of course, but children imagine the strangest things."

Now Lamprophyre cruised down in a wide spiral around the coliseum and observed the passersby thronging the streets surrounding the coliseum. The streets radiated out from it like spokes on a cart wheel, with a single street wide enough for two dragons to sit side by side—she and Flint had checked—completely surrounding the coliseum, and a similar street circling that one about two dragonlengths away. When she had first come to Tanajital, she'd stayed in the coliseum until the embassy was ready, and those circular streets had been empty because the citizens all feared her. Now, even though she was circling low and Flint and Orthoclase were already in the coliseum, those streets were as full as ever with humans heading home to their suppers or out for an evening's entertainment. Just like she was.

She landed lightly at the back of the coliseum, near the wooden box where the royal family sat to observe races or performances. Large openings framed with wood allowed her to see inside the box easily. It was bare as far as decorations went, the walls unpainted and lacking the woven hangings she'd seen looking through windows at the homes of the well-to-do. Some chairs with fat yellow cushions on their seats were lined up in two rows facing the coliseum floor. If you were human, those chairs would be an extremely comfortable way to watch the races held here weekly.

A round platform about two handspans high had been erected in the center of the coliseum, with unlit torches flanking it. A couple of plain wooden stools like Lamprophyre had seen outside buildings near the embassy, the buildings where humans went to buy meals, were arranged in a loose grouping around its circumference.

Flint and Orthoclase had settled nearby, comfortably settled on their haunches with their tails wrapped around their hindquarters. "Isn't anyone else coming?" she asked.

"Bromargyrite will be here any time now," Flint said. He shuffled over to make room for Lamprophyre next to him. "Dolomite and Porphyry flew home for a few days, and you know Coquina has no interest in poetry."

Lamprophyre privately thought that however little interest Coquina had in poetry, she certainly had a great deal of interest in Flint, but she would never embarrass him by referring to Coquina's pursuit of him. "I wonder if it will ever be anyone but our clutch coming to Gonjiri," she said. "I don't know if they're not interested, or they don't feel welcome."

"Most of them don't think humans have much to offer us," Orthoclase said. "That will change over time."

"And once they realize—oh, it's Bromargyrite," Flint said, looking up at a descending figure that glowed orange and yellow in the last light of the sun. "Everyone duck and cover."

"Funny," Bromargyrite said, but he landed more carefully than Lamprophyre had and stood well away from the wooden box. "This human city seems made of intentionally fragile things. I swear I never mean to step on anything, but it's like things appear just where I mean to step."

"You're not too far off," Orthoclase said. "Obviously Tanajital wasn't built for dragons, but it's almost as if some human builder wanted to make us uncomfortable."

"And yet humans themselves can be very friendly," Flint said. "As I was about to say, once the rest of the flight realizes how interesting humans are, they'll spend more time in the lowlands. I've gotten to know a human male, a builder of stone houses, and he's taught me a lot about why humans build the way they do. I've even helped with some of his construction. We flew south yesterday—"

"Flew?" Lamprophyre said.

"I'll admit it was uncomfortable at first, having a human perched back there," Flint said, reaching around absently to rub the base of his neck, "but I liked having someone to talk to on that long flight. And Lokun wasn't afraid at all. I think we might become friends."

"I suppose if Lamprophyre could manage it," Orthoclase said. "I'm not sure I could be that close to a human, but it's also true I've made acquaintances among the stone merchants. So maybe I'm wrong about that."

Torchlight flared at the far end of the coliseum, and Lamprophyre's attention was drawn by three humans in short, sleeveless robes, circling the walls and lighting the torches that hung at intervals there, then crossing to the center and lighting the torches on the platform. The sun was nothing more than a yellow glow in the western sky, and the torches were a welcome illumination. They cast their dancing shadows on the ruddy earth that floored the coliseum, lighting the space well enough that Lamprophyre could have read by their light.

She heard voices approaching from the east, murmuring too low for her to identify the speakers, so she listened for their thoughts and found Rokshan, Dharan, and Rokshan's sister Anchala. To her surprise, one of the remaining thinkers was Rokshan's mother, Queen Satiya. She didn't recognize the fifth person and guessed it must be Nevrita. Excitement made her pulse quicken. The fifth person wasn't thinking anything coherent, which meant she was listening to someone else speak. Lamprophyre hoped the speaker was Rokshan. Her earlier stupid jealousy of someone who might theoretically take Rokshan's time away from her vanished in her eagerness to meet this woman Rokshan was interested in.

She was also aware of a few other presences who didn't speak and whose thoughts were preoccupied with an awareness of their surroundings that to Lamprophyre sounded like a light, lilting hum punctuated with the occasional *shadow* or *keep back*. The group of speakers' voices became muffled, echoing like water dripping into a pool deep within a lightless cave. Soon enough, though, she heard them clearly, their voices coming from somewhere at her eye level. Someone laughed.

Then a door at the back of the wooden box opened, and a couple of guards walked through. Lamprophyre realized immediately they had been the preoccupied thinkers. They checked the box thoroughly, then stood to either side of the door and stood as still as trees. All the dragons were watching now, Bromargyrite a little farther from the wooden box than the others.

Rokshan walked through the door and gestured for someone to follow him. That someone turned out to be the queen, who came forward to the front of the box. "Lamprophyre," she said in her sweet, soft voice. "How good to see you. And these must be your...clutch-mates, is it?"

"That's right, your majesty," Lamprophyre said. "These are Ortho-clase, Flint, and Bromargyrite."

The three male dragons bowed. Bromargyrite's bow wasn't at all clumsy. He must have practiced. "We appreciate the welcome Tanajital has given us," Flint said.

"I hope to continue to welcome dragons to our country," Satiya said. "It's unfortunate you've had to stop racing around the city wall. I wish I could have seen it."

"We're trying to find a solution, your majesty," Orthoclase said. "Dragon racing is something humans have shown an interest in, and we think it would build dragon-human relations if it could be a commonplace."

"When you figure it out, let me know," Satiya said. She seated herself in the front row of chairs and straightened her robe, not the colorful one she wore for official functions, but something soft green and flowing.

Anchala took a seat next to her mother with a nod for the dragons, all of whom she'd met before. Dharan sat beside her without a hint of reservation, something that amused Lamprophyre. She knew very well that Anchala had set her sights on Dharan in a way that made Coquina's flirtation with Flint look like mild interest. Since Dharan had no intention of marrying any time soon, and even less interest in Anchala, Lamprophyre thought it remarkable that he could sit so calmly beside his pursuer. Dharan must like paraveti tangal more than she realized.

She turned to look at the last woman emerging from the corridors behind the royal box. She was tall for a human female, almost as tall as Rokshan, and rather than arranging her hair high on her head as Anchala had done, or in loops and coils the way Satiya's hair was, she had pulled it back from her face and secured it at the back of her neck with a golden clasp—real gold, Lamprophyre smelled. Her skin was a lighter brown than most Gonjirians Lamprophyre had seen, almost as light as the queen's, and her loose robe with the deep neck concealed her figure enough that Lamprophyre could barely see the bumps on her chest that meant she was female.

"Lamprophyre, I want you to meet Nevrita," Rokshan said, beckoning the female forward. "Nevrita, this is my friend Lamprophyre."

"It's a pleasure to meet you," Nevrita said. Her voice was deep and flowing like water over stone. "Rokshan speaks of you constantly." *Too constantly*, she thought. *It's enormous.*

The spiteful thoughts startled Lamprophyre. "It's nice to meet you finally," she said. "Rokshan says you know a great deal about this performance tonight. I'd appreciate your insights." Nevrita must be as uncomfortable as Lamprophyre, to think so negatively about someone she'd only just met.

"Of course. Though Rokshan is more experienced than I." *Separate them, how?*

Lamprophyre's mouth nearly fell open in shock. She heard Rokshan laugh and say something about his experience, but her mind made no sense of the words. Separate her and Rokshan? Why the Stones would Nevrita want to do that? Then she had to choke back a laugh. Of course. Nevrita liked Rokshan, and she had the same fears

Lamprophyre had—that Rokshan wouldn't be able to make room for more than one close relationship. Lamprophyre relaxed. Nevrita would realize she wasn't a threat to Nevrita's relationship with Rokshan, and they would eventually become friends.

"...so I asked them to perform some of the most famous roles," Rokshan was saying. "I think it's best if you dragons experience the tangal without any explanation at first, so we'll hear a few performances. Then we'll explain some of the subtleties. Then the last ones, Nevrita and I will explain as they go. All right?"

"I feel as if we're making history," Flint said, making his clutchmates chuckle, all except Lamprophyre. She'd caught the tail end of Nevrita's thought: *boring, don't know why I agreed.* She examined the woman closely. Nevrita was laughing at something Rokshan had said, and her hand rested lightly on his forearm in a caressing, intimate gesture. Lamprophyre eyed it warily. Why the woman's demeanor was so at odds with her thoughts, she didn't know, but she had a very bad feeling that it couldn't be explained away as Nevrita's jealousy.

Humans, two male and one female, had taken seats on the stools on the platform when Lamprophyre turned around. They wore strange clothing, black trousers with wide legs, tunics with sleeves equally wide, and gauzy black cloths tied around their heads to cover their hair completely. She almost asked Rokshan what the clothing meant, but remembered Nevrita was sitting next to him and changed her mind. Nevrita might be superficially pleasant, but Lamprophyre was reluctant to draw the woman's attention to herself in any way.

She settled in to listen to the performance, telling herself to block out the intruding thoughts that made it impossible to appreciate the poetry. But her seat below the royal box put her directly in front of Nevrita, and her awareness of the woman was like an itch between her shoulder blades, impossible to reach. Her knowledge that she would ask Rokshan to scratch a real itch of that kind drove that awareness to new heights of discomfort. She would shut out Nevrita's thoughts for a hundred beats or so, until she couldn't bear not knowing what Nevrita was thinking any longer, and then, with a furtive feeling of guilt, she eavesdropped for another hundred beats before blocking her again like flinching from a blow. Sometimes the thoughts were good ones, like *wish we were alone*, but even the good thoughts were followed by ones that tarnished them: *never going to make him mine if we're always surrounded by people*. And some of them were terrible: *stupid dragons, never appreciate art* or *blue dragon's a fool to think he'll choose her over me*.

By the end of the first round of performances, Lamprophyre's head ached and her body felt as if she'd been poisoned, weak and sick and with acid flowing through her veins instead of blood. She turned to look at Nevrita, who was smiling as pleasantly as if she was genuinely enjoying herself. As she watched, Rokshan put his hand on Nevrita's elbow, guiding her forward, and Lamprophyre felt she might actually be ill. She swallowed, put on a cheerful smile, and tucked her misery away where she could indulge it later.

"What did you think, Lamprophyre?" Rokshan said.

"I think maybe you need to have human experience and knowledge to truly appreciate it," she managed, which was true; she'd enjoyed the poetry, what she'd heard of it, but with the consciousness that there were rivers of meaning flowing deep beneath the surface.

"Let's hope that's not true," Rokshan said. "I chose these roles because they require very little knowledge of history to appreciate. The subtlety lies in understanding that the events narrated in the poems are shaped by the experience of the character doing the recitation. Did you notice that all three of them described the same event?"

"I didn't, actually," Orthoclase said. "But now that you say so, I can see how the first and the last, at least, were about two sides to the same situation."

"The middle one isn't as obvious," Dharan said, "because the speaker, Mindai, was a servant who worked in the great estate that was overrun. She saw things the general and the ruler didn't."

"I understand now," Lamprophyre said, then shut her mouth, unable to continue because she'd heard Nevrita think *much handsomer than Rokshan, too bad he's not the prince*. Her heart ached with her secret knowledge.

Nevrita was holding forth on some stupid detail of the performance, and Rokshan was listening to her with a little smile on his lips like he was very pleased not just with what she said, but with his closeness to her as well. Lamprophyre once more wanted to be sick. This wasn't something she could conceal from Rokshan. He had to be told what Nevrita was really like. But if Rokshan liked Nevrita, and he clearly did, he would be so upset to learn the truth. She could imagine how he would feel to learn that Nevrita only wanted him because he was royalty, that any prince would do.

Heartsickness gave way to anger. How dare this woman hurt her friend? How dare she pretend to care about him for the sake of—what? Becoming a princess? Gaining wealth? It didn't matter what Nevrita's actual motives were; she was a grasping opportunist, and Lamprophyre wished she dared denounce her right here and send her screaming out of the coliseum, pursued by dragons.

The rest of the performance passed Lamprophyre in a blur. By finally and resolutely blocking all thoughts, she managed to pay enough attention to the final recitation and Rokshan and Nevrita's commentary to make intelligent responses to the questions Rokshan posed. When the last recitation was over, and the discussion had died down, Lamprophyre said, "I should be going. I had an early morning, and I'm almost falling asleep now."

"Of course," Rokshan said. He sounded so concerned Lamprophyre for the first time ever wished she were a human, to break down in a sobbing fit. She'd seen humans weep for sadness or frustration, and it seemed to bring them comfort. But dragons couldn't cry, so she smiled, said goodbye to Nevrita without listening to hear whatever spiteful thoughts she might be entertaining, and flew straight to the embassy without looking around at Tanajital by night, normally a sight that pleased her.

Depik had left the lanterns by the doorway burning, and Lamprophyre extinguished them, careful not to break the delicate glass. Then she settled down on the nice earth floor of her embassy, curled her tail around her flank, rested her head on her folded arms, and closed her eyes tight to invite sleep to come quickly. But her mind persisted in running through Nevrita's horrible thoughts, over and over again until Lamprophyre wished she were mentally deaf like the dragon Massicot, unable to hear thoughts. But then Rokshan would have no way of knowing what Nevrita was really like. Without that knowledge, he might even marry her, and what a nightmare that would be.

Lamprophyre sighed, blowing out a cloud of smoke, then intentionally breathed out more of it until the ceiling of the embassy was comfortably foggy. As horrible as her knowledge was, she could endure it if it meant helping Rokshan. She clung to that thought until she eventually fell asleep.

CHAPTER SEVEN

L amprophyre woke with a headache and a horrible taste in her mouth that wasn't cleared by the deliciously greasy sheep Depik prepared for her. After breakfast, she retreated into the embassy. She knew the building was called a hall, but today it suited her to think of it as a cave, comforting and dark and isolated from humans.

Now that she'd slept, she found herself more horrified by Nevrita than she had been the night before. No dragon would ever behave that way. Of course, that was because dragons were from birth accustomed to their surface thoughts being perceived by others, and they learned to make their thoughts match their demeanors. But it was also because the idea of entrapping someone into a pair-bond as Nevrita clearly intended to do to Rokshan was so alien as to be incomprehensible. Any dragon who managed to fool another about her affection for him would have the deception revealed the first time they were sexually intimate. Lamprophyre's thoughts the previous night about wishing to be human vanished. She wouldn't be human if it were a choice between that and a grisly death.

She picked over her books, but didn't feel like reading any of them. She was in the process of copying out dragon poetry, but that required Dharan to write everything down, since there were few papers big enough for her to write on. She settled down to lie full-length on the floor and flexed her wings. Maybe she should go flying. That always cleared her head. If she were careful, she could avoid her clutchmates and go for a nice solitary flight.

She heard footsteps and suppressed a groan. Rokshan. How to tell him the terrible news? She had a feeling there was no good way to do that.

"Are you still feeling poorly? You looked a little wan last night," Rokshan said. He dropped to the ground beside her head and crossed his legs under him. "It went really well, don't you think? Nevrita couldn't stop talking about how much she liked you. I hope you liked her. I never realized how much I enjoyed talking about paraveti tangal until I met someone who shares my appreciation for the art. And Mother seemed to like her too, though Mother is so reserved it's hard to tell." He rested his elbows on his knees and propped his chin on his hands in the pose Lamprophyre thought of as Contemplative Monkey. "I was wondering, do you think you might be willing to fly with Nevrita? I know it's a very personal thing, but I want the two of you to be friends."

It was too much. "Rokshan, I have to tell you something," she said, "and you're not going to like it."

Rokshan's smile vanished. "You didn't like Nevrita."

"It's not that." She knew her expression was unconvincing.

"Lamprophyre, she's a good person, and I know if you give her a chance, you'll like her. This is important to me, can't you see that?" Rokshan scooted closer. "You know this doesn't affect our friendship, if I have a close relationship with someone else."

Lamprophyre couldn't keep in a laugh. It sounded shrill and false, as if she'd only ever heard about laughter from other people. "You know, until last night that was my biggest worry," she said. "I'll admit I was a little jealous of Nevrita before I met her. But now... Rokshan, you know I care about you, right? And I would never do anything to hurt you without a reason?"

Rokshan's face looked like a wooden mask. "And you think you have a reason?" he said, sounding formal and distant and making her heart hurt worse.

Lamprophyre swallowed. "I listened to her thoughts. Nevrita's thoughts. I'm glad I did and I wish I hadn't at the same time. Rokshan, she's not who she seems to be. She's cruel and sarcastic and—"

"You listened to her thoughts? How dare you intrude on her privacy!"

"I do it all the time and you never complain!" Lamprophyre exclaimed. "Rokshan, she doesn't like me at all. She sees me as an impediment to your relationship with her and was thinking about how hard it would be to separate us. She thinks dragons are stupid because we don't understand your art. And she was bored at even being there. She wondered why she'd agreed to it."

Rokshan was so still he might have been carved of brown agate. Lamprophyre wished he would do something, say something, even if it was yelling at her. "That's not the worst," she went on, feeling her voice shake. "She thought how Dharan is handsomer than you, and how she wished...wished he was a prince. Rokshan, I'm sorry. I'm so, so sorry. But I couldn't not tell you."

Rokshan blinked. He worked his jaw a couple of times. Then he stood. "Forgive me for not thanking you," he said. His voice was as cold as any winter cavern, and as quiet as if he were on the other side of the courtyard instead of standing next to her.

"At least...at least you're not pair-bonded. Married," Lamprophyre said, and instantly regretted her stupid words when he turned the bleakest, darkest look she'd ever seen on her.

"You couldn't have kept this to yourself," he continued in that still, cold, dead voice. "Were you that jealous? Jealous enough to want to rip my heart out?"

"What? Rokshan, no!"

"I might have guessed your ability would end up causing me misery. I'd rather have gone on ignorant. So maybe I can thank you, after all." Rokshan turned his head to look out at the distant street, already working toward a noontime heat. "Thank you, Lamprophyre, for ruining my life. Thank you for intruding where you weren't wanted. And thank you *so* much for not keeping your enormous mouth shut." He'd started walking before the last words fell from his lips, treading across the courtyard with his head bowed and his shoulders hunched as if she'd thrown a punch at him instead of her terrible words.

Lamprophyre watched him until he was swallowed up by the crowds thronging the street. Her head ached more than before, and the tension through her shoulders burned. She laid her head down and covered herself with her wings. She knew Rokshan well enough to know when he was speaking out of pain, and she knew he didn't mean any of what he'd said to her. His words still felt like icy spears aimed at her heart, miraculously capable of piercing dragon hide and freezing her solid.

She lay like that for several hundred beats until she heard approaching footsteps. Not Rokshan, whose tread she would know anywhere. She closed her eyes and pretended to be asleep. Maybe whoever it was would be afraid of disturbing a dragon at her rest. Everyone knew dragons were dangerous. They just didn't know they were only a danger to their best friends.

"Lamprophyre?" Dharan said. "Is something wrong?"

She sighed and raised her head. Dharan wouldn't be balked by something so simple as sleep, and he was one of only three humans in Tanajital who knew she could hear thoughts. "Something terrible," she said. "I listened to Nevrita's thoughts."

"Oh," Dharan said. "Then you know she was only interested in Rokshan for his title."

Lamprophyre sat up. "You knew?" she exclaimed. "Why didn't you tell him?"

"I only met her last night. I came on purpose to meet her. Or did you think Anchala had grown on me?" Dharan settled himself on the ground next to her. "I wasn't sure that's what was going on. I absolutely wasn't going to suggest the possibility to Rokshan unless I was sure. But I can only think of one way in which Nevrita's thoughts could be considered terrible."

"He hates me. I told him what I heard, and he said—oh, it doesn't matter. He was hurt, and he lashed out. But I don't think he'll ever forgive me for being the one to tell him."

"He will. But he needs time to get past feeling like a fool. That's not an easy feeling." Dharan sighed. "Damn Nevrita. I wish women would stop thinking Rokshan is an easy target, just because he's a prince."

"I don't understand. Why would that make him a target?"

Dharan sighed again. "Most nobles marry for political consideration. Love doesn't come into the picture. So there's a certain kind of woman—man, too, to hear Anchala tell it—who believes a prince is a prize to be won instead of a human being with needs and desires like everyone else. They figure love is irrelevant if it means they can be a princess. And Rokshan—" He shook his head. "Rokshan may be the best man I've ever known. He's generous, smart, compassionate, and skilled at making other people into the best versions of themselves. But he's also wary of any woman who expresses an interest in him. That he let Nevrita get close—I don't know what he was thinking. This is going to wound him deeply."

"Is he not handsome? Because Nevrita thought you were more handsome than he."

Dharan scowled. "You didn't tell him that, did you?"

Lamprophyre flinched.

"You did. Well, nothing we can do about that now. Yes, he's handsome, though I'm sure whatever scars he bears have convinced him that's not true. But it doesn't matter. Between this and the last time, I'd be surprised if he's willing to take a chance on love ever again."

"There was a last time? Another Nevrita?"

"Worse." Dharan let out a short, curt laugh that had no humor in it. "Never bring this up with him, understand? We don't talk about it. Ever."

"All right," Lamprophyre said, feeling a little frightened at his vehemence.

"About five years ago, Rokshan was involved with a woman who told him she was carrying his child. He intended to marry her, but I was suspicious. The whole situation was too easy. So I investigated, and discovered that the child had been fathered by another man, someone she still had a relationship with. She wanted a royal pedigree for the brat."

Lamprophyre felt sick again. Knowing that humans could have sex without being married was hard enough to comprehend. That anyone would do something so monstrous as lie about the father of her child made her head spin. "But he's a prince. Could she get away with that?"

"She was destined for execution as soon as the baby was born. Rokshan intervened and sent her into exile without his father knowing. And then he left Tanajital for three months. I have no idea where he went. When he came back, he asked to join the Army and was his old self—so long as nobody brought up that fiasco."

"He said he wasn't going to have sex again until he was married," Lamprophyre said.

"Yes. I can hardly blame him. Wait—he told you that?"

"He was explaining about prostitutes and how it's bad to accuse a man of having sex with one."

Dharan cleared his throat. "You ask the most interesting questions, Lamprophyre. Anyway. This thing with Nevrita will devastate him. He'll need friends when he finally overcomes his instinct to flee."

Lamprophyre's heart ached more fiercely. "He doesn't want to be my friend."

"He's upset because you revealed the truth. He won't stay angry with you, if only because he's too smart not to realize who actually deserves his anger. In fact, I imagine right now he's looking for a reason to end the relationship without revealing that a dragon read Nevrita's mind. I know, it's not reading."

"He can't just stop speaking to her?"

"He introduced her to his mother last night. He's going to need a plausible excuse for why he would do that and then break things off." Dharan rose. "I'll go look for him. Maybe I can help with that. And, Lamprophyre?" Dharan put a hand on her shoulder. "Thank you. I know this seems like disaster now, but you saved him a lifetime of misery. Remember that."

Lamprophyre watched Dharan cross the courtyard as she had Rokshan and was struck by the difference in their gaits, one dejected and angry, the other confident. It made her suddenly furious with Nevrita, that the woman could so callously use Rokshan, treat him as a prize. She rushed from the embassy and took to the skies. She would find Nevrita and scare her senseless, teach her why it was a mistake to hurt the people Lamprophyre loved.

Almost immediately, she remembered she had no idea where Nevrita lived or where she might go during the day. But flying soothed her, and she decided to follow the river downstream a ways, letting her mind wander far from her troubles. She felt a pang at not having Rokshan perched behind her shoulders, but it faded as she swept across the sky, high enough that the air was cool and the sun's warmth was comforting rather than a brutal weapon.

When it was nearly noon, she turned around and flew back toward Tanajital, this time swooping low enough to startle a herd of deer. She almost snatched one up, just for fun, but she wasn't hungry and it would be a waste of good meat.

As she approached the city, she saw orange and red and midnight blue forms making slow loops and occasionally hovering on its far side. Hopefully her clutchmates wouldn't want to converse or race or anything else social, because she still felt a little downcast. But Bromargyrite, Porphyry, and Flint ignored her, and she returned to her embassy without encountering anyone.

She entered the coolness of the hall and stopped with her tail and hindquarters still outside. "Hello," she said to Rokshan, and couldn't think of anything else to say.

Rokshan was sitting next to the slate, flipping the pages of a book in a way that said he wasn't seeing them. "I'm sorry to intrude," he said.

"You're never an intrusion."

Rokshan shut the book and tilted his head back, closing his eyes. "I'm sorry," he said, his voice as quiet as it had been that morning. "I didn't mean any of that—but that's not the point, is it? I was hurt, and I wanted to hurt you so I wouldn't feel alone in my pain. I'm sorry I did that to you."

"I understand." Lamprophyre came fully into the embassy and sat. "I don't blame you."

"Don't worry, I blame myself enough for both of us." He ran his fingers through his hair and opened his eyes. "I just felt so stupid. I swore I'd never get caught like that again, but Nevrita—she was perfect. And maybe that should have been the clue. Nobody's that perfect unless they're trying to be."

"She was very good. If I hadn't listened to her thoughts—I'm sorry I did that."

"I'm not. Forget my self-righteous outburst earlier. If you hadn't found out what she truly is, I might have..." His voice trailed off. "I seem to recall that you offered to do exactly that months ago—listen to the thoughts of any young woman I might be interested in. I should have remembered that sooner, brought her to meet you after the second time we met, and everything would have been simple."

"Dharan said you have to come up with a good, public reason for not seeing her anymore."

"Was Dharan here?" Rokshan laughed the same short, curt laugh Dharan had. "He's probably afraid I'll disappear again. Yes, I've made enough of the 'relationship' with Nevrita that I have to get out of it gracefully and publicly. Much as I wish I could just stop seeing her."

"I'll help if you need me."

This time, his laugh was unforced. "You're still my friend?"

"Of course. You'll have to do worse than say horrible things to me to drive me away."

"God's breath, Lamprophyre, I hope we never find out what it *would* take to drive you away." He got heavily to his feet. "I'll figure something out, or Dharan will. Don't worry about it."

"Do you want to go flying? Or have you eaten yet?"

"I'm not hungry. And flying would be a release. Thanks."

Bromargyrite, Porphyry, and Flint were gone when Lamprophyre and Rokshan rose above the towers of Tanajital. Feeling relieved because she still didn't feel like conversation with anyone, even Rokshan, she flew south and then circled the great city wall around to the north. The fields below were lush with greenery that made her wish she knew the names of the plants, though none of them were edible by dragons. The afternoon rains were on their way, and Lamprophyre cast an expert eye on the clouds; the storm would arrive by midafternoon. She and Rokshan had time for a leisurely flight.

When she reached the northernmost edge of the city, she was surprised to see her clutchmates sitting on the ground that lay between the wall and the first of the fields. Bromargyrite was lying flat on his stomach with his head tucked low near his shoulder. Porphyry and

Flint sat upright, and the sound of a conversation drifted to Lamprophyre's ears. More disturbing were their thoughts, which were all three sullen and angry. Flint looked up when Lamprophyre flew past overhead, but didn't wave. Concerned, Lamprophyre circled back around and landed a dragonlength from the three.

"What's wrong?" she asked. She crouched to let Rokshan climb down. "You're all disturbed by something."

"We've been discussing what to do," Flint said. Porphyry grunted and let out a sharp, acid-scented stream of air from both nostrils. The smell dissipated quickly in the breeze that blew intermittently from the direction of the river. Bromargyrite had his eyes closed and appeared to be asleep, but Lamprophyre could hear how angry he was. For Bromargyrite, the most easygoing dragon in the flight, to become that angry, something must be very wrong. She didn't want to eavesdrop past the general drifting surface emotions dragons didn't care about concealing, but she'd never been so tempted to do so before.

"Do about what?" she asked.

Flint glanced at Bromargyrite as if waiting for him to speak. Bromargyrite put an arm over his face. "The ecclesiasts," he said. "Stones take them. Two of them accosted me while I was in my warehouse."

"*Accosted* you?"

"Challenged him verbally," Flint said, anger touching his words. "Called him a heretic and a godless animal, among other things. Insisted that he worship this stupid Katayan person—sorry, Rokshan, I mean no offense."

"I understand you," Rokshan said. "Did they threaten violence?"

"Against a dragon?" Flint laughed. "They're stupid, but they're not that stupid."

"I think they were trying to goad me into attacking them," Bromargyrite said, his voice muffled by his arm. "I nearly did. They were drawing all sorts of attention, though, and I knew it would go worse for me if I gave in to my instincts. So once I recovered from the surprise of the attack, I flew away." He moved his arm so he could look at Lamprophyre. "Why would anyone do that? I know the ecclesiasts are upset that we don't worship their god, but this felt like they cared more about hurting me than convincing me they were right. I don't understand it."

"I think I do," Rokshan said. "They want to drive you all out of Tanajital. Out of Gonjiri, if they can manage it."

"How is attacking Bromargyrite going to accomplish that?" Lamprophyre asked.

Rokshan paced the ground between Lamprophyre and Flint. "You dragons have proved you're not violent," he said, "and the ecclesiasts know your response to being attacked is to remove yourselves from the situation. Like Bromargyrite did. They probably also know the odds of converting you to the worship of Katayan are vanishingly small. But you're still a threat to their power. So they're going to keep attacking until you're so uncomfortable you leave the city." He stopped pacing and looked up at Lamprophyre with his hands on his hips. "No more dragons, no more challenge to their authority, no more dealing with people doubting their teachings."

"But we don't want to leave," Porphyry said. "Humans are interesting, the ones that aren't calling us names, anyway. And I'm still learning to read."

"I don't want you to leave, either, and I'm sure my father feels the same," Rokshan said. "Your presence here supports the alliance he needs to keep Fanishkor from attacking. But he has very little power over the ecclesiasts. If all they do is call names and insult you, well, there's no law against that. But there has to be something we can do to counter them."

"Something," Flint said irritably. "It had better be something effective, because I don't know how forbearing I can be if this goes on much longer."

"We can't attack humans, even the ecclesiasts," Lamprophyre said.

"I know." Flint sighed, and more acid-tinged air drifted toward Lamprophyre. "But we can fight back. Actively challenge their authority. We can show them we aren't helpless targets."

"That would just make things worse," Rokshan said. "They'd feel even more justified in trying to get rid of you. But being humble and courteous won't work either, not if the ecclesiasts are determined to anger you." He rubbed a hand over his face. "I'm sorry. It's been a bad day and I'm not thinking clearly."

"Bad day?" Flint asked.

Rokshan shook his head. "It's not important. What matters is deciding what to do next. For now, you need to stay away from the ecclesiasts. I can have a detachment of soldiers guard the streets surrounding the warehouses who will turn everyone away, including the ecclesiasts, and that will contain the problem for now. Let me and Lamprophyre work on a more long-term solution. I think diplomacy is the key."

Lamprophyre didn't feel like being diplomatic with anyone who called her friend an animal, but she nodded agreement. "Maybe we can figure out something else the ecclesiasts want," she said. "Some compromise. Much as I feel we shouldn't have to."

"Can you three wait outside the city until sunset?" Rokshan asked. "That will give me time to post guards. I'm sorry to have to ask that of you."

"We'll go for a swim," Bromargyrite said. "I want to wash away the nasty feeling those ecclesiasts gave me. I hate being angry."

"Those ecclesiasts were lucky in their choice of targets," Flint said. "Any of the rest of us might have lashed out. The Gentle Giant is more temperate."

Bromargyrite's orange scales darkened to red as he blushed. Lamprophyre hadn't heard anyone call him that in over twenty years, but his size—he was as big as Lamprophyre, very big for a male—and his placid temperament had earned him the nickname when he was very young. Probably his clumsiness was related to his size. She smiled fondly at him. "You'd never hurt anyone, however provoked you were."

"Let's hope that stays true," Bromargyrite said gruffly, but he smiled, too.

The three males flew off south and west toward the river while Lamprophyre and Rokshan returned to the embassy. "I think I could eat," Rokshan said as he dismounted in the courtyard. "And then we can discuss the problem further."

Lamprophyre nodded. She headed for the cool darkness of the hall, then stopped, startled, because someone was already within.

"Coquina?" she said. She couldn't think of any way to ask what the dragon was doing there without making it an accusation. "Are you all right?"

Coquina emerged from the hall, and Lamprophyre's surprise turned to alarm. She'd never seen Coquina look so distraught. Her eyes were wide, the pupils dilated almost to circles, her breathing was heavy, and she moved restlessly, as if she weren't in control of her limbs. "Lamprophyre," she said, "I'm afraid I've killed someone."

CHAPTER EIGHT

"*Stones*," Lamprophyre swore, and took Coquina by the shoulders and hustled her back inside the embassy. The hall was big enough to comfortably fit no more than two dragons, but right now Lamprophyre felt crowded, as if Coquina were twice her size and had her wings spread wide instead of folded forlornly along her sides. "What happened? Who was it? A human, yes?"

"I don't know," Coquina said. "I mean, yes, humans, but I don't know if they're dead—"

"*They*? More than one? Coquina, *what happened?*"

"Take a breath, both of you," Rokshan said. Lamprophyre hadn't noticed him follow her inside. "Coquina, tell us from the beginning."

Coquina nodded. "It was about a thousand beats ago. I was at the coliseum." Her voice was so subdued it was hard to believe this was the same brash dragon who'd made Lamprophyre's life a misery for years. "There's a game some humans and I invented, where they throw things in the air and I burn them before they touch the ground. People come to watch. But today, three of those ecclesiasts in their carrying cages—"

Lamprophyre groaned and closed her eyes. Rokshan said a few of the human swear words he refused to teach her the meaning of. "They harassed you," he said in a flat, angry voice.

"How did you know?" Coquina asked. "Yes. They came right onto the floor in the middle of the game. That's so dangerous, and I nearly set the royal box on fire by accident. I swear it was an accident. They startled me. And then they started shouting things about me. Horrible, stupid insults. But they were so stupid I just laughed." She laughed now, a brittle, almost hysterical sound. "That made them so angry. And my friends—the players—they were laughing too, and they yelled insults back at the ecclesiasts. Then the ecclesiasts told the humans who carry them to attack my friends. And it wasn't funny anymore."

She took a deep breath and made a visible effort to control her trembling. A shadow passed over her face, and Lamprophyre glanced up, but saw only the storm clouds gathering in preparation for the afternoon rains.

"Those human males who carry the cages are much bigger than my friends, and have those strange bulging muscles," Coquina continued. "And most of my friends are females and not very strong. Fast, but not strong." She breathed in deeply again, this time blowing out a puff of smoke. "I couldn't let them hurt my friends. So I got between the two groups and spread my wings so I'd look bigger and hopefully scarier. But I moved too fast, and I knocked over one of my friends, and when I turned to help her up, I swung my tail and hit two of the large males. I really didn't mean to, I swear, Lamprophyre. But they fell, and they didn't get up. Then the ecclesiasts were shouting again, and my friends were pressing me closely, and the next time I moved, it was one of my friends I hit."

Coquina's trembling had all but stopped, but her eyes were still dilated and her gaze darted everywhere but at Lamprophyre. "I tried to help her up, and the ecclesiasts' servants started hitting me. It didn't hurt, obviously, but between that and the shouting and the fact that I couldn't turn anywhere without hurting a human, I panicked. I backed away carefully, and once I was free of everyone except the males hitting me, I flew away. And then I came here." Another puff of smoke jetted from her nostrils. "I don't know what to do. If I killed them—"

"Let's worry about one thing at a time," Rokshan said. "You did the right thing in coming here. This embassy is legally dragon territory, and you can claim asylum if you need to."

Coquina looked at Lamprophyre in puzzlement. "He means Gonjirian soldiers can't take you away to prison, or—yes, I know, there's no way they can confine a dragon, but that's the idea. That you're safe from retaliation here."

Coquina nodded. "But I'm worried about Melika," she said. "The female I knocked over. If I killed her, I don't know if I can live with that."

"Lamprophyre and I will find out what happened to all of them," Rokshan said. "And we'll bring word."

"It's all right, Coquina—or, rather, it will be all right," Lamprophyre said. Consoling Coquina struck her as the most ludicrous thing she had done all day—weren't they enemies? She looked into Coquina's fear-stricken face and remembered the day, years and years ago, when Coquina had brushed past her rather than greeting her and had gone on to ignore her invitations to play, sighing dramatically and saying she'd outgrown childish things. If they were enemies, it was past time they put that enmity behind them. "The ecclesiasts are trying to force dragons out of Tanajital. They attacked Bromargyrite today, too. This is entirely their fault."

"Morally, maybe," Coquina said. "I'm not sure human law would agree. I'm the one who did the damage."

"You let us deal with that." Lamprophyre gripped her shoulder briefly. "We'll be back soon. Stay here, don't let anyone see you, and try to calm down. If Dharan shows up, tell him what happened and ask him to wait for us to return. He might have a solution none of us have thought of."

Coquina nodded and settled herself on the floor of the hall. Lamprophyre followed Rokshan into the courtyard and crouched for him to climb up. "Where do we go first?" she said.

"Over a thousand beats. That's nearly an hour ago," Rokshan said. "Let's try the coliseum anyway. There might still be people there who saw what happened and know where the victims were taken."

The coliseum was empty when they arrived. Rokshan swore again. "That makes it harder," he said. "We might have to go to the Archprelate's palace and demand to see the ecclesiasts responsible. I doubt very much they were acting on their own initiative."

"Maybe not," Lamprophyre said, listening to the ebb and flow of human thoughts. "I mean it might not be that hard." She descended on the western side of the coliseum to land on the street outside, very slowly to give the humans time to move out of her way. The last thing they needed was more human injuries.

"Excuse me," she said to the crowd, which had gone very still. "There was an accident here about an hour ago involving some ecclesiasts and the big grass-green dragon. Can anyone tell me what happened?"

No one moved. No one spoke. "Please," Lamprophyre said. She could still hear their drifting thoughts, and many of them were about Coquina's accident. "This is important. My friend Coquina is very worried that she hurt humans, and we need to know what happened here."

"She should've been more careful, big brute like that," someone called out from the center of the crowd. People immediately moved to give the speaker space, as if they were afraid of being too near her. Calling Coquina a brute was a bad choice of words that might justifiably provoke her fellow dragon, though of course Lamprophyre wasn't going to take offense and retaliate.

"I understand she was pressed closely on all sides," Lamprophyre replied politely. "Aren't humans sometimes injured by accident in large crowds like this? I promise Coquina was trying to be careful, and this was a terrible accident. Did you see what started the conflict?"

The woman glared at Lamprophyre, but said nothing. Lamprophyre, listening to the woman's thoughts, said, "So you didn't see it. Wasn't there anyone here who did?"

"I did," a man said. Once more the crowd shifted so he stood alone. He was tall for a human and built like the swaying willows that grew by the riverbank. "I go to all the dragon games. Never seen an ecclesiast take an interest until today, and then three of them show up."

Relief flooded through Lamprophyre. "Three? In litters?"

"Yes, but with the drapes tied back. They came right onto the floor in the middle of the game, which is damn dangerous if you ask me. All that fire flying around. But they came in shouting for the game to stop, which made the audience angry."

"Why is that?" Rokshan asked.

Lamprophyre thought the answer was obvious, but to her surprise the man ducked his head furtively. "We wager on the game," he said, "begging your pardon, your highness."

"I'll pretend I didn't hear that," Rokshan said. Lamprophyre hadn't thought there was anything wrong with wagering, given how humans seemed compelled to wager on almost anything, but clearly there was something shameful or possibly illegal about it. "So the game was interrupted. I take it the players all stopped what they were doing?"

The willowy man nodded. "The ecclesiasts verbally attacked Coquina right away," he said. "Told her she ought to worship Katayan, and then yelled insults and demands when she refused. Look. It's not my place to say, but I think Katayan is pleased that there are dragons in the world again, and I don't know why dragons don't worship him. But you can't force anyone to believe a certain way, and Jiwanyil knows if you did, that belief wouldn't be worth anything."

"That's very wise," Rokshan said, nodding. "So the ecclesiasts were yelling and insulting Coquina?"

"She laughed at them," the man said with a smile. "Probably not the best idea, since nobody likes being laughed at, but it got the other players laughing, and then the audience was laughing too because the ecclesiasts actually got out of their litters and were shaking their fists and acting like a bad performance of Falat."

"A paraveti tangal role," Rokshan murmured to Lamprophyre. "And that angered the ecclesiasts more."

"Right." The smile fell away from the man's face. "I'm not right sure what happened next. The ecclesiasts ordered their bearers to arrest the players—I don't think ecclesiasts have that power—"

"They don't. Go on."

"Anyway, the bearers attacked, Coquina got in the middle of the fight to protect the players, and next I knew there were bodies on the ground and the watchers in the lowest tier were climbing over the wall to join the fight. Coquina flew away somewhere in the middle of that, but the fight kept going until the city guard broke it up. They arrested the bearers and anyone else they could prove had been in the fight, and the bodies were taken away. Don't know where."

"Were they still alive?" Lamprophyre asked.

The man shrugged. "Don't know. I think so. They were more careful with them than if they'd been corpses."

That relieved Lamprophyre's mind. "What happened to the ecclesiasts?"

"They left on foot." The man laughed. "Guess I shouldn't be amused by that, but I've never seen an ecclesiast walk anywhere. It made them seem more like ordinary people, and that's...I don't know. Almost like seeing Jiwanyil himself treading the streets."

"I understand," Rokshan said. "Thank you, sirrah. We hope to have this misunderstanding cleared up shortly, and for the games to resume so you can, of course, not wager on them." He kept a perfectly straight face as he said this, but the man chuckled and nodded as if Rokshan had said something else. "Anyone who witnessed the events is invited to come to the dragon embassy to have your story recorded. We and Coquina appreciate your testimony and your assistance in seeing justice done."

He climbed back up to his seat, and Lamprophyre, having checked carefully for humans pressing too near, leaped into the sky. "Where now? The Archprelate's palace, to find those ecclesiasts?" she asked when they were high enough not to be overheard.

"They'll be protected there, almost as well as Coquina will be at the embassy," Rokshan replied. "The next step is to find where they took the injured and learn if any of them survived. There are centers for healing throughout the city, and I'm guessing our three victims were taken to the nearest one."

"Good idea. Where is it?"

"A few streets over from the coliseum. But you can't accompany me there. The streets are too narrow."

Lamprophyre scowled. Stupid human city with no regard for the needs of large creatures. "So what do I do?"

"Go to the central guard post and find out who was responsible for arresting the brawlers. We'll need their testimony as well."

"I don't understand why we're asking all these people to tell the story. Don't we just need Coquina and the ecclesiasts, and maybe Coquina's human companions?"

"Because those ecclesiasts will try to spin the story their way, and we need as many witnesses as possible to counter them. An ecclesiast's testimony carries more weight than it should, since people assume as Jiwanyil's voices, they're honest and infallible."

"You mean they might lie."

"Absolutely." Rokshan leaned forward along her right side. "Why, don't dragons have problems with two dragons giving different versions of the same event?"

Lamprophyre shook her head. Below, Tanajital was a dull brown under the storm clouds that blocked most of the sun's rays, and she cast no shadow on the buildings. "Dragons don't lie. Hearing thoughts means lying is pointless. If two dragons understand a situation differently, they work together to understand why. Gaining that understanding is considered a gift, and it brings the dragons closer. We only know about lying from stories of humans."

"That's disheartening, that lying is something we might be known for, but not unjustified." Rokshan pointed. "The center of healing is down there. If you let me off near the park, I can walk the rest of the way. You know where the guard headquarters is?"

"On the west side, in that big open plaza, yes."

She descended to land outside the park that circled the palace. From above, it looked like a green moat dividing the palace from the rest of Tanajital. At ground level, it smelled richly of leaves and thick emerald grass, and trees grew thickly enough that most of the palace was invisible. All that showed were its golden roofs, angled or domed and giving off whiffs of tangy metal. It was still a few thousand beats before suppertime, but the smell roused Lamprophyre's hunger.

Rokshan hopped down without waiting for her to crouch. "We'll meet back at the embassy before supper, all right? Remember, you want the witnesses of the guards who broke up the fight."

"I understand."

Rokshan saluted her with a wave and ran off northward. Lamprophyre beat the air with her wings until she was just above the trees, then headed west.

CHAPTER NINE

S he had never visited the guard headquarters, but its enormous stone construction, mountain-like in its peaked shape, was an obvious landmark from the air. Rokshan hadn't known why it was so big, or if it had been something other than guard headquarters once as Lamprophyre suspected. Her familiarity with the buildings and towers of Tanajital told her that most structures that size and height belonged either to wealthy individuals or to the government or royal family. She was still fuzzy on the difference between the last two.

The guard headquarters was shaped like a pyramid of stone, but perfectly regular, as if someone had cut square sections out of a mountain, each smaller than the last, and stacked them atop each other. The topmost level was a little more than two dragonlengths in each direction and made a perfect landing platform, but Lamprophyre had a feeling the city guard would take offense at her intruding on their territory. So instead, she landed on the plaza—Dharan's word—in front of the guard post.

The plaza was a great sweep of stone wide enough for all of Lamprophyre's clutch to sit close together, if they weren't concerned about trampling the plants that grew in stone boxes at regular intervals across it. It, too, was evidence to Lamprophyre that the headquarters hadn't always belonged to the guard, because it didn't strike her as necessary to their work. The plaza looked more like a place where street performers would gather, and that turned out to be true.

Today, the musicians who performed with a variety of musical instruments Lamprophyre had no names for scattered as she descended, though at nearly midafternoon, the hottest part of the day even when a storm loomed, most humans were indoors. She felt sorry for the musicians and wondered if they made so little money from their efforts that they couldn't afford to go inside. Maybe some of them visited the embassy in the evenings for free food.

She looked around carefully to make sure there were no humans in her way, then crossed the plaza to the guard headquarters. To her surprise, there was no one guarding the doors, which were too small for her to enter. Though maybe it wasn't so surprising, because who would attack a building full of armed men?

She knocked politely on the doors and sat back. Nothing happened. She was about to knock again, more loudly this time, when the doors flew open and a dozen men wearing the sky-blue tunics and short tan pants of the city guard emerged at a run. They all held short, fat sticks above their heads in preparation to attack. When they saw her, they stumbled to a halt, some of them running into their companions and staggering from the impact. Wide-eyed, they spread out slowly, never taking their eyes from Lamprophyre. Their thoughts were a muddle of confusion and fear, and from a few of them Lamprophyre gathered her gentle knocking hadn't been so gentle, and they'd thought she was a battering ram. The image amused her, or would have if she hadn't still felt so tense.

"I beg your pardon," she said in her least thunderous voice. "I seem to have startled you. I'm not attacking, I promise. I'm here to ask some questions about the, um, incident at the coliseum earlier today."

None of them lowered their sticks, but their thoughts became less fearful and more confused—all but one man, who was thinking *should have expected this, don't know what to say to a dragon.* Lamprophyre focused on him. Unlike the others, he wore a bronze circle of metal too small for Lamprophyre to see in any detail attached to the left side of his blue tunic. "Are you the leader?" she asked. "I'm sorry, I don't know much about the city guard except that you are a kind of soldier and that you report to one of General Sajan's commanders. And that you keep the peace."

The man stepped forward, finally lowering his stick. "If you're here for revenge, you're in violation of Tanajital's laws," he said in a harsh voice that concealed fear. "And you should tell the green dragon to give itself up for judgment, because it's in violation too."

"*Her* name is Coquina," Lamprophyre said, "and she wasn't at fault. She has sanctuary in the dragon embassy while we sort this out."

"Protecting a criminal makes you guilty as well," the man said. "We have laws, and you dragons have to follow them while you live here. Don't think you can get away with killing people."

Lamprophyre sucked in a breath. "They're dead?"

The man shrugged. "Not sure. They were alive when they were taken to the healing center. But one of them was in a bad way."

Lamprophyre closed her eyes and sent up a quick prayer to Mother Stone for patience. "I'm not here for revenge, and we're not interested in breaking laws with impunity," she said. "I just want to talk to the guards who broke up the riot. We need their testimony to prove that the ecclesiasts were as much at fault as Coquina and her friends, or more so. Though if the guards arrived after the fight started, they don't know what caused it."

"Not our business," the man said. "We're responsible for keeping the peace." A tendril of doubt and the words *knew something was up* threaded through his thoughts.

"I know, and all I'm asking is for your men to tell the truth," Lamprophyre said. "Those ecclesiasts baited Coquina, and when she tried to protect her friends from the men the ecclesiasts ordered to attack them, she accidentally hurt people."

"That wasn't part of the report."

"As I said, I'm sure your men didn't witness that. But they did arrest some of the bearers as well as the game players and probably the watchers who got involved in the fight. So they know the ecclesiasts had something to do with it."

"Those bearers were defending themselves!" another man said. The guard captain, as Lamprophyre assumed he was, glared at the speaker. The man ignored his captain. "That dragon is dangerous!"

Lamprophyre felt sick. She hadn't considered that the guards might have misunderstood the situation. She could tell the man wasn't lying to protect the bearers, but if he was a religious man who believed the lies the ecclesiasts were spreading, his testimony would damn Coquina rather than exonerate her.

"Did you see Coquina—the dragon—attack anyone?" she asked as calmly as she could manage.

The man swallowed hard, his fear at having Lamprophyre's attention making his thoughts incoherent. "She was gone when we got there," he said.

"Then you didn't see what she did, and you shouldn't make accusations about something you didn't see," Lamprophyre said. "Dragons believe in being honest, and that means not claiming witness of events they weren't present for. Are humans different?"

"No, they are not," the guard captain growled, directing another glare at the man. "And guards are meant to be impartial in their enforcement of the law. Turn the dragon over to us, and we'll see that she receives justice."

"Sirrah, you can't confine a dragon."

"If it's—she's—innocent, she won't try to escape."

"Even so, she has asked for sanctuary and I've granted it. I promise she won't leave Tanajital until this is straightened out. Will you accept my word?"

The guard captain's scowl became truly ferocious. "You don't trust us?"

"Have you arrested the ecclesiasts who incited the riot?" Lamprophyre asked, inspired.

"Arrest ecclesiasts? Are you mad?" the guard captain exclaimed.

"Then you can't arrest Coquina either," Lamprophyre said. "If you're so concerned about fairness and impartiality."

The guard captain let out a deep breath. "Damn," he said, so quietly she almost couldn't hear him. The wind had picked up and was doing its best to carry their words away from the oncoming storm. "All right," he finally said. "She doesn't leave Tanajital." *Doesn't matter, not like we can execute a dragon for murder.*

"I promise she'll stay here," Lamprophyre said. "Will you send the guards who controlled the riot to the dragon embassy to have their witnesses recorded?" She privately hoped he wouldn't send the outspoken man, but even his word counted. Maybe not for the right side, but it counted.

"I will," the guard captain said. "I don't like disorder in my city. Are there going to be more incidents like this one?"

"That's up to the ecclesiasts," Lamprophyre said, feeling unspeakably grateful that Bromargyrite was as easygoing as he was. "Dragons haven't incited any riots and will continue to be inoffensive and interested in coexisting peacefully with humans. You have my word on that."

The guard captain was thinking hard about ecclesiasts, and Lamprophyre heard *so many of them in the streets these days, any more problems and I might have to kill my career arresting an ecclesiast.* She hadn't realized there were more ecclesiasts about than usual, but then most of the streets of Tanajital were too narrow for her to walk, and she hadn't thought to watch for their litters as she flew overhead.

"I'm returning to the embassy now, and I'll watch for your men's arrival. Please tell them not to be afraid. We won't hurt them, and we won't be angry no matter what their witness is." Lamprophyre spread her wings. The copper membranes caught the wan light dimly, turning almost brown. She waited for the guards to retreat before flapping hard to lift herself into the sky, feeling as if she were fighting the leaden, wet air of the storm. With a few last beats of her wings, she glided toward the embassy.

CHAPTER TEN

With the guard captain's thoughts in mind, Lamprophyre flew slowly, examining the narrow streets for the conspicuous colored rectangles of the ecclesiasts' litters. She knew most of them had yellow curtains, and that the High Ecclesiasts like Khadar each had their own color. Almost immediately, she saw a yellow one, moving rather quickly in the direction of the Archprelate's palace. She suspected it was racing the storm. These afternoon storms poured rain down hard and fast enough that flying was impossible, and she imagined the downpour would saturate the curtains and get the ecclesiast inside very wet. It was a cheering thought.

She saw no other litters, but the streets were almost empty of ordinary traffic, so if there were more ecclesiasts about than normal, she would have to try searching for them another time. Making another slow, wide turn, she descended to the embassy courtyard and furled her wings just as the first heavy drops fell.

She hurried inside and nearly bumped into Coquina, who was drawing pictures on one of Lamprophyre's slates. "Oh! Sorry."

"No, I was in the way." Coquina dropped the chalk and shifted to the back of the embassy. "Did you find out about Melika?"

"We think she was taken to a place where they have adepts who heal people. It's too narrow for a dragon to fit, so Rokshan will inquire. I guess he's not back yet."

"No, and Dharan hasn't come either. I've just been sitting here wishing I could wind back time and make different choices." Coquina settled low on the ground, looking so dejected Lamprophyre's heart went out to her.

"We've spoken to people who witnessed the event, and they're going to speak—maybe not in your defense, precisely, but they'll tell the truth, and that should be enough."

"Enough for what?" Coquina let out a puff of smoke. "I don't know anything about how humans deal with criminals. And don't they think ecclesiasts are above the law?"

Lamprophyre remembered the guard captain's shock when she'd suggested he arrest the ecclesiasts who'd started the riot. "I'm sure King Ekanath doesn't think so, and we can take this to him if we have to."

Outside, the rain hammered down on the courtyard and struck the roof with a hissing, rattling sound as if someone were pouring gravel over the steeply slanted roof tiles. Lamprophyre half-turned away from Coquina to watch the water sheeting down from the sky. "But the ecclesiasts were at fault, and we'll prove that," she added, speaking loudly to be heard over the clatter.

Coquina said nothing. Lamprophyre settled her head on her arms and breathed in the smell of water mixing with the hard earth of the courtyard. It reminded her of the river near her mountain home that swelled its banks in spring and carried with the rapid, icy flow a rush of sediment that gave the water a loamy, rich scent. It was impossible to drink, of course, coating the tongue with a fur of soil particles, but it smelled delicious, like living stone.

"Why did we stop being friends?" Coquina said.

Lamprophyre jerked upright in surprise. Coquina was tracing circles on the packed earth of the floor and wasn't looking at her. "What do you mean?" she asked, stupidly.

"We were such good friends as dragonets, and then everything changed. But now I can't remember what happened. Only that we've been at odds for years."

"Because you treated me like an inferior, and mocked me, and never let me forget it when you beat me at something," Lamprophyre replied, hot anger replacing her stunned amazement.

"That, I remember," Coquina said, still not looking up. "But you stopped wanting to do things with me. You didn't want to give up childish games, and all I wanted was for us to start acting like adults. Together. We were the only females in the clutch, Lamprophyre, it's not like I had anyone else my age to share things with. And you weren't interested. I felt so betrayed, and I didn't know how to talk it out. So I pretended it didn't matter because I felt stupid about letting your behavior get to me."

Lamprophyre realized her mouth was hanging open and shut it with a snap. "That might make sense for a first reaction," she heard herself say, "but it doesn't excuse all the years after that."

Coquina shrugged, a strange gesture from someone lying nearly prone. "It felt like once I'd started down that path, I didn't know how to stop. And you were smarter than me, and better at poetry recitation, and I was sure Hyaloclast wanted you for her successor and then you really would be superior, because you'd be my queen—"

Lamprophyre laughed. "Hyaloclast has never shown any interest in making me her heir. I was thinking it would be Chrysoprase."

"You're smarter than Chrysoprase, too."

"Maybe, but I'm sure intelligence isn't the most important quality in a queen."

Coquina shrugged again. "I'm sorry," she said. "I didn't behave very well. We should have done the honorable thing and talked it out with the flight, and I don't know that my youth is any excuse."

"I wasn't honorable either," Lamprophyre said. "I was ashamed of being so jealous of you—"

"Jealous of me? Why?"

"Please. You're beautiful, you win all the races, you're witty. I always felt so stupid around you."

Coquina got heavily to her feet. "That's hilarious. I was jealous of you. I don't think you realize how admired you are for your memory. Nobody in the flight knows as much poetry as you do, except maybe old Scoria, and you're far better at recitation than she is."

Lamprophyre blushed. "I didn't know anyone thought that way."

"It's true." Coquina laughed, a weary, bitter sound. "I can't believe I had to nearly kill someone to become humble enough to ask your forgiveness."

Guilt flooded through Lamprophyre, chilling her hot, embarrassed blood. "Hyaloclast chastised me for being jealous of you," she said, "but even that wasn't enough for me to humble myself, either. I'm sorry, Coquina. I should have remembered that early friendship and tried to get it back."

"So should I," Coquina said. "Can we? Be friends again, I mean?"

"We are," Lamprophyre said. "And it's not so bad. We only have twenty-seven years of lost time to make up for."

Coquina laughed. "No time at all."

She settled herself beside Lamprophyre, and the two of them watched the rain in silence. Pale sunlight slanted through an unexpected gap in the clouds, lighting a spot on the courtyard that shifted gradually as the clouds moved. It looked like a yellow leaf, floating along the surface of the courtyard as if it were a deep pool and not an expanse of earth whose top layer was being churned into mud. The falling raindrops plinked into the mud and were soaked up, making Lamprophyre imagine the courtyard was desperate for moisture and wished to be a green field of human crops instead of a sterile landing ground for dragons.

After a few hundred beats, the rain changed from being a waterfall downpour to a steady sprinkle and then passed entirely, heading westward toward distant Fanishkor. Lamprophyre propped herself on her elbows. "I wonder how long it will take those humans to come here," she said. "We really do need Dharan and Rokshan. Someone will have to write down their witnesses, or something. I don't know how it works."

"I just want to know that Melika's all right, and that the other players don't hate me," Coquina said. "I never imagined I would be friends with humans, but it's not that remarkable, is it? They're rational creatures just like we are."

Lamprophyre thought of the guard who'd been so adamant about the ecclesiasts being victims and wondered about the "rational" part of that statement. "Rokshan is my best friend," she said. "I certainly didn't expect that. Though sometimes I wish he was a dragon. He'd be a good one." She'd occasionally imagined them flying together, side by side, and it was a satisfying daydream.

"I almost wish I were human," Coquina said, "or at least human-sized. It would be fun to be able to play with my human friends on their terms."

Lamprophyre shuddered. "I wouldn't be human if you paid me," she said, using one of Dharan's favorite phrases, and then realized she'd spoken like a human and blushed.

Coquina shifted her weight. "There's Rokshan," she said, "and it looks like he found Dharan." She got to her feet and exited the embassy. She didn't seem to care about the thin mud clinging to her feet and the underside of her tail. Lamprophyre followed her, more reluctantly.

Rokshan and Dharan were both damp, as if they'd left shelter before the rain had fully stopped. "Nobody died," Rokshan called out from across the courtyard. Coquina stopped where she was, her shoulders slumping in relief. "There were five people injured, three by Coquina and two by the fighting, which is damn near miraculous."

"It sounds bad," Lamprophyre said.

"You've never seen a riot," Dharan said. "People get hurt who aren't even throwing punches. Probably more of the participants were injured, just not badly enough to require healing attention."

"So Melika is all right?" Coquina asked.

"She was fully healed right after I arrived. I paid for the healing with embassy money, Lamprophyre," Rokshan said.

"That's acceptable," said Lamprophyre. "What about the ecclesiasts' bearers?"

"Also healed, though I didn't offer to pay for them. There were a couple of ecclesiasts there speaking with the adepts, and I saw the bearers walk out with them, so their healing was complete as well."

"I'm so glad," Coquina said.

"I'm not," Rokshan said. "Oh, all right, I'm glad for your sake, Coquina, but they deserved a beating. Being willing to attack others, some of them women smaller and weaker than they—that's reprehensible. But it doesn't matter. Since no one died, this situation has become much less complex."

"And we may be in a position to go after the ecclesiasts," Dharan said. "I found Rokshan returning here just before the storm hit, and we discussed things while we were hiding from it. If we can get enough witnesses to swear to the ecclesiasts' behavior, I'm sure we can accuse them of inciting riot, and that *is* a crime. One they won't be able to hide from behind ecclesiastical privilege."

"But will we find enough witnesses?" Lamprophyre asked. "It's a big city, and I get the feeling most people don't like coming to the attention of the law, even indirectly."

"We have all of the men and women who play that game with Coquina," Rokshan said. "I told Melika to bring them here. And there's the man we spoke with outside the coliseum. If he comes here, we can ask him about others he knows who were present, and invite them to speak up as well. Ten or twelve witnesses to match the twelve bearers—"

"Which is also a point in our favor," Dharan said. "Twelve strong men were ordered to attack a group half their size and not as strongly built. That suggests the ecclesiasts had this outcome in mind from the start."

"This might work," Lamprophyre said. "Because aside from clearing Coquina of any legal charges, we want to keep the ecclesiasts from continuing to attack dragons. If they know they can be arrested for breaking the law, they'll be less likely to do so."

"Leaving them to try something they can't be caught at," Coquina said.

The others stared at her. "It's obvious," she said. "The ecclesiasts won't stop until they get rid of dragons in Tanajital. If it's a matter of religion, they'll be devoted to that cause. We can't stop being alert for whatever they try next."

Her words brought Lamprophyre down to earth. "She's right," she said. "They'll try something we can't defend against."

"Let's worry about that later," Rokshan said. "We still need to resolve Coquina's problem. And I haven't yet arranged for soldiers to guard the warehouses."

"Why soldiers, and not the city guard?" Lamprophyre asked.

"The city guard are soldiers whose first responsibility is to keeping the peace in Tanajital," Rokshan explained, "but keeping the peace means non-lethal force. It's why they carry truncheons rather than swords. The soldiers of the Army are intended to fight non-Gonjirians, but they are also deployed in times of extreme domestic crisis. Setting them to defend dragons sends a different message than if I asked for a detachment of guards. It says Gonjiri sees a threat to dragons as a threat to the country. Also, they won't be intimidated by the ecclesiasts unless the Archprelate himself shows up demanding to be let through. And that's not going to happen."

"Why can't we talk to the Archprelate? He has to be the one who gave the ecclesiasts their orders."

"Lamprophyre, nobody talks to the Archprelate. He lives in seclusion so he's untainted by the ways of the world and capable of receiving the purest revelations."

"Or because he's being manipulated by the High Ecclesiasts," Dharan murmured. Rokshan glowered at him. "All right," Dharan continued, "I don't actually believe that. I *do* believe it's a mistake for the person entrusted with the spiritual well-being of a nation to be so isolated he doesn't know what the people need."

"Jiwanyil knows what the people need. Are you saying the Archprelate doesn't speak with Jiwanyil? All his prophecies are on record," Rokshan said.

"I don't want to get into a religious debate, Rokshan. What matters is that you're right about this problem not being able to be resolved by someone talking to the Archprelate. We'll just have to be careful."

Rokshan nodded, though Lamprophyre could tell he wanted to go on arguing about his faith. "Then I'll go speak to Sajan and arrange for troops to block off the dragons' territory. Dharan, will you wait here and take down any witnesses from people who arrive? Lamprophyre, if you'll fly with me, that will speed things up. I don't want your clutchmates forced to spend the night outside the city."

Lamprophyre nodded. Coquina said, "I suppose I have to wait, still. It's all right, I don't mind, I just wish there were more I could do."

"Time enough for that when the ecclesiasts invent a new plan," Rokshan said.

Lamprophyre crouched, muddying an elbow, and Rokshan climbed up. His sandals left streaks of mud down her side. A bath was in order just as soon as everything dried out enough that she wouldn't get muddy again immediately. In this weather, that wouldn't take long. She took off with a powerful push of her hind legs, flapped hard to gain altitude, and headed for the Army buildings on the far side of the palace. It felt good to take action. It would feel better to stop those ecclesiasts for good.

COOL NIGHT AIR BRUSHED LAMPROPHYRE'S FACE, AND THE HUM OF the wind blowing past the window openings near the embassy's ceiling was as soothing as a lullaby. Beside her, Coquina breathed softly enough that if not for her body's heat, Lamprophyre might have imagined her gone back to her own warehouse.

It had been a busy afternoon. She and Rokshan had returned from arranging for soldiers to block the entrances to the dragons' warehouses to find the courtyard full of humans. Some of them were Coquina's friends, and they'd been chattering animatedly beside the dining pavilion, surrounding Coquina like bees courting a rose. Others were men and women who'd been in the coliseum, more than Lamprophyre had anticipated. Their thoughts were all indignant, but not at Coquina; they were upset that the game had been interrupted and angry with the high-handedness of the ecclesiasts.

"I respect them because they speak with Jiwanyil," one of those women had said, "but some of them seem to think that means they're better than the rest of us. We're all Jiwanyil's creations, aren't we? I'm more comfortable with the reverend who lives four doors down from my family. He's generous and he cares about seeing that the children get a good religious education."

"The ecclesiasts are frightened of dragons," Lamprophyre had replied, "and frightened people do stupid things. At least, dragons are that way."

"Humans too," the woman had said. Craning her neck to look Lamprophyre in the eye, she'd added, "And why don't you worship Katayan the way any right-thinking creature would?"

She hadn't sounded accusatory despite her choice of words, just curious, and Lamprophyre, feeling uncomfortable, had told her, "Dragons are raised to believe in Mother Stone. I had never heard of Katayan before coming here."

"Which is a blessing. Now that you know about him, you can worship properly."

"We do worship properly," Lamprophyre had said, hotly, "and why is it you're so convinced you're right? Dragons are older than humankind, so shouldn't that mean we know the truth?"

The woman had stiffened and turned away without saying anything else. Lamprophyre had feared she'd made a mistake—but she wasn't going to deny her faith just to keep humans happy, and it was past time they learned that.

At suppertime, Lamprophyre and Coquina had eaten and watched the beggars come for a meal. Coquina had looked sad when the old man arrived. "His mind is broken," she'd said. "It's like a mass of shattered stone, some of it with sharp edges. How terrible for him. Suppose he was someone brilliant once?"

"I think it's tragic no matter who he used to be, but I take your meaning," Lamprophyre had said. She'd chosen not to explain the Sister of the Red prostitute, feeling too bone-weary from the excitement of the day to deal with Coquina's probable shock when she learned about humans and sex. It seemed as if her fight with Rokshan was years in the past.

Just before sunset, a runner dressed in royal livery, yellow and green, had come rushing into the courtyard looking for Rokshan. The child had a folded paper in an oiled packet he gave to Rokshan. Rokshan had read the paper's contents silently. "Coquina is to present herself to the king on the training grounds tomorrow at ten o'clock. That's midmorning," he clarified. "With any witnesses to provide her side of the story."

"Does that mean the rest of us can't come?" Lamprophyre had asked.

"No, you're to attend as Coquina's guarantor, I suppose you could call it," Rokshan had said. "The one who stands surety for her appearance and for her harmlessness. I'll be there to put all the statements together and to argue with whoever the ecclesiasts send. Please, Jiwanyil, let it not be Khadar, though that might be good as he's not very bright and I could talk circles around him. Forgive me, Jiwanyil, but let me change my last plea."

Dharan laughed. "And I'm coming along as legal consultant," he'd said, "as I know slightly more about the details of the law than Rokshan, and might see possibilities he doesn't."

"I'm relieved," Coquina had said. "I didn't want to face the king alone."

"No fear of that," Rokshan had said, "though between us, I believe he's on our side."

Now Lamprophyre looked through the doorway across the dark courtyard and considered that. The king ought to be impartial, shouldn't he? And yet Rokshan had said more than once things that suggested the king wasn't fond of ecclesiasts. That didn't make any sense, given that Ekanath had more than once requested a prophecy from those ecclesiasts, and would he have done that if he were opposed to them? It was confusing, and Lamprophyre hated being confused.

She settled down and closed her eyes. Tomorrow this would all be resolved, one way or another. They had witnesses, they had truth on their side, and that would be more than enough.

She hoped.

CHAPTER ELEVEN

The training grounds were a wide stretch of bare earth behind and to the right of the palace, hemmed in on its far side by the parkland circling the palace. Low buildings with dark red roofs nestled into the trees, creating a contrast with the bright and dark greens of the leaves that was almost dragon-like in its brilliance. In fact, the colors reminded Lamprophyre strongly of Chrysoprase, whose dark green scales and maroon wing membranes were unique not only in the current flight, but in the memories of the oldest dragons. Rokshan had told Lamprophyre that some of the buildings were for housing soldiers, and some were for the officers, but they all looked the same to her: low to the ground, lined with window holes, with roofs bright enough that Lamprophyre might have used them as a beacon to land at night. Boring.

The platform erected on the training grounds, on the other hand, roused Lamprophyre's curiosity. It was wood, and not very sturdy from her point of view; she would almost certainly crush it if she tried to stand on it. But it was sturdy enough to support the king's seat and a handful of other chairs, so it wasn't something to be put up and taken down in only a hundred beats. Temporary and not temporary at the same time. That struck her as typically human. She wondered who was responsible for building it and taking it down, and whether it came in pieces that could be stacked together. Maybe Rokshan knew.

She looked down at him, thinking to ask the question, but he was deep in conversation with Dharan and she didn't feel like interrupting just for idle curiosity. The training ground was as dry as if the previous day's storm had never happened, and the sun shone in a clear sky, edging its way toward midmorning. The heat, already unpleasant, weighed on her head and shoulders and made her wish for a canopy like the one shielding the king's seat. She needed something she could carry with her. That wasn't so unlikely, was it?

On her other side, Coquina sat on her haunches, talking quietly with one of her human friends. The rest of them milled around her, restless as dragonets ready for their first flight. Lamprophyre wondered which of them was Melika. None of them acted like they'd been injured, though Lamprophyre supposed a good healer would take care of that. The only healing Lamprophyre knew anything about was Rokshan's, after he'd been burned, and that had been interrupted because the two of them had had to stop a war.

She glanced around. So far, the only people who'd arrived were Coquina's defenders, including three men who'd witnessed the fight at the coliseum. It made her nervous that maybe Rokshan had mistook the time, that they'd been supposed to arrive at some other of the many human hours that all had numbers assigned to them.

But—no, there was movement at the corner of the palace where the road curved around from the park. A handful of—she didn't actually know what they were, except she didn't think they were ecclesiasts and they didn't dress like reverends—anyway, five or six of the people dressed in ecclesiastical yellow with the strange upside-down bowl-shaped haircuts preceded two litters. Fluttering yellow drapes caught the scant breeze, but didn't move enough to reveal the ecclesiasts inside. Two litters, not three. That might be significant, though Lamprophyre didn't know how. Right now she felt she was grasping at anything that might give Coquina an advantage.

The people walking ahead of the litters carried musical instruments, pipes and drums and a piece of metal hanging from a cord, but they weren't playing any of them except the piece of metal, which the person holding it tapped with a slim brass rod every fourth step. The procession, and the tiny *ting* sounds, put Lamprophyre's back up. She knew very little about human customs, but her instincts told her this behavior was the ecclesiasts' way of establishing dominance.

"What does that mean?" she said, nudging Rokshan.

Rokshan regained his balance and looked over his shoulder. "God's breath," he swore. "I don't know what to make of that."

"Does it mean something? I feel like it means something."

"It means," Rokshan said, tilting his head to look up at her, "the ecclesiasts intend to make this a sacred affair. They want to claim that Coquina's actions were intended as a blow at them in their religious capacity and not as defending herself and others from an attack. Which could be a problem for us, if Father decides he doesn't want to offend the ecclesiasts."

"Or he'll be angry at their blatant attempt at manipulation and tell them off," Dharan said. "Let's not be pessimistic. It could go either way."

"You said the king might be on our side. Is that because he dislikes the ecclesiasts?"

"I would never say that," Rokshan said, but his face was expressionless in a way that suggested he meant the opposite of what he'd said. Since the ecclesiasts' procession had nearly reached them, and they might be able to overhear Rokshan, Lamprophyre guessed he didn't want to give their enemies any reason to protest unfair treatment if the king's judgment went against them.

The ecclesiasts' bearers set their burdens down about a dragonlength away from Dharan and the same distance from the platform as Lamprophyre and the others were. The attendants put their musical instruments away in their belts, which were simple cords of twisted red silk, and tied back the yellow curtains with more red cords. From Lamprophyre's perspective, the men inside the litters were almost invisible; she was enough taller that she could see only the knee of the nearest ecclesiast and the hand he rested on it. She decided not to crouch so she could see inside, because that would look like she cared, or possibly like she was nervous.

Coquina appeared to have drawn the same conclusion Lamprophyre had, because she ignored the litters entirely. "Why only two, I wonder?" she said in a low voice for Lamprophyre's ears alone.

"That's what I was thinking. If there were three ecclesiasts at the coliseum, shouldn't all three have come to this?"

Coquina shrugged. It was a gesture they'd all picked up from humans, versatile and communicative. "I'm so nervous I don't dare move, because I'd either trample someone or start shaking."

"It's all right. It's not as if they can hurt us. If King Ekanath does decide you were at fault, he'll probably just send you home."

"Which will hurt our presence here and make all dragons look weak. And I don't want to go home, certainly not under these conditions."

Lamprophyre cast her a startled glance. Coquina might or might not be less intelligent than Lamprophyre, but she was smart enough to see to the heart of the problem: ecclesiasts driving one dragon away would open the door to casting out others.

A pause settled over the training grounds, a moment in which no one spoke or moved restlessly. The only sound was that of the breeze rustling the distant leaves, something Lamprophyre suspected only she and Coquina could hear. She knew her hearing and sight were superior to a human's, but not how much more acute, and now she tilted her head and listened to the rushing sound, a hissing like scales rubbing over stone. If only the breeze would become a wind, and stir the heavy air so Lamprophyre didn't feel quite so much like falling asleep! As it was, only responsibility and nervousness kept her from giving in to her impulse to return to the embassy and nap.

Behind her, a loud noise somewhere between a squawk and a moan shattered the stillness. Lamprophyre jumped and half-turned to see what strange creature had such a call. Two men in the green and yellow that marked them as royal servants strode forward at a measured pace, pausing between each step. Curved horns with large, round mouths hung by long cords around their shoulders to bounce at their hips. As Lamprophyre watched, one man raised his horn to his lips without unslinging it, and that same peculiar sound rang out.

Behind the men with the horns came four women, shorter than the horn-blowers and with their long hair gathered up in horse's tails at the back of their heads. They made four points of a square, or two short columns lined up behind each of the horn-blowers. Each carried a book nearly too big for her, bound in leather with gilding on the page edges and locked shut with a strap and a clasp. The leather smelled old, the gilding smelled as fresh as if it had just been applied, and Lamprophyre wished she knew what it all meant, because this was clearly a ceremony that said King Ekanath was taking this very seriously.

The king's litter, borne by four muscular men unclad from the waist up, followed the four women. The white curtains were tied back, and Lamprophyre caught a glimpse of the king, sitting in that uncomfortable-looking legs-folded pose, before he approached too near for her to see beneath the litter's roof. He didn't look happy, but he didn't look angry, either. Lamprophyre hoped his expression wasn't one of the many she still couldn't interpret, and that he was on their side, after all.

The group of men and women dressed richly in court attire, white shirts and short trousers under heavy silk robes in a variety of colors, that followed the king weren't as orderly as the procession in front. Lamprophyre risked listening to their thoughts—there were already enough humans present to make eavesdropping impractical, much as she wanted to know what the ecclesiasts had in mind—and gathered that most of them were extremely curious about what the king would decide, though a few were already thinking about their midday meal. As it wasn't even mid-morning yet, she thought those few were, as Dharan sometimes said, slaves to their stomach. If they were here to help the king pass judgment, they ought to have the decency to focus their attention on Coquina's fate and not on roast chicken.

The bearers set the king's litter on the ground at the base of the steps leading to the top of the platform, and one of them assisted the king to his feet. Ekanath climbed the stairs and took his seat in the golden chair, covered with the canopy that cast such a lovely shade. A few of the crowd following the litter ascended as well and sat in the chairs to either side. As soon as all of them were seated, the women holding the oversized books carried them up the steps, where Ekanath's followers each accepted one. They set the books on their laps, front side up, but didn't open them.

The horn-blowers took up positions at either side of the base of the steps. Both blew an even longer, louder note that sounded like the cry of a strangled goose. Lamprophyre swallowed an inappropriate laugh. She welcomed her mirth even if she couldn't indulge in it, because the ceremony was impressive and alien and very, very human and she felt so out of place she was grateful for anything normal like a laugh.

When the last echo of the dying goose cry had vanished, the king leaned forward slightly and said, "Ladies and gentlemen, the books of the law."

As if guided by invisible hands, the four people holding books in their laps unlatched the straps and opened the books simultaneously. None of them spoke, but Lamprophyre observed they had all opened to different points in their books, and she hoped that meant this was more symbolism and not that they'd already made a decision, whoever they were.

"What is the charge?" Ekanath said. His words carried through the still air, which impressed Lamprophyre. She hadn't realized humans knew the trick of projecting their voices far using the power of their diaphragm muscles.

One of the horn-blowers spoke. His voice was nearly as loud as Ekanath's. "The ecclesiasts claim a challenge to their religious authority in the person of the dragon Coquina, accused of attacking their servants in an unprovoked manner."

Coquina shifted restlessly, but said nothing. Rokshan had told everyone not to react, no matter what the ecclesiasts claimed. Lamprophyre was glad of the warning, because she otherwise might have shouted denials and angry retorts.

"And what is the counter-charge?" Ekanath said. He still looked and sounded as if none of this mattered to him.

"The dragon Coquina claims ecclesiasts taunted her and ordered their servants to commit violence against innocent humans. In the process of defending herself and those innocents, she accidentally injured three humans. She counters that the ecclesiasts are ultimately responsible for the injuries and other damages sustained," said the other horn-blower.

"Very well," Ekanath said. "Witnesses for the accusers?"

One of the bowl-haircut attendants stepped forward. "Ecclesiasts Nendan and Sarthak have submitted the ecclesiasts' statements and stand ready to answer questions."

"I have received and read their statements," Ekanath said. "Witnesses for the defender?"

Rokshan took a few steps forward. "Your majesty has the statements of six witnesses who were present in the coliseum for the riot," he said, "and we have nine others present here today who are ready to answer questions."

It was all so calm and civilized Lamprophyre wanted to scream. Surely the king, if he'd read all those witnesses, knew the truth?

But the king still looked perfectly placid. "Ecclesiast Nendan," he said, turning slightly in his chair to more directly address the ecclesiast's litter. "Repeat your claim to these auditors." He gestured at the man seated nearest him, who still held his book resting open on his lap as if prepared to read from it at any moment.

"Your majesty," the unseen ecclesiast said, "we—"

"Please stand before your king," Ekanath said in a pleasant voice.

"I—yes, your majesty," Nendan said. He clambered out of his litter, not very gracefully, and had to grab hold of the roof pole to keep his balance. "We had heard tell of an...event...occurring at the coliseum, featuring that dragon." He gestured at Coquina without looking at her. "We saw an opportunity to invite her to renounce her godless ways and pay devotion to the Living God of the Dragons, Katayan. She rejected our words and cast insults and vicious laughter at us, inciting the crowd to do the same. Your majesty knows a challenge to an ecclesiast is a challenge to Jiwanyil himself. We attempted to reason with her, but she dealt two of our men a blow, knocking both unconscious, then in her rage turned on other humans."

Coquina made a sound deep in her throat that might have been the beginnings of a snarl. "But—" one of Coquina's female friends began, and was hushed by a glare from Rokshan.

"So you claim innocence in all of this," Ekanath said.

"We do, your majesty. In Jiwanyil's name."

Even though she was blocking the thoughts of everyone present, Rokshan was near enough and familiar enough to Lamprophyre that she could feel a pulse of satisfaction run through him at those words. She was certain she understood it. Claiming to tell the truth in the name of their God when they were lying would certainly work against them.

"And why are there only two of you?" Ekanath said in that same mild tone.

"We judged this situation simple enough to resolve that it did not need the presence of three ecclesiasts," Nendan said. He sounded like someone confiding in a friend some obvious truth that they both understood without saying.

Ekanath nodded. "Prince Rokshan," he said, turning to Rokshan. "Have you anything to say in Coquina's defense?"

"The ecclesiasts' actions were not innocent or benign," Rokshan said, "and I have witnesses to prove it. While they may have intended only to invite Coquina to follow their teachings—which, by the way, I doubt—"

"We are not here to read the minds of the ecclesiasts," Ekanath said. "Go on."

"As I say, they may simply have wanted to convert a dragon, but they did so using harsh and insulting words designed to goad Coquina into anger. And they ordered their men to attack innocents, thus inciting riot."

"We dispute this claim utterly," Nendan shouted.

"Ecclesiast Nendan, do not interrupt," Ekanath said. "And the dragon's attack on the ecclesiasts' men?"

"Was an accident," Rokshan said. "Coquina moved to interpose herself between the attackers and her friends, and she struck those men without intending to."

Ekanath eyed Coquina, who returned his regard fearlessly. If she was shaking, it wasn't evident. "I can see how that would be possible," he said.

"Your majesty," Nendan said, in the tones of someone who'd been bottling up his rage for several beats, "you cannot think to credit this creature's account over that of representatives of Jiwanyil! We have sworn to our statement in Jiwanyil's name, and that gives us an impeccable witness that trumps all others."

"That is true," Ekanath said. "There is legal precedent for what you say."

Lamprophyre felt numb. He was going to take their word—their lying word—for truth even though their witnesses were weak compared to Coquina's. Beside her, Coquina shifted, and Lamprophyre felt her take her hand and squeeze it tightly.

"I have only one more question for you, Ecclesiast Nendan," Ekanath said. "Do you take me for a fool?"

Another hush fell over the training grounds. Nendan's mouth fell open. "I," he said, then licked his lips nervously. "Of course not, your majesty. I don't know what you mean."

"Then you swear that you were at the coliseum during the event in question?" Ekanath leaned slightly forward again, and this time his words were sharpened steel.

"I," Nendan said again, his gaze flicking in all directions as if seeking help and finding none. "I am a representative of the ecclesiasts—"

"Who was not present for the attack," Ekanath said. "I believe—Vanga, correct me if I am wrong, but I believe I asked for the presence of the ecclesiasts who were part of the attack."

"You are not wrong, your majesty," the first horn blower said. "You summoned the three ecclesiasts who were in the coliseum, who are Golzar, Saral, and Barindra."

"But you—" Nendak sounded utterly astonished. "How did you know—"

"I may only be king," Ekanath said, "but I am very concerned about law and order in my city. I made sure to know the names of those I intended to question. Why, I ask again, did the Archprelate choose to mock my justice by hiding those three ecclesiasts?"

"The Archprelate didn't—that is, we thought—Sarthak and I are experienced with speaking the law—"

"But I am interested in hearing eyewitness testimonies." Ekanath sat back. "You spoke as though you personally were present. You thought to usurp my authority by manipulating the process of justice."

Now Nendak sounded terrified. "Your majesty, I swear—"

"By Jiwanyil?" Rokshan said placidly. The four book-bearers on the platform chuckled.

Nendak pulled himself together with a visible effort. "We misunderstood the situation," he said. "We believed wrongly that we should show our respect for the law by presenting our claim through those with legal experience. We apologize for our mistake." He bowed deeply.

"I expect the Archprelate—I beg your pardon, the High Ecclesiasts—to learn from this mistake." Ekanath turned back to Rokshan. "I wish to question your witnesses."

"Of course, your majesty." Rokshan stepped back to stand beside Lamprophyre again.

Ekanath fixed one of the men with his gaze. "Who attacked first?" he said.

The man showed no sign of nervousness at addressing his king. "The ecclesiasts' bearers did, your majesty, under order from their masters."

Ekanath turned to the next man in line. "How many humans did the dragon Coquina attack?"

"None, your majesty. She knocked over two of the bearers by accident, and she stepped on Melika when she tried to back away from the bearers," the man said.

"Is one of you Melika?" the king asked.

The woman Coquina had been talking to stepped forward. "I am, your majesty."

"You seem very well for someone who's been stepped on by a dragon."

Melika smiled at his humor. "Coquina paid for my healing, your majesty. It was a terrible mistake. She would never hurt any of us intentionally."

"I see. You," the king said, pointing at another woman. "Did you participate in the riot?"

The woman stilled. "Your majesty, I didn't think those bearers ought to be allowed to get away with attacking people, just because they work for the ecclesiasts," she said, somewhat nervously.

"Your majesty, I protest," Nendan said. The king waved him to silence.

"So you believe the violence was justified," Ekanath continued.

Lamprophyre closed her eyes briefly and hoped the woman would have the sense to shut up.

"No, your majesty," the woman said, "but I don't believe anyone should be asked to lie down and take a beating. They attacked us, we fought back."

"Ecclesiast Nendan? Anything to add?" Ekanath said to the ecclesiast.

"Your majesty, these people have been coached in their responses," Nendan said. "I believe the dragon ambassador paid them to speak in her friend's defense."

"Excuse me?" Lamprophyre said.

"That is a bold accusation," Ekanath said. "Ambassador, what do you say?"

"I say that people are always quick to accuse others of their own worst failings," Lamprophyre retorted. "The ecclesiasts are angry because dragons don't worship the way they want them to, and they have attacked more than one dragon with words and threats. Now they've attacked a dragon physically and gotten humans hurt. That's taking their anger too far. Dragons respect human religion, but we have our own faith, and we're not going to sacrifice it just to keep the ecclesiasts from attacking us. I don't need to pay people to entice them to speak the truth, and I think, your majesty, that you should consider what it means that these witnesses were very eager to speak out against the excesses of the ecclesiasts."

Nendan was sputtering with rage. "Well spoken, ambassador," Ekanath said. "Ecclesiast Nendan, Ecclesiast Sarthak. I have great respect for those who hear the voice of Jiwanyil, and my respect and that of my predecessors is enshrined in law. But I have no respect for those who seek to trade on those legal protections to the point of disregarding both my instructions and the law itself."

Ekanath stood, prompting the four others to stand as well, though they didn't close their books. Ekanath said, "I judge that the dragon Coquina is innocent of the charge of willfully attacking humans, as well as the charge of inciting riot. The High Ecclesiasts, as guarantors of the ecclesiasts as a whole, are ordered to repay Coquina the money spent on healing this young woman, as well as a fine of two hundred rupyas in restitution for having harassed a guest of the royal house."

Nendan had gone perfectly silent. His fists were clenched by his sides, and he was breathing heavily, but he said nothing.

"In addition," Ekanath said, "I order the High Ecclesiasts to pay a fine of five hundred rupyas to the Crown, for attempting to usurp the king's authority and for taking advantage of the law's very generous provisions with regard to ecclesiastical authority." He smiled. It was not a nice smile. "Please relay my best wishes to your superiors, and my hopes that they will continue to serve Gonjiri in the way Jiwanyil expects." He walked down the steps and climbed into his litter. Behind him, the four men and women closed their books and strapped them shut. Lamprophyre reminded herself to ask Rokshan what the books were for, but later.

She stood patiently while the king's litter receded into the distance. It hadn't yet disappeared beyond the palace before Nendan, swearing viciously under his breath, climbed into his own litter and signaled the bearers. The two ecclesiasts retreated rapidly, this time without their musical accompaniment. The bowl-cut attendants almost had to run to keep up.

When they were gone, Rokshan sagged against Lamprophyre's side. "That outcome was not nearly so much a given as it seems," he told her. "We were lucky the ecclesiasts were so arrogant they assumed they had everything going their way."

Nearby, Coquina's friends cheered and hugged her. Lamprophyre caught Coquina's eye and smiled. Coquina's answering smile was wobbly, but it was still a smile.

CHAPTER TWELVE

Lamprophyre and Rokshan flew with Coquina back to the dragons' warehouses. Lamprophyre felt superstitiously that if she let Coquina out of her sight, the ecclesiasts would descend again. But aside from seeing three yellow-topped litters following various streets on the flight from the training grounds, nothing happened. Coquina settled into her warehouse and said, "I'm going to sleep. I feel as if I haven't rested properly since all of this happened."

"We should race later today," Orthoclase said. He and the other males of the clutch had been waiting impatiently for news, and now they stuck their heads out of their warehouses like so many inquisitive badgers. "Then see if we can't bring food to the clearing north of the city so we can all eat together properly."

"I like this idea, if you can get Depik to cook enough for all of us," Bromargyrite said, licking his lips in anticipation.

"I'll see what I can do," Lamprophyre said. "Meet at the river mid-afternoon?"

"A swim and a race, and then another swim," Flint said. "There are benefits to lowland living. The water is always warm."

Lamprophyre waved goodbye to her clutch and flew back to the embassy, where she let Rokshan off with a sigh. Dharan came out of the embassy and leaned against the door frame, watching the two of them. "I can't believe the ecclesiasts didn't even obey the king's instructions," Lamprophyre told Rokshan.

"I can," Dharan said. "I realize this means nothing because I'm a heathen, but ecclesiasts are full of their own privilege and don't care anything for their religious responsibilities."

"That's not true of all ecclesiasts," Rokshan said.

"All right, it's only true of some, but what does that say about religion if Jiwanyil is willing to deliver prophecies even to those who aren't good examples of his servants?"

"We don't know that that's true, Dharan. For all we know, those corrupt ecclesiasts are never possessed of a prophecy."

"It would be interesting to look into," Dharan mused. "Something you could show the High Ecclesiasts, maybe get them to chastise the worst offenders."

"Unless the High Ecclesiasts are like that, too," Lamprophyre said. "What about Khadar?"

"Now you've corrupted her," Rokshan said, glaring at Dharan.

Dharan held up his hands in a "don't hit me" gesture. "You have to admit Khadar is not the best example of a worthy ecclesiast," he said.

"I know." Rokshan sighed. "And yet he was possessed of a prophecy. I don't understand the divine mind, and sometimes I question whether anyone does."

"You said the Archprelate receives the purest revelation," Lamprophyre said. She ducked into her hall and rooted around her stone supplies for a hunk of feldspar, which she bit into with pleasure. Eating at midday, or nearly midday, felt so decadent.

"I did, and I believe that," Rokshan said. "So if he hasn't chastised those ecclesiasts, I have to conclude even their behavior is part of a divine plan."

"That's a level of faith I will never understand," Dharan said, "but it heartens me to know there are still honorable believers in the world."

Rokshan clapped Dharan on the shoulder. "I'll convince you yet."

"I don't know. I'm thinking I might convert to the dragon faith."

"That would be so strange," Lamprophyre said. "I'm not sure you could make it all the way to Mother Stone when it's your time to die. You're already so fragile."

"I'd depend on you to help me," Dharan said with a smile. "I'm off to lectures now, but tell Porphyry I'll be here tomorrow by nine—by morning—for another reading lesson. And to take down another poem. We almost have enough to publish a book."

"I look forward to it," Lamprophyre said.

When Dharan was gone, Rokshan said, "I wish we knew what the ecclesiasts will try next. Coquina's right, they won't stop because of one defeat. However definitive a defeat it was."

"Do you think we should take extra precautions?" Lamprophyre asked. "We could continue to post guards, maybe make sure nobody goes anywhere alone—Stones, I can't believe I'm suggesting that. We shouldn't have to behave like victims!"

"I think we'll maintain a military presence by the warehouses for a while, just in case." Rokshan paced the courtyard, his head lowered in thought. "We can't do that here because people have to be able to reach you, but it's not as important because that street is already a bottleneck. But other than that, I think dragons should behave as if they have every right to be here. Which they do."

"So we need to know how the ecclesiasts will attack next."

Rokshan sighed. "I hate fighting a defensive war, but we have no idea how the ecclesiasts will strike next. We'll just have to stay alert and ready to fight back the instant they strike."

"Staying alert all the time sounds exhausting."

"It is, but we don't have much choice." Rokshan stretched. "I'm off now. I'll be back this afternoon, if I'm invited for swimming."

"Of course you are," Lamprophyre said. She hesitated, then added, "It will be secluded, and nobody approaches us dragons when we're all together."

"Don't start on that again, Lamprophyre."

His voice was a warning, but the tension of appearing before the king and her fear of Coquina being punished found sudden expression in anger. "Why not?" she exclaimed. "Rokshan, why are you hiding your body? I don't understand why you're so self-conscious about looking different than you used to. You know we won't—"

"That's *enough*," Rokshan snarled. "I don't like being stared at—"

"None of us would do that."

"And it's my body, not yours—"

"True, but it makes me sad that you're so ashamed of yourself."

"I'm not ashamed!" Rokshan half-turned so his face was in shadow and spat out a blistering curse. "I don't expect you to understand. Dragons don't scar. Nothing hurts that impenetrable hide of yours."

"Other dragons can," Lamprophyre said.

He turned back to face her. "But dragons don't fight each other."

"No, but there are sometimes accidents. Dragon claws and teeth are stronger than dragon hide. Those accidents leave scars."

He shrugged. "Nevertheless. I don't like being reminded of my, well, weakness, I suppose."

"Weakness? Because you were burned?"

He shrugged again. "Fragility, maybe? I'm not as strong as I thought I was."

"Rokshan, that makes no kind of sense. As if suffering burns was the same as letting someone hit you without fighting back. You almost died from those burns, but you survived. I would think you would see those scars as a reminder of that. Of how strong you are."

Rokshan let out a long, deep breath, his head thrown back so he was facing the sun. Then he walked into the embassy without a word. Lamprophyre followed him. He walked all the way to the back door so he was only dimly lit by the sunlight coming through the window holes near the ceiling. Then, still in silence, he pulled his loose linen shirt off over his head and dropped it on the floor. He gave Lamprophyre a challenging look, daring her to see what he'd kept hidden.

Lamprophyre came closer and lowered her head to look at her friend. She remembered what he'd looked like before the fire, his smooth brown skin the color of chestnuts, the defined muscles that weren't so ridiculous-looking as those of the king's bearers. Now she swallowed to keep from saying something compassionate he would take as a terrible insult.

Streaky marks not as dark as the rest of him, ridged and irregular, radiated out from a spot at the middle of his chest. They ran thick ropy tendrils of scars down into the waistband of his trousers, and up over his shoulders, and spidered like bony fingers up the side of his face. Lamprophyre had seen that much of the scars, those marks on his formerly smooth cheek, but seeing them connected to the rest of the terrible ridges and streaks made her feel she'd only thought she knew what they looked like.

Rokshan turned around slowly, holding his arms slightly away from his body. More scarring, not as heavy as on his chest, made stripes across his back and circled his arms. The scars didn't seem to pain him, but she looked at one thick patch over his left biceps and tried to imagine how it would feel to have fabric constantly rubbing against it. She almost reached out to touch the ridges, to see if they felt rough or smooth, but realized in time what a terrible mistake that would be.

"My left thigh is a mass of scars," Rokshan said. He sounded as if they were discussing the weather. "I don't know why it's so much worse than the right one. I suppose I should be grateful it's not that bad everywhere."

Lamprophyre's throat ached with sorrow, and the muscles of her shoulders were in knots. She swallowed again, and said, "It's my fault. I'm so sorry."

Rokshan turned around. "What are you talking about?"

"I didn't put out the fire fast enough. You might have been fine if I'd been faster. I'm sorry."

"You're—" Rokshan bent and retrieved his shirt, but didn't put it on. "I showed you so you'd stop nagging me, not so you could blame yourself. I don't blame you at all."

"You should. No wonder you didn't want to show me. I had no idea the damage I'd done."

Rokshan chuckled, normally a sound that cheered her. Now it just made her more miserable. "I've been really stupid," he said. "Vain and selfish and stupid. I don't know what I was thinking." He ran a hand lightly over his chest. "Lamprophyre, you saved my life. You were in pain I can't even comprehend and you still only thought of saving me. And I repaid you by resenting—not you, I never resented you—but the loss of my old appearance. You're right. Nobody who matters will look at me differently."

Lamprophyre nodded. "Certainly not dragons. We don't have any idea of human beauty. Yours is just a different kind of body."

"You're still blaming yourself. I can tell."

She shook her head, then nodded. "It will pass. Mostly I'm grateful I didn't let Harshod go. If I'd seen this before encountering him, I'm sure I could have killed him without a single reservation."

"He's dead. We're not. Let's make that cause for celebration." Rokshan shook out his shirt and put it on. "I really do have to go. I'm arranging for an excuse to stop singling out Nevrita."

"Oh."

This time, his laugh was hearty and free of any negative emotion. "You really are my best friend," he said. "Don't think I don't know you wanted to tear into Nevrita, metaphorically speaking, for using me."

"I would have, but I don't know where she lives."

"It's all right. I'll take care of it." Rokshan gripped her forearm briefly. "Thank you for not letting me continue to wallow in self-pity. Now—stop blaming yourself. Take a nap or something. I'll be back in a few hours."

Lamprophyre settled on the floor when he was gone and closed her eyes. It was hard not to see Rokshan's scarred body when she did. She resolutely tried to think of other things, feeling that dwelling on his scars was the opposite of what she'd promised him. Swimming this afternoon, that would be fun. Maybe tomorrow she and Rokshan could go over what Dharan had learned in the Hall of Visions. That would be less fun, but at least she would feel she was accomplishing something.

A shadow passed over her face, and she blinked at the young woman—maybe an older child, she was so short—who stood there, balanced on the balls of her feet like she wanted to flee. "Yes?" Lamprophyre said.

The child jerked, startled, and took a step backward. Her thoughts were full of nervousness but not fear, and Lamprophyre heard *trample me without noticing.* Well, that was better than outright terror.

"Did you need something?" she went on. "A question, or something dragons can do for you? Or did a dragon cause you injury? I promise we don't intend to hurt humans, but we are very large and sometimes it happens by accident. If it was Bromargyrite, he's really sorry."

The girl shook her head. "It's a message," she said in nearly a whisper. "From Princess Manishi. She asks that you come to her workshop imm—as soon as you're able."

Lamprophyre concealed a smile at the girl's amendment of Manishi's message. "I don't suppose she said why she wants to see me?"

"No, my lady ambassador."

So at least the girl had been coached in the correct form of address, almost certainly not by Manishi. "Will you return to her highness and tell her I'll be there shortly?" Lamprophyre could outfly this messenger, but she felt it was good for Manishi not to develop the expectation that Lamprophyre would drop everything at her command.

The girl nodded and was gone before Lamprophyre could get to her feet. Lamprophyre stretched and picked up a book from the piles. Give it a thousand beats or so, and she'd see what Manishi wanted. She had some reservations about going unaccompanied by Rokshan, because he was more suspicious than she and better at keeping Manishi from cheating them. Manishi's strange quality that blurred her thoughts and made them impossible to hear meant Lamprophyre couldn't use her secret edge. But Lamprophyre had had several encounters with Manishi over the last dozen twelvedays, and she felt less worried about dealing with her than she originally had.

Lamprophyre opened her book and settled in to read. Whatever Manishi wanted, it would almost certainly be interesting.

CHAPTER THIRTEEN

Though Manishi lived in the palace with the rest of the royal family, she spent most of her time in the slums of Tanajital. Slums, Lamprophyre had learned, were old or run-down neighborhoods where very poor people lived. Rokshan had said there was much crime in the slums, which confused Lamprophyre; poor people didn't have anything worth stealing, and she didn't know why people were more likely to attack each other just because of where they lived. It wasn't something that concerned her personally, but it did make her wonder what power Manishi had that she wasn't afraid of walking those streets alone.

Manishi's workshop was a wooden building weathered silver with age and a dozen years' exposure to the storms of Gonjiri summers. It slumped as if worn down by life, with even its roof sagging and what was left of its paint peeling in thin strips where it had been partly protected by the eaves. The workshop was nearly as big as a warehouse, but it was built differently from the ones the dragons had rented as temporary caves. Its roof wasn't quite as high, it had no windows, and its double doors opened outward rather than inward. One of those doors hung crookedly on leather hinges, inviting thieves, but when Manishi opened the door to Lamprophyre, shoving hard to get it to move, she showed no sign that she was concerned about people breaking in.

"You took your time coming," Manishi groused. She was dressed, as always, in knee-length trousers and a sleeveless shirt, both of which were made of coarsely woven ivory cloth, and her hair was piled messily atop her head.

Lamprophyre opened the other door and managed to squeeze through the opening, ducking her head and furling her wings close to her body. "I do have other responsibilities," she said, "and you didn't say it was urgent."

Manishi shrugged. Her irritation had vanished as quickly as if it had been manufactured rather than genuine. "Close the doors, and have a seat," she said.

Lamprophyre tugged the doors shut and made herself as comfortable as possible in the cramped workshop, wrapping her tail around her hindquarters and keeping her wings furled. Lanterns glowed on the walls, two flanking the door and four more spaced throughout the workshop. Their warm light wasn't enough to fill the large space with more than a twilight glow, but Lamprophyre's vision was better than a human's, and she had no trouble seeing the cabinets filled with drawers of all sizes and the obsidian slab hanging in one corner. This was the only adept's workshop she'd ever seen, and she'd occasionally wondered if they all looked the same, or if Manishi's single-mindedness with regard to magic manifested itself in this orderly environment.

Manishi dragged a low stool out from under the work table shoved against one wall and sat. For a few beats, they examined each other, princess and dragon. Lamprophyre was by now burning with curiosity about what Manishi wanted, but she wasn't so stupid as to speak first and give up her advantage. Someday she really needed to learn Manishi's secret for turning her thoughts into an indecipherable hum.

"You've been selling kyanite to others," Manishi abruptly said. "We had an arrangement."

"What?" Lamprophyre hadn't anticipated anything like that. "I don't recall any such arrangement."

"It was implicit. You provide me kyanite privately, so no one else knows I have it, and you don't tell any other adept you can get it."

Lamprophyre was certain she'd never agreed to those terms, but she knew Manishi well enough to be aware the woman constructed her own reality and clung to it. "It doesn't matter. I haven't sold kyanite to anyone else. No one's asked for it, for one, and I'm not so desperate for coin as to need to sell my own private stock. Kyanite is delicious."

"Eating it. What a waste." Manishi frowned. "Then why is it at least three other adepts have stopped looking for it at the market?"

"I have no idea. Maybe they don't want it anymore. What's it for, anyway?"

Manishi's gaze flicked speculatively at Lamprophyre. "It wouldn't mean anything to you," she said. "An experiment."

Manishi was right; Lamprophyre wouldn't appreciate the details. From asking other adepts, she knew kyanite had mind-focusing powers, but so did sapphire, and sapphire was more potent than kyanite. She'd originally suspected Manishi wanted the kyanite because it was cheaper than sapphire, but some careful inquiries had turned up the surprising fact that kyanite was among the more expensive stones humans traded for. Lamprophyre doubted Manishi wanted the stone for anything so mundane as improving mental focus and clarity.

"So how do you know these other adepts have stopped looking?" she asked. "Since I don't imagine they came out and told you."

"I have my ways," Manishi said with a smile. "I want you to find out which of your dragon friends are selling kyanite, and make them stop."

"Excuse me?"

"I want you," Manishi said in the slow, deliberate tones of one speaking to an unusually dim child, "to make them stop."

"I can't do that. What my friends do is their own business."

"True, but you can...encourage...them to change their business. Tell them you have more need of kyanite than they. I don't care. Just get them to stop."

Lamprophyre let out a deep breath and suppressed the urge to shout. "In the first place," she said, "I'm not going to lie to my friends." She almost told Manishi why lying to a dragon was impossible, but revealing that secret to this woman struck her as a very bad idea. "In the second place, don't you think that would make them suspicious? And that they'd pass that suspicion on to whoever's buying the kyanite from them? If you're so concerned about secrecy, you ought to think before doing something that will draw attention to yourself."

Manishi frowned. "Good point." She stood and paced the small area between the door and Lamprophyre. "Very good point. I suppose I'll just have to increase my supplies of kyanite. There's a chance my rivals will notice the depletion of the supply, but I'll have to risk it."

Irritated, Lamprophyre said, "You say that as if I'm a tap you can turn on and have kyanite come flowing out. Suppose I don't feel like going after more for you?"

"I'll pay you well."

"I don't need money." This was not strictly true. With the addition of six more dragons to Tanajital, Lamprophyre's needs for the embassy, for entertaining as well as paying reparations for accidents, had increased substantially. But she didn't like Manishi's attitude.

"Everyone needs money." Manishi turned to face Lamprophyre. "Very well. If you're not interested, I suppose I'll have to tell Father what that dark blue dragon has been up to."

Puzzled, Lamprophyre said, "Flint? What are you talking about?"

"He's made several long flights out of Tanajital since he arrived. Him and a human rider. Some of them have been over the Fanishkorite border."

"I don't understand. Is that a problem?" Lamprophyre's uneasiness grew.

"Of course it is. We're almost at war with Fanishkor—even a dragon ought to know that. Fanishkor is *very* interested in any information that will give them an edge over Gonjiri. With all that flying, scouting overhead, I'm sure the blue dragon and his rider have a very good sense of where our military presence is. Do you suppose Father will believe he *didn't* sell information to Fanishkor the last time he landed there?"

Lamprophyre's chest ached with tension. "That's ridiculous. Flint has no interest in giving Fanishkor information. Fanishkor attacked dragons and tried to bring us into a war with Gonjiri. Flint would have no reason to help them even if we weren't allied with Gonjiri."

Manishi shrugged. "I suppose we can put it to Father. Who do you think he'll believe?"

"But—" Lamprophyre shut her mouth. The idea of Flint as a spy was ludicrous. It didn't make sense even if she assumed he'd done what Manishi suggested, but had been an innocent dupe of his human rider. And yet... "You have no evidence," she said.

"I have plenty of evidence," Manishi said. "I observed that dragon landing in Fanishkor and meeting with humans, and I made a record." She crossed the room to her enormous slab of polished obsidian, which rested in a frame that could be rotated vertically or horizontally. At the moment, it was upright and reflected the room dimly, an imperfect mirror that made Lamprophyre look like a fuzzy-edged blue blob.

Manishi took a thin wand of rose quartz the length of her forearm from a sheath connected to the mirror's frame and ran its tip across the surface of the obsidian, from upper right to lower left. It made a faint scratching sound, but left no mark on the shining, flawless stone.

Light flickered from deep within the obsidian like a torch coming to life, warm and glowing. It spread and grew lighter until the entire surface glowed pale yellow with a radiance that made Lamprophyre close her nictitating lids briefly. Manishi held the wand to her lips and whispered something across its tip, then held it to the mirrored, glowing surface.

Color bled outward from the tip of the wand, blues and greens and browns spreading like ink dropped into a puddle of water. Unlike ink, the colors stayed discrete; if anything, they became more coherent the farther they flowed across the mirror. After only a few beats, Lamprophyre realized she was seeing a picture of a hilltop, gentle and low, unlike the foothills near her rocky home. Greenish-yellow grass burned by the summer sun covered the hilltop. Five darker shapes, one very large, filled the view. Lamprophyre blinked and squinted to bring them into focus; the image wavered as if Lamprophyre had ducked her head underwater without closing her nictitating membranes.

Then the image became clear, and Lamprophyre gasped at the sight of Flint and four humans gathered together on the hilltop. For a beat, nothing moved, and then the image jerked into motion, looking for all the world as if Lamprophyre were looking through a window at the real Flint. She couldn't hear anything, but the figures' lips were moving, and Flint lowered his head to listen to one of the humans.

Another of the humans handed something small and square to the speaker; Lamprophyre couldn't make it out, but the speaker reached into it and thumbed through its contents, convincing Lamprophyre that it was paper.

Then the human who'd handed the paper over climbed onto Flint's shoulders, and Flint took off, soaring out of the picture. Manishi touched the wand's tip to the mirror, and the image shivered, then dissolved into a swirling mass of color which flowed in reverse back into the wand.

Lamprophyre stared at the obsidian mirror until all the light drained from it. "How did you do that?" she demanded. "*Why* did you do that? Have you been spying on all of us?"

"I have my methods," Manishi said. "And it hardly matters why, not when the evidence is so strong."

The blank face of the obsidian mirror reflected Lamprophyre poorly, but her aghast expression was clear, if only to her. "It doesn't mean anything," she finally said, cursing how weak her voice sounded.

"I'm sure Father will agree. Let's ask him." Manishi regarded her with a pleasant smile. Lamprophyre wished she dared smack that smile off the adept's face.

She considered her options. She was certain Flint hadn't done anything wrong and almost as certain that he hadn't even done anything wrong unintentionally. But proving that would be difficult. Manishi's father, King Ekanath, might want his dragon alliance, but he was unlikely to give anyone, dragon or not, the benefit of the doubt when it came to apparent espionage. Lamprophyre felt confident that eventually, she'd be able to convince Ekanath of Flint's innocence. It was "eventually" that worried her. So much turmoil would ensue between now and that eventual time, and who knew what kind of other, permanent repercussions there might be?

"Fine," she said. "I'll bring you more kyanite. But you'll pay the standard rate. I don't believe Flint is guilty."

"Of course. I'm no blackmailer," Manishi said, her smile broadening.

CHAPTER FOURTEEN

Lamprophyre arranged with her blackmailer the details of providing Manishi with the stone she wanted and flew off toward the warehouses. Fury had taken over irritation. What the Stones had Flint been thinking? She was going to tear him apart.

When she arrived at the warehouses, only Flint, Dolomite, and Coquina were there. "Where are the others?" she asked. She still felt wary of letting any of her friends wander Tanajital freely when there were still ecclesiasts around. Then she felt angry again, for a different reason. Dragons shouldn't have to alter their behavior out of fear of the ecclesiasts.

"Porphyry and Bromargyrite left to buy cows for Depik to cook," Dolomite said. His dark green scales looked nearly black in the dimness of his warehouse, so he was virtually invisible except for the silver-shot blue of his wing membranes, the exact color of a summer sky over the mountains laced with impossible lightning. "Orthoclase had to see someone about an exchange of stone."

"Exchange of stone? Was he selling kyanite?"

Dolomite and Flint exchanged wary glances. She realized she'd sounded a little too shrill and intense.

"I don't think so," Dolomite said. "Why?"

Lamprophyre shook her head. "It's not important. Flint, why have you been flying to Fanishkor?"

Flint now looked alarmed. "Lamprophyre, are you angry about something?"

"Just answer the question."

"Lokun likes flying, and he has friends all over the world, not just in Gonjiri." Flint's gaze on Lamprophyre was steady and not at all guilty. "He's introduced me to many of them."

"And he gave the ones in Fanishkor information? Confidential information?"

"How do you know that?"

Lamprophyre's heart felt leaden. "Tell me the truth, Flint. Have you and Lokun been spying for Fanishkor?"

Flint's eyes widened. "Of course not! Why would you even think that? Fanishkor's government is our enemy."

"And yet Lokun handed a Fanishkorite documents containing secret information he gained from what he saw when you flew all over Gonjiri." Her words tasted sour, as if she were male and bubbling over with acid from her second stomach instead of fire.

"He did not! Lamprophyre, who told you these lies?" Flint was breathing heavily now, and the scent of acid wafted from his lips.

Lamprophyre settled back on her haunches, feeling as weary as if she'd flown to Mother Stone and back without stopping. "I saw you," she said. "Princess Manishi has some way of observing people at a distance and preserving that observation so others can see it. I watched you and Lokun hand over a packet of papers to Fanishkorites. I know you've flown over the land enough to make detailed records of where Gonjiri's military is deployed. Flint, please. Tell me I'm wrong."

Flint settled back as well, his mouth a tight, angry line, his wings furled close about him as if for protection. "We gave papers to those Fanishkorites, yes," he said, "but they were plans for a house Lokun designed for his friend. Lokun is famous as a designer of human build-ings, not just as a mason. Fanishkor may be our enemy, but a lot of its people just want to live in peace. I can't believe you'd take the word of some human over mine."

His surface thoughts were hurt, and angry, and Lamprophyre felt guilt tangle with her ebbing fury. "I'm sorry," she said. "But you don't understand how damning those images were. If Manishi wants to, she can take them to her father and claim what I just accused you of, and Ekanath would almost certainly believe her."

"But we'd tell him otherwise," Dolomite said. "It's just a misunderstanding."

"The king is still worried about war," Coquina said, drawing every dragon's attention. "He's not going to take chances. If he finds out about this, it won't matter if we tell him the truth. He'd send Flint home and probably do awful things to Lokun to get him to reveal his supposed contacts in Fanishkor."

"I wouldn't let that happen," Flint said, spreading his wings to make himself look bigger.

"But I don't understand why Manishi would care," Dolomite said. "I've only met her once, but she struck me as completely uninterested in politics."

"She cares," Lamprophyre said wearily, "because she can use those images to make me do what she wants."

"So what does she want?" Coquina asked. "It must be something awful if she has to force you to do it."

"It's not awful—at least, I don't think it is. Manishi is experimenting with kyanite and she needs a large supply of it. Without telling any other human she wants it or has it. I've brought her some in the past, but you can imagine I don't like selling it when we could eat it instead."

Dolomite smiled reflectively, apparently reminiscing on past meals. Flint said, "So she threatened you so you'd supply her with kyanite. Is that why you wanted to know if Orthoclase was selling it?"

"Yes. She suspects some of her rivals have private suppliers, because they aren't looking for it in the market anymore, and of course she assumed one of us was that."

"It's not me," Dolomite said. "I've been working on a way to allow dragons to race, and no one's even approached me asking me to provide them with stone."

"I spend all my time in Tanajital in the coliseum," Coquina said.

"You already know what I've been doing," Flint said. His voice was calm, but his thoughts were still angry. Lamprophyre's fury became directed at Manishi. How dare she make her doubt a clutchmate?

"Flint, I'm sorry I accused you," she said. "I didn't believe you'd done anything wrong, but I was angry at being blackmailed and I was angry you'd done something so careless as dealing with Fanishkorites. But of course there's nothing wrong with having friends, even if those friends are citizens of the wrong country. Please forgive me not trusting you."

"I accept your apology," Flint said. "And I think we should be grateful for one thing to come out of this misunderstanding, which is that we now know Manishi is capable of spying on us and ruthless enough to use that against us. Is there anything we can do about that, do you think?"

"I have no idea," Lamprophyre said. "Though it did seem she kept the images inside a wand, like ink in a bottle, only when she poured them out, they made pictures instead of a pool of ink. I suppose, if we stole the wand—"

"Careful," Coquina said. "What if she's watching us now?"

"It's just images, not sound. If it had sound, I'd have heard what Lokun was actually saying and the king would know it was an innocent transaction." Lamprophyre sighed. "And we can't steal the wand, because Manishi has protections on her workshop that are powerful enough to blow even the palace apart, or so she told me once. Even a dragon might take damage from that."

They all fell silent, their thoughts somber and melancholy. Eventually Flint roused himself to say, "There's nothing we can do about it, save provide Manishi with the kyanite she wants. And see if Orthoclase has been selling it to others. I know he has any number of deals going with human merchants, but last I heard, he was buying varieties of granite from all over Gonjiri, not dealing in crystals. But he has to fund those purchases somehow, and it's probably by selling stone from the home gleaning fields."

A large shadow swept over them, temporarily blocking out the sun. Orthoclase landed neatly on the street beyond and turned around, tucking his tail close to his body and furling his wings. "Who's selling stone?" he asked. "I know all the major buyers now, and what they're looking for. I have to say, collecting coin is far more satisfying than I ever imagined back when old Scoria told us stories of humans and their obsession with it."

"What have you been selling?" Lamprophyre asked.

Orthoclase's elegant eye ridges flared. "A lot of different stones. Why? Am I in trouble? Because you're all looking at me like I'm the last cow in the herd."

"We have a problem," Lamprophyre said, and quickly explained Manishi's blackmail.

Orthoclase's expressive eyes grew cold and hard as she spoke. When she finished, he said, "And there's nothing we can do about it."

"We'll think of something," Lamprophyre said. "Right now I think we should find out who's been selling kyanite. I take it it's not you, Orthoclase."

"Definitely not. Kyanite is one of my favorite foods, and there's never enough of it. A human would have to offer me a pile of vahas to get me to part with it." Orthoclase stood and tried to pace, but came up against Coquina in just two steps and had to subside. "But is that really a good idea? It sounds like Manishi fears any investigation will lead back to her, and she might decide to tell her father her story as revenge if she thinks we're responsible for revealing her interest."

"We know humans get kyanite from places other than our mountains," Coquina said, "because they knew what it was before Lamprophyre brought it to Tanajital, right? So if there are other adepts who are experimenting with it, and they've suddenly stopped, they're getting it from secret sources. And wouldn't a human do better bringing something that valuable to market and letting humans compete to pay her the most for it? Like in the story about the pearl?"

"That suggests those other sources are illicit," Flint agreed. "And it makes me wonder if humans aren't going to our mountains secretly and mining things for themselves."

Lamprophyre's breath caught in her throat. "They couldn't. Could they? Wouldn't someone have noticed?"

"There are a lot of mountains, and our flight only occupies some of them." Flint stood and stretched his wings, barely missing Dolomite's head. "Now that humans know dragons are allies, and not inclined to attack humans, there might be some daring enough to sneak into the mountains for stone. Some of those stones aren't available in the lowlands, even from merchants from other countries, and some of them are closer and more plentiful than in other places. I know Lokun said something about our garnet being cheaper than the stone from Sachetan."

"Which might make Sachetan angry," Coquina pointed out. "Not that that's relevant now, but it might mean Sachetan is looking to undercut us." She laughed. "I'm talking like a human merchant. I blame Melika. Her family sells artifacts, and she knows all about how stone sales work."

Lamprophyre sat up. "She does? Would she be willing to explain it to us?"

"You think Melika might be able to find out who's supplying kyanite?" Orthoclase said.

"She'd be discreet, and she wouldn't want the information getting back to Manishi," Coquina said. "I can ask her."

"There is one other thing," Dolomite said. "Don't we want to know *why* Manishi and all those adepts want kyanite? If they're experimenting with it, that means they intend it to do something. To be an artifact. And if Manishi is so underhanded as to blackmail us, I don't trust her to only create artifacts that are harmless."

"I have a book on magic," Lamprophyre said, "something general for beginners. It will provide a foundation for me to understand more complicated magic. And there's a scholar-adept at the academy named Sabarna who's helped me in the past. I think I can ask her questions. Though..."

"Though, what?" Flint asked.

"She wasn't forthcoming about the uses of kyanite either. *And* I couldn't understand her thoughts the same way we can't understand Manishi's. Maybe I don't want to involve her, after all."

"I think it's past time we figured out why those two humans' thoughts are impossible to hear," Flint said. He laughed. "Seems like we just gave ourselves assignments the way Dharan does Porphyry."

Lamprophyre nodded. "Find the suppliers of kyanite. Figure out what the adepts are trying to do with it. Discover Manishi and Sabarna's secret ability. Oh, yes, and make a trip home to collect kyanite for our blackmailer." She sighed. "You're right, that sounds like a lot of work."

"I think it's exciting," Coquina said. "Solving a mystery. It's like the stories about the human female Veena from before the Great Cataclysm, how she would find things that were stolen or learn who attacked someone. It must be so challenging, not being able to tell what someone's thinking or whether they're lying. Of course, if she could do that, there wouldn't have been stories."

"I agree," Flint said. "I never knew you liked those stories, too."

Coquina shot a glance at Lamprophyre. "I suppose I didn't want anyone thinking I was childish for liking children's tales."

"Nobody thinks that," Flint said. "Let's all go race. I feel the need to shake the dust of this human city off my feet."

"I'll wait at the embassy for Rokshan, and we'll join you by the river at the usual place." Lamprophyre stood and stretched. "Maybe next time you could bring Lokun. If he's such a good friend, we'd all like to meet him."

"Good idea," Flint said.

Lamprophyre watched her friends fly off southward, then headed back to the embassy. She felt much less confident than she'd let on, though she was sure those feelings were buried deep enough no one had heard them. Manishi was clever, and Lamprophyre was sure her amity toward dragons would last only until they turned on her, or made themselves useless to her. They would have to be very careful not to give Manishi any reason to tell the king what she knew.

And yet as she alit neatly on the courtyard and entered the embassy, she couldn't help feeling her clutch was on the right track. If they were going to counter Manishi, they needed information, preferably information that would allow them to blackmail the adept in return. It might be their only hope of stopping her. Lamprophyre lay on the cool earth of the hall's floor and sighed. Dragons blackmailing humans. The thought made her feel itchy and guilty. She had no desire to be human, but it seemed humanity had overtaken her, at least in this one way.

CHAPTER FIFTEEN

Lamprophyre lay in the clearing to the north of Tanajital and tore a mouthful of cow free from its carcass. While Depik had been willing to cook for all seven of the dragons plus Rokshan, his kitchen wasn't large enough to handle three cows without the first one getting cold while the second cooked. So in the end, Flint, Coquina, and Bromargyrite had each carried a butchered cow to the clearing, and Lamprophyre and Coquina had roasted the meat for everyone.

"This feels so homey," Flint said around a large bite of tender meat. "Like when we were thirty and finally old enough to go off on our own. That one night we spent in the lowlands west of home—remember?"

"I remember," Coquina said. "We were so excited about catching our own meals we killed too many boars and had to haul the extras back to the flight the next morning. That was a long and tedious journey."

"But it was the best meal I'd ever had," Dolomite said, smiling lazily as if the memory was as fresh as yesterday.

"I remember a time," Rokshan said from his position leaning against Lamprophyre, "when Dharan and Baleran and I traveled south to Sunital on our own, without our families. We were barely sixteen and we thought we were the lords of creation, adults doing adult things."

"That sounds like you thought wrong," Lamprophyre said. "What happened?"

"Some thief took Baleran's money. Slit the bottom of the pouch and lifted the coins neatly as you please. With only two-thirds of our resources left, we couldn't afford three separate rooms at an inn, so we crammed into a tiny garret with only two beds. Dharan snores like a woodcutter with a rusty saw, and Baleran talks in his sleep, so you can imagine how restful the night wasn't." Rokshan laughed. "And in the morning, the innkeeper insisted we'd burned a hole in the bedclothes and extorted an extra five rupyas from us. We hurried back to Tanajital as fast as our feet would carry us and vowed never to take our lives for granted again."

"I don't understand," Dolomite said. "If you're a prince, how were you able to travel so simply and privately? Shouldn't you have had bodyguards, or attendants, or something?"

"I didn't exactly have permission." Rokshan sat up and reached for a second leg of turkey, which Depik had cooked. "Though as the youngest son of the king, I'm not as closely watched as, say, Tekentriya is as heir. And I think, looking back on that escapade, my teachers might have been deliberately less observant, to give me a chance to get away from the scrutiny."

"That could have gone badly for them, if you'd been hurt," Coquina pointed out.

"It could. But really, there was no danger. I'm not—well, wasn't then—very recognizable as Prince Rokshan. You'd be surprised at how easily Anchala and I can get away with moving through a crowd without drawing attention. Or—I can't really anymore." He gestured at the scars on his cheek. "People know about what happened to me, and there aren't so many scarred men in Tanajital that I can pass unremarked."

Lamprophyre nodded, keeping her expression neutral. That Rokshan could allude to his disfigurement so casually told her he really had started to come to terms with it. He'd also taken off his shirt and trousers to go swimming, keeping only the short pants he wore to protect his male parts, and behaved as if nothing were wrong. Lamprophyre had had a tense moment when Dolomite, guileless and bad at knowing what not to say, had asked "Do they hurt?" with a gesture at Rokshan's thigh (which was, in fact, more severely scarred than the rest of him). But Rokshan had simply said, "No," and when Lamprophyre broke her own rule about not listening to her friend's thoughts, she'd heard only a peaceful reflection on how strange burn scars did feel.

"I can imagine there are benefits to that as well as drawbacks," Flint said. "Being recognized, I mean."

"Well, I spend a great deal of time with Lamprophyre, and she's definitely recognizable," Rokshan said, "so it doesn't take much intelligence to guess who the man flying with her is." He looked up at Lamprophyre. "I was wondering the other day," he continued, "whether there are any duplicates among dragons. Of colors, I mean."

"Sometimes," Coquina said. "Porphyry and Nephrite come closest, but Nephrite is a much darker red than Porphyry. For us, at least, there's a huge range of colors even among ones you humans might simply call red. So if there were another dragon with blue scales and copper membranes, her color wouldn't be the exact shade of Lamprophyre, and we could easily tell them apart."

"But it doesn't happen often," Orthoclase said. "And we certainly don't have identical dragons the way humans have sometimes. I was so startled when I saw a human female the other day with two children who looked exactly the same. I thought the child had some kind of magic that moved it instantly from one place to another."

"Twins," Rokshan said. "Yes, sometimes human women give birth to more than one child at once, and sometimes those children are identical."

"That must be so uncomfortable," Lamprophyre said. "Having more than one baby inside you. Women already look enormous when they are ready to give birth to just one child."

Bromargyrite stirred his enormous self, but said nothing. Lamprophyre could hear enough of his thoughts to know he'd been about to ask something about human childbirth, or the sex that led to childbirth, but had changed his mind when he remembered it was Rokshan he'd meant to ask. For someone who'd actually had sex, Rokshan was remarkably easy to embarrass with mention of it.

She wondered if he'd be more frank with the dragons if she and Coquina weren't present, since he'd told her more than once that among Gonjirians, it was considered crude to discuss sexual matters with members of the opposite sex. Lamprophyre, who wasn't yet on the verge of being pair-bonded, hadn't had the discussion with Hyalo-clast about the practicalities of dragon sex, so it wasn't as if she had anything to compare the human kind to.

"Female dragons become large, too, just before expelling an egg," Orthoclase said. "Not as large as female humans, proportionately."

"It's not something I'm looking forward to," Coquina said. She didn't glance at Flint the way she normally did when discussing anything even remotely related to pair-bonding, which surprised Lamprophyre. Maybe Coquina wasn't interested in him, after all. Or maybe she'd finally realized she had a better chance of winning his heart if she wasn't so obvious in her pursuit. Either way, Lamprophyre hoped for Coquina's happiness, and was pleased to find no bitterness in the thought.

Bromargyrite got heavily to his feet—he'd eaten more than the rest of them—and stretched so his arms were flung wide, his back was arched, and his wings were spread to their fullest. "I'm ready for some stone," he declared. "What did you bring, Orthoclase?"

Orthoclase grinned and opened the heavy leather sack at his side, bigger than a human torso and smelling deliciously of a dozen delicate stone flavors. "Granite," he said. "But not just any granite," he went on quickly as Flint and Coquina groaned. "I've been experimenting with the different kinds of granite available throughout Gonjiri, and the subtleties are really remarkable."

"I was ready for marble," Flint complained. "I know you have some in there."

"That's the other thing," Orthoclase said, ignoring his plaintive tone. "I've worked on some delicious pairings to take advantage of the granite subtleties." He dug about in his sack and removed a couple of fist-sized stones, one white and veined with gray, one rough and nearly black. "Granite from near the Sachetan border, combined with some marble waste I got from a sculptor here in Tanajital."

Flint accepted both stones and cracked each in half. He bit into one of the marble chunks, then took a bite out of the granite. His eye ridges rose. "That *is* good," he said, his words muffled.

Orthoclase handed around more paired stones. Lamprophyre chewed hers, pink granite that looked like the walls of Tanajital and a slab of silvery mica, with pleasure. "I've wished I could take a bite out of the city wall from the day I arrived," she murmured. The mica fractured pleasantly in her mouth, crunchy and light. She swallowed and added, "I'm surprised the adepts don't use granite in their magic. There's so much of it, and there are as many kinds are there are of feldspar and quartz and agate, which I know they do use."

"Adepts are strange," Bromargyrite said. "I got to talking with one about a twelveday ago and he had the oddest questions."

"Questions? Like what?" Lamprophyre sat up, scattering stone crumbs.

"Oh, like do dragons work magic from eating stone. Do we need stone to fuel our second stomachs. What stones do dragons prefer to eat. The sort of question that reflects more about the asker than anything else. He was clearly convinced we gain some benefit from eating the kinds of stone that an adept would use for magic."

"But he didn't ask about kyanite?"

Bromargyrite shook his head. "Didn't ask about any stone in specific."

Lamprophyre glanced at Rokshan. She had told everyone about Manishi's blackmail while they were swimming, and none of the others had been approached about kyanite. "I feel we keep accruing more questions," Rokshan said, "and don't have answers for the questions we had before. I wish adepts weren't so secretive. We don't dare ask the questions we most want to know the answers to."

"We'll harvest Manishi's kyanite tomorrow," Lamprophyre said, "and Coquina, you'll ask Melika about it?"

"She's been asking if we could go flying, and that would be a good, private way to discuss it." Coquina blushed, tinting her grass-green scales light brown. "It just feels so intimate, letting a human that close. I consider Melika a friend, but I wasn't sure I wanted to single her out from the others. Or maybe I'm wrong, and it will feel perfectly natural."

"It's strange at first, like having a fly perched just out of swatting range," Flint said, "but you wouldn't believe how nice it is to have someone to talk to while you're flying."

"And it's fun to see how much Rokshan enjoys it," Lamprophyre said.

"Do I?" Rokshan asked with a smile.

"You shout when I do something daring, like you're half scared and half exhilarated."

"That's true. But not every human feels that way. Dharan wouldn't want to fly with a dragon unless it was a choice between that and a horrible death." Rokshan set his turkey leg aside and wiped his hands on the grass.

Lamprophyre took another bite of mica. "They don't use mica, either," she said, returning to the previous line of conversation. "But quartz..."

Porphyry, who'd been silently lying nearby with his eyes closed, stirred and asked, "What about quartz?"

"I thought you were asleep!"

"Just digesting." Porphyry sat up and took a chunk of streaky lavender quartz from Orthoclase. "I've noticed a lot of adepts carry quartz artifacts, but never by themselves. That is, if they only have one artifact, it won't be quartz, but if they have two or more, at least one of them is likely to be."

"I didn't know you'd paid that close attention to adepts," Flint said.

Porphyry shrugged. "They interest me. And I've read some of that book Dharan brought you, the one about magic for beginning adepts. The fact that humans place such value on different stones that to us are just food is fascinating, don't you think? It's made me wonder how they figured it out in the first place. They certainly didn't learn it from dragons."

"When I compared Manishi and the scholar-adept Sabarna, back when I first came to Tanajital, I noticed they both had artifacts in common. Chlorite, and quartz." Lamprophyre settled down more comfortably. "And they both have incomprehensible thoughts. I wonder if one or both of those stones is responsible?"

"Maybe that's something we can find out," Bromargyrite said. "Though we'd have to be careful not to give our secret away."

"I'd like to look into it," Porphyry said. "I can be discreet. I wish I'd thought to make note of the artifacts the other adepts were carrying, the ones whose thoughts are unintelligible, I mean."

"Me too," Orthoclase said. "I've encountered a few adepts in the course of buying stone, and some of them are like Manishi. Who, if we could hear her thoughts, would be less of a threat."

"It sounds like we have direction," Flint said. "Coquina will talk to Melika, Porphyry and Orthoclase will investigate the adepts, and Lamprophyre and Rokshan will harvest kyanite. I think I might come along on that trip. While you're getting the stone, I'll talk to the flight and see if they've noticed anything strange in the gleaning fields. If humans are secretly stealing our stone, they might have left signs."

"I'll visit with that adept again," Bromargyrite said. "He said he was interested in learning about dragonkind. I'm sure I can get some answers out of him without him knowing that's what I'm doing."

"This is exciting!" Dolomite said. "What should I do?"

Lamprophyre exchanged glances with Rokshan. Dolomite was no younger than she was—older by a couple of days, even—but his eagerness and guilelessness made him seem as if he belonged to a younger flight. He would be so hurt if she told him there was nothing for him.

An idea occurred to her. "Actually, there's something I was meaning to do before Manishi interfered," she said. "The guard captain thought something about there being more ecclesiasts in the streets than usual. I had planned to fly over the city and see if that was true, but would you be interested in doing that instead? I don't want it to wait for me to get back, and the kyanite is going to take all day."

"Why do we care?" Dolomite asked, though with curiosity rather than the sullen resistance that would have said he saw her offering as makework. "It's not as if they can hurt us anymore."

"Maybe not the way they tried with Coquina and Bromargyrite, but we're sure they haven't given up on driving us out." Lamprophyre stepped closer. "I think it's very important that we know as much about their movements as we can find out. If the guard captain thought their increased presence was potentially a problem, that tells me the ecclesiasts are a danger to more than just us."

Dolomite nodded. "All right. I can mark down what I learn on one of your slates. I may not know how to read yet, but I've seen how humans tally things and it's not much different from our counting."

"Thanks, Dolomite." Lamprophyre stood and stretched. "I think I'll turn in early, so we can make an early start tomorrow. Rokshan, can I take you to the palace?"

"Please."

Rokshan climbed swiftly to his usual seat, and Lamprophyre waited for everyone to collect the picked-clean carcasses and Rokshan's turkey bones before leaping into the sky and heading for the palace. "How early is an early start?" Rokshan asked.

"Around dawn? I want to have plenty of time to search for kyanite."

"I'll be there." Rokshan shifted in a way that suggested he was looking behind them. "It's still remarkable to see so many dragons in the sky all at once."

"Even more remarkable when it's the whole flight." Lamprophyre felt an unexpected pang of homesickness. A ridiculous pang, given that her clutch was almost always here, and she liked Tanajital, and she was free to return home whenever she wanted, but still a pang. It was just as well they were making that trip tomorrow. She would have to make time to visit with the flight. How awful, if she only ever returned home because of Manishi's demands.

She scowled. Maybe she shouldn't have given in to the blackmail. The king wasn't irrational, and he wanted the dragon alliance; he was unlikely to expel them on so flimsy a piece of evidence as Manishi's magic mirror. But she would have been making that decision on behalf of other people, and that wasn't fair. No, they were better off letting Manishi think she'd won, and secretly working to neutralize her power over them. And if Manishi thought she was cleverer than seven dragons, she was going to be profoundly surprised.

CHAPTER SIXTEEN

It was barely midmorning when Lamprophyre swept over the foothills below her mountain home. The summer sun had burned the short grasses golden, and she knew from experience that they were also stiff and dry and prickly-ticklish even against the thick, rough skin of her feet and hands. Her shadow kept pace with her, lumpy and distorted by the curves of the hills and by Rokshan's silhouette. Farther away, Flint followed, his shadow appearing to race hers.

She flew on, past the foothills into the beginnings of the rocky peaks, furred with the remains of scruffy short plants and prickly with stunted pines that were all that could grow on that ground. The smell of the stone, dry and dusty in this season, cheered her. It was the smell of home.

She rose higher into the mountains until the air was cool and fresh and she had left even those few plants behind. Rokshan leaned forward so she could hear him over the sound of the rushing wind. "We're going straight to the gleaning field, yes?"

"Yes, and it should be warm enough for you, this time of day." Lamprophyre banked and wheeled right, waving at Flint, who kept on going. "Though we'll stop at the caves on our way back to Tanajital. If

Flint discovers that humans have been secretly mining our mountains, we may need to do something about that immediately."

"Is it bad that I hope it *is* humans mining the mountains for kyanite? That would be an easy solution, not to mention Manishi can hardly gripe about dragons cracking down on theft regardless of what stone they're stealing."

"I was thinking something like that. All the other possibilities are more complicated." Lamprophyre scanned the peaks below. Even for her draconic eyesight, the small exposed patch of kyanite was hard to spot. "I want—oh, there it is." She furled her wings and dove so Rokshan would give that shout of terrified excitement that made her laugh.

She pulled smoothly out of her dive and hovered above the blue bands streaking the gray surface of the mountain. A rockfall sometime earlier that year had exposed the kyanite, and Lamprophyre and other members of the flight had been carefully chipping away stone to expose it further. The sweet, rich scent wafted to her nostrils, and she inhaled deeply, letting the smell fill her with satisfaction.

There was a ledge about half a dragonlength deep below the gleaning field, and she landed there and carefully let Rokshan down. "I'm afraid this is going to be boring," she said. "Stay on the far end of the ledge so the rocks don't hit you. They'll be small, but it's still no fun being pelted with gravel."

Rokshan nodded and walked to where the ledge tapered to no more than a handspan wide. He withdrew a sack from where several were tucked into his belt and shook it out, then sat with his legs dangling over the ledge. If the height—it was another three dragonlengths down to the next flat spot—bothered him, he gave no sign. "This is an amazing view," he said.

With her feet, Lamprophyre grabbed the lip of the rock beneath the gleaning field, carved out for the use of dragons cutting away the stone, and swiveled to look out over the rocky heights. "I suppose," she said. It looked the same as always, stark rocky slopes descending to the softly rolling foothills and then the vast plains stretching out into misty yellow-gray dimness. Tanajital was too far away to be seen even from this height, but she imagined she could perceive it, straddling the banks of the Green River that lay west of where they were.

"I suppose," Rokshan scoffed. "How jaded do you have to be not to be amazed by this vista?"

"Jaded? More like I've seen this view every day for the last sixty years. That's just experience." She swiveled back to face the kyanite. When she and Rokshan had first found it, the dusty blue crystals had been visible only one or two handspans' worth. Now, after several twelvedays of careful excavation, the sweep of kyanite stretched nearly a dragonlength across the sheer surface of the mountain. Sheer except where dragons had removed crystals, of course, and in those places the mountain was pitted and rough like a worm-eaten tree. It was not an image Lamprophyre would have had before living among humans.

She took hold of a protruding knob designed to steady someone cutting the crystal and extended the strong, powerful claws of her left hand. As she carefully cut along the long side of one of the exposed kyanite crystals, she said, "I meant to ask how it went, freeing yourself of Nevrita, but I wasn't sure it was something you wanted to talk about. So you don't have to say if you don't want."

"My plan is in motion. I'd rather not discuss the details." Rokshan leaned back against the rough face of the mountain so the stone plucked at his black hair. "I still feel like such a fool for being caught like that."

"I understand. When it's something you've done before, and you think you've learned from your mistakes, but it turns out otherwise—you're not the only one who's done that, you know."

"Really? What have you done that you swore you wouldn't do again?"

Lamprophyre paused in her cutting. "Oh, Coquina was always good at goading me into pitting myself against her. Racing, specifically. I've never beaten her in a race, and after every loss I always swore I wouldn't try again, but then I'd tell myself it must have been a fluke and challenge her, or accept her challenge, and of course I'd lose again."

"But you're friends now."

"I think so. We have a lot of years of anger to get past, and I still have flashes of jealousy of her, so I don't know that our relationship is totally repaired. But we finally both want to be friends, and that's the beginning of fixing things." Lamprophyre carefully thumped the stone above the crystal to free it, then handed it down to Rokshan to put in his sack. "That was faster than I anticipated. Maybe we'll be back at the embassy in time for supper."

"That would be nice." Rokshan sat down again. Lamprophyre shifted her position and spread her wings to keep her balance. The smell of kyanite made her stomachs rumble, and she resisted taking even a small bite. She knew very well how it worked: one small bite led to another, and another, until you were logy and over-full from eating a whole crystal of the rich stuff.

"Lamprophyre," Rokshan said, and the too-casual sound of his voice made her stop her cutting again. "Are you, um, interested in any of your clutchmates?"

"What? You mean, as a mate?"

"Never mind. I shouldn't have asked."

Lamprophyre realized how shocked she'd sounded. "No, it's all right, you just startled me. What makes you ask?"

"I was curious. Now that I've gotten to know them, and I understand you're likely to choose one of the males as your mate, I can't help trying to see them as a dragon would. But I have no more understanding of dragon beauty than you have of human, except what you've said about Flint being very attractive." Rokshan chuckled. "I still say you have the nicest coloring, but Flint comes close."

Lamprophyre smiled. "Thank you. Flint's colors are attractive, yes, but he's also handsome because his shape is nice, and his muscles are defined without being obvious, and his eye ridges are very expressive. Though Orthoclase's eyes are actually prettier than Flint's. Orthoclase can even do that trick with his eye ridges that some of you humans do with your eyebrows, waggling them independently. He learned from watching Dharan."

"I see. So you're attracted to Flint?"

Lamprophyre handed Rokshan another crystal. "I'm not. I'm not attracted to any of them, which is hard because I'm so close to all of them. But there's still time for that to change. Or I'll find a mate in the next older clutch. I'm not worried."

Rokshan looked her in the eye, making her hesitate rather than returning to her task. "Aren't you?" he said, in a tone of voice inviting her to say more.

Lamprophyre sighed. "All right, I'm a *little* worried," she said. "Hyaloclast and Aegirine were pair-bonded when they were my age. Aegirine told me when I was little that he'd never so much as looked at another female, that he'd loved Hyaloclast from the time he was old enough to understand what love was. I don't know how Hyaloclast felt about him, because she and I don't talk about personal things, but I think she loved him enough that she hasn't pair-bonded again even though he died many years ago. So if my parents had such an immediate and lasting connection, I feel there's something wrong with me that I haven't."

"If they were human, I'd say what your parents had is pretty rare," Rokshan said. "My parents had a political marriage, and Mother said it was a miracle they fell in love. She said my father believed she only married him to be queen, and *she* believed he'd chosen her because he needed a mother for his three children. According to her, it took them more than a few years to realize they were wrong about each other. But now they're very close, for all Father seems hard and unyielding and Mother is diffident."

"But it's not quite the same for dragons. It's like, oh, I don't know. I'm always afraid the males of my clutch are waiting for me to choose one of them, and that it changes how they see me. It's a burden that I'm not interested in any of them. And what if I never find anyone I'm attracted to? We have so many stories about the beauties of the pair-bond. I want to experience them for myself."

"You still have plenty of time," Rokshan said. "Though I understand why you'd feel their regard was a burden. They're all good people and worthy of you, except maybe Dolomite, and that's not his fault."

"Yes, he's just too innocent for me to think of him seriously as a potential mate." Lamprophyre resumed cutting, licked her claws for a taste of the sweet crystal, and added, "I do sometimes think about each of them as if they were my mate, testing the idea, you know? And if I had to pick one—if love weren't an issue—I don't know who I'd choose, because they're all interesting in different ways. It's probably different for humans, but with dragons, a mate will know if you're not completely honest, and that includes how you feel about him. I couldn't do that to any of my friends, choosing them just to have chosen someone."

"Yes, humans are better at being deceptive," Rokshan said drily.

"Sorry, I forgot. It's too bad humans aren't more like dragons that way."

"Oh, I don't know," Rokshan said. "Humans are made for deceit. Not in an awful way, just that our society is built around little white lies and we're used to that. So if we were suddenly incapable of lying without it being found out, I think our civilization might collapse."

"That makes sense." Lamprophyre sniffed the next crystal, taking a deep breath and closing her eyes in pleasure. "Oh, that is good. It's unfortunate you can't smell this, though really it's just as well because you'd want to eat it if you could smell it, and that would be a disaster."

Rokshan took it from her and set it gently in his sack. "What does it smell like? Or is that an unanswerable question?"

"Maybe not. It smells a little like that brown stuff they had at the Rezmish ambassador's reception. The stuff that melted immediately when I touched it."

"Like chocolate?" Rokshan grinned. "If that's true, it's no wonder you dragons are crazy for it. Chocolate's only been readily available here in the last seventeen years, I think. At least, I can remember being a child and tasting it for the first time when the ambassador from Sachetan gave some to my father as a sample of what they wanted to start trading. I think it's much more valuable than garnet, but then I have no need for a contraceptive or a virility enhancer."

"You said that Sister of the Red wore her garnet artifact openly, so people would know she can't have children. Now you say it enhances someone's sex abilities. How can the same stone do two opposite things? And don't say it's not polite to discuss it with a female, because *you* brought it up."

Rokshan groaned. "I did, didn't I? Well, there's not much to tell. All I know is that garnet has an inherent quality that affects reproduction. So I imagine cut one way, it can make someone more fertile, and cut a different way, it can inhibit fertility."

"I don't understand why someone would want not to have children. That's not a dragon thing at all."

"Well, it's mostly women who use those, because the burden of childbearing falls most heavily on them. They endure nine months of increasing discomfort, then the agony of childbirth—"

"Childbirth hurts humans? I suppose that makes sense, but expelling an egg is supposed to be a pleasurable sensation."

"The woman has to push the baby out of her body through a very small passage, and no, Lamprophyre, I am not going to elaborate on that for you. Anyway, yes, childbirth is painful. And then there's years of taking care of the baby until it's old enough to be left with someone not the mother. Human women produce milk for their babies, and although there are other foods you can feed an infant, that milk is still the most nutritious substance it can get. Which is all a very long way of saying that a woman who has a demanding job, or doesn't have a husband to help support their family, might not want to be tied down to a baby."

"I understand." Surprisingly, she did. She cut one more crystal free and said, "I think that's enough. And we should only give Manishi half of what we gleaned. I don't want her thinking we have access to an unlimited supply, because she might become more demanding."

"Very smart. And half of this is more than we've provided her before in any case." Rokshan got to his feet. "Shall we look for more stones? It's not even noon yet, and we can always use the money."

"Orthoclase said there was a lot of extra turquoise when he was here last. Turquoise is fairly valuable." The ledge wasn't big enough for her to fit and give Rokshan a leg up, so she hovered just beside it and extended her arm. Rokshan clambered easily up and settled himself in the notch. Lamprophyre took another long sniff of the kyanite before wheeling away and descending to the lower heights.

There was enough turquoise she didn't need to cut any free from the mountain. She and Rokshan tossed chunks of it into a different sack so they wouldn't break the long kyanite crystals. When they'd taken as many as Lamprophyre judged the flight could spare, she said,

"I wonder who harvested this much. Leucite, maybe. He loves turquoise." She made a face. "I've never understood the appeal, because it tastes bitter, but there are a few dragons who are crazy for it."

"What I don't understand," Rokshan said, "is how there are so many valuable stones in these mountains. South of here, the mines only produce one or maybe two types of stone, and that's all there is in that area. Yet up here, it's like you scratch the surface and there's a different precious or semi-precious stone."

"I never thought about it," Lamprophyre said. "I didn't realize the southern mines were so limited." She weighed a lump of turquoise in one hand and let it fall. "But Mother Stone is different, and so maybe her children are, too."

"I thought dragons were her children. You mean the mountains around Nirinatan—Mother Stone?"

"Yes, but they're different kinds of children. We believe that when a dragon dies, her bones enrich the mountain, and so the lower peaks are like the essence of dragons who came before. Except the mountains are far too big to be nothing but dragon bones. So they're really only metaphorically her children, unlike dragons, whose spirits come from Mother Stone."

"That's fascinating," Rokshan said. "I wonder why human legends don't say anything about that. It's not like humans and dragons didn't live together centuries ago. And yet we have stories of Katayan instead."

Lamprophyre shrugged. "Who knows what else we've lost over the centuries? Dragons have no memories of human religion at all." She crouched. "Let's see if there's any jade. I was thinking we could sell directly to the adepts who supply stone to the healing centers."

Rokshan clambered up. "Manishi won't be happy."

"I never promised to deal exclusively with her, whatever she says. And she doesn't use jade, anyway."

"True." Rokshan swiveled in his seat. "There's Flint. Maybe he learned something."

Lamprophyre pushed off with her powerful legs and rose to meet Flint. His unexpectedly rapid flight brought him even with her before she could ascend very high. "You look like you're in a hurry," she said. "Is something wrong?"

"Nephrite and Heliodor said they saw humans on the lower slopes a few days ago," Flint gasped. "They—the humans—moved like they were trying to go unobserved. So Nephrite concealed himself long enough to watch them, and then Heliodor swooped low overhead to see what they'd do. They scattered, but Nephrite saw they had pack animals laden heavily with lumpy sacks. And a bunch of tools Nephrite described as 'sticks with metal teeth.' I wish memories were visual, because I could have seen what he meant, but I'm sure they were mining tools."

"So we were right," Rokshan said. "I'm surprised it was that easy."

"It's not easy at all," Flint said. "The humans left three or four days ago, and they might be anywhere now. There's no way for us to catch them and prove they were stealing stone."

"Except that Rokshan is an excellent tracker," Lamprophyre said.

"I'm honored at your faith in me," Rokshan replied, "but it's rained here at least twice in the last four days, and that rain will have obliterated any trace of those thieves."

Lamprophyre grimaced. "I guess it doesn't matter, then. Though we know—you did tell the flight to watch for more thieves, yes?"

"Of course." Flint drew in a deep breath and expelled acid-scented air. "But that will matter only for the territory around the caves. They didn't seem concerned about watching the length of the mountains, and why would they? There's only so much territory we can defend."

"Then we'll have to track the thieves at the other end," Rokshan said. "In Tanajital, or in the other large cities. And that's only the Gonjirians. There's no way to know if Fanishkor is sending miners to the mountains abutting on their country."

He sounded frustrated, and Lamprophyre said, "But we're not worried about stone theft in general, are we? Just people mining kyanite illicitly and selling it in secret. Though I am angry about the thefts. I almost had Hyaloclast convinced that we could allow humans to mine in our territory. Now she'll be angry and forbid it, and we'll miss out on all the artifacts we could have traded for."

"You're right, though." Rokshan leaned forward so she and Flint could hear him more clearly. "As infuriating as the idea of theft is, we're really only concerned about the influx of kyanite. Was there any of it in the area Heliodor and Nephrite saw the thieves?"

"No," Flint said, brightening. "Nor in any of the adjacent areas."

"So they aren't the ones we're after." Rokshan absently patted Lamprophyre's shoulder. "We can go home and see what the others learned."

"First, I want to say hello to the flight," Lamprophyre said. "I want to catch up on all the gossip."

"I didn't know dragons gossiped," Rokshan said as Lamprophyre turned and flew westward. "What with hearing each other's thoughts."

"We only hear surface thoughts. Listening in on purpose is bad manners. So there's still talk, and people's art creations, and new pair-bond announcements. And seeing how the dragonets fare." Lamprophyre felt a proprietary interest in the dragonet Opal, whom she and Rokshan had rescued from human bandits before her hatching. But whenever she was close to Opal, the dragonet burst into alarmed chatter about anything that flitted across her mind, and Lamprophyre had to settle for reports from Bromargyrite, who was Opal's brother.

They stayed and talked with the flight until midafternoon, at which point Lamprophyre and Flint headed back to Tanajital. The journey home was a silent one. Lamprophyre felt she'd talked herself out in her conversations with her friends, and talking to another dragon while flying was difficult, as you had to shout to be heard over the distance dragons necessarily had to be separated by so they wouldn't collide. Rokshan, too, was quiet, but he was probably thinking about the next step in finding out where the mysterious kyanite was coming from.

At nearly sunset, they separated at the city wall, Flint heading for the warehouses, Rokshan and Lamprophyre flying to the embassy. Before splitting off, Flint had said simply, "Come to the warehouses after you eat, and we'll discuss with the others."

Lamprophyre had nodded, feeling too hungry and weary from the long flight to speak.

The courtyard was full of beggars eating soup, so Lamprophyre landed atop the embassy roof and scrambled awkwardly down behind the embassy. She crouched so Rokshan could climb off and said, "Do you want soup, or are you going to the palace for supper?"

"Soup. I want to hear what everyone learned." Rokshan stretched and yawned. "Besides, the soup smells incredible."

Lamprophyre crept past the kitchen into the dining pavilion and settled herself on the dusty flagstones. The woman with two children was supervising washing their faces at the water barrel. The old man with the wispy white hair sat cross-legged beside the embassy's front door, drinking soup as was his custom. He seemed untroubled by whatever pained his head tonight. Lamprophyre didn't see the one-legged man, Sumaan, but the Sister of the Red had her bowl in one hand held close to her lips and was eating tidily, her attention on her meal.

Rokshan returned to her side with his bowl and spoon just as Depik wheeled out the trolley with a beautifully sectioned and roasted pig on it. The smell was incredible. Lamprophyre tore into the meat and nodded thanks at Depik, her mouth too full to speak. Hot meat juices dripped down her chin, but she was too hungry to care about what she looked like.

Rokshan paused in his eating. "That's a reverend," he said, pointing with his spoon at a portly man wearing ordinary trousers and a sleeveless shirt. The only thing that set him apart from the beggars, aside from his confident bearing, was a length of fabric the color of buttercups draped over one shoulder and secured in a knot at the opposite hip. The fabric was thick and wide and fell in a long drape from that knot to brush the ground. The reverend held it gathered in one hand and let it sway as if he were using it to sweep the street.

"Surely reverends aren't beggars?" Lamprophyre said.

"Not to my knowledge."

Rokshan set his bowl aside and got to his feet. He hadn't taken more than a couple of steps toward the reverend when the man released his grip on the fabric and raised both hands high above his head. "O beloved of Jiwanyil," he shouted. His voice wasn't deep and had a slightly nasal quality to it, but it filled the courtyard nonetheless. "Our God is all-knowing and all-merciful. He wants all his children to return to him. But his understanding has a limit. Jiwanyil has declared what the children of Katayan must do to return to their God's embrace, and he sorrows at their recalcitrance."

"Now, wait just a minute," Lamprophyre said, rising.

The reverend ignored her. "Katayan weeps for his children, and Jiwanyil weeps with him. Jiwanyil fears the disobedience of the children of Katayan will corrupt his children. He has warned many times, but to no avail. Therefore, he has instructed his ecclesiasts and the reverends who are their right arm to take stronger measures."

Rokshan had halted. Lamprophyre, watching him, was caught by the odd look on his face, as if he anticipated a blow.

"As the voice of the ecclesiasts," the reverend continued, "I instruct the worthy children of Jiwanyil to have no dealings with the children of Katayan. Anyone found violating this instruction will be considered an unworthy follower. And the destiny of unworthy followers is to be cut off from Jiwanyil's blessings."

CHAPTER SEVENTEEN

Rokshan let out a hiss that made him sound almost draconic. "You," he said, striding forward to face the reverend, "what exactly are you saying?"

Rokshan towered over the portly reverend, but the man looked at him without a trace of fear. "Jiwanyil's instructions are clear," he said. "Have no dealings with dragons, and you will partake of Jiwanyil's grace. Continue to consort with them, and be denied his blessings."

"You can't be serious."

The reverend turned his gaze on the men and women filling the courtyard. All of them stood frozen, some with full spoons half-raised to their lips, others gripping their bowls in taut-knuckled hands. "When Jiwanyil's warnings go unheeded, God must speak more loudly," he said. "He pleads with you to return to the true faith. You have been warned." He turned his back on Rokshan and walked out of the courtyard, his yellow drape once more sweeping the street into puffs of dust rising wherever he trod.

Lamprophyre hurried to Rokshan's side. "What does it mean, be denied Jiwanyil's blessings?" she said in a low voice. "Rokshan. Talk to me."

Rokshan shuddered as if a chill had touched his spine, impossible to imagine in this sultry weather. All around them, beggars came back to life, gathering together into small murmuring groups. Some of them cast wary glances at Lamprophyre.

"It means," Rokshan said in the same low voice, "not being allowed to worship in congregations. Denied the rites of marriage or burial. Shut out from religious ceremonies and celebrations. It means excommunication."

She had never heard the word before, but it sounded like a death knell. "Can they do that?"

"Of course they can do that, Lamprophyre. The ecclesiasts are told what behavior is in harmony with Jiwanyil, and they proclaim that to the people."

He sounded so angry Lamprophyre recoiled. "But you don't believe that, do you? That spending time with me angers your God?"

Rokshan wasn't looking at her. He had his gaze fixed on the courtyard. People were setting down their bowls and walking toward the street, their heads lowered as if they felt shamed. Lamprophyre watched the woman drag her two children away. The younger one was screaming and fighting her, and the older child cried something about being hungry still that made Lamprophyre feel sick.

"Rokshan, you have to stop them," she said. "They need this food. Tell them it's a mistake. That Jiwanyil doesn't mean them to go hungry just because it's a dragon providing the food."

Rokshan shook his head. "They won't believe that." He bent to put his own bowl on the ground. "I don't know. Lamprophyre, I'm sorry."

"Sorry? Sorry for what?"

By this time, only a handful of people were left in the courtyard. One was the Sister of the Red. The old man still sat by the embassy door, slurping soup as if he hadn't understood the reverend's warning.

"Rokshan," Lamprophyre said, feeling desperate, "look at me. Look at me!"

He turned, and the look on his face was so empty, so hollow, it made her feel even sicker. "I have to go," he said, and turned away.

"Rokshan, wait!"

He paused without turning around. Desperate words whirled

through her mind, but she couldn't think of anything that might convince him to stay.

"You know this is wrong," she finally said. "No God who loves his children would demand such a sacrifice."

Without looking back, Rokshan said, "God sees farther than we do. He gives us instruction because it will benefit us, even if we don't know why. That's the kind of love Jiwanyil has for us." He walked away across the courtyard and vanished down the street.

Lamprophyre let out a terrible, anguished cry and leaped into the air, heedless of the people remaining in the courtyard. From above, she could see Rokshan making progress down the streets, headed toward the palace. She thought about descending on him, catching him up and carrying him away as she had the day she'd met him. If she could get him alone, she could convince him the reverend was wrong. She could remind him that their friendship mattered more than the foolishness of the ecclesiasts. But the crowds pressed him too closely, and he never looked up even though he could surely hear her beating the air above him. With another cry, she wheeled around and arrowed toward the warehouses.

Most of her clutch was there, though Porphyry and Bromargyrite were absent. Lamprophyre stumbled to a halt in the street and cried out, "The ecclesiasts have struck again!"

"Did they hurt you?" Orthoclase asked. "You look terrified."

"No, it's Rokshan—they didn't—oh, I don't know what I'm saying, it's all so terrible and muddled." Lamprophyre drew in a breath and tried to calm herself. "A reverend came to the embassy and told everyone if they associate with dragons, they can't receive religious blessings anymore."

"I don't understand. Why would they do that?" Dolomite asked.

"Because it's an excellent threat," Flint said. "Humans won't want to lose their connection to Jiwanyil, certainly not over dragons. Imagine if someone told you you couldn't return to Mother Stone when you die."

Dolomite shuddered. "So the humans won't want to deal with us anymore."

"But that can't include the friends we've made," Flint said. "They have to know better."

Lamprophyre's throat ached with misery. "Rokshan walked away from me. He just left. I don't understand. This has to be a ruse by the ecclesiasts. I don't believe Jiwanyil wanted it at all."

"The people won't care," Coquina said. She looked as stunned as Lamprophyre felt. "They believe the ecclesiasts speak for their God. Dealing with us was fine so long as it was just a matter of what dragons believe being wrong. Humans might even have thought they were doing God's will in associating with us and maybe bringing us to the truth. Now..." She let out a hot burst of smoke. "And there's nothing we can do about it. I don't know much about human law, but I'm sure it doesn't govern ecclesiasts doing purely ecclesiastical things."

Flint gripped Lamprophyre's shoulder, steadying her. "It will be all right," he said. "Rokshan is too good a friend to let this come between you."

"He also has tremendous faith in Jiwanyil," Lamprophyre said miserably. "I know he's said he's comfortable with not knowing the entire truth—that if dragons worship Mother Stone, there's probably a reason humans believe in Katayan—but I doubt that extends to believing the ecclesiasts are lying to everyone in Gonjiri just to drive dragons away."

"But that's what we think, right?" Dolomite said. "We know we're not evil."

"No, but maybe the human God is threatened by us, and he really does want us gone," Coquina said.

"I don't think so," Orthoclase said. "I've given the religious situation a lot of thought, and it occurred to me that if the human God Jiwanyil really exists, he would know the truth about dragon religion, that Mother Stone is real and Katayan is made up. Or maybe Katayan is a corruption of what humans used to know about Mother Stone." He shook his head impatiently. "The important thing is, if Jiwanyil is real and really does want dragons gone, he wouldn't dress it up in terms of an imaginary God demanding we worship him. He'd just tell us to get out of Gonjiri."

"So it really is the ecclesiasts trying to get rid of us," Flint said. "But why?"

"It doesn't matter," Lamprophyre said. "Those ecclesiasts are lying, and worse, they're using people's honest faith to compel them to do what the ecclesiasts want. I refuse to let them manipulate me and I am absolutely not leaving Tanajital, not when I'm still needed here. I'll just have to prove what they're doing."

The four other dragons stared at her. "Prove, how?" Flint asked.

"I don't know. It makes me sick to think that usually I have Rokshan to help me come up with plans." She swallowed, trying to ease the ache in her throat. "Not everyone in Tanajital is devout. We'll still be able to interact with some humans. And then I'll think of something."

Coquina laughed, startling the others. "Sorry," she said. "I was just thinking how Manishi is one of those humans, and I was actually relieved by the thought."

Orthoclase chuckled. "She definitely won't care about being cut off. Neither will Dharan."

This thought comforted Lamprophyre, though not by much. "I want to talk about what we learned today," she said. "I don't want to think about this until morning. I'm going to have trouble sleeping as it is."

"I told these three what we learned about stone theft," Flint said. "Porphyry is still out investigating. We think. He's been gone since morning."

"Bromargyrite left after noon to talk to that adept he knows," Orthoclase said. "I spent the afternoon at the market, sniffing for stone. I'm afraid I didn't learn much, aside from how common certain stones are. Nobody was actively using magic, so I couldn't compare the effects to the stones and work out what they're for."

"I talked to Melika this morning," Coquina said. "She's going to look into the kyanite situation for us and let me know if she finds out who's selling it. At the very least, she thought she could discover who's *buying* it." Coquina's lovely face hardened. "Assuming she's willing to speak to me again after this."

Lamprophyre nodded. It seemed everything led back to the ecclesiasts' terrible pronouncement.

"I don't know if I learned anything helpful," Dolomite said. "I flew over the city several times, watching for ecclesiasts, and I saw a lot of them. But the pattern they made didn't mean anything."

Lamprophyre sat up. "Pattern?"

"Well, patterns," Dolomite said. "I drew them on the slate. I hope you don't mind that I borrowed one of yours, Lamprophyre." He ducked inside his warehouse and returned holding one of the giant slates Lamprophyre and Porphyry practiced their handwriting on. It was covered with a roughly circular design filled with an intricate, multicolored pattern. A wrist-thick line cut off the left side of the circle, and Lamprophyre, looking at the design in puzzlement, felt the image click into focus. It was an aerial map of Tanajital, rendered beautifully in Dolomite's distinctive artistic style.

"Where did all the colors come from?" she exclaimed.

"Oh, humans make chalk in dozens of colors," Dolomite said eagerly. "I bought some so I could draw on the inside of my warehouse. They're amazing, aren't they? But today I used the colors to show the path of each ecclesiast I saw." He traced a blue line without touching it, his finger hovering just above. "This one followed this path. She was moving really slowly, so even though I was watching half a dozen of them, it was easy to keep track of her. The pattern looks like a six-pointed star, see? And she traveled the path four times before returning here. This is the Archprelate's palace." This time he did tap the slate, smearing the fat chalk circle slightly.

Flint stepped closer to examine the blue line. "It does look like a star."

"All the ecclesiasts I saw made patterns," Dolomite said, "and they all traveled over those paths four times before returning. Like wearing a groove in the streets or something."

"And they covered the entire city in their patterns," Lamprophyre said. "Did you only draw the streets the ecclesiasts followed, Dolomite?"

"No, the white lines are the large streets they didn't use." Dolomite tilted his head curiously. "There aren't very many of them. I was so interested in the patterns I didn't realize."

"It's interesting, but what does it mean?" Coquina said. "Do those patterns matter?"

"We don't know enough about human religion to answer that question," Flint said.

The sound of flapping wings made them all look up. "Sorry that took so long," Porphyry said. "That's beautiful work, Dolomite. What is it?"

"A map of Tanajital, and the progress of the ecclesiasts Dolomite saw," Flint said. "What does it look like to you?"

Porphyry narrowed his eyes. "Like colored patterns. But in truth, if that represents several paths, it looks like someone searching for something."

Lamprophyre gasped. "You're right! They're covering the whole city in a tight pattern the way they would if they were hunting."

"But then why make patterns?" Coquina said. "They could achieve the search pattern more efficiently if they weren't constrained by those smaller patterns. See, this one is really small, and it's entirely within this other one."

"Coincidence," Lamprophyre snapped. Of course Coquina had to step on Lamprophyre's discovery. She never could bear to see Lamprophyre succeed.

"It's too regular to be coincidence," Coquina said irritably. "If you'd let go of your need to be right all the time—"

"Only when I'm actually right!"

"So you're going to insist on your interpretation even though—"

"Both of you, stop right now," Orthoclase said, spreading his wings with a snap that cut across their argument. "You're upset because you have human friends who might desert you because of the ecclesiasts' decree. Don't let that affect what we're doing. Or your friendship."

Lamprophyre closed her mouth. Across from her, Coquina dipped her head low so Lamprophyre couldn't see her face. Hot, embarrassed blood turned Lamprophyre's scales lavender.

"I'm sorry," she told Coquina. "Orthoclase is right. And I guess I'm not as comfortable around you as I claimed. Forgive my harsh words."

"No, it's my fault," Coquina said. "I'm the one who turned our disagreement into a personal attack. I'm sorry."

Silence fell for a few beats, until Lamprophyre managed to look at Coquina and found the other dragon gazing back at her, somewhat dejectedly. "If Rokshan doesn't come back, I don't know what I'll do," Lamprophyre said.

Coquina nodded. "I was supposed to go flying with Melika tomorrow morning for the first time."

"So let's figure out how to stop the ecclesiasts," Flint said. "I think it's obvious that the ecclesiasts were looking for something today, and it's equally obvious that they used these unusual patterns for some reason as part of that search. Dolomite, will you watch again tomorrow and see if the patterns are the same?"

"Of course. This is so exciting!" Dolomite said, fairly bobbing in his excitement.

"Then, Porphyry, what did you learn today?" Flint asked.

Lamprophyre and Coquina exchanged wry glances. For a male, Flint was certainly bossy—though if he were female, they'd consider him assertive. But he was smart, and saw to the heart of things quickly, so what did it matter that he wasn't female? Lamprophyre decided she was just as happy to let him coordinate their efforts.

"I flew to the academy and talked to the students," Porphyry said. "And I observed them and their teachers. I'm certain it's chlorite that makes certain humans' thoughts incomprehensible."

"So why quartz, too?" Lamprophyre asked.

"That one, I just asked someone about," Porphyry said with a grin. "Turns out quartz amplifies the effect of whatever stone you pair with it. Which is why you never see it as the only artifact someone has. There would be no point because there's nothing for it to work on."

Again, the flapping of giant wings made them all duck and then shift to make room for Bromargyrite. "You won't believe what I learned," he said without waiting for anyone to greet him. "Chlorite blurs human thoughts."

"Not to diminish your findings, but Porphyry figured that out," Coquina said.

"But did Porphyry also figure out that it's related to the kyanite?" Bromargyrite said smugly.

The clutchmates burst out talking all at once. "All right, quiet down and I'll tell you what I learned from that adept," Bromargyrite said. "This time, I couldn't hear his thoughts. I did a quick sniff and realized he'd added a chlorite pendant to his array of artifacts, so I guessed that was responsible. That also told me he had no idea dragons can hear thoughts, or he'd have been wearing it the last time."

"At least we've managed to keep that secret," Orthoclase muttered.

"Anyway," Bromargyrite said with a warning look at Orthoclase for the interruption, "I steered the conversation around to specific stones. Got him to take off the chlorite so I could 'see it more clearly,' and then distracted him so he never remembered to put it back on and I could eavesdrop. I pretended dragons got benefits from eating certain stones and asked to compare those effects to what human artifacts do. And he gushed out information like a rushing river."

"I hope you were cautious," Lamprophyre said.

"I did not mention kyanite, so stop glaring at me, Lamprophyre, but I didn't have to because he thought about it. We were talking about sapphire, and how it improves mental focus, and he thought 'if I only had some kyanite, I could prove the communication theory.' So I pushed a little harder, asked him about chalcedony because of that communication stone you have, Lamprophyre. And he thought, 'chalcedony is well enough, but someday I'll read others' minds.'"

Everyone fell silent. "Don't you see?" Bromargyrite said. "Those adepts looking for kyanite are trying to develop an artifact that will let them hear thoughts!"

"That's kind of a stretch," Flint said.

"Not so much of a stretch, if you put all the pieces together," Coquina said. "We know sapphire and kyanite have similar mental effects. That adept wanted kyanite for a 'communication theory.' A mental communication isn't that far a leap from listening to thoughts."

"Ohhh," Lamprophyre said, realization striking. "We wondered why some adepts would have incomprehensible thoughts when they don't know dragons can hear them. Obviously, if they are trying to develop a thought-hearing artifact, they know others are too. What if they invented a way to block that artifact before it was even created?"

"That makes a lot of sense," Coquina said. "But now I'm concerned about what happens when they succeed with the kyanite. There's no reason to believe that artifact will work only on humans. And I really don't want someone like Manishi hearing what I'm thinking."

Once again, silence fell. Finally, Flint spoke. "There isn't anything we can do about it, save getting some of those chlorite artifacts for ourselves. And even that's impossible because it would give away that we know the secret. But at least now we know what we're facing."

"I haven't given Manishi the kyanite yet," Lamprophyre said. "If we're willing to face the potential catastrophe, I can refuse to hand it over."

"I don't think we should risk angering the king, not now that the ecclesiasts have struck another blow," Flint said. "I don't mind for myself, but Lokun could be in trouble."

"And really, what's the worst that could happen?" Porphyry asked. "We know what Manishi is after, and we can keep an eye on her. If she develops the kyanite artifact, we'll be aware of it and we can counter her. Not giving her the kyanite just means someone else will develop it first, someone we don't know to ward against."

Lamprophyre scowled. "I hate giving her an advantage in anything. Rokshan—" She stopped as the terrible heartache descended on her again.

Orthoclase put a hand on her shoulder. "It will be all right," he said. "This will pass. The ecclesiasts are lying, and we'll prove it."

She nodded and put her hand over his. "Thank you."

The sun had almost set, and lanterns were coming on in the neighborhoods surrounding the warehouses. The dimness didn't impair the dragons' vision much, but Lamprophyre said, "I'm going to sleep. We can talk more in the morning. Maybe things will sort themselves out overnight."

The others murmured what she hoped was agreement and feared was the same discouragement she felt. She waved goodbye and flew off to the embassy.

In her heart, she imagined Rokshan waiting for her inside, ready to explain that it was all a mistake. But the embassy was empty, and the courtyard was dark because no one had lit the lanterns. That was usually something Depik did—but he'd have left, too, wouldn't he? The ache in Lamprophyre's throat redoubled. She crept slowly into her hall and settled herself to sleep.

CHAPTER EIGHTEEN

She woke to the smell of roasting cow and lay quietly for a dozen beats, drifting between sleep and wakefulness. Then the memory of the previous night struck her. Confused, she left the embassy and stepped into the dining pavilion. "Depik?"

"One moment, my lady," Depik called out, and shortly he appeared, trundling the cow on its trolley. "Sorry about that. I'm afraid I got a bit of a late start."

"But, didn't you hear?"

"Hear what?"

Lamprophyre almost didn't tell him. It felt so good to speak to a human who didn't hate her, she didn't want to give that up. But it wasn't honorable to keep this secret. "The ecclesiasts have said anyone who associates with dragons is denied Jiwanyil's blessings."

"Oh, *that*." Depik said the words as if dismissing everything she'd just said. "I'm not giving up the best job I've ever had for the sake of religious trappings. Now, would you prefer sheep or cow for your supper?"

Lamprophyre gaped. "Religious trappings? But you won't be able to worship!"

Depik gave her a serious look. "Worship is what you make of it," he said. "I've kept Jiwanyil's teachings for years even though I rarely go to services. I'm willing to take a chance on that satisfying God." He turned and entered the kitchen.

Lamprophyre stared after him for a few beats. Then she absently tore off a large bite of cow, her eyes never leaving the kitchen door. She expected people like Dharan and Manishi, people who didn't really believe in God or his teachings, to reject the ecclesiasts' demands. But Depik was faithful, or as faithful as someone could be who disobeyed what he had to believe was God's command. Lamprophyre tried to imagine denying Mother Stone and came up blank. It would mean not being a dragon anymore. Obviously it wasn't the same for humans, but if they truly believed the ecclesiasts heard the word of Jiwanyil, how could they justify refusing to obey their commands?

She ate slowly, wishing the food could dispel the horrible ache that lingered in her throat and had moved behind her eyes. Rokshan would come back. He had to. She clung to that thought until common sense prevailed. Of course he wouldn't. She didn't know what humans believed about what happened to their souls when they died, but being denied Jiwanyil's blessings almost certainly meant their souls would be cut off from their God. That wasn't something anyone faithful would want to risk. And that alone would keep him away.

She found herself unable to finish her meal and pushed it aside without summoning Depik to remove the rest. Wearily, feeling a million years old, she trudged back to the embassy and sorted through her piles of stone. Her eye fell on the sack containing the kyanite crystals, and another pang of sadness pulsed through her. She opened the sack, removed a long, rod-like crystal, and bit off the end. The sweet flavor made her gag, but she choked it down where it would no doubt sit in her stomach, lumpy and indigestible. She tossed the rest of the crystal back and lay down beside the stone stores, breathing in their mingled odors.

She heard footsteps approaching and looked up to see Dharan running across the courtyard. "I heard," he said, panting, as he drew up even with the doorway but did not enter. "Are you all right?"

Lamprophyre shifted to be able to look at him more directly. "He left," she said. "I don't know where he went."

"I haven't seen him since two days ago. I would have thought—but no, he wouldn't talk to me because he knows what I'd say."

"What would you say?"

"That he's a fool," Dharan said. "This is clearly a ploy by the ecclesiasts."

"I agree, but, Dharan—"

"No 'buts,' Lamprophyre." Dharan sounded furious. "You know the ecclesiasts want dragons gone. They've hit on the perfect way to accomplish that. I never knew they were this corrupt."

"Yes, but what if they're not?" Lamprophyre exclaimed. Orthoclase's words of the previous day had faded to nothing in memory. "Ecclesiasts *do* receive prophecies—we've seen that. There's no reason to think this isn't one more prophecy except that we don't want it to be!"

"I may or may not believe in God, but I do believe in logic. And a principle of logic is that you shouldn't ignore the obvious answer in favor of a more convoluted one. You dragons threaten the ecclesiasts' power. They need you gone. And they just happen to be possessed of a prophecy that gives them what they want?" Dharan started pacing the doorway, turning rapidly on his heel every time he came up against the frame. "It's ridiculous. It can't possibly be true."

Lamprophyre sighed. "It doesn't matter. There's nothing we can do about it. Besides, we have other things—I mean, we dragons do—to investigate."

"More important than convincing Rokshan to pull his head out of his ass?"

"We can't force him to believe our way, Dharan. It has to be his decision." She sighed again. "Come inside. I don't want to talk about this where people can hear."

Dharan glanced around the courtyard. "Nobody is here. And that's not likely to change so long as the ecclesiasts' edict is in place."

That made Lamprophyre's heart feel like cracking in two. "Even so, I don't want to risk it."

Dharan walked past her and sat next to the second slate. It still had Porphyry's handwriting scrawled across the upper half, unrelated words he'd found visually appealing. "So what do you dragons have going on?"

Lamprophyre settled herself so her hindquarters blocked the doorway and most of the light. The dimness comforted her. "We found out a few things. One is that the ecclesiasts are searching Tanajital for something, and they're traveling in mysterious patterns we don't understand. The other is that some adepts are trying to invent an artifact that will let them hear thoughts. Manishi is one of them."

Dharan's mouth fell slightly open. He said, "Even one of those things would be astounding. Are you sure about the mind-reading? I know, it's not reading. Or maybe it is, if it's adepts inventing the thing."

"We're reasonably sure. It fits all the evidence." Lamprophyre fumbled around until she found the kyanite bag. "This crystal is what they're experimenting with. I'm supposed to give some to Manishi."

"You can't do that," Dharan said. "Manishi is smart and ruthless. If anyone could invent a mind-reading artifact, it's she. And Manishi capable of hearing people's thoughts doesn't bear thinking about."

"I have to. She's threatened to hurt Flint if I do."

Dharan laughed. "How in God's name does she expect to hurt a dragon?"

Lamprophyre explained everything. "And we can't risk the king getting angry with us now, even if I'm sure we can prove Flint's innocence eventually," she concluded. "We're already in such a precarious position. And there's Flint's human friend Lokun to think of, too."

"But giving in to a blackmailer is dangerous. Manishi will go on holding that over your heads forever, and her demands will grow more terrible."

"It won't be forever. We'll figure out a way to stop her. At worst, we'll find a time to tell the king ourselves what Flint and Lokun did. That has to be better than him finding out some other way."

"I don't know." Dharan shook his head. "It doesn't sit well with me to give in to blackmail."

"Me either, but we don't have a choice right now."

"You always have a choice, Lamprophyre. You just don't have a *good* choice right now." Dharan leaned back with his head tilted against the wall in a pose that reminded Lamprophyre so much of Rokshan it made her want to fly away from him. She closed her eyes and willed herself calm. Nothing she could do.

"Tell me more about the other thing," Dharan said. "How do you know the ecclesiasts are searching? What for?"

"We don't know. Dolomite was watching them yesterday and he saw the patterns." Lamprophyre stood and stretched. "We should go to the warehouses so you can see. Maybe a human will understand better than a dragon."

At the warehouses, when Dharan finally appeared—he had flatly refused to fly with Lamprophyre, which had secretly relieved her mind, because she didn't want to fly with anyone but Rokshan—he examined Dolomite's slate with interest. "It's definitely a search pattern," he said. "I'm not sure about these smaller patterns, except that they seem to outline certain districts within the city. And they're avoiding some places entirely. The streets surrounding the dragon embassy, for one." He traced the white lines surrounding the spot Dolomite had marked, smearing the chalk slightly.

"That makes sense," Orthoclase said. "If they're so keen on dragons being evil, they wouldn't want to contaminate themselves."

"They're also avoiding the slums," Dharan continued, "and that makes sense too, if you consider what a high opinion of themselves ecclesiasts have. It's not as if anyone in the slums will attack an ecclesiast, so it's not a matter of personal safety, but that's what they have reverends for, to take Jiwanyil's light into dark places they'd rather not venture."

"So the embassy, the slums, and...what's this?" Bromargyrite asked, pointing.

Dharan tilted his head and squinted. "The academy," he said. "But that might just be because there aren't any large streets within the academy's boundaries, just footpaths. The ecclesiasts certainly circle it. You said they trace their paths four times?"

"That's what Dolomite observed," Orthoclase said. "He's out watching the ecclesiasts again. I think he enjoys the challenge."

"So they might not follow the same paths today," Lamprophyre said. "And who knows how long they've been doing this?"

"The question is, what are they looking for?" Dharan said. "I don't know how to answer that."

"We could just ask," Flint said.

Lamprophyre laughed. "I doubt they'd be willing to talk to a dragon. Or a known heathen," she added, gesturing at Dharan.

"So we watch them, and see what we can learn," Flint said.

A shadow passed overhead, and the dragons looked up. Lamprophyre caught sight of Coquina's face, set and hard, before the dragon landed, took a few trotting steps to slow herself, and ducked inside her warehouse without saying a word. Lamprophyre looked at the others. "Coquina tried to talk to Melika this morning," Flint said in a low voice.

Lamprophyre took a few cautious steps, being careful to make noise so Coquina wouldn't think she was sneaking up on her, and paused just outside Coquina's warehouse. Coquina was a dark shadow inside the windowless building. "Um, did something happen?" Lamprophyre asked.

A puff of hot smoke emerged from the doorway. "She wouldn't see me," Coquina said. "Her mother told me I wasn't welcome and slammed the door in my face. So I don't know if that was Melika's decision, or her mother's, or—"

"I'm sorry," Lamprophyre said, the ache beginning in her throat again. "I'm sure Melika is still your friend, even if this decree means she has to stay away."

Coquina burst out of the warehouse. "She's a stupid human, and she believes the lies her false god is telling her," she shouted. "I don't know why I ever thought we could be friends."

Lamprophyre faced her down, unmoved by her outburst. "I know it hurts," she said. "If we can find a way to change the ecclesiasts' minds..." Even to her, that sounded facile and improbable. She blew out a smoke cloud of her own. "Let's worry about the things we have power over. Rokshan and I were going to meet with Manishi around late afternoon to deliver the kyanite. Am I still doing that?"

"We're not in a position to defy her yet," Flint said. "Can you put her off for a few days?"

"I think so. She might not know I've already harvested it. I can tell her I won't have it until three days from now. Any later than that and she might get suspicious, or angry, and go to the king." Lamprophyre looked up to where Dolomite swept past, a dark green speck against the cloudless summer sky. "I wonder what he sees up there?"

The others followed her gaze. "It's hard to remember he's our age," Coquina said. "And then he comes up with something brilliant like seeing those patterns."

"Once he's drawn today's paths, we'll have something to compare yesterday to," Dharan said, "and that might be revelatory."

"But what does it matter?" Coquina burst out. "So the ecclesiasts are looking for something. It's not as if we can do anything with that."

"Maybe not," Flint said. "But if they've lost something, they don't want anyone to know about it, or they'd have made another of those obnoxious announcements. Suppose we figure out what it is and find it first? That gives us a weapon to use against them."

That hadn't occurred to Lamprophyre at all. "That would be fantastic," she breathed. "But it's going to take time. And we still have to figure out how to keep Manishi from going to the king with what looks like evidence of treason."

"It gives us something to do," Orthoclase said with a shrug.

Coquina spread her wings with a sharp crack. "I'm joining Dolomite. If we can bring down these ecclesiasts, I say we should." She leaped into the sky with a great swirling of wind and dust.

"I'll talk to Manishi," Lamprophyre said, "and the rest of you get to work thinking how we can outmaneuver her."

"Be careful," Dharan warned. "She's suspicious and paranoid. You can't give her any hint that you intend to deceive her. Even pretending to be downcast and submissive might tip her off."

"I'll do my best."

Lamprophyre was halfway back to the embassy before remembering she likely couldn't get a human to take the message to Manishi that she wanted to see her. Muttering curses under her breath, she changed direction and headed for the slums. Dragons didn't lie, but they knew about pretending—putting on a show the other person knew was false, but accepted in the spirit of the game—and she was sure she could trick Manishi. But pretending wouldn't be necessary. Lamprophyre was angry and hurt and bewildered, all of which she could display to the adept without giving anything away.

She descended slowly, giving the humans time to clear the streets. The slums were never as crowded as the richer parts of Tanajital, as if the residents were ashamed of where they lived and didn't want anyone to see them. Men and women slunk off down narrow alleys leading from the street in front of Manishi's warehouse, their thoughts a muddled tangle of surprise and fear and even resentment, which puzzled Lamprophyre. After some consideration, she decided the humans might not like being invaded by a creature the ecclesiasts had declared outcast. Suppose the reverends and the ecclesiasts considered them tainted by proximity to her, even if they didn't speak or interact in any way? Anger flared within Lamprophyre. It was all so unfair she wanted to scream.

Manishi's workshop was as quiet and still as it ever was, giving no sign that anyone was within. Lamprophyre hesitated before knocking on the door. Suppose the workshop's protections were sensitive to any outside force? She didn't think she was in danger, but the surrounding buildings and the people hiding from her within them might be. She thought about this for a moment, then knocked gently on the wood. The protections couldn't be that sensitive, because for all this neighborhood wasn't busy, there were enough people that casual contact with the buildings was possible. Manishi didn't want her workshop blown up for no reason.

The door swayed a little under her knocking, though she hadn't used much force. Lamprophyre heard no one moving around inside. She waited a few beats, then knocked again, more forcefully. "Manishi?" she said. "I need to talk to you."

Still nothing. Lamprophyre looked around. She couldn't sit in the street, waiting who knew how long for Manishi to return. She had no way of leaving a message, nothing to write with, and Manishi might get angry if Lamprophyre scrawled all over her door and walls. And she couldn't leave a message with one of the humans, even if there had been any about. But she didn't like the idea of returning here repeatedly until she found Manishi. Lamprophyre let out an impatient puff of smoke from both nostrils. She was close to leaving this city, and Stones take the alliance between her people and Gonjiri.

"You looking for the adept?"

Startled, Lamprophyre looked over her shoulder. A human child, male or female, Lamprophyre couldn't tell, stood hesitantly in the shadow of the nearest alley. The child's eyes were wide, its face filthy, and it wore a ragged shirt that fell all the way to its knees that Lamprophyre thought was actually an adult's tunic. The child wiped a hand across its nose and repeated, "You want the adept?"

"I, well, yes," Lamprophyre said. "You shouldn't speak to me."

"Why not?" Another swipe across the nose. "I heard as dragons don't eat people. So I ain't scared of you."

"Because you'll be in trouble with the ecclesiasts."

The child shrugged, one shoulder rising higher than the other. "Don't never see the ecclesiasts in here. Ain't scared of them, neither."

Lamprophyre turned to face the child more directly. "Your parents will be angry with you, though."

The same odd shrug twitched through the child. "No parents. Just me and Kavari."

Rokshan—she closed her eyes briefly as she thought of him—had told her many of the children who came alone for soup were orphans, a word Lamprophyre had never heard before. He'd also said that children whose parents died and who had no other family were usually in the direst of straits among Tanajital's beggars. "Who is Kavari?"

"Little sister. We live just down there. Do you breathe fire?"

"Sometimes, but never to hurt people," Lamprophyre assured the child. Its thoughts were clear and untroubled by fear, but there was an edge of hunger to them Lamprophyre recognized, and it broke her heart. "What's your name?"

"Rassika," the child said. That sounded like a girl's name, though Lamprophyre hated to jump to conclusions with humans and their strange prickliness about having their sex misidentified.

"Rassika," Lamprophyre said, "are you hungry? You and your sister?"

Rassika's eyes widened. "We do fine on our own," she said. "Ain't no one taking her away."

"I wasn't going to do that. My friend Depik makes soup every night for anyone who needs it. I was wondering if you and Kavari might want some."

Now the girl's eyes narrowed suspiciously. "Why?"

"Because Depik and I like helping. Because we have lots of food, and Depik used to be a beggar and he knows how it feels to be truly hungry. I would be pleased for you and your sister to visit me."

"But you want something out of us," Rassika said, suspicion still tingeing her voice and her thoughts.

"No, I—" Lamprophyre paused. She didn't know how old this child was, but she knew plenty of adult humans whose pride wouldn't let them accept help without giving something in return. "Actually, yes," she corrected herself. "I need to tell Manishi—the adept who works here—something important, but I don't think I should wait around here for her to return. If you give her a message, I'll give you and Kavari a good meal tonight. Is that fair?"

Rassika regarded her in silence for a moment. "Fair," she said. "What message?"

Good question. "Tell her the delivery will be in three days," she said. This was actually an excellent solution; Lamprophyre wouldn't have to encounter Manishi, or lie to her, and Manishi would have no option but to wait the three days, lacking anyone to argue with.

"Delivery in three days," Rassika said. "Delivery of what?"

"It's private."

Rassika nodded as if privacy was something she understood and held dear. "Where do we go for food?"

Lamprophyre considered her mental map of Tanajital and translated it into something a landbound creature could use. "The old customs house, north of here," she said, and gave a handful of directions Rassika took in without looking or sounding confused. "You can come any night you want. And we can talk again, if you want. I like talking to humans."

Now Rassika did look puzzled. "Why?"

"Because humans are interesting, and I'm here in Tanajital to explain about how dragons live and their customs so humans and dragons will understand each other." Something that could not happen so long as the ecclesiasts' edict was in force. This made her angry again, so she took a deep breath and said, "Can I meet your sister?"

Rassika shook her head. "Tonight," she said, and slipped away deeper into the alley.

Lamprophyre listened to her thoughts—*dragon big, maybe not eat but it would crush Kavari, don't know if I trust it*—until Rassika was too distant to be more than a thread in the tangle of humanity surrounding her. Then she flew for the embassy. Depik needed to know they were still serving soup that night, even if no one came.

She landed in the courtyard and stretched out her wings and back. Even if Rassika didn't deliver the message, she could justify not going back as a response to the ecclesiasts' demands. Yes, make Manishi come to her. Manishi might be blackmailing her, but Dharan was right that giving in readily would just make Manishi step up her "requests."

She took a few steps toward the embassy, but stopped when something moved within, something no more than a shadow in the dim interior. "Can I help you?" she asked, squinting into the darkness.

The shadow moved forward to stand in the doorway. It was Rokshan.

CHAPTER NINETEEN

"**R**okshan*," Lamprophyre breathed, and fell silent. Rokshan stood stiffly, like someone unsure of his welcome and ready to flee if necessary. His silence was the sort that swallowed words, his own and those of everyone around him. It didn't matter, because Lamprophyre couldn't think of anything to say.

They stared at each other for a dozen beats, not moving, not speaking. Finally, Lamprophyre managed, "We should go inside. It's too hot out here."

Rokshan nodded and retreated into the shadows. Lamprophyre followed him, furling her wings closely so she wouldn't accidentally knock him down. She settled on the floor and lowered herself until her head was level with his. What to say? Everything in her heart felt like an accusation. *You left. You cared about your religion more than about me. You wouldn't even say goodbye.*

She waited for Rokshan to sit as he always did, with his legs crossed in that painful position, but he stood, still looking uncertain, with his hands clasped loosely behind his back and his head bowed. More silence stretched out between them like a river, with both of them on opposite banks and no way of crossing or even meeting halfway. The silence wore on Lamprophyre, but she knew it was a mistake for her to be the first to speak, and override whatever had brought Rokshan back.

Finally, without looking up, Rokshan said, "I had to go, Lamprophyre."

Lamprophyre drew in a breath. "But you knew it was wrong, didn't you? Jiwanyil couldn't possibly want what the ecclesiasts said!"

"It's not faith if you only obey the instructions you like," Rokshan said. "Or the ones you already intended to follow. I believe the ecclesiasts speak the word of God. I couldn't not—God's breath, Lamprophyre, don't you understand?"

"I do," Lamprophyre said. "I do understand. But something is very wrong with that pronouncement. Dharan said—"

Rokshan's head came up. "Dharan," he said through gritted teeth, "has no idea what it means to live a faithful life."

"It's not that. He said it's an unlikely coincidence that the ecclesiasts want dragons to stop threatening their power, and then they receive a prophecy that gives them what they want. Don't you think that's strange?"

"Unless they were right all along."

"Stop it!" Lamprophyre shouted. "Why did you even come back if you were just going to repeat what you already said? You believe I'm evil? Then get out of here, and never come back!"

"You're not evil," Rokshan said. "But don't you see the position I'm in? Either I believe the ecclesiasts and lose my best friend, or I question the ecclesiasts and lose everything I've believed my whole life. And—God help me, Lamprophyre, but I think the ecclesiasts are wrong. I think...I think they're lying."

The words sounded as if they were wrung out of him. Lamprophyre's anger vanished, replaced by a terrible sorrow. She rested her hand gently on his small shoulder—he was so fragile, she could break him without even realizing—and said, "You shouldn't have to make that choice. Stones take those ecclesiasts for what they've done."

Rokshan shook his head. "I don't know where that leaves me. Heretic, maybe. But I've thought about this, and I spoke to Khadar—"

She'd almost forgotten he had a close relationship with one of the

High Ecclesiasts who were responsible for the edict. "What did Khadar say?"

"It's what he didn't say that convinced me. He was nervous. Khadar is never nervous. He was born arrogant, and he's convinced that everything he does is right. But he wouldn't meet my eyes, and he didn't take the opportunity to lecture me on how my evil ways consorting with dragons had finally caught up to me. He just said prophecy is prophecy and Jiwanyil's word is infallible. And then he made an excuse and left. It was so unlike him it made me wonder..."

"Wonder what?"

He finally lifted his head to look at her. "Wonder what game the High Ecclesiasts are playing at. I would have sworn that despite their love of power, they have enough respect for God and the responsibility of their positions not to abuse the trust we all have in them. And I believe the Archprelate really is Jiwanyil's voice to all of Gonjiri, and that he would rein them in if that became necessary. But this—Lamprophyre, how is it possible? And if the High Ecclesiasts have lied to us, how long has that been going on?"

"But the ecclesiasts are possessed of true prophecies. We've seen it. So they can't possibly be lying about everything."

Rokshan's mouth thinned into a hard, straight line. "Just lying about one thing is enough."

Lamprophyre lowered her hand. "All right," she said. "The ecclesiasts are pretending Jiwanyil told them dragons should be shunned. That doesn't mean Jiwanyil doesn't exist, or that he doesn't reveal prophecies to worthy ecclesiasts. It just means your religion is in the hands of people who don't believe in it. You shouldn't doubt what you know is true."

"What makes you say they don't believe?"

Lamprophyre struggled to put into words ideas that had only just come to her. "If they believed," she said slowly, "they wouldn't fake prophecies to get what they want. They would leave it to Jiwanyil to decide how humans should relate to dragons. They would have faith that even though they thought dragons were a problem, Jiwanyil sees more than they do and would guide them to the right outcome."

Rokshan smiled. "You're wiser than every ecclesiast in Tanajital," he said. "Even so, it still doesn't make sense. Either they haven't been possessed of any prophecies on the subject, or they have, and they're lying about what Jiwanyil told them. That's another thing I would have sworn was impossible."

"There isn't anything we can do about it, though, is there? Short of pinning Khadar down and beating his secrets out of him, which, by the way, I would love an excuse to do."

Rokshan's smile turned into a laugh, and Lamprophyre felt giddy with joy to hear it. "I don't know," he said, "but if they're lying, I believe Jiwanyil will eventually intervene. Somehow."

"You really do have tremendous faith," Lamprophyre said. "If I found out—I don't know. If I found out dragons don't return to Mother Stone when they die, I think it would shake my faith to its core."

"I never knew whether I really believed until that reverend delivered that decree." Rokshan lowered himself to the floor. "I don't know that I recommend having your faith tested that way."

"I'm just glad you're back," Lamprophyre said. "And I have so much to tell you."

ROKSHAN EXAMINED THE PATTERN DOLOMITE HAD DRAWN THE DAY before. "It's strange," he said. "They're obviously looking for something, but these search patterns, they're a complete waste of time and energy."

"Why is that?" Flint asked.

Rokshan tapped the six-pointed star. "This path requires the ecclesiast to stop halfway down a street and retrace his steps before moving to the next street. Someone else examines the rest of the street, as part of another small pattern. It's a terribly inefficient way to search for anything." He laid a finger to his lips and then made a face as he tasted the bitter chalk dust.

"So they're doing something else as well," Lamprophyre said.

"Yes..." Rokshan drew the word out on a long hiss. "Yes, something else, but what?"

The sound of wings drew everyone's attention. Coquina and Dolomite landed in the street near the slate. They both looked exhausted. "We should be taking turns," Lamprophyre exclaimed.

"The patterns aren't apparent unless you watch for a long time," Dolomite said. Wearily, he reached for the second slate, transported to the warehouses by Lamprophyre, and gestured to someone to hand him his chalks as if he were too tired for more speech.

The others watched as he swiftly sketched the view of Tanajital from above, a rough circle with its left side cut off by the fat line of the Green River, and drew in the major streets. Then he picked up a pale red chalk piece and roughed out a trapezoidal shape as if he were sketching someone's portrait. "Nine patterns, not seven like yesterday," he said, "and they were different patterns this time."

"Why do you orient the map that way?" Rokshan asked. "With north at the top?"

"Because north points to Mother Stone," Lamprophyre said. "Your maps are different?"

Rokshan nodded. "We have west at the top, looking toward where Jiwanyil entered the world."

It took Dolomite about a hundred beats to finish drawing all the patterns, but when he'd dropped the last piece of chalk, Flint lifted the slate and set it to lean against a warehouse next to the first. "Is there any correlation between the colors?" he asked.

Dolomite brightened. "Oh! That would be good, if I knew which ecclesiasts went where and drew which patterns!" Then he looked dejected. "Except they all look the same from above."

"Don't worry about it," Flint said. "This is amazing."

"I flew lower than Dolomite," Coquina said, "getting a better look at the individual ecclesiasts. Scared the Stones right out of some of them, too." She grinned nastily. "All the groups were identical. Three musicians, four bearers, two reverends, and the ecclesiast in his or her litter. Every one of them had the curtains tied back. And none of them were High Ecclesiasts. I couldn't get close enough to see if the ecclesiasts were paying close attention to any place in particular, and I couldn't pick their thoughts out of the general noise. But since most of the time ecclesiasts travel with the curtains hiding them, I think it's safe to assume they are definitely looking for something."

"What about the attendants? Did they appear to be searching?" Orthoclase asked.

Coquina looked thoughtful. "That's a good question," she said. "I'd have to say I don't think so. The musicians always have that glazed stare, like they're seeing something nobody else can, and the bearers are the same. The reverends might have been, but—no, they couldn't, because they were reading aloud from big books they carried. Taking turns reading, I mean."

"That sounds like the ecclesiasts are taking care to conceal their interest," Rokshan said. He was staring at the slates, examining first one and then the other. "Traveling in the same pomp they always do so no one will think anything about this journey is different."

"That's seriously paranoid," Bromargyrite said. "Nobody in Tana-jital is likely to question anything an ecclesiast does, right? So I don't see why they'd worry about behaving strangely."

Rokshan took a quick step back and tilted his head sharply to the right. "God's breath, I have it," he said. "Somebody rotate these slates one turn to the right. Put west at the top like a human map."

The dragons all looked at him in confusion. "Quick, or I'll lose it again," Rokshan demanded. Lamprophyre picked up one slate and Bromargyrite took the other. They swiftly turned the slates until the west side of the city was at the top, making the city look like a blob clinging to the branch that was the thick line of the Green River.

Rokshan took a piece of white chalk and quickly drew small versions of the patterns, now rotated to the right, along the top of the slate, above the river. "They're not searching the west bank, which means they know whatever they're looking for can't cross the river," he said, "and they're not searching properly because they can't. Not if they want their search to succeed." He finished drawing the seventh pattern and moved on to the second slate.

"I'm confused," Lamprophyre said. The patterns he'd drawn looked almost like letters, some of them. "How can their search succeed if they're not efficient?"

Rokshan drew the last pattern with a flourish and stepped back.

"Those are all symbols relating to the High Ecclesiasts and their responsibilities. Each of the High Ecclesiasts represents one of the gods—Nirinatan, Katayan, and so forth—and each has symbols pertaining to his or her god. In certain ceremonies, they use these symbols to invoke the gods. They're prayers." He gestured at the slate. "The ecclesiasts are using the city to power their prayers."

The others fell silent. Finally, Lamprophyre said, "And no one would notice except a dragon, who wouldn't know the significance. Honestly, I still don't know the significance. Is it dangerous to do something like that?"

"I feel very uncomfortable being in the center of some other religion's prayers," Porphyry said.

"It's not dangerous," Rokshan said, "and it doesn't affect the people in the city. I've seen it done—well, not seen, it's too big for a human to see—at any rate, I know of it being done twice before in my lifetime. One was when the previous Archprelate was dying, and the prayers were to speed him on his journey back to Jiwanyil. The other was when my father was very sick, and everyone joined together to plead with God for his recovery. Oh, and I know they did it when my father's first wife was killed in an accident. That time, it was for mourning. But in every case, they made an announcement so the people could participate in their own small way."

"And they haven't said anything this time."

Rokshan glanced at Lamprophyre. "No. Though I don't think we needed any more evidence that the ecclesiasts are up to something shady."

"But it does tell us they are very concerned about finding whatever they've lost," Flint said.

Lamprophyre sighed. "This is progress," she said, "so why do I feel we haven't gained any ground? We still have no idea what the ecclesiasts are looking for."

"Or who," Coquina said. "It could be a person."

"True, and that complicates things," Rokshan said. "Do you have any idea how many thousands of people live in Tanajital? And a person can hide in ways an object can't. If I were an ecclesiast, I'd recognize what, specifically, these prayers are for, but I can't read the symbols, just recognize them."

"I can't think of a way to locate whatever or whoever it is," Flint said. "Maybe this is a problem for tomorrow. Sleep on it, and see what occurs to us."

"I have to return to the embassy," Lamprophyre said. "If anyone shows up for supper, I want to reassure them that they're doing the right thing." She also hoped Rassika and her sister would arrive, and not just because she wanted to know if Rassika had delivered her message.

CHAPTER TWENTY

The courtyard was virtually empty when she arrived, empty enough that she had no trouble landing. Rokshan hopped down and said, "I'm starving. I forgot about breakfast."

"Have some soup." Lamprophyre settled herself in the dining pavilion and examined the few beggars who'd dared the ecclesiasts' wrath. There was the Sister of the Red—well, she was already outcast, no doubt. She didn't see one-legged Sumaan, but the old man was there, holding his bowl in both hands and swaying to music only he could hear. A few others, all strangers, ate swiftly and didn't meet her eyes. That hurt, but she reminded herself that she cared more that these people be fed than that they liked her.

Furtive movement at the mouth of the street caught her attention, and she stepped forward out of the dining pavilion, startling two of the strangers into fumbling their bowls and sending splashes of soup to soak the ground. Lamprophyre ignored them. "Hello, Rassika," she said. "Is this Kavari? Welcome to my embassy."

Rassika clutched the arm of a much smaller child, one who looked up at Lamprophyre in stunned amazement. She moved as if trying to escape her sister's grasp, but Rassika held on more tightly. "I told the adept what you said," she told Lamprophyre. "She ain't happy."

"With you, or with me?" Lamprophyre asked.

"With you. She di'nt care about me 'cept that I stay out of her place." Rassika wiped her arm across her nose. "You got food?"

"Come with me, and we'll see about that," Rokshan said, startling Lamprophyre because she hadn't heard him approach. Rassika dragged Kavari with her, making the child stumble along because her round brown eyes were fixed on Lamprophyre's wings. Lamprophyre suppressed a laugh. She hadn't felt much like laughing in the last day.

She turned from watching the children follow Rokshan and was arrested by the sight of more people entering the courtyard. It was the woman with two children. She held their hands as tightly as Rassika had gripped Kavari, and she halted about a dragonlength from Lamprophyre and stood watching her as warily as she might a dangerous predator. Lamprophyre reminded herself that to this woman, she might actually *be* a dangerous predator, and settled back on her haunches rather than approaching.

"I'm glad you came back," she said politely. "I know it's hard, feeding two children, and I'm glad for any help I can provide."

The woman's eyes looked haunted. "We're outcast now," she said in a hoarse voice, "but I—we need this food. Need it more than Jiwanyil's blessings."

Lamprophyre looked at the children, a boy and a girl. Their clothing was dirty, but their faces were clean, though Lamprophyre could see traces of tears on the boy's face. All three of them looked unnaturally gaunt for humans, and Lamprophyre had the sudden horrible suspicion that this meal was all these people got, all day long.

"Come in and eat," she said, "and tell me about yourselves."

The woman's name was Bhakriya, and her children were Preyanka and Abhit, and they had come from Kolmira looking for work. At first, Bhakriya was reluctant to speak—or maybe she was just busy eating—but gradually she relaxed enough to let her children stray from her side. She and Lamprophyre and Rokshan watched the two approach Rassika, whose grip on Kavari hadn't weakened and who ate her soup by tipping the bowl one-handed to her mouth. "Whose children are those?" Bhakriya said.

"No one's. They're orphans," Lamprophyre replied. "I asked

Rassika to help me today in exchange for food. No, it's not like that," she went on hastily as Bhakriya's eyes widened in alarm, "the food is free, without obligation on anyone. But Rassika is very proud and she didn't want a handout."

"Even so, I should have thought of that," Bhakriya said. "What can I do to repay you?"

Lamprophyre looked at Rokshan, caught off guard by the question. "Well—"

"You could help Depik wash up," Rokshan said. "There's not many dishes tonight, but usually it's a big chore. I'm sure he'd appreciate the assistance."

"I'll do that," Bhakriya declared. She set her bowl beside her and rested her arms on her drawn-up knees. "God's breath," she said. "I'd forgotten there are those who have it worse off than I." She was looking at the four children, who now sat in a circle talking. "Time was my children would be off running in a place like this. Now they haven't the strength for it. And those other two—not even a parent to watch out for them. No wonder she's clinging so tightly to the little one. The child can't be more than three, and her sister's not full grown yet."

Lamprophyre looked away in embarrassment from the tears welling up in Bhakriya's eyes. "Can I ask about your children's father?" she said, hoping it wasn't a forbidden subject. Rokshan shifted, but said nothing, so it was probably all right.

Bhakriya wiped tears from her eyes. "Gone, if Jiwanyil loves us," she said, her voice hard and cold. "He used to hurt me and was working his way up to hurting the children when we fled Kolmira. I hope he never finds us." She laughed bitterly. "Though I suppose Jiwanyil doesn't love us anymore if we're consorting with you, so maybe our luck's run out."

Lamprophyre stared at Bhakriya, her mouth hanging open in surprise. "I don't understand," she said. "He hurt you? Aren't you his mate?"

"Lamprophyre," Rokshan said quietly, "humans don't—sometimes they do terrible things to each other—"

"I know that. But to his own mate?"

Tears once more filled Bhakriya's eyes, and she lowered her head to her knees. Lamprophyre heard her thoughts, full of pain and sorrow and, to her astonishment, shame.

"Why are you embarrassed?" Lamprophyre asked, not caring that it revealed her secret ability. "Your mate has a duty to protect you and your family—at least, that's how it works for dragons. If it's all right for a human to hurt his mate—"

"It's not," Rokshan said. "Let it go, Lamprophyre. I'll explain later."

Lamprophyre didn't want to let it go, but she trusted Rokshan. "I'm sorry I made you cry," she said to Bhakriya. "There are so many things I don't understand about humans." Inspiration struck. "You know, I'm sure Depik would appreciate having more frequent help in the kitchen, cleaning up. Why don't you come back in the morning? There's always leftover food, and you could wash dishes in exchange for that."

Bhakriya looked terribly torn. "I don't want you making work for me, out of pity," she said.

"It's not pity. I want to help. And you don't have work, do you?"

She shook her head. "Not regular work. We have to keep moving so my husband doesn't find us."

"So you can work for me, and I'll watch your children while you do, and we both benefit." Lamprophyre leaned closer. "I'm very good at hide and seek," she confided.

Bhakriya looked Lamprophyre up and down, clearly contemplating her size, and just as clearly deciding not to ask questions. "All right," she said. "In the morning. And I'll wash up tonight, too."

"Wonderful! Here, let me introduce you to Depik. He really will be happy for help washing all the bowls."

Depik came out of the kitchen when Lamprophyre called his name. "Depik, this is Bhakriya," Lamprophyre said, prodding the woman forward. "She's going to help clean the dishes and the kitchen every morning and night. Bhakriya, this is Depik."

Depik extended his hand to Bhakriya. "Welcome," he said. "I could use the help. My lady is a messy eater." He grinned up at Lamprophyre to show it was a joke.

"You haven't seen messy yet," Rokshan said. "Bhakriya, we'll keep an eye on the children if you want to set to work now."

Bhakriya nodded and followed Depik into the kitchen. "Well, *that's* interesting," Rokshan said in a low voice.

"What is?"

Rokshan cast a glance back at the kitchen. "Nothing. Maybe. Ask me again next week."

Sometimes he mystified her. "All right."

She sat watching the four children as dusk settled on the courtyard. At some point, Depik came out to light the lanterns, and their glow cast odd shadows over the children's faces that made all four of them look even gaunter. Maybe she should offer Bhakriya the use of one of the servants' houses behind the embassy. No, better wait until she was sure this unusual arrangement would work out.

"You're unexpected," a voice said from beside her. Lamprophyre turned to see the Sister of the Red watching her, that peculiar smile on her lips.

"Am I?" Lamprophyre said. "How is that?"

The Sister of the Red drifted forward, kicking up her filmy skirts with each step. Lamprophyre observed that her sandals and her toenails were the same shade of bright gold. "You're no human," the woman continued, "but that doesn't stop you treating humans the way you would your own kind."

Her words were innocuous, but her tone irritated Lamprophyre. "You don't know anything about dragons, so I'm not sure how you think I treat them."

The woman's smile broadened. "Humans reserve their sympathy for those closest to them," she said. "Family, lovers, friends. Anything else is Other. I'm sure dragons are the same. Most dragons." She drew a shallow line in the dirt with the toe of her sandal. "I'm intrigued by a creature who cares enough about people not of her species to go out of her way to protect them. What good will that woman and her brats ever do you? Or that old man whose brains flew away with the wind?"

"Why should they have to do me good?" Lamprophyre said, feeling seriously nettled now. "I have resources and I choose to spend them on helping others. And I find humans interesting. Even awful humans like *you*."

The Sister of the Red laughed. It was, surprisingly, not a nasty sound. "I admit I'm not a nice person," she said. "I've been looking out for my own interests since I was fourteen. So I don't think the way you do. But that's why you interest me. We're so different I can't help wondering what the world looks like from your perspective. And not just because your perspective is fifteen feet high." She laughed again. "Maybe if I visit here often enough, I'll figure it out."

"Wait," Lamprophyre said as the woman turned to leave. "You don't need food. Why come here?"

The woman paused. Over her shoulder, she said, "Food's not the only thing you supply, Lamprophyre."

Lamprophyre watched her go, stunned into silence. What else did she supply? Companionship, maybe; she'd seen some of her regulars make friends with the other beggars. Safety, certainly. Bhakriya's horrible mate would have trouble hurting her here, under a dragon's watchful eye. But she couldn't imagine anything she had that the Sister of the Red would want, unless it was the perspective the woman had mentioned.

She shook her head and entered the embassy, where Rokshan sat watching the children. As she passed the old man, he smiled vacantly at her, and she returned the smile even though he probably wasn't really aware of her. People came for food and they stayed for the company. Maybe she was doing more for Tanajital than she thought.

CHAPTER TWENTY-ONE

Lamprophyre woke early the next morning to the smell of roasted cow and the sounds of rapidly pattering feet. She opened one eye to see a small figure dart past the doorway, followed by a slightly larger one. So Bhakriya was here. Lamprophyre closed her eye and stretched, flexing her wings. She didn't have to get up immediately. Besides, after the turmoil and stress of the past two days, she felt entitled to sleep in.

Thoughts intruded on her peaceful morning, not terrible ones, but ones focused on her: *big as a house* and *could squish us* and *smells like fire*. Lamprophyre sighed, and realized she'd breathed out smoke when the thoughts became agitated. "It's all right, it's just smoke," she said, opening her eyes. Bhakriya's children regarded her from the doorway, their thoughts uncertain but curious. Lamprophyre couldn't remember their names.

"Do you want to come in?" she asked.

The girl shook her head vigorously and grabbed the smaller child, the boy, by the shoulder to keep him from advancing. "Mama said not to disturb you," she said.

"I'm awake, so it's no disturbance," Lamprophyre said. "My name is Lamprophyre. I'm sorry, but I don't remember yours."

The little boy wrenched free of his sister's grasp and walked to within touching distance of Lamprophyre. "I'm Abhit," he said. "I like blue. You're very blue."

"I am," Lamprophyre agreed. "Did you eat breakfast? Because it smells like mine is almost ready, and you can have some of it if you like."

"Depik made porridge for all of us," the girl said. She took a few tentative steps forward. "I'm Preyanka."

"It's nice to meet you both," Lamprophyre said. "Now, I don't want to step on you, so if you'd move to the side, please?"

Preyanka took Abhit by the hand and towed him rapidly to where Lamprophyre's books lay piled on their cloth. Abhit's eyes widened. "You have books!" he exclaimed.

"I do. If you want, you can look at them. Just be very careful, because they're expensive and some of them aren't mine."

Preyanka nodded. "We had a whole room of them in our house in Kolmira," she said, then shut her mouth and ducked her head as if she'd said something she shouldn't. Lamprophyre guessed she didn't want to talk about the home they'd left behind, particularly if her father was as awful a person as Lamprophyre imagined.

"Well, enjoy yourselves," Lamprophyre said, as if she hadn't noticed Preyanka's confusion, and strolled to the dining pavilion, where Depik had just wheeled out the trolley. Steak. Depik must be feeling very well today.

Bhakriya emerged from the kitchen with a wooden bowl in her hands and a scrap of cloth she was drying it with. "Thank you again, my lady," she said. "It wasn't necessary to provide us with special food. Scraps are fine."

"That was Depik's idea, not mine, and I leave those decisions to him," Lamprophyre said around a mouthful of steak. "Besides, I don't think porridge is expensive, if that's what you're worried about, and all of that aside, I want the people who work for me to be well-fed so they won't want to be hired away."

"I've had trouble finding employment that will support all three of us. This work is a blessing." Bhakriya tucked the cloth into her waist-band, but stood there holding the bowl instead of returning to the kitchen. "I hope you understand how very grateful I am. How grateful we all are."

Her words made Lamprophyre uncomfortable. "Well, I'm grateful for your help, because Depik is sick sometimes and can't always keep up."

Bhakriya looked concerned. "Sick? What kind of illness?"

"It's not contagious, if that's what worries you. He has trouble getting out of bed some days, and sometimes that lasts for a while. But he's a hard worker."

"My lady is generous," Depik said, coming up behind Bhakriya. "I was destitute for years before she took a chance on me. I'm better than I used to be, but I have days where it's not so good."

"Then I'll help on those days," Bhakriya declared. "I don't have much experience cooking, but I'm sure there's something I can do."

Depik glanced at Lamprophyre. "If my lady doesn't mind."

"You can't be worse a cook than I am," Lamprophyre said. She didn't like the expression on Depik's face; it was unfamiliar, but his thoughts were tinged with unhappiness that made no sense. He'd been cheerful about having Bhakriya help, he'd gone out of his way to provide her and her children with breakfast; could it be that Bhakriya helping on his bad days was a reminder of his weakness? Lamprophyre knew human males in particular could be embarrassed at being made to look weak or inferior in front of human females. But Depik was sensible, so that seemed an unlikely explanation. She determined to pay attention to his thoughts, and task him with it if his unhappiness persisted.

She devoured her steaks a little too rapidly—she preferred her food hot, and the small pieces of meat cooled off quickly—and washed her claws and face. She heard voices coming from within the embassy, and went inside the hall to discover Preyanka reading to Abhit from the book of constellation stories. "Go on," she said when Preyanka paused to look at her, and settled down where she could listen. Preyanka had a nice, clear voice, and Lamprophyre enjoyed hearing the story.

Preyanka was almost finished when Bhakriya entered, standing in the doorway with her hands clasped before her. She didn't say anything until the story was over, and then she clapped her hands and said, "It's time to go, children."

"I like this place. Why can't we stay here?" Abhit complained.

"Because my lady has better things to do with her time than supervise children," Bhakriya said.

"I won't be here most of the day, or I'd invite the children to stay," Lamprophyre said. "So you can do your other jobs without worrying about them."

Bhakriya looked up at Lamprophyre and blinked rapidly to clear away tears. "I don't understand why you are so generous," she said. "Thank you. We'll be back this evening. Early, so I can help with supper."

"I look forward to seeing you then," Lamprophyre said.

She settled comfortably on the floor and flipped the pages of the largest book without reading it, thinking about what the Sister of the Red had said last night. She hadn't done anything for Bhakriya that she wouldn't do for a dragon of the flight, but Bhakriya was human, so maybe Lamprophyre's generosity was unusual. It was just that humans interested her, that was all, and their needs were so different from hers it was fun to see how she could help.

She saw Rokshan approaching from the street and walked to meet him in the courtyard. "I saw Bhakriya and her children," he said. "Did everything go well?"

"I think so. Depik made porridge. I'll have to make sure he doesn't run through his own supplies too quickly."

"Depik made porridge, did he?"

Rokshan's tone of voice was heavy with meaning, as if porridge were somehow significant. "Should he not have?"

"What? Oh. No, of course not. In fact, I was betting on it."

"Why?"

Rokshan glanced past her at the dining pavilion. Lamprophyre looked, but no one was there. "Maybe nothing," he said. "Don't worry about it."

"Rokshan, I hate secrets unless I'm the one keeping them."

"It's not a secret, just something I'm not sure about, and I don't want to discuss it until I am. Understand?"

"Unfortunately, yes." Lamprophyre breathed out two puffs of smoke, impatient as much with herself as with him. "Are you ready to fly? I want to see where the ecclesiasts go."

Rokshan clambered up. "I thought Dolomite was doing that."

"He tracks the patterns. I just want a sense for how many ecclesiasts are involved. There were seven, then nine, and suppose that number keeps increasing?" She pushed off with her powerful legs and beat the air to gain altitude.

"Like I said, I don't know enough about the symbols to be able to tell what kind of prayers they are," Rokshan said. "But if they're searching as well as praying, they might send out more searchers if they aren't immediately successful."

"That makes sense."

She rose high above Tanajital and made a slow right-handed circle, following the wall of the city and altering her course to fly above the river rather than crossing it to the west bank. Below, Dolomite flew lazily in the opposite direction, making a great spiral that would cover most of the city. It was fortunate for everyone that he loved flying, because Lamprophyre couldn't imagine a more tedious job.

From her height, humans were visible only as movement through the hair-fine streets, and not even the ecclesiasts' litters were distinguishable. She sank lower and still lower, descending below Dolomite to where she was only a few dragonlengths above the streets. Now she could see the ecclesiasts, traveling through the streets surrounded by what looked like bubbles of air separating them from the masses. She focused on one and swooped lower until she could hear the music the ecclesiasts' attendants were playing. "Can you hear that?" she asked Rokshan.

"Not over the noise of the crowd."

She hummed a snatch of the tune. "Does it mean anything?"

"Nothing unusual. It's an auditory warning that an ecclesiast is coming. Standard practice."

Lamprophyre rose about half a dragonlength and beat her wings lazily, but even at her slowest she was faster than the ecclesiast's litter, and soon outpaced it. She continued in her flight path until she'd spanned the entire city and was back where she'd started. The bearers didn't react as if they were worried about her. "I counted," she said. "Twelve ecclesiasts in the streets. The guard captain believed there were more of them around than usual, but I don't know how many is usual."

"Neither do I, but twelve seems excessive," Rokshan said. "So others have noticed it, too. At least, they've noticed the increased numbers. I think you're right that it would take a dragon to see the patterns."

"I wonder," Lamprophyre said. She'd been watching the street the ecclesiast had chosen. It widened out three dragonlengths ahead into a street big enough to fit her, if she didn't mind displacing the people.

"Wonder what?" Rokshan asked.

"Wonder what they'd do if I confronted them."

"I'm not sure that's a good idea, Lamprophyre. You might start a fight."

"How? It's not as if they can hurt me. And I have some very reasonable questions."

Rokshan was silent for a moment. Finally, he said, "Is it bad that I want to see this?"

Lamprophyre grinned. "Of course not. You humans are so bloodthirsty, I'd be concerned if you *didn't* want to see it."

"We're not bloodthirsty. We just like watching a good fight."

"I'm not sure where the distinction is, but I'll let you have it."

She flew a tight circle over the litter. None of the ecclesiast's attendants looked up at all. Lamprophyre remembered what Coquina had said about the musicians' and the bearers' glassy stares. Maybe they didn't even know she was there. Well, that wouldn't last long.

When the litter was barely a dragonlength from the wider street, Lamprophyre descended slowly, calling out, "Make room! Please, give me space! I don't want to hurt anyone!" as Rokshan yelled similar warnings. Men and women scattered, though they didn't go far. Lamprophyre found herself in an empty spot on the sun-heated white bricks of the street, circled by more empty space, enough that there might have been room for another dragon so long as he was male and not Bromargyrite. People surrounded that space in a ring, watching tensely, their thoughts full of fear and curiosity and (from those near enough to see the approaching ecclesiast) worry about whether standing and watching a dragon could constitute consorting with her.

The ecclesiast's procession hove into view, musicians, bearers, litter, and reverends, exactly as Coquina had described. Lamprophyre rose to her full height, which gave her a good view of the humans' heads and the top of the litter, and said, "I'd like a word with you, your Holiness." She didn't like to give him any kind of respect, considering how the ecclesiasts had treated her species, but it was always better to start with politeness because it gave you more options for descending into rudeness.

The bearers didn't put down the litter. The reverends walking behind it closed their books, which were big enough to require two hands to hold them. One of the reverends, a woman whose dark hair was tinged with red, said, "Dragons are outcast, and no ecclesiast will speak with one. Step aside." Her thoughts were as stolid as her voice, with no fear of Lamprophyre.

Lamprophyre didn't move. "But no ecclesiast will fear Jiwanyil's wrath simply for speaking to me, because they're more holy than the average person and not vulnerable to whatever taint you think I have. I just have a few questions, and then I'll be on my way."

The other reverend said, "Dragons are outcast, and no ecclesiast will speak with one. Step aside."

"What are you afraid of?" Rokshan asked. "Surely you're not going to miss an opportunity to convince a dragon to follow the true path in worshipping Katayan?" He appeared to address the ecclesiast, who was invisible from Lamprophyre's perspective.

The first reverend said, "Dragons are outcast, and—"

"I will answer no questions except those pertaining to true doctrine," the ecclesiast said, interrupting the reverend, who fell immediately silent. The ecclesiast's voice was the high-pitched one of a woman, and was perfectly calm in a way that in anyone else Lamprophyre would have found soothing. But this was her enemy, and Lamprophyre tamped down her irritation. Politeness, until rudeness was necessary.

"Why does Jiwanyil hate dragons?" she asked.

"Jiwanyil does not hate dragons." The ecclesiast's voice was even smoother. "Jiwanyil hates no living creature. He wants all to live in harmony with God and worship their creator according to the laws of their creation." Her thoughts were as placid as the reverends' and as fearless.

"But dragons don't believe in your religion. Why should we change to suit you?"

The ecclesiast's thoughts didn't waver. "Dragons have lost the true faith in the years of their isolation. It is not your fault that you have forgotten Katayan. The fault is in those who, having had the truth revealed, fail to return to Katayan's worship."

"That only sounds reasonable," Rokshan said. "Dragons are older than humans. Why shouldn't their religion be the true one?"

The ecclesiast's thoughts became unfocused with anger, and Lamprophyre caught a flash of thoughts: *apostate, heretic, he is in a position to sway many, must stop him.* "You are in violation of Jiwanyil's teachings, Prince Rokshan," the ecclesiast said, her voice taut with the same anger. "You were warned of the consequences, and you are now outcast, denied Jiwanyil's blessings. If you want to be restored to full fellowship with Jiwanyil's light, walk away from this creature now."

"I'm not going to do that," Rokshan declared, his voice carrying to the watching crowd. "I don't believe those teachings came from Jiwanyil. I think you're lying."

Lamprophyre jerked, trying to twist around so she could see her friend who had apparently just lost his mind. He had been the one who didn't want to start a fight! "Rokshan? What—"

"Don't you *think* so, Lamprophyre?" Rokshan said, putting heavy emphasis on "think." Lamprophyre listened. The ecclesiast's thoughts were nearly incoherent with rage, but fragments of thought emerged: *how dare he* and *deserves what he gets* and *wish we could drive the creatures out faster.* To her surprise, nothing in the ecclesiast's thoughts suggested that she knew the decree was false. So not all the ecclesiasts were in on the plot. Maybe it was just the High Ecclesiasts, after all, and she needed to track down Khadar.

"What are you searching for?" she asked, hoping to take advantage of the woman's fury to goad her into revealing something.

"You dare address me after speaking blasphemy?" the ecclesiast shouted, thinking *holy, must find*. It was all Lamprophyre could hear before the crowd's agitation grew too great. Their confused, frightened thoughts overwhelmed her to the point that she had to block everything out, but it didn't take a dragon's mental hearing to know Rokshan's words had stirred them to the point of incipient riot.

"We have to get out of here," she said, and took off without another word. Looking back, she saw the wind of her passage had knocked two of the musicians over, and the bearers seemed to be struggling to keep the litter upright, but no one seemed hurt. That relieved her mind.

"What were you *thinking?*" she demanded. "Challenging an ecclesiast in public? Did you want to start a riot?"

"I was thinking," Rokshan said placidly, "that it might be a good idea to plant the idea that the ecclesiasts are lying."

"Won't that just cause civil unrest? We don't want people to disbelieve their entire religion."

"No, but if enough people challenge the ecclesiasts, the Archprelate will have to intervene." Rokshan shifted his position and leaned forward so he could speak directly into her ear. "Wherever this false teaching came from, the Archprelate can put a stop to it."

"Unless—" Lamprophyre shut her mouth on *the Archprelate is corrupt.*

Rokshan knew what she meant without her speaking. "I don't believe that," he said. "The Archprelate has guided Gonjiri for twenty years, and his wisdom has blessed our country. If he was possessed of a prophecy that said dragons should be shunned, he wouldn't try to justify it by saying it was Katayan's will, because he has always been very clear that he speaks only for Jiwanyil. So I think it's someone else. One or more of the High Ecclesiasts."

"Which means we really should go after Khadar."

"Yes. I'll seek him out this afternoon. Did you learn anything from that ecclesiast's thoughts?"

"That she doesn't know the decree is a lie, which implies that you're right about the High Ecclesiasts. Oh, and that they're searching for something holy."

"That's not much help, is it?"

Lamprophyre blew out a puff of impatient smoke. "No. It doesn't even tell us whether they're looking for a thing or a person."

"It's more likely they're looking for a thing, because a holy person would be in the Archprelate's palace. I can't imagine an ecclesiast running off." Rokshan blew out his breath. "But I don't know what a holy thing might be. As far as I know, things are only holy when they're in use."

"I don't understand what that means."

"Oh, well, if a thing contains the power of God, like a prayer wheel, it only does when someone directs that power into it. Things don't store up holiness the way an artifact stores magic. Unless I'm wrong about that."

"So we're no better off than we were before."

"We confirmed they're searching for something. That's good."

Lamprophyre alit outside the warehouses and let Rokshan down. "I hope you're right about stirring people up. I don't want to be responsible for a riot."

"You started a riot?" Orthoclase said, poking his head out of his warehouse. "On purpose?"

Lamprophyre explained about the encounter with the ecclesiast. By the end of her story, Porphyry and Flint were listening, too. "That actually makes sense," Flint said when she finished. "If the ecclesiasts are teaching something that isn't true, people should know about it. It might even confirm what they feel deep down about that teaching."

"You think humans can tell the difference between a true teaching and a lie?" Orthoclase said.

"Why not? Dragons can," Flint responded.

"I like to think Jiwanyil's light touches all of us," Rokshan said, "and that light illuminates the truth of his prophecies. But I was also thinking that this might get people searching the Hall of Visions for the record of the prophecy that supposedly says dragons are outcast. If it's not a true prophecy, it might appear different from others. And that will encourage more people to question the false decree."

The beating of giant wings and an enormous shadow drew everyone's attention upward to Coquina, descending rapidly. She landed hard and crouched on hands and feet, breathing heavily as if she'd been racing. "I'm fine," she said when Orthoclase tried to support her. "Just didn't shed momentum fast enough. I'm fine."

"Why were you in such a hurry?" Lamprophyre asked.

Coquina turned to face her. Her chest was still heaving, and her wings trembled from exertion. "Melika's been hurt," she said. "Her mother wouldn't tell me more than that. It's my fault."

"How could it be your fault?" Lamprophyre said. "You haven't seen her for days."

Coquina laughed, a shrill, almost hysterical sound. "They found her in the slums, badly beaten. There's only one reason she'd be anywhere near there. She was investigating the kyanite. For us." She drew in a deep, shuddering breath. "She was hurt because she was helping us."

CHAPTER TWENTY-TWO

"But she's alive?" Lamprophyre asked.

Coquina nodded. "I don't know more than that she was taken to her home and treated by a physicker. I offered to pay for them to take her to a healing center, but her mother slammed the door on me after telling me not to come back." Her hands and wings trembled with agitation. "I don't even know if it's something she might die of."

"Try to calm down, Coquina," Flint said. "There's nothing we can do for Melika now."

"Except find the humans who hurt her and destroy them," Coquina snarled.

"We can't kill humans even if they deserve it," Lamprophyre said, feeling uncomfortably guilty at saying it. After all, she'd been indirectly responsible for a human's death and she didn't even regret it. "They have to go to trial."

"And if human justice finds them innocent? That's unacceptable." Coquina stood to her full height and flexed her wings.

"We don't know that, and we can't act before we do," Lamprophyre said. "Besides, how are we to find the guilty humans? The city is teeming with people, and Melika's attackers could be anywhere."

"We go to the slums and we question humans until we find

someone who saw the attack. Maybe they even know the attackers." Coquina's eyes were narrowed in anger, and her voice shook.

"That's a good plan," Orthoclase said. "And it gives us a reason to pursue the kyanite smugglers, or whoever they are. They have to have some connection to the adepts. If Melika was close enough to the truth that they beat her to stop her investigating—"

Coquina growled, deep in her throat, and didn't even look embarrassed at her atavistic reaction. Orthoclase glanced her way, then continued, "If we can find her attackers, it probably won't be much of a reach to find the adepts who are buying kyanite, or the people selling it. Whatever it is Melika found."

"The problem is the slums have mostly narrow streets," Flint said. "It's going to be difficult to fit into some of those spaces."

"I can handle that," Rokshan said. "I'll arrange for an investigation. A private one, so the slum dwellers aren't frightened by uniforms. They'll learn the truth and report back to me."

"A private investigation?" Lamprophyre had thought he would send in soldiers under his authority as a military commander. "What does that mean?"

"My sister Tekentriya despises me, but she is rabid on the subject of violence against women," Rokshan said. "It won't take much to convince her to send out a few of her agents to look into the attack."

That left Lamprophyre feeling wary. Tekentriya was heir to the throne and supervisor of a network of confidential agents, and she not only despised Rokshan, she feared Lamprophyre. "She would have to be very rabid to overlook the fact that it's you asking," she said.

"Trust me, she is," Rokshan said. "Coquina, do you know where in the slums Melika was attacked?"

"I don't know where it is, but Melika's mother said she was attacked in South Narrows, like that was a landmark," Coquina said.

Rokshan nodded. "I'll go now to get that investigation moving. Then I'll see if I can find Khadar." He ran off northward and was soon lost to sight.

"Why does he want to find Khadar?" Flint asked, making a disgusted face.

"We, um, talked to an ecclesiast, and her thoughts indicated that she didn't know the decree is a lie. So we think it's the High Ecclesiasts responsible." Lamprophyre settled back on her haunches and sighed. "Coquina, I'm so sorry. If those idiots hadn't spread that false prophecy, we could arrange for Melika to get proper treatment."

"It's infuriating," Coquina said, but she sounded less angry than before. "I hope a physicker is good enough. If she dies because she was helping us—"

"Let's not worry about that," Flint said. "Until we know more about the attackers, all we can do is continue to watch the ecclesiasts and hope they give something away."

Coquina spread her wings again. "I'll see what I can learn," she said, and leaped into the sky.

The others watched her fly away in silence. Finally, Porphyry said, "I'm going to the market to see what kind of artifacts are for sale."

"We don't need artifacts. Do we?" Orthoclase said.

Porphyry shook his head. "I don't intend to buy. I want to confirm that no one sells chlorite artifacts. I doubt they do, since they're related to the race to create the first mind-reading artifact, but if I'm wrong, we might want to question anyone who is."

"Be careful," Lamprophyre said.

Porphyry grinned. "I always am."

When he was gone, Lamprophyre and Flint looked at each other. Lamprophyre wondered if Flint felt as discouraged as she did. "I'm going to fly," she said. "If Manishi is as upset with me as I think, there's a chance she'll try to track me down. So I'm not going to settle anywhere very long."

"I had an idea about her," Flint said, "but I don't want to talk about it until I'm sure. Good flying, Lamprophyre."

Lamprophyre nodded and took to the skies.

IT WAS LATE AFTERNOON BEFORE SHE RETURNED TO THE warehouses, tired from her wanderings and ready for a meal. But she didn't want to return to the embassy until she knew what the others had learned. She swept low over the city, breathing in the smells of dust and cooking fat and the sour smell of thousands of human bodies all packed together. It was strange how individual humans smelled nothing like the sour odor. Rokshan, for example, smelled like the pines that grew on the hills below the mountain peaks, and Manishi smelled of a dozen different stones plus a whiff of something Lamprophyre couldn't identify that she thought of as the smell of magic. So unusual.

Humans looked up and pointed as she passed overhead, but there were too many of them for her to make out coherent thoughts. She didn't need to; she could guess they were thinking about how her presence in Tanajital was a potential contamination. That made her angry and determined to prove the ecclesiasts wrong. Strange as the scents of humans were, what was even stranger was how fond she had become of the human city and the people who lived in it. It would never be home, but it was more welcoming than she'd imagined possible when she'd first arrived.

Everyone was there when she arrived, all but Dolomite settled in their warehouses. Rokshan had also returned and was drawing symbols on a sheet of paper secured to a board. Lamprophyre had seen one like that used by Dharan as well, something he called a blank book that was bound on one end like a regular book, but with pages that weren't written on and only one cover. Rokshan's fingers were gray from the charcoal stick he held, as if he'd been writing for a while. Lamprophyre bent to peer at the tiny writing.

"I don't know if there's anything I can learn from this," Rokshan told her. "But the more information we have, the more likely that is."

Dolomite finished his sketch, drawn on the back of the first slate, and sat back as if exhausted. "Twelve patterns," he said, "and three of them are repeated from the last two days. And they're covering more ground, though they still haven't ventured into the slums, the embassy, or the academy."

Lamprophyre examined the new sketch. "You're going to run out of chalk colors if they continue increasing their numbers."

"Oh, I don't think so. There really are a lot of chalk colors. Humans are so inventive." Dolomite idly drew a dragon in flight, tiny but so detailed it might have flown off the slate and winged around his head.

"Did Tekentriya's people find the attackers?" Lamprophyre asked Rokshan.

He shook his head. "Not yet. It may take a few days, and then I'll have to coerce the information out of someone. Tekentriya made it clear that even though she appreciated my bringing the problem to her, it wasn't my business anymore. And of course I couldn't tell her why it mattered that I learn the results of her investigation."

"But they did start investigating."

"Yes. Like I said, violence against women is something Tekentriya takes very seriously."

"That's so strange," Coquina said. "I mean that that's something common enough that it's a special category of violence."

"Humans use violence to get their way sometimes," Rokshan said. "Some men see women as an easy target because women are generally smaller and weaker than men. Tekentriya would like the law to recognize this tendency and provide special protections for women because of it."

"I'm trying to imagine being shoved around by Coquina and failing," Flint said with a smile.

Coquina arched her neck to look at him. He was half a dozen handspans smaller than she, and his wingspan was narrower. "So much easier to keep you in line by outflying you."

Flint's smile broadened. "I didn't realize that's what you've been doing all these years, keeping us in line."

Coquina smiled back. "Five males and two females in our clutch. You males have us seriously outnumbered. We have to keep you in line, right, Lamprophyre?"

"Naturally," Lamprophyre said with a straight face. "Teach you who's boss."

"You're not bossy," Dolomite exclaimed. "You're assertive."

Lamprophyre and Coquina exchanged glances. Dolomite really was guileless and innocent. "That's a nice way of saying 'bossy,'" Lamprophyre said, "but I'm glad you don't feel intimidated by us, because we don't want to control you males. It's so much more fun when we work together."

"Like now," Orthoclase said. "I never realized how close we all are until we were aliens in a human city."

"I hadn't considered that, but it's true," Lamprophyre said. "All of us trying to solve this puzzle, and defeat the ecclesiasts, and thwart Manishi—Flint, did you work out what you were thinking about her?"

"I don't know her well enough to guess what approach will be best," Flint said, "but we have a few options. One is to steal that crystal wand she has the images stored in. That would be ideal, but requires us to get inside her workshop, and that's unlikely. We could threaten her with violence, but from what you've said, she doesn't think like ordinary people and might not care."

"That's true," Rokshan said. He was twiddling the charcoal stick between his fingers, blackening them further. "Besides, she knows dragons won't hurt humans."

"The third option is to find something we can blackmail her with. But that has two problems. We'd have to investigate her, and that's not something we're equipped to do, and if she doesn't care about a threat of violence, she might not care about blackmail."

"That makes sense," Orthoclase said. "Though it would be a satisfying option."

Flint nodded. "So we come to the option I'm leaning toward, which is that I go preemptively to the king and tell him what Lokun and I did."

Lamprophyre sat up. "That isn't a good idea," she said. "Suppose King Ekanath decides you're a threat and has you banished? Or, worse, what if it gets him thinking in terms of what dragons might do, and gets rid of all of us so we can't spy on him?"

"That's not what he'd think," Rokshan said. "If Flint tells him the truth, and it gives Father ideas, those ideas will almost certainly be that he can enlist dragons to spy on *Fanishkor*. He'll want to turn you over to Tekentriya for use in her spy corps."

Horrified, Lamprophyre said, "But we don't want to do that! We're not Gonjirians, and I don't think the terms of the human-dragon alliance allow us to act so directly as human auxiliaries."

"That doesn't mean he won't put pressure on you. It could be uncomfortable."

"Uncomfortable enough that Manishi blackmailing us is a reasonable alternative?" Flint asked. "We should consider it. Manishi having a hold on us is dangerous. Personally, I'd rather the king tries to make us his spies than that Manishi forces us to work for her. We can turn the king down."

"We have a few days before Manishi becomes a problem. We'll think about other possibilities until then." Lamprophyre sighed. "It's almost suppertime. Is there anything else we need to discuss?"

"I'm too tired to think straight," Dolomite said. "Bromargyrite, were you going to bring us a cow or three?"

Bromargyrite stood and stretched. "Porphyry, help me out," he said. "Lamprophyre, we'll see you in the morning?"

Lamprophyre felt a little guilty that she was going to have a perfectly cooked meal while her friends would eat what Coquina roasted. Though Coquina was a more meticulous cook than Lamprophyre, so it wasn't as if they'd eat poorly. "In the morning," she said, and when Rokshan had climbed up, she flew away to the embassy, taking a higher path so she could see the city the way Dolomite had drawn it. She saw no ecclesiasts' litters, nothing but the usual streams of people heading for home and their own suppers.

The courtyard was as sparsely populated as it had been the previous night, but there were still people there, which relieved Lamprophyre's mind. Most of them were strangers, and those men and women stayed well away from Lamprophyre, but the Sister of the Red was there, smiling her enigmatic smile as she observed the courtyard. Her smile grew more amused when she met Lamprophyre's gaze. Lamprophyre watched her for a few beats before looking away. She didn't want the women thinking she'd won some battle.

She said to Bhakriya, who stood at the cauldron ladling soup into bowls, "I wish Rassika and Kavari would come back. I think Rassika needs a safe place where she doesn't have to worry so much about her sister wandering away."

"She did come back," Bhakriya said. "She said she had a message for you, and I told her to wait in the embassy hall. That's all right, isn't it?"

"Of course." Lamprophyre's mood brightened. "Did she eat?"

Bhakriya shook her head. "She said she should speak with you before that. She really is very independent. I don't think she wants to rely on anyone but herself."

"I suppose that makes sense." Dragons relied on their clutch, on the whole flight, without worrying about the kind of reciprocity that seemed to define Rassika's life. Lamprophyre crossed the courtyard without difficulty and ducked her head inside.

Rassika was curled up on the cloth the books lay on, limp and boneless with exhaustion. In the dim light, her face looked rounder, less tense, and her resemblance to Kavari was stronger. Kavari sat next to her sister, looking at the illustrations of the constellations book and occasionally touching the bright colors. She looked up at Lamprophyre, and her eyes grew wide.

"Hello, Kavari," Lamprophyre whispered.

Kavari stood, pushing the book aside. She took a few tentative steps toward Lamprophyre, then a few more. Lamprophyre held out her hand, which was big enough to fit completely around Kavari's head, though she didn't know why she would do that. Kavari reached out, slowly, and closed her hand on Lamprophyre's finger, as far as it would go. The touch was barely palpable, the child's hand cooler than Lamprophyre's, but it made Lamprophyre's breath catch in her throat as if she'd been handed something precious.

Rassika stirred. Her hand closed slowly on nothing. Then she sat up, all her tension returning in the space of a beat. "Kavari!" she shouted, her voice filled with such fear Lamprophyre's heart ached for her.

"She's right here," Lamprophyre said. "She's safe."

Rassika scrambled awkwardly to her feet. "Shouldn't've slept," she said. Her breathing was ragged with what was left of her fright. "Anything could've happened. Shouldn't have slept."

"You were so tired, I'm not surprised you slept." Lamprophyre wished she could adequately reassure this proud, frightened girl. But she knew in her bones that Rassika wouldn't forgive herself for not protecting Kavari, even if it hadn't been necessary. "And Kavari is smart. She knew not to go anywhere. See, she was looking at the pictures. You've taught her well."

Rassika took Kavari's hand and held onto it so tightly Kavari cried out and tried to pull away. "Can't let her go," Rassika said, ignoring her sister's cries. "Dada said, don't let go. She's all I have left."

"I understand," Lamprophyre said. "I—" There really wasn't anything Lamprophyre could say, much as she wished she could make the girl's life easier. "Did you have news for me?"

Rassika nodded. "Heard the adept woman talking. Don't know to who. But she said as you dragons ain't done what you said, and she had to teach you a lesson."

Lamprophyre's blood froze. "Stones," she breathed. "Rassika, when was this?"

"Don't know hours. It was just before I come here."

Lamprophyre stepped back out of the hall. "Rokshan?"

"Over here," Rokshan said. He was crouched beside the old man, holding the man's soup bowl while he keened a thin, weak cry of pain and gripped his head in his hands.

Lamprophyre waited for the old man to stop making noise and impatiently gestured to Rokshan to join her. "Manishi is going to 'teach us a lesson' for not bringing her the kyanite," she said. "What do we do?"

"I'll go back to the palace immediately and see if I can forestall her," Rokshan said. "I'll tell her we'll bring the kyanite in the morning. There's no time for anything else."

"But—"

"It will have to be Flint's plan," Rokshan insisted. "If he tells Father the truth, it won't matter what Manishi says. You'll just have to stand firm against any plans he wants you for." He turned and ran from the courtyard before Lamprophyre could offer to fly him to the palace. Well, it was better, if he was going to confront Manishi, that Lamprophyre not be present to make Manishi wonder why they hadn't brought the kyanite with them.

Rassika was looking at her speculatively. "You ain't scared of the adept, not someone as big as you, right?"

Lamprophyre sighed. "Big doesn't always mean powerful. I can't hurt a human without causing a lot of trouble, which means humans who want me to do something for them can sometimes force me to do things I don't want to. Thank you for bringing me that news. I owe you."

Her words made Rassika's eyes widen as if Lamprophyre had said something more startling. But all she said was, "You said we could have soup if I told you things."

"You can have soup any time you want, whether or not you give me information."

Rassika nodded and dragged Kavari past Lamprophyre to where Bhakriya stood at the soup cauldron. Preyanka stood next to her mother, holding the bowls to be filled. Lamprophyre wished she knew how to tell human ages. She only knew that humans with white hair and wrinkled faces were older than those with black hair and smooth faces, and she knew a child's height indicated years, but dragons lived so much longer than humans Lamprophyre wasn't good at judging the relative maturity of two adult humans. Rokshan had told her that in human years, she would be about eighteen. It was interesting information, but not helpful.

Even so, if heights were anything to go by, Preyanka was older than Rassika, Rassika was older than Abhit, and Kavari was younger than all of them. Lamprophyre was fairly certain Kavari was old enough to speak—there was another difference; dragonets came out of the egg able to speak, but human babies took a year or more to say their first words—but she'd never heard a word out of the child. Maybe she was as frightened as Rassika in her own way.

Preyanka handed the bowl of soup to Rassika with a smile the younger girl didn't return. That didn't seem to bother Preyanka, who watched Rassika and Kavari walk away as if curious. It was too bad Rassika was so isolated, because Preyanka might be a good friend. Lamprophyre had observed Bhakriya's daughter closely over the twelveday the little family had been coming for soup, and she was impressed at how kindly she treated her brother and how respectful she was of her mother.

Preyanka picked up another bowl and held it for Bhakriya to ladle soup into it. The man standing before her took hold of it, then came up short when Preyanka didn't let go. "I've got it, girlie, thanks much," the man said. He tugged on the bowl, making soup slosh up the sides and trickle down over the lip. Preyanka stared past him, her lips moving as if she were chewing something.

Bhakriya flung the ladle down with a splash and snatched the bowl out of Preyanka's hands. "I beg your pardon," she said to the man, "she hasn't been feeling well," and steered Preyanka through the dining pavilion and past the kitchen to the rear of the embassy. Lamprophyre, curious and a little concerned, followed.

Bhakriya glanced back and saw Lamprophyre. A look of terror just like the one Rassika had had at thinking Kavari was missing flitted across her face. "It's not—please don't—" she said.

"Is Preyanka all right?"

"It's nothing—"

Preyanka closed her eyes and swayed as if she were about to faint. When she opened her eyes, they were the green of new leaves, pupils, irises, whites and all. "*Find the lost,*" a voice that was not hers said. Lamprophyre couldn't tell if it was male or female; it reverberated as if echoing off invisible walls. "*That which is spoken by the old stone is true and false, and the hearers wander like lambs. Faith is not enough.*" Preyanka drew a deep breath. "*The skies will burn.*"

CHAPTER TWENTY-THREE

"What," Lamprophyre began. Preyanka, an ecclesiast? Preyanka licked her cracked, dry lips to moisten them. Bhakriya held her by the shoulders, either supporting or restraining her, Lamprophyre couldn't tell. Preyanka's head sagged, and a trickle of blood ran from her nose. Then she jerked sharply, nearly tearing free of her mother's grasp. She flung her head back, sending blood flying to spatter Bhakriya's cheek, and then her whole body went into spasms, her arms flopping and her head twitching as if some invisible force were shaking her. Bhakriya cried out and held Preyanka close enough that she, too, jerked and spasmed. It looked as if the two were dancing some horrible, unnatural dance. Lamprophyre hovered nearby, afraid to touch them and possibly hurt them by accident.

After what felt like a thousand beats, Preyanka's convulsions slowed, and when she opened her eyes, they were her normal brown, though she didn't appear to see anything. Bhakriya still clutched her tightly, tears trickling down her cheeks. She, too, stared into the distance as if looking at something invisible to Lamprophyre.

"Bhakriya," Lamprophyre said, "what can I do? Bhakriya, talk to me."

Then Depik was there, gently easing Preyanka free of her mother's blind grip. "This way," he said, carrying the girl around the rear of the embassy to the rows of little houses meant for servants. Depik nudged open the door to his house and entered it. Lamprophyre leaned down and peered through the window. Depik had laid Preyanka on his bed and now stood looking down at her. His back was to Lamprophyre, so she couldn't see his expression.

Bhakriya followed Depik, her hands clenched together tightly in front of her. "Don't say a word," she told him. Her voice was fierce with anger and fear. "Not a word, or I'll—"

"Or you'll what?" Depik said.

Bhakriya flinched and took a step backward. "Nothing," she said, sounding as bleak as Lamprophyre had ever heard. "I'm helpless. Please, don't tell. I beg you."

Depik turned to look at Bhakriya. "I won't betray you," he said, "and neither will my lady. But I don't understand why you're afraid. This is nothing to be ashamed of."

Preyanka twitched, drawing Lamprophyre's attention. "Mama?" she said weakly. "Did it happen again?"

Bhakriya dropped to her knees beside the bed. "Yes, sweetness, but there's nothing to worry about. Just rest."

"But he'll find us now." Preyanka sounded near tears.

"He won't, I swear. It's all right. Rest now."

"Where am I?" Her tearful voice sounded frightened.

"It's my home," Depik said. "It's all right. Try to sleep, if you can." He gestured to Bhakriya. "We're going outside, but I promise your mother won't go far."

Bhakriya squeezed Preyanka's hand, then followed Depik out to where Lamprophyre waited. "Now you know our secret," she said. "You can't tell anyone. Please. It's her life at stake."

"I'm confused," Lamprophyre said. "Isn't Preyanka too young to be an ecclesiast? And why are you begging in the streets when she could be living in the Archprelate's palace?"

"She's young, yes, but that just makes her remarkable." Bhakriya's voice shook. "My lady, the ecclesiasts—oh, it's a long story."

"Neither of us have anywhere to go," Depik said. "Talk. It might do you good."

Bhakriya nodded. "My lady," she said, "nobody knows who an ecclesiast is until he or she is possessed of a prophecy. So it's always a surprise. Usually ecclesiasts are young adults when it happens, but sometimes they're in their teens or even younger. The young ones, the ecclesiasts are always excited about because their prophecies are considered purer." She made a noise of disdain. "I think it's nonsense, but it doesn't matter. What matters is that young ecclesiasts are taken from their families and brought to the Archprelate's palace. The families are well compensated for the loss, but the children still go."

"They wanted to take Preyanka away," Lamprophyre said, understanding dawning.

Bhakriya nodded again. "My husband—he was thrilled. We're not poor people, but he loves money more than anything else, and he was eager to increase his fortune by way of selling his only daughter." She laughed bitterly. "I didn't care about the money. I don't want that life for Preyanka, to be praised and worshipped for the next sixty or seventy years. But I would have endured it if we could have stayed near her. Ecclesiasts can see their families if they want. And my husband refused to leave Kolmira. So I took the children and fled."

"To Tanajital," Depik said flatly. "The very place the ecclesiasts would have taken her."

"It was the only place in Gonjiri big enough for us to be lost in," Bhakriya said. "I was afraid to go to Fanishkor, what with them being on the verge of war with Gonjiri and maybe interested in taking out their anger on a displaced woman with two young children, and Sachetan is too far. So I decided to take my chances."

A terrible idea was taking shape in Lamprophyre's mind. "Would your mate—your husband—have told the ecclesiasts about Preyanka?"

"Of course," Bhakriya said. "He'd already sent word when we left."

"Is it possible he guessed where you went?"

"I don't know." Bhakriya's brow furrowed. "I suppose he might. We left over a month ago, so if he searched Kolmira first, he might have worked out by now that we're not there." Her voice choked on a sob. "I should have sent her away, protected her from her father's fists, but I couldn't bear to lose my little girl."

"Nobody blames you," Depik said. "You were in an awful position, you and the littles, but you're safe now. My lady won't let anyone near you."

"He's right," Lamprophyre said, but her mind was working furiously. *Holy, must find.* Who was it who'd said there was no chance the ecclesiasts were searching Tanajital for one of their own? It didn't matter. If Bhakriya was right about the ecclesiasts valuing a very young person for her purer prophecies, no wonder they were sweeping the city. The High Ecclesiasts must be going out of their minds at having lost Preyanka.

"No, wait," she added swiftly. "I can only do so much. If your husband comes here, or if the ecclesiasts find Preyanka, I can't commit violence against them even if they deserve it. We have to find a way to keep anyone from learning where she is."

"We can move on," Bhakriya said, sounding uncertain.

"You won't have better protection anywhere else," Depik said. "I'm sure o' that. And my lady may not be able to hurt them, but I've no reservations about it."

"Depik, you can't fight them. The guard will take you into custody," Bhakriya said.

Depik shrugged. "If it spares you time to get away, might be worth it."

"Nobody's fighting anyone," Lamprophyre said. How she wished Rokshan hadn't left! Stones take Manishi and her stupid greed and selfishness. "Bhakriya, the ecclesiasts are searching the city for Preyanka. It's just good fortune they haven't seen her yet. It's also good fortune they don't ever come this way. You'll have to stay here until we can figure out what to do."

"I can't do that." Bhakriya's voice sounded tearful again. "I shouldn't involve you in my troubles."

"Why, because the ecclesiasts will condemn me? Too late to worry about that." Lamprophyre laughed. "What's happening to you isn't fair, and I don't like unfairness. Rokshan and I will work out how to solve your problem, and until then you'll go on working for me. There are plenty of these little houses for you to use."

Depik put a hand on Bhakriya's shoulder. "It will be all right," he said.

Slowly, Bhakriya raised her hand and rested it over Depik's. "I believe it will," she said.

"All right. Let's finish serving food and clean up, and then tomorrow we'll discuss your problem with my clutch—the other dragons—and find a solution." Lamprophyre didn't want to tell Bhakriya she was relieved to learn what the ecclesiasts were looking for, in case Bhakriya took it the wrong way. But she felt more cheerful than she had since the day that reverend had brought his terrible decree to the embassy.

While Bhakriya and Depik returned to serving soup, Lamprophyre helped Preyanka and Abhit choose a house to sleep in. Preyanka had recovered completely from her prophecy, though the way she refused to meet Lamprophyre's eyes and her tumbled thoughts told Lamprophyre the girl still felt awkward and embarrassed and hoped the dragon wouldn't push her to talk about it. Lamprophyre stayed tactfully silent.

Rassika, towing Kavari behind her, followed the other two children, not saying anything. Lamprophyre caught a glimpse of her face and felt incredibly torn. Rassika's longing for even so impermanent a home as the embassy was obvious, but Lamprophyre knew there was no way Rassika would accept charity, even if Lamprophyre couched it in terms of keeping Kavari safe. She wished Rokshan were here, because he might see a solution—and just like that, the answer came to her.

While Preyanka and Abhit were settling themselves in their chosen house—the houses weren't really very small, but each had only one bed, so they couldn't share with their mother—Lamprophyre drew Rassika aside and said in a low voice, "Rokshan needs to know what happened, and I don't want to wait until morning. Do you suppose you could run to the palace for me and ask him to come? I'll watch Kavari until you return."

Rassika's gaze darted to her sister, then back to Lamprophyre. "I guess I could," she said, warily.

"Thank you. And it will be late when you return, so I was thinking, maybe you could sleep here for the night? I worry about you and Kavari traveling the slums in darkness."

"I been doing that for years," Rassika said, but in the tone of someone who wanted to be convinced.

"Yes, but surely this is easier? And Depik makes porridge in the morning, so you could have a meal—and of course I'd pay you for running the errand," Lamprophyre pressed on relentlessly.

Rassika looked at Kavari again. Kavari's eyes were fixed on Lamprophyre's wings. "All right," Rassika finally said. "You watch her right, yes?"

"I promise."

Rassika released Kavari and bolted. Kavari never stopped staring at Lamprophyre. "We'll wait for Rassika in the embassy hall," Lamprophyre said.

"Butterfly," Kavari said, reaching out a tiny hand toward Lamprophyre's wings. Her thoughts were wordless, but filled with wonder.

Charmed, Lamprophyre picked Kavari up and lifted her to where she could touch the copper membranes. She could barely feel Kavari's fingers brushing against the sensitive spots. She'd wondered, from things Rokshan had said, whether humans' sense of touch was more refined than dragons', and now she felt that had to be true.

Carrying Kavari, she walked through the courtyard and settled herself just inside the embassy so she could watch the stragglers coming for food with the last rays of sunlight. Depik and Bhakriya were talking in low voices near the soup cauldron, and Lamprophyre idly listened to their thoughts. Bhakriya was exhausted, but hopeful, and Depik—*oh*. That must be what Rokshan had thought might or might not be something.

Lamprophyre looked at Depik more closely. If he had affection for Bhakriya...actually Lamprophyre didn't know what that meant, in human terms. It sounded as if Bhakriya was still pair-bonded to her husband, and dragons, at least, couldn't have more than one mate at a time. Though maybe it didn't matter, since Bhakriya's thoughts about Depik weren't along those lines. Lamprophyre examined the two of them more closely. She found herself wishing Bhakriya returned Depik's regard, because how beautifully simple a solution to have the two of them pair-bonded! Depik would never hurt anyone, and he was kind and loyal, a perfect mate for Bhakriya. If her husband were gone, of course.

The Sister of the Red finished her soup and nodded at Lamprophyre as if they were equals before leaving. Lamprophyre still wasn't sure how she felt about the woman. Others drifted away until the only humans still there were Depik, Bhakriya, and the children—oh, and the old man, who seemed to have fallen asleep sitting up. Lamprophyre left him alone. It felt as if she were sheltering half of Tanajital tonight. She glanced at Kavari, who was looking at the constellations book again, settled herself across the doorway so Kavari couldn't get out without her knowing, and closed her eyes, not to sleep, but to listen to the voice of the city as it hummed along into night.

She didn't open her eyes when Kavari climbed over her and settled in the nest made by her folded arms, but soon Kavari fell still and quiet, and when Lamprophyre peeked, she saw the child was curled up asleep. She was no bigger than a hatchling dragonet, and Lamprophyre had a sudden vision of herself with her own child, sometime in the future. She still had no idea who she would choose for a mate, but the idea of being pair-bonded, of tending a child, was less uncomfortable now.

She closed her eyes again and listened. There was Depik, clattering away in the kitchen, and Bhakriya swishing dishes through water. At the limits of her hearing, Preyanka and Abhit were breathing quietly in sleep. Past that, the murmur of thousands of people going about their nighttime business soothed her spirits. One of those people might be Bhakriya's husband, but Lamprophyre found it impossible to worry about that, what with the calm of the warm, humid air and the dim purple twilight. Something for the morning, when she could discuss it with the clutch.

She roused from her doze at the sound of running footsteps, one light, the other heavier. Blinking, she looked up to see Rokshan coming toward her, trailed by Rassika. Conscious of Kavari's sleeping weight in her arms, she didn't move more than to raise her head. "Did you find Manishi?" she asked.

"She wasn't at the palace," Rokshan said. "Father hadn't seen her. Whatever she has in mind, it's not telling Father about Flint."

"That's a relief. Sort of. I guess it was easier when we knew what she planned." Lamprophyre carefully slid her arms from beneath Kavari until the child rested in her hands. She gave her to Rassika, who staggered slightly. Maybe the girl wasn't as rested from her sleep as Lamprophyre had thought. "Bring Kavari, Rassika, and I'll show you where you can sleep."

Rassika stared at the little house, clean but furnished only with a bed, an oil lamp, and a small chest, as if it represented the height of luxury. "We can sleep here?" she asked, her voice tinged with awe.

"Yes, and have a meal in the morning. And—" It was an impulsive, rash thought, but the girl's plight and the memory of cradling Kavari spoke to Lamprophyre. "If you don't mind, you might run more errands for me. There are so many places in this city I don't fit, and I imagine you know it well."

"Sure I do." Rassika didn't take her eyes off the bed. "I'm fast, too, faster'n most my age."

"That is exactly what I need." She resolved to think of errands for Rassika to run. "Now, sleep, and we'll talk more in the morning."

She walked in silence back into the embassy and closed the back doors as quietly as she could manage. Then she leaned against them, making them creak, and rubbed her hands over her face, pressing the ridges above her eyes to relieve the tension at the back of her skull. "I've never been so tired."

"Don't sleep yet," Rokshan said. "I need to tell you what I learned."

"I thought you said Manishi wasn't at the palace." Thinking about what Manishi might be doing right then made her head hurt more.

"Not Manishi. Khadar," Rokshan said. He sat cross-legged next to her and stretched out his back with a series of pops that made Lamprophyre shudder. "I searched for him earlier today. Usually he's either at the palace or at some pleasure house, doing un-ecclesiastical things. But he wasn't in any of his usual haunts. I think he's gone to ground in the Archprelate's palace."

"Where we can't get at him." Lamprophyre sighed. "It doesn't matter. I found out what the ecclesiasts are searching for."

Rokshan's head jerked up. "You what?"

Lamprophyre lowered her voice, though there was no one around to hear. "Preyanka is an ecclesiast. She was possessed of a prophecy right in front of me. Bhakriya fled with her to keep the ecclesiasts from finding her and taking her away."

"But—Lamprophyre, we have to take her to the Archprelate's palace. She has a destiny she can't avoid."

Lamprophyre recoiled. "You can't possibly be on their side. Not after what they've done."

"What they've done is separate from the duties of an ecclesiast. Preyanka is going to go on being possessed of prophecies for the rest of her life. That's Jiwanyil's voice speaking to humanity through her. It's not fair to anyone to deny the world the word of God." Rokshan closed his eyes and let out a deep sigh. "No wonder the ecclesiasts have been out in force, though it doesn't explain why they didn't make an announcement and enlist the city's help."

His placid certainty angered Lamprophyre. "They were going to take her away from Bhakriya," she said, feeling a growl build within her. "She would never see her daughter again. *That's* not fair."

"That's not true. It's not like the ecclesiasts are thieves. Bhakriya could see Preyanka whenever she wanted."

"Not if Bhakriya is living in Kolmira with that awful husband of hers. He only cares about the money the ecclesiasts would pay for Preyanka. And you know if they find Preyanka, it will be easier for Bhakriya's husband to track her down. I refuse to let that happen."

"Lamprophyre—"

"Don't sound like that."

"Like what?"

"Like I'm the unreasonable one."

Rokshan rubbed his face the way Lamprophyre had rubbed hers. "All right, you're not unreasonable. But you also don't understand everything about this situation. You've seen how a prophecy takes the one possessed of it. Receiving prophecy is hard on a human body, and the ecclesiasts have things, medicines, that ease that burden. If Preyanka doesn't receive that treatment, one of her prophecies could injure her, maybe even kill her. Does Bhakriya know that?"

Lamprophyre involuntarily glanced over her shoulder as if she could see through the walls to where Bhakriya slept. "I don't think so."

Rokshan sighed again. "There has to be some way to keep Preyanka safe without alerting her father. I don't know why Bhakriya hasn't taken steps to annul her marriage. Any ecclesiast who knows the truth would see to it. Though if her husband is powerful enough, he might continue trying to hurt her regardless of whether or not they're still married."

"Wouldn't the law protect her?"

Rokshan looked away. "It should. But it's complicated. The law wants to see families stay intact, and sometimes that means over-looking or ignoring good reasons for a marriage to end. It's not right, Lamprophyre, I know, but humans can't hear people's thoughts. They have to go on what they see. Even ecclesiasts. Bhakriya's husband—like I said, if he's rich and powerful, he might be able to conceal what he's done to her and escape punishment."

Outrage choked Lamprophyre's reply. "That is so unfair," she said. "I—" She managed not to say *I'm glad I'm not human*. The failings of human society weren't Rokshan's fault.

"Bhakriya is in a much better position now," Rokshan said. "With the two of us behind her, she's protected from her husband simply snatching her away. I'll spend the night here, and speak with her in the morning about a divorce—that means legally ending her marriage. She might not have pursued that option out of fear her husband will try to keep the children from her."

"We can stop that, too, right?"

"If you're willing to spend some money, yes." Rokshan's face was grim. "I'm embarrassed to say this, but the whole thing would be easier if Bhakriya had some fresh bruises."

"That's disgusting."

"Like I said, humans can't hear thoughts to know if someone's evil. Even if Bhakriya is granted a divorce, a judge bribed sufficiently might rule that Abhit has to go back to his father. But we won't let that happen." Rokshan put his small hand over Lamprophyre's. "I hope Bhakriya trusts us. Finding a permanent solution for her means she'll have to face her husband eventually. And let Preyanka go."

His somber tone of voice told her he was warning her that she had to trust him. She hated his words. Expose Bhakriya to the man who'd hurt her, force her to give Preyanka up to the ecclesiasts—nothing about this was good. But he was right that hiding Bhakriya and her children was a very impermanent solution. And the draconic solution —making Bhakriya's husband flee in terror from dragons who would tear him to pieces if he hurt her again—was impossible in a human world.

"I think I liked it better," she said, "when all we had to worry about was Manishi's blackmail."

CHAPTER TWENTY-FOUR

Lamprophyre banked left and made a long, sweeping turn that brought her once more over the street leading to the embassy. According to Dolomite's maps, the ecclesiasts never came closer than two dragonlengths from the courtyard, but Lamprophyre didn't want to risk not knowing that had changed, not now that they knew the ecclesiasts' intent. She saw a yellow-shrouded litter a good distance away, and one about ten dragonlengths away on a direct line to the embassy and headed their way. She followed it until it turned east and was clearly heading for the palace. For now, they were still safe.

On her return, she found the courtyard empty, hot and humid even at not quite midmorning. Voices came from the sheltered dining pavilion, and when she ducked into its shade, she found Bhakriya and Rokshan facing one another, speaking in loud voices. Depik stood nearby, watching in silence, but his thoughts were all about Bhakriya and his worry for her.

"I won't do it," Bhakriya said. She looked at Lamprophyre. "Thank you for your generosity, my lady," she said, her voice tight and angry, "but we have to leave now."

"You can't leave! The ecclesiasts are still out there, looking for Preyanka," Lamprophyre exclaimed.

"His highness wants to turn her over to them," Bhakriya said, without a hint of respect or awe over Rokshan's title. "If we run now, we can escape them. We'll go to Sunital, or somewhere—"

"Preyanka can't keep her gift secret forever," Rokshan said, sounding much calmer than Bhakriya, "and if you don't take her to the ecclesiasts, it could kill her. If you go now, with me—"

"We're both outcast, remember, your highness? They won't do you any favors. They'll take Preyanka and tell Jagen where we are. I'd rather die on the road than go back to him."

"We won't let that happen." Rokshan glanced at Lamprophyre. "Whatever the ecclesiasts say about religious matters, we're not outcast from the law's protections. We can help you receive a divorce, and protect you from your husband. You can't keep running forever."

"I can't," Bhakriya said. Tears welled up in her eyes. "You don't understand. It took everything I had to run away, every scrap of courage. You don't know what it's like to live with someone who thinks nothing of a slap or a punch to make us fall in line. I can't go back to that. If I didn't have the children to think of, I might have..." She shook her head. Behind her, Depik's hand closed slowly into a fist. "I want to be truly free, but I can't risk it. You know the law isn't always fair. I can't prove what Jagen is, and he has wealth and power—"

"I can't bear this," Lamprophyre told Rokshan. "What can we do?" Bhakriya's thoughts were filled with the black despair she had only ever heard from Depik when he was deep in the grip of his illness.

Rokshan looked from Lamprophyre to Bhakriya. "You're right that I don't understand," he said, "but I know something about being trapped by a life you can't escape. However frightened you are, your suffering will go on unless you do something to change it. Do you want to go on living in fear, always running, never knowing if this is the day someone catches up to you? Or do you want to take the next courageous step, and reach for a future you can bear to live with?"

Bhakriya stared at him. "It's not just me," she said.

"I know. It's terrible for children to be mixed up in this. But I promise you—" Rokshan took her hand and squeezed it. "Lamprophyre and I will stand with you. You won't lose Preyanka, because the ecclesiasts will treat her with respect in every way, including finding a place for you and Abhit to live where you can see her often. You're not the first family to be in this position. And as for your husband...damn it, I shouldn't say this, but if the law doesn't support you, Lamprophyre will make sure no one ever sees him again."

Bhakriya's eyes widened. "My lady, you would..." Her thoughts finished the sentence she couldn't bring herself to say.

"I would," Lamprophyre said. "But I have faith in Rokshan. We'll try the law first. And we will protect you until it's all resolved."

To her surprise, Bhakriya turned to Depik. "What do I do?"

He blinked. "Why ask me?"

"Because you've been helped by them, and you know what they're capable of. Am I mad not to run?"

Depik came forward. "I trust my lady. She gave me a chance when no one else would. If she says she'll support you, that's not nothing. And I..." He swallowed. "If it were up to me, I'd want you to stay."

Bhakriya's thoughts changed from agitated to confused. She ducked her head slightly. Depik's face became impassive. He opened his mouth as if to speak, then seemed to think better of it. Lamprophyre felt awkward about having witnessed his moment of vulnerability. She cleared her throat, drawing everyone's attention and breaking the strained silence. "Will you trust us?" she asked. "Because I'd worry so much if you left."

Bhakriya let out a deep breath. "I will, Jiwanyil help me," she said. "He may not love me and mine, but I say you've done more for us than any ecclesiast."

"The ecclesiasts," Lamprophyre said. "Rokshan, what does it mean if an ecclesiast is outcast?"

"You mean, because Preyanka has consorted with dragons, and been possessed of a prophecy under those circumstances?" A wicked smile touched Rokshan's lips. "That's an interesting question. I look forward to asking it."

"Is that what we do first? Tell the ecclesiasts about Preyanka?"

"The first thing is to rid Bhakriya of Jagen. Whatever money they pay for Preyanka—to compensate the family for the loss of her labor—"

"Preyanka doesn't have to work," Bhakriya said.

"Legally, a child is recognized as a resource a family may or may not use," Rokshan said, "and that money is due regardless. You'll need it to help support you and Abhit, since you don't have your husband's support anymore. If you're divorced before the ecclesiasts take Preyanka in, and your children are legally yours, that will make the financial side of this less complicated."

Bhakriya nodded. "I'm afraid I don't know anything about divorce. I was always too frightened to ask questions, because if Jagen knew —anyway."

"I'll handle the first inquiries," Rokshan said. "For now, you need to stay concealed, you and the children. Lamprophyre, you and your clutch will need to find out what Manishi is up to. If it means Flint has to tell Father his story, that will have to happen immediately."

To Lamprophyre's surprise, Bhakriya laughed and immediately muffled it with her hand. "I'm sorry," she said, "it's just that a dragon and a prince are intervening on my behalf. I never would have dreamed it. Thank you, my lady, your highness."

"We're happy to help," Lamprophyre said. "Depik, you'll watch them while we're gone, yes? And I'll tell Rassika she's to find me if anything happens, like if the ecclesiasts come this way."

Depik nodded. His face was still impassive, but Lamprophyre could hear his thoughts, and Bhakriya was preeminent in them. She found herself hoping Bhakriya could see what a good man he was.

She found Rassika eating porridge in the kitchen with the other children. Rassika took in Lamprophyre's request with a solemn expression. "So you see it's important that you're fast," Lamprophyre concluded. "That will be so important if anything happens here."

"I'm fast," Rassika said with a nod. "But Kavari—"

"Bhakriya will care for her," Lamprophyre said, feeling confident in her promise. "She's a mother, so she knows how to take care of children, right? You don't have anything to worry about."

Rassika looked at Kavari, who was feeding herself rather messily. "You don't need me for true, do you?" she asked.

"If you mean, am I making up jobs for you out of charity, then sort of, in the sense that I could hire anyone to run errands for me. But I want to help you because you're brave and I think that's deserving of respect. And, well, look at me." Lamprophyre stepped back, away from the overhanging roof of the dining pavilion, and spread her wings wide. "This city was made for humans, not dragons, and there are so many places I can't go. I trust you to go where I can't, Rassika. That matters to me. So I'm willing to pay you and provide you shelter in exchange for your labor. And that's not charity."

She folded her wings and sat down again. Rassika examined her closely. Then she set her empty bowl aside and stood. "Ain't had no one care what happens to us for years," she said. "I'll run for you if it's what you want."

"It is," Lamprophyre said. "Do you know where the dragons live? The ones not me?"

Rassika nodded. She looked poised to dart off immediately despite Lamprophyre's instructions.

"That's where I'll be. Come for me if Depik or Bhakriya tell you." Lamprophyre backed away into the courtyard and found Rokshan waiting. She crouched to let him up. "Where should I take you?"

"The central guard post. The judiciary is next to it. I'll start those proceedings and then join you at the warehouses." He gripped her ruff hard as she launched herself into the sky. "Would you really kill Bhakriya's husband?"

"I don't know. I don't want him to escape justice, but I'm not comfortable being the instrument of justice myself. Among dragons, that's what the queen does. It feels presumptuous." But she couldn't help remembering Bhakriya's black despair at the thought of returning to where her husband could hurt her or her children. What was worse: sending three people she cared about into danger, or ending the life of a horrible criminal? It disturbed her that she didn't have a ready answer for that question.

They flew the rest of the way to the monstrosity of the guard post in silence. Though the plaza was thronged with people, they all moved aside to give Lamprophyre space to land. Silence filled the plaza as she crouched and Rokshan hopped down, silence dense enough that the noises of the city were a more distant hum than usual. A rush of wings filled the air as a flock of gray and white birds swooped past and settled on the stones less than a dragonlength away. They were too ignorant or too stupid to realize they were in danger, even if it was only theoretical danger because they smelled verminous and didn't tempt Lamprophyre's hunger at all.

"This shouldn't take long. I'll return soon," Rokshan said. Lamprophyre didn't wait around to see where he went, though she was mildly curious about what the judiciary building looked like. She wanted to get away from all the silent humans and their wary, watchful eyes that said she was a threat. Stones take those ecclesiasts who'd ruined all the hard work she and her clutchmates had done to stop humans from being afraid of dragons.

Hot, muggy air enveloped her as she flew toward the warehouses. Bhakriya and her children were safe for now, which meant it was time to worry about the other threat. Lamprophyre couldn't begin to guess what Manishi might try next, except that it would be something manipulative. Maybe she should just give the adept the kyanite. So what if she created a mind-reading artifact? She was only one person— all right, a ruthless, self-centered, amoral person who wouldn't think twice about using that ability to ferret out secrets and use them for further blackmail. No, they couldn't give Manishi what she demanded. Lamprophyre refused to dwell on the other problem: that there were possibly dozens of other adepts, in Tanajital and beyond, all set on being the first to listen to thoughts. Nothing the dragons could do about them.

By the time she reached the warehouses, she was hot and tired as if she'd flown much farther than not even halfway across the city. The day was shaping up to be the hottest this year. Mentally cursing the weather, the lowlands, and the humans who'd thought settling here was a good idea, she landed and then stood for a beat or two, breathing heavily. She needed to make time for a swim later.

She heard voices coming from Flint's warehouse and wearily walked in that direction. "...won't do it," an unfamiliar voice said. It was high-pitched enough not to have come from a dragon, but she didn't recognize it as belonging to any of the humans she knew.

"We're out of choices," Flint said. "If we take action, we cut her off at the knees, so to speak."

"You may be confident of your chances, but I'm nobody," the stranger said. "I'll end up in prison no matter what."

Lamprophyre poked her head through the open doorway. "Flint?"

Flint glanced up. He looked as if he'd been having this argument long enough to become frustrated. "Lamprophyre," he said. "This is my friend Lokun. He had an unexpected visitor last night. Tell her, Lokun."

Lokun was short by human standards and stocky, but his eyes gleamed with intelligence as well as anger. "You trust this dragon?"

"She's my clutchmate, Lokun. I trust her with my life." Flint sounded superficially calm, but Lamprophyre knew him well enough to tell when he was ready to start shouting.

"Was your unexpected visitor a woman?" she asked. "With messy hair, dressed like a laborer but with speech like a noble?"

Lokun's brow furrowed. "How did you know?"

Lamprophyre exchanged glances with Flint. "How did she threaten you?" she asked Lokun.

He stared up at her as if expecting her to come out with more information. "She told me she'd seen me and Flint selling secrets to Fanishkor. I thought she was mad at first, but then she told me details of that visit with Parhit no one could have known unless they were there. So I called her a liar, and she asked who I thought the king would believe, a nobody like me or a powerful adept."

"Odd," Lamprophyre said. "She didn't tell you her name or true identity?"

Lokun shook his head. "She just said to tell my dragon friends to do as they'd promised or it would go ill for me. Now Flint tells me she's the Princess Manishi and she wants you to deliver a crystal she offered to buy. Flint, just give her the damn crystal and be done with it!"

"I told you she will use it to hurt people," Flint said. "We can't be party to that."

"You don't know that's what she'll do." Lokun turned to face Flint. "Right now, the king doesn't know anything about the princess's lies. If we go to him, tell him we didn't sell information to the enemy, it will get him thinking about the possibility that we might have. He might even think we're trying to deceive him, pretending honesty and openness to gain his trust and get him to overlook what seems like treachery. He can't hurt you, but he can stick me in a dungeon and torture me to get me to tell secrets I don't have!"

"I won't let that happen," Flint said. He flexed his wings as best he could in the confines of the warehouse. "I'd take you to hide somewhere."

"Hiding is short-term thinking. My whole life is in Tanajital. I can't up and move somewhere else, take a false name and start a new life!"

"He's right," Lamprophyre said. "And it's not fair, even if it were practical."

Flint blew out an acid-scented breath of hot air. "But the alternative is giving Manishi a hold over us forever. She's not going to be satisfied with one delivery of kyanite. She's going to go on demanding things of us, and suppose someday those things are criminal? I know you're scared—"

"Damn right I'm scared." Lokun didn't sound scared. He sounded furious.

"But you know this is the only answer." Flint crouched to put himself on a level with Lokun's face. "You don't have to come along. I can refuse to reveal who my human companion was. But the king will trust us more if we're both there, completely honest with him. And if he does threaten to hurt you, I'll stop him."

"Flint—" Lamprophyre began.

"I know we're not supposed to harm humans, but if it's a choice between that and letting them harm an innocent, I know where I stand," Flint said.

It was so much like what Lamprophyre had been thinking about what she would do to keep Bhakriya and her children safe it shut her mouth on more objections. "All right," she said. "And I'll come with you."

"Come with you where?" Dolomite asked, startling Lamprophyre with his silent approach. "Is it swimming? Today should be a day for swimming. I feel like the air is trying to drown me."

"We're talking about going to the king to preempt Manishi's threat," Lamprophyre said. "I think it should just be me and Flint, though. It's my duty as ambassador, and we don't want to make the king feel like he's on the defensive."

"I wonder why Manishi doesn't come here to challenge us," Dolomite said, with the air of someone contemplating an idle question he didn't much care about answering. "Do you think she's afraid of all of us together?"

"I think she doesn't want to give up her advantage," Lamprophyre said. "She feels stronger when she's in her own place." She wished they dared threaten to destroy the adept's workshop, but Manishi would just laugh at that.

"So do we have an agreement? Or will you stay behind?" Flint asked Lokun.

Lokun's jaw was set tight. "You're manipulating me."

Flint jerked as if the man had punched him between the eyes, not that a human could do much damage even there. "I'm just being logical. Please, Lokun, don't give in to fear."

In the silence that fell, Lamprophyre could hear the dull hum of the city, punctuated by the occasional shout of a street vendor. Lokun looked as if he'd been turned to stone. "Fine," he finally said. "Fine. I'll do it. But I think you're wrong, and this is all going to be a disaster."

"It won't. I won't let it," Flint said.

"I'll request an audience with the king," Lamprophyre said. "I hope it won't take long." She couldn't send Rassika, in her overlarge adult's tattered shirt and dirty face, for this. She would have to go herself. "In fact, I'll do it now. Rokshan is coming here when he finishes his business—would you ask him to wait for me?"

She caught a glimpse of Flint's thoughts—*maybe Rokshan can talk sense into him*—as Flint said, "We'll all wait."

"Let's get this over with quickly," Lokun said. He sounded calmer now, but his thoughts were still agitated, and Lamprophyre felt a pang of sadness for both Flint and Lokun. Manishi had a lot to answer for.

CHAPTER TWENTY-FIVE

S he flew as fast as she dared to the palace, so fast she stumbled when she alit in front of its great double doors. At this hour, they stood open, and men and women passing through in both directions shrieked and fled when she made her precipitous appearance. A couple of soldiers in uniform, dark blue shirts and knee-length tan trousers, stood to either side of the door, holding their halberds in an awkward semi-defensive position, as if they wanted to ward against a potential attack but didn't know how they could hurt a dragon. More humans, braver than the rest, hovered near the doorway, staring at her.

"I'm sorry I startled you," Lamprophyre said politely. She addressed the soldier on the left, whose thoughts were more wary than frightened. "I need to get a message to King Ekanath immediately. It's urgent diplomatic business. Could you send someone to ask him if the dragons can meet with him privately, at his earliest convenience?"

The soldier nodded slowly, his eyes never straying from her face. He snapped his fingers twice, then once more in what sounded like a signal. A boy about Preyanka's height came forward from the crowd at the door. He, too, wore the dark blue and tan clothing, though in his case it looked less like a uniform than the soldiers'. Lamprophyre repeated her request, and the boy nodded and shoved through the crowd to disappear into the palace.

Lamprophyre took a few steps backward and settled herself to wait. "It's all right, I'll just sit here until he returns."

The soldiers slowly returned to their ready and alert position, halberds gripped in one hand with the butt grounded beside their feet. The rest of the humans continued to stare, but one or two detached themselves from the crowd and descended the stairs, staying well away from Lamprophyre as they continued on to wherever they'd been going. Eventually only a few people remained, and their thoughts were curious rather than afraid. Lamprophyre thought about inviting them to ask her questions, but she was still on edge from the argument with Lokun and deeply unsure, now that she was here, that they were doing the right thing.

She blocked out the distracting thoughts of the humans and listened to the city's hum, more distant now that she was in the palace grounds and away from most of the traffic. It occurred to her that the ecclesiasts hadn't avoided this place in their search, even though it was as closed to regular traffic as the academy. So they weren't intimidated by the king. They must feel secure in their power.

More people came to the doors and stopped short at the sight of her. Whispered conversations too distant for her to hear clearly carried with them thoughts she could hear all too easily; the newcomers wanted to know why the dragon was there. She ducked her head to hide a smile as the watching humans speculated about why she might want to speak to the king. Obviously they couldn't know the truth, but their guesses were amusing: she wanted a trade agreement, she intended to declare war on Gonjiri, she wanted the king to give her part of the palace to live in. Humans had strange ideas about what dragons wanted.

Eventually, she heard running footsteps, much more rapid than those of the other humans, and the boy emerged, once more pushing past the people clogging the doorway. He trotted down the steps and halted only a few handspans from her. His thoughts were free of fear, being mostly taken up with awe that he'd spoken to the king and was about to speak to a dragon. "My lady ambassador," he said with a bow, "the king requests your presence this afternoon at three o'clock in the great hall."

"Please tell the king I and my companion Flint will be there at that time," Lamprophyre said. She had no idea when three o'clock was, but Rokshan ought to come with her anyway, as her diplomatic liaison. She bowed to the boy, sending up a flutter of startled thoughts from everyone watching, and backed away so she could fly off without knocking the boy over.

When she returned to the warehouses, Rokshan had arrived and was talking quietly with Lokun. Lamprophyre broke her own rule about not listening to Rokshan's thoughts just long enough to establish that he felt calm despite Lokun's evident agitation. "He'll see us at three o'clock," she said, interrupting their conversation.

Flint, seated within his warehouse, nodded without saying anything. He was upset, Lamprophyre could tell, his surface thoughts preoccupied with Lokun's anger and fear. Lamprophyre wished there was something she could do. She didn't know how close Flint and Lokun were, and maybe their friendship wasn't as established as hers and Rokshan's was, but she feared this attack of Manishi's had dealt it a blow it might not recover from.

"I assume you want me along," Rokshan said.

"Of course. Though I don't know that either of us should do more than introduce Flint and Lokun. And I don't think we should bring Manishi into it."

"Why not?" Lokun said. "Since the bitch is responsible."

"She *is* my sister," Rokshan said mildly. "And I think mentioning her will make you both seem weak. It implies that you would have kept the secret if Manishi hadn't intervened, rather than realizing the implications and choosing to speak in the name of patriotism and honesty."

"Understood," Flint said. "What does three o'clock mean?"

"Between midafternoon and late afternoon," Rokshan said. "I'll warn you when it's time to go."

Flint roused himself and stepped out of the warehouse. "I'm going for a flight," he said. "Lokun, will you join me?"

Lokun looked up at him. "Not right now," he said. "I need to think some things through."

A flash of pain crossed Flint's handsome face. Then his expression hardened. "I'll be back after noon," he said, and leaped into the sky.

"That was cruel," Lamprophyre said without thinking.

Lokun was watching Flint fly away and didn't look at her. "I thought we were friends," he said. "He's asking too much of our friendship."

"That's not true," Lamprophyre said, shamelessly eavesdropping on Lokun's thoughts. "I think you feel responsible for leaving Flint open to blackmail. It was your request that took you both into Fanishkor. Lokun, you're both innocent of anything but wishing ordinary people didn't have to suffer because of their governments' enmity. It's Manishi who's to blame."

"And yet I'll take most of the punishment if the king decides to be an idiot," Lokun said.

"He *is* my father," Rokshan said in that same mild, slightly amused tone. "And he's not cruel or stupid. I really do think if you're honest and open with him, he'll respect that."

"Just—please don't blame Flint for this situation," Lamprophyre continued. "I would hate to see you lose your friendship over someone else's evil behavior."

"I..." Lokun sighed. "I shouldn't have turned him down just now, but I need some time alone. Look, I'll be back around two, and maybe he and I can talk then. I'm sorry." He trudged away down the street, his head hanging low as if his toes were the most interesting thing around him.

Beside her, Rokshan let out a deep sigh. "Manishi needs to be taught a lesson," he said.

"I was thinking something like that myself," Lamprophyre said. "She can't go on thinking we're helpless. And she deserves a thrashing for hurting Flint and Lokun."

"Removing the possibility of blackmail will go a long way toward doing that. And when that's done, we can discuss her future relationship with dragons."

"You can't mean we should continue trading with her?"

Rokshan smiled. "Of course not. But I want her to clearly understand that she ruined her excellent trading position because she was greedy and paranoid."

Lamprophyre relaxed. "I agree."

"Where is everyone?" Rokshan said. "It's remarkably quiet."

"I'm sure Dolomite went flying, either to the river or to watch the ecclesiasts. I suppose we should still do that, even though we know what they're looking for now." Lamprophyre peered into a few more warehouses. "Everyone else is gone, too. I bet they left before Flint and Lokun started arguing, maybe to give them some privacy. Coquina might have gone to see if she could convince Melika's mother to accept her help in getting Melika healing treatment."

"It might be too late," Rokshan said. "No, I don't mean she's dead," he added hurriedly as Lamprophyre gasped in horror. "I mean that magical healing is more effective if it happens soon after the injury is received. The healers who worked on me the second time, after we stopped the war, told me if the body's natural healing mechanisms are engaged, they fight with the unnatural effects of jade or moonstone. It's been long enough that healing might not help Melika."

"Coquina will be furious if that's true," Lamprophyre said.

"With good reason. The ecclesiasts have a lot to answer for."

Lamprophyre stepped inside Flint's empty warehouse and settled into the slightly cooler dimness. "What happened at the judiciary building?"

Rokshan sat beside her and leaned against her flank. "I asked for information on divorce." He chuckled. "Made a lot of people very confused until they understood I wanted the information for someone not myself. I'm sure some of them still think I'm trying to get rid of a secret bride."

Lamprophyre laughed. "And is it simple? Please say it's simple."

"It's unfortunately not simple. We have to have the original decree of marriage, which bears the name of the reverend or judge who performed the ceremony. Bhakriya has to come before a different judge, accompanied by the one who married her and Jagen, and declare her reasons for wanting a divorce. Then Jagen can either counter or agree to the dissolution."

"But that means he can prevent her from being free! Because I'm sure he won't admit to beating her."

"It's a safeguard so no one can get rid of a spouse just because they feel that person is a burden on them. Men sometimes try that when they want to get rid of their wives to marry younger women. The good news is that if Bhakriya can show evidence, like the testimony of other people that Jagen beat her, Jagen's consent is no longer necessary."

Lamprophyre sagged. "The bad news being that anyone like that is in Kolmira, and out of our reach."

"Let me worry about that. You keep an eye on Bhakriya and be alert to anyone who might try to drag her back to Jagen. We need to keep her safe until she can appear before a judge. The one thing we have in our favor right now is that Bhakriya and Jagen were married here in Tanajital. I had the records clerk check, just in case. So we should be able to find the reverend who married them."

"Someone who won't like that you're both apostates."

Rokshan shook his head. "This is a legal matter as well as a religious one. The reverend won't be able to refuse to do her duty even if she thinks Bhakriya is a contaminating influence."

Lamprophyre sighed. "I feel a little better now, though really nothing's changed. We still have only a small chance of freeing Bhakriya from her husband, we have to turn Preyanka over to the ecclesiasts, Manishi is still a threat, and the king might not see things our way."

"You're so pessimistic sometimes." Rokshan tilted his head back and closed his eyes.

Just after midafternoon, Flint returned. Coquina had come back a few thousand beats earlier, frustrated at her failed attempt to get Melika's mother to see reason. "I offered her a pile of rupyas and she turned me down," she'd growled. "I'd be impressed at her commitment to her religion if she wasn't obeying a false decree."

Porphyry and Bromargyrite had returned just after Coquina. They'd been searching for Manishi and they, too, had to admit failure. "She wasn't at her workshop, and no one in the neighborhood admitted to seeing her recently," Porphyry had said. "We think she might have left the city. She goes off on buying trips all the time."

Lamprophyre had felt unexpected relief at the idea. She didn't relish having to face the woman, even though she and her clutchmates were clearly in the right. Manishi was so erratic and unpredictable, she felt like more of a threat than she probably was.

Now Flint landed neatly outside his warehouse and ducked inside without saying a word. Lamprophyre thought *Let's leave him alone* and hoped the others were paying attention.

"I think we should go for a swim after this meeting with the king," she said. "We deserve a nice rest."

"And another supper together," Bromargyrite said. "I miss that."

"Good idea," Porphyry said. "Coquina?"

Coquina shrugged. "I'm not going to be good company."

Flint poked his head out of his warehouse. "Neither am I."

"We don't care if you're angry so long as it's not with us," Porphyry said. "Let's sit around and grouse about things. That's always satisfying."

Coquina gave a reluctant half-smile. "True," she said. "Humans call it 'bitching.' I like that word."

"Then we'll bitch together," Lamprophyre said. "Does anyone know where Orthoclase went?"

"Picking up more stone, I hope," Bromargyrite said. "He knows this marble sculptor who gives him her waste stone for free. He says she likes not having to deal with it."

"I could use some marble right now," Flint muttered. Lamprophyre glanced at the others. All of them clearly had decided not to draw attention to their clutchmate's bad mood.

"Let's hope he brings some—oh. Hello, Lokun," Lamprophyre said to the man approaching down the street.

Flint stirred and sat up, but said nothing. Lokun came to a halt before the dragon. "I'd like to talk," he said. "Privately."

"We don't have a lot of time," Lamprophyre said.

"This won't take long." Lokun's thoughts were direct and clear, not muddled with anger as they'd been earlier, but Lamprophyre couldn't tell if he had decided to say something that would destroy his friendship with Flint.

Flint stretched. "We'll meet you outside the palace in a thousand beats. Will that be soon enough?"

Rokshan nodded.

Flint crouched to give Lokun a leg up, then flew away in a nearly vertical ascent. Lamprophyre watched them go, shielding her eyes from the sun's glare with her nictitating membranes. "I hope," she said, then fell silent.

"Me, too," Coquina said. Lamprophyre caught a snatch of Coquina's thoughts and was struck by the unexpected depth of feeling Coquina had when she looked at Flint. Maybe there was possibility there, after all.

Rokshan cleared his throat. "I hope they resolve their problems," he said, "because they'll be more convincing if it's clear they are in accord."

Lamprophyre blew out a big puff of smoke. "I'm tired of being afraid and worried. Rokshan, let's fly for a bit before we have to meet the king. I need to relax and pretend there's nothing more wrong with the world than pig for supper instead of cow."

Rokshan laughed. "Tragedy indeed."

They flew across the city, waving to Dolomite in his endless spiral—he would definitely need a rest after this—and downriver a few hundred dragonlengths. The smell of cool running water relaxed Lamprophyre, and she imagined swimming in it, soaking her scales and her wings and not even caring about the uncomfortable feeling wet membranes gave her. It also made her wonder what winter was like in the lowlands. Surely not as cold as it got in the mountains, but was Tanajital ever not humid? She almost asked Rokshan, but decided it was more fun to speculate.

Eventually, Rokshan told her, "It's time," and they headed to the palace. When they arrived outside the great doors, Flint and Lokun were already there. Lamprophyre risked listening to Lokun's thoughts, but heard only agitation and *if this doesn't work* and concluded his relationship with Flint wasn't topmost in his worries right now.

Rokshan hopped down and strode toward the doors. "There's room enough for all of us, but you dragons will need to keep your wings furled," he said over his shoulder. Lamprophyre followed him inside.

The hall beyond the doors was as cavernous as she remembered, though those memories were tainted with the fear she'd felt for Rokshan the first time she'd entered. Her non-retractable toe claws clicked over the floor, made of hard, flat, perfectly square stones that weren't really stones. They smelled almost like pumice, dusty and dry, and she was sure eating them would be as unsatisfactory.

Behind her, Flint ducked to avoid the metal web that gleamed with fire and failed to light the hall fully. It was pretty, but odd, and Lamprophyre didn't know why the king didn't have proper lanterns with nice clear glass to light his hall. Probably it was a human royalty thing.

She came to a stop in the center of the hall, and her mouth fell open. The king stood at the top of the dragon-wide staircase on the right side of the hall. His expression was forbidding, and his thoughts were angry, filled with horrible words like *betrayal* and *lies* and *death*.

Beside him, wearing a smile that made Lamprophyre think of a predator, stood Manishi.

CHAPTER TWENTY-SIX

"You dare show your faces here," King Ekanath said. His thoughts were angrier than his tone of voice, which confused Lamprophyre. It made no sense for him to conceal his anger, if Manishi had told him everything—which, by the look of her, she almost certainly had.

"Flint and Lokun came to explain," Rokshan began.

Ekanath cut him off with a curt gesture. "If they think anything they have to say will exonerate them of espionage, they are sorely mistaken. I've seen what they did."

"You've seen what Manishi showed you," Lamprophyre protested. "An exchange that could have been anything."

"So you knew what these two had done and you didn't come forward immediately?" Ekanath said. He took two steps so he stood at the edge of the platform at the top of the steps. "That makes you complicit."

"Your majesty," Rokshan said, and his use of formal address rather than calling the king Father told Lamprophyre they were deep within the realm of diplomacy, "perhaps we should take a step back. We assert that Flint and Lokun are innocent of espionage. You are committed to the rule of law, which says no one can be convicted without a fair trial."

"You want to drag this through the courts?"

"You are the ultimate judge and the voice of the law," Rokshan went on, unperturbed by the interruption. "I ask only that we be allowed to defend our actions before you."

Ekanath gazed down at his son. "The evidence against these two is strong."

"And circumstantial," Rokshan shot back. "I would like to know what Manishi told you."

Ekanath glanced back at Manishi, whose smile had vanished. Now she looked sad and a little uncertain. Lamprophyre wished she dared attack the woman. She settled on her haunches and glared at Manishi, though as Manishi was looking at Rokshan, it was a wasted glare.

"I didn't want to believe such foul behavior of an ally of the kingdom," Manishi said, her voice low and confiding. "But after considering the possible consequences of those two's actions, I realized I had to do my duty and speak up."

"So you showed him what you showed me? Flint—the dark blue dragon—and that man, meeting with a stranger and handing over papers?" Lamprophyre said.

Ekanath's eyebrows raised. "How did you know?"

"I admit I showed the evidence to Lamprophyre first," Manishi said smoothly. "I hoped she would convince the criminals to turn themselves in. But when she did nothing, I was forced to act."

"That's not true, your majesty," Lamprophyre said. "Manishi used that evidence to blackmail me."

"Lies," Manishi said, sounding perfectly calm.

Ekanath's gaze traveled from Manishi to Lamprophyre. "Blackmail you, how?" he asked.

"She wanted me to provide her with stone I didn't want to give. It was supposed to be a secret from the other adepts that she had it."

"I don't need blackmail to get what I want. I have enough money to pay for things legally," Manishi said.

"This is irrelevant," Ekanath said. "Regardless of motive, the facts remain that those two—" he pointed at Flint and Lokun—"sold state secrets to Fanishkor."

"We didn't," Flint said, stepping forward. "I don't know what

230

Manishi showed you to convince you otherwise, but the one time we traveled to Fanishkor, it was to meet a friend of Lokun's."

"I designed a house for him, your majesty," Lokun said. "I'm well-known as an architect, and I've designed houses and public buildings for many people, including some in other countries." He glanced up at Flint. "This whole mistake is my fault. I didn't want to take the overland route to Fanishkor, especially since the border crossing is difficult, and I thought it wouldn't be wrong if all we did was meet my friend for five minutes to hand over the designs."

"It's my fault, because I knew it would look bad, but I wanted to help Lokun," Flint said. "I admit we made mistakes, but I deny we did anything to betray Gonjiri. I don't know if you remember, your majesty, but Fanishkor used dragons to very nearly start a war, and we were all furious at being made their tools. There is no way I would do anything to help that country." He was breathing heavily, filling the air with the sharp stench of acid.

"Your majesty," Lamprophyre said as the king opened his mouth to speak, "if you saw the same thing Manishi showed me, you know it was a visual record only. There's no record of what the two groups said to each other."

"Which means nothing," Manishi said. "They were in Fanishkor speaking to Fanishkorites. They handed over documents. A dragon can spy out military secrets easily."

"It means," Lamprophyre said as if Manishi hadn't spoken, though anger made her voice shake, "it comes down to Flint and Lokun's word against Manishi's. The word of two people who were present versus the word of one person who was not. Your majesty, did you ask Manishi why she happened to have that visual record?"

Ekanath's eyes narrowed. He turned to Manishi, who still looked calm. "Well?" he said. "Did you have some reason to suspect these two?"

"I," Manishi said, "of course I knew they fly all over Gonjiri, and it occurred to me that they must be spying—"

"Rokshan and I fly all over Gonjiri. Are you going to accuse *us* of spying next?" Lamprophyre said. "Your majesty, doesn't it make more sense that Manishi, wanting a hold on us dragons, went looking for something she could use to blackmail us?"

"Of course not," Ekanath said. "Manishi has no need to stoop to blackmail."

"Your Majesty," Rokshan said, startling Lamprophyre into silence when she would have shouted something inappropriate, "Manishi wanted kyanite from Lamprophyre. Do you know why? I *think* you might."

Lamprophyre caught the emphasis on *think* and listened closely to Ekanath's thoughts. Clear as a ringing bell, she heard *kyanite, what is kyanite* and *no idea what Manishi does ever.* Rokshan caught her eye, and she gave a minute shake of her head.

"I don't see how that's relevant," Ekanath was saying.

"It's relevant," Rokshan said, "because she wants to develop an artifact that will let her read minds."

Lamprophyre gasped. She heard the horror in Flint's thoughts and the confusion in Lokun's, but Rokshan remained as placid as if he'd just commented on the weather. Maybe he was placid because he'd lost his mind. Revealing that secret, and to the king, of all people—yes, Rokshan had gone mad without her noticing the descent.

"She what?" Ekanath said. He, too, sounded puzzled. Clearly he didn't realize his youngest son was insane. "An artifact? That can't be possible."

"Of course it isn't," Manishi said, glaring at Rokshan from behind her father's back.

"The dragons discovered a secret cabal of adepts who are engaged in a race to be the first to develop that artifact," Rokshan said. "The dragons realized kyanite was key to the discovery and, knowing what a dangerous weapon that would be, refused to provide the crystal to Manishi. That's why she blackmailed Lamprophyre. I take it she didn't tell you? Because I'm sure Tekentriya's spies would love something like that, as would the military, and someone as...loyal...as Manishi ought to have created that artifact to serve her country."

"You liar," Manishi snarled.

"Can you prove this assertion?" Ekanath asked Rokshan.

Rokshan shrugged. "I can prove Manishi wanted kyanite from the dragons, and I can show you the evidence that kyanite is key to developing the mind-reading artifact. Whether Manishi was acting out of self-interest or out of patriotic duty, only Manishi knows that."

Ekanath turned to Manishi. "Well?"

Manishi's face had smoothed into her original sad but determined expression. "I wanted it to be a surprise," she said. "I don't like having people breathing down my neck while I'm working, and I haven't proved the theory yet. I can't believe Rokshan could do something so terrible as ruin my efforts."

"But—" Lamprophyre began.

Rokshan overrode her with, "I don't think this project is benefited by secrecy. You don't like working with others, but surely if you collaborate with, say, some of the adepts attached to the military, you'll have quicker success? I know you want to beat your rivals to the discovery."

Manishi's face twisted briefly with malice. Glancing at Ekanath, she said, "I suppose that's true."

"I'm astonished," Ekanath said. "I had no idea such a thing was possible. If you knew about it, why didn't you bring it to my attention sooner?" he said to Lamprophyre.

"We only discovered it a few days ago," Lamprophyre said, "and we were working out what to do with the information when Manishi attempted to blackmail me. I'm sorry if we didn't act fast enough." It stunned her how easy it was to lie to someone who couldn't hear her thoughts. Well, it was only partly a lie, and maybe that helped.

Ekanath looked at each of them in turn, dragon and human, reserving his longest gaze for Manishi. "You are correct that Manishi's evidence hinges on knowing what passed between Flint and Lokun and their Fanishkorite friends," he finally said. "In the absence of any more evidence, I choose to believe the dragon's account of what happened is true, if only because dragons do not, to my knowledge, lie."

Lamprophyre kept from flinching with guilt.

"My judgment is that this was an innocent, if foolish, transaction, and I instruct all dragons living in Gonjiri not to fly into Fanishkorite territory in future. I realize I cannot control where you fly, and I can only make it a request, but you should consider it a binding part of our treaty—a gesture of goodwill on the part of dragons, just as my leniency in this instance reflects goodwill on the part of humans."

"Thank you, your majesty," Rokshan said with a bow.

"Oh, get up," Ekanath said irritably. "No more 'your majesty,' Rokshan, unless you want me to believe you're making fun. Manishi, I'll ask General Sajan to choose his best adepts to work with you. I expect you to proceed as quickly as possible, if it's true there are others interested in making this discovery first."

Manishi's smile was bitter. "Certainly. But I will need kyanite," she added, shooting a poisonous glare at Lamprophyre. Lamprophyre's heart sank. All that work, and she'd still have to hand over the stone to their enemy.

"Oh, and Manishi can show you how to protect against having your thoughts read," Rokshan said cheerfully. "Ask her to explain what chlorite does."

That wiped the poisonous look off Manishi's face. Stunned, she said, "How did you—"

"Dragons are thorough when they want to learn a thing," Rokshan said.

"This is extraordinary," Ekanath said. "I want full reports every day. I know you don't like being monitored, Manishi, but the needs of the kingdom outweigh your preferences." He made a gesture Lamprophyre interpreted as indicating the "court" was over and walked away through the little door at the top of the stairs.

Manishi's left hand, the one wearing the quartz and chlorite ring, was clenched into a fist as if that would somehow hide it from notice. "You dare," she snarled. "Everything was fine until you had to defy me."

"No, everything was fine until *you* got greedy. Greedier," Rokshan said. "You should have been more obliging and less quick to attempt blackmail."

"You're a fool," Manishi said. "Why do you think I didn't take this to the military? The secret will come out in days, and so much for my edge."

"Exactly." Rokshan tilted his head back to look at her more closely. "Mind-reading isn't a secret anyone should have. It's not safe. Better a thousand adepts develop it than one or two. If everyone knows it's possible, everyone can potentially defend against it. You've lost, Manishi."

To Lamprophyre's surprise, Manishi shrugged. "I suppose. But I still get what I wanted. You can deliver the kyanite to my workshop this evening. And I'll have another order for you at that time."

Lamprophyre laughed. "You really believe we'll still deal with you after what you tried?"

"Please. You've won this round. That doesn't mean we stop playing the game."

"Yes, actually, it does." Lamprophyre walked to the base of the stairs and leaned forward. If she stood at her full height, she was almost eye to eye with Manishi. "I'll sell you the kyanite because you're working for the government now. But I'm done being your errand runner. After this, no dragon will sell to you, ever again. You're stuck with rock sniffers and merchants now."

Manishi raised one eyebrow. "I'm your most reliable client. You think you can afford to alienate me?"

"Alienate—? Manishi, you're mad. *You* alienated *us* when you tried to blackmail me. We'll be just fine. You, on the other hand, are going to have to compete with your fellow adepts for resources." Lamprophyre turned away. "I predict you're in for a miserable year. And that's just the beginning."

She ducked past Flint and left the palace, taking a few steps away from the door to leave room for her clutchmate to exit. Breathing in the warm, wet air that smelled of inedible green things and not dust and pumice and acid, she said, "Rokshan, the next time you decide to run mad, would you warn me first? Why the Stones did you tell the king about the kyanite?"

"For exactly the reason I gave. So long as the mind-reading artifact is a secret, it gives a tremendous advantage to anyone who develops it. If everyone knows about it, particularly if they know there's a defense against it, it's useless." Rokshan stretched, making his back pop. "I admit there's a risk in turning it over to the military to develop, but it's less of a risk than letting Manishi continue to work on it in secret. I'm sorry you have to give her the kyanite."

"That's all right. It's not like it's really going to her, if she's working with General Sajan's adepts." Lamprophyre crouched to give Rokshan a leg up. "Shall we go back to the warehouses and tell everyone the good news?"

"We're going for a flight down river for a few hundred beats," Flint said. Lokun was already perched in the notch behind his shoulders. "We never did finish our talk. I'll be back soon."

"All right—wait, what's Porphyry doing here?" Lamprophyre beat the air and flew to meet her clutchmate, who was flying awkwardly in their direction. When she neared the bright red dragon, she discovered his awkwardness was because he had a passenger. To her amazement, the passenger was Rassika, her eyes wild with terror and her small hands gripping Porphyry's ruff so tightly the color bled away from his scales.

"We need to land," Porphyry shouted; he was still far enough away that the sound of wings beating drowned out some of his words. Lamprophyre followed him down to the soft grass of the parkland surrounding the palace, where he knelt and twisted gently to get Rassika as close to the ground as possible. Rassika rolled off and crouched on her hands and knees, breathing heavily.

Her heart thumping against her ribs, Lamprophyre crouched beside the girl and said, "Rassika, what happened?"

"He came," Rassika panted. "Bad man came and took them all."

CHAPTER TWENTY-SEVEN

"Stones," Lamprophyre breathed. "When? How long ago?"

"She reached the warehouses about three hundred beats ago," Porphyry said, "shouting things about people being taken and asking for you, Lamprophyre. I flew as fast as I dared—Stones, but she's small. I could barely feel her. Left me terrified she'd fall and I wouldn't notice."

"I run as fast as I could," Rassika gasped. She pushed herself to her feet. "The bad man had a mort o' others with him. He went after Bhakriya, Depik attacked him, and that's all I saw because I run to where you said." Tears streaked her thin cheeks. "I left Kavari. I don't know where she is. Bad man said, take 'em all, but I couldn't stop for her because you *said* go fast—"

Rokshan picked up the girl and held her close. "Kavari will be fine," he said. "They won't hurt a baby. But we need to go quickly. Rassika, I'll hold you and we'll fly with Lamprophyre, all right? You don't need to be afraid. I won't drop you."

Rassika, her face buried in his shoulder, nodded vigorously. Lamprophyre crouched to take on her double burden. "Porphyry, go back to the warehouses and warn everyone we may have to face down the ecclesiasts. Ask Bromargyrite and Coquina to come to the embassy. And go quickly."

Porphyry nodded and took to the skies. Lamprophyre took off as gently as she dared, though her heart was pounding more rapidly than when she'd faced down Manishi and she wanted to speed through the air to find out what had happened. If Depik had attacked…he was strong, she thought, but one human male couldn't stand up to a handful of them. She flew faster. Depik hurt, the others taken. How could they find four humans in a city full of them?

The courtyard teemed with people when Lamprophyre arrived, forcing her to alight on the roof of the embassy. "Everybody *out!*" she shouted in her deepest, most sonorous voice. Startled, the crowd shifted and pressed to the edges of the courtyard, though very few people fled. A few still huddled around an unmoving form near the dining pavilion. Lamprophyre's breath caught.

She leaped down from the roof and leaned over to let her passengers off, then hurried to Depik's side. Blood trickled from his nose and from a long cut on his cheek that was the center of a spreading bruise, and more bruises splotched his forehead and chin. His eyes were closed, but a second glance showed her his chest was rising and falling, too slowly, but at least he was still alive. "What happened?" she demanded. "Depik, what happened?"

"Don't disturb him. He's badly injured," a woman kneeling next to Depik said.

"I can see that," Lamprophyre said irritably. "There were four other people here, most of them children. Does anyone know where they went?"

Rassika shoved past the people surrounding Depik and grabbed his shoulder. "Where's Kavari?" she shouted. Tears once again flowed down her cheeks, but she didn't spare a hand to wipe them away.

Depik stirred. His eyes fluttered open briefly, then closed tight against the bright sunlight. "Fought," he whispered. "Give them time to run. I don't know what happened after."

"I only saw the ending," the kneeling woman said. "There were a lot of men beating on this fellow, and one of them fighting with a woman. I didn't see children."

"Lamprophyre!" Rokshan shouted. Lamprophyre looked in his direction. He stood in the embassy doorway, his hand on—Lamprophyre gasped and hurried to where Abhit stood, clutching Kavari. He was shaking and his eyes were wide with fear. Then Rassika was there, grabbing Kavari from Abhit's arms and clutching the child to her heart. Kavari burst into tears. With all the people present, Lamprophyre couldn't pick out Kavari's thoughts, but she judged the child was crying out of fear and confusion and not injury.

"Preyanka and I were playing with Kavari in the embassy," Abhit said. His voice was as shaky as the rest of him. "I heard Depik shout that we should run. Preyanka went to the door, and she started screaming, so I grabbed the baby and ran out the back. We hid under the bed —was that right? I don't—" He burst out sobbing. "Where's Mama? Did he take her? He's going to hurt her again!"

"We'll find her, Abhit, don't cry," Lamprophyre said.

She turned back to the watching crowd. "Did *anyone* see where those men went? They would have been dragging a woman and a girl not yet full grown. Please, this is important." A possibility occurred to her. Maybe it was a bad idea, but the faces surrounding her showed no inclination to help a dragon. "The girl is an ecclesiast," she shouted, and a loud murmur sounded among the watchers. "That man kidnapped her to take her away from her mother. I know the ecclesiasts aren't friends to dragons right now, but nobody should treat an ecclesiast that way, least of all a young girl who can't defend herself. Now, *please*, didn't anyone see anything?"

A tall, gangly woman stepped forward. "I saw," she said. "They came down the street and spread out in front of the embassy. That man stepped up to defend the others, and they all ran, but while some of the men were beating on that fellow, others caught hold of the woman and slapped her around until she stopped fighting. They dragged the girl out of that tall open place, but they didn't hurt her. Then when they were finished with the beating, they dragged the woman and girl off down the street."

Lamprophyre chose not to yell at the woman for keeping this to herself for so long. "Did you see which way they went?"

The woman pointed right. Westward. Lamprophyre's heart sank. There was a lot of city in that direction. But it was all she had.

The sound of wings beating the air drew her attention upward to where Coquina and Bromargyrite filled the sky. Lamprophyre drew back to give Coquina room to land, while Bromargyrite, clearly unwilling to hurt the humans still thronging the courtyard, settled on the roof ridge. "Did that woman's mate steal her away?" Coquina asked. "Porphyry didn't have many details."

"He took Bhakriya and her daughter. Rokshan and I are going after them. I need you two to watch this place in case someone comes looking for Abhit—that's Bhakriya's son." Lamprophyre didn't know how much of a problem this might be, but with Depik looking the way he did, she didn't want to take chances.

She turned back to Depik, who was moving feebly as if he wanted to rise. "Lie still," she told him, pressing him gently to the ground. "I'll give you five vahas if you'll arrange for a healer to tend him," she said to the kneeling woman. "You can keep whatever the healer doesn't take. And if it's not enough, find me and I'll make it right."

"*Five* vahas," the woman breathed. "I don't need paying to help someone."

"Nevertheless," Lamprophyre said. Rokshan dug in his belt pouch, the one containing the embassy funds, and handed over five square gold coins. "I'm asking a lot of you, because I also need someone to help watch these children while I track down their mother." Rassika, Abhit, and Kavari still looked terrified, and Lamprophyre didn't think it was a good idea to leave them supervised only by two dragons they didn't know. This close, if she focused on the one mind nearest her, she was able to pick out her thoughts from the seething mass filling the courtyard, and the woman's thoughts were full of compassion for Depik and the children. "I think you can be trusted."

"The ecclesiasts—" the woman faltered, then firmed up her chin and said, "I'll do it."

"Thank you," Lamprophyre said. "Rokshan, let's go."

With Rokshan securely settled behind her shoulders, she climbed to the embassy roof and leaped from there into the sky. Almost immediately, the despair she'd been holding at bay threatened to overwhelm her. The streets were as full as they always were, there was no sign of Bhakriya or Preyanka, and it had been more than five hundred beats since Jagen and his men had attacked the embassy. "They could be anywhere," she said.

"Could be, but in reality there's only one place they are," Rokshan said.

"Can you track them?"

"Not in the city. We can ask around, but let's use our heads first." Rokshan leaned well out so he could see the streets. "Jagen's not from around here, so he'd have to hire rooms to stay in while he searched for Bhakriya and the children. He's wealthy, so they will be nice rooms in a nice inn. But he also knows hurting his family is wrong, so he'll want to keep that a secret, and the only way to do that is to hire a house instead of taking rooms at an inn. By the same logic as before, it will be a nice house. And he'll have gone back to it by the most direct route."

"That all makes sense, but how does it help?"

Rokshan shifted to look over her other side. "We need just one more piece of information, which is that taxes on personal property are assessed according to how elaborate a house you own."

"Now I'm confused."

"Turn right at the next corner. Can you go any slower?"

"Maybe, but at some point I'll go so slow I'll fall out of the sky. Why do we care about taxes?"

"We care," Rokshan said, "because people who own property they rent out make that property as bland and uninteresting as possible, to minimize the taxes they pay. They can't disguise its size, but they can paint it a boring color with no decorations, and not plant a roof garden, things like that." He pointed, and Lamprophyre saw the edge of his hand and looked where he indicated. "They look like that."

"But we don't know if that's the right one. I saw three other houses of that type when we were flying."

"It narrows down our search considerably, though, and we can start by asking questions of the people in the vicinity. And I've been keeping count. This is the farthest they could have gotten in the half hour since the attack, and we haven't seen them on the streets, so we know they went to ground somewhere in this quarter-mile area."

"Rokshan, you're brilliant," Lamprophyre said.

"I know. It's a curse," Rokshan replied.

The neighborhood they now flew over had wide streets and large houses separated from each other by narrow alleys, signs that it was a wealthy neighborhood. Lamprophyre only cared about the wide streets that allowed her to walk without her tail smacking the walls. The streets smelled cleaner, too, freer of the refuse and human waste stench that plagued other parts of Tanajital. If she hadn't been so agitated, it would have been a pleasant walk.

People ran when she and Rokshan approached, not because they feared her, but because they feared the ecclesiasts, as Lamprophyre discovered when she stopped to listen to their thoughts. Frustrated, she said, "Those ecclesiasts have a lot to answer for."

"We have Abhit, and men like Jagen don't give up their heirs easily," Rokshan said. "Particularly since Preyanka, as an ecclesiast, can't inherit more than basic personal property. Jagen can't leave Tanajital until he retrieves Abhit, and at worst, we can lay a trap for him."

"But there's no reason to think he won't hurt Bhakriya to punish her for running away," Lamprophyre said. "We can't leave her with him."

"I know. I'm trying not to think about it."

Lamprophyre growled deep in her throat. "This is ridiculous," she said, and swiftly pounced on a portly man hurrying past. He squeaked, a high-pitched noise at odds with his physique. "We're looking for someone," Lamprophyre said. "We won't leave until we find him. So if you're worried about dragons contaminating your home, well, help us find him and we'll go. It's that simple."

"Who?" the man asked in a shaky voice.

"That house," Lamprophyre said, pointing at the nearest house that matched Rokshan's deduction. "Who lives there? Is he home now?"

The man shook his head. "Vacant," he whispered. "Been vacant two weeks now."

Lamprophyre listened to his thoughts and heard no echo of lies.

She released her captive and turned away. "Next neighborhood," she said.

The next neighborhood had two houses that might be Jagen's hideout. Lamprophyre didn't bother with the niceties this time; she grabbed a young woman and the man strolling hand in hand with her and said, "Tell me what I want to know and I'll be out of your hair. That is the expression, isn't it, Rokshan?" she asked her friend.

Rokshan rubbed his mouth as if concealing a smile. "That is correct, Lamprophyre."

Lamprophyre shook the pair gently. "Those houses. That one across the street, and the one five places down. Those are for rent?"

The two looked at each other as if they thought she might intend to rent one. "Yes?" the man said. "Please don't eat me."

"Dragons don't eat people, Rabhan," his female companion said. Her thoughts were completely free of fear, even fear of the ecclesiasts. "What of it?"

"Who's living in them now?"

The woman jerked her chin, as her arms were pinned at her side by Lamprophyre's hand. "Close one, it's a family, parents and three children. Farther one is a man with a lot of servants."

"That farther one," Lamprophyre said. "Did you see him return?"

"Saw him leave," the woman said. "Left about an hour ago, him and six of his men. I didn't like the look of them. Not our kind of people at all, not for this neighborhood. They looked the sort of men who enjoy causing pain, if you take my meaning."

"So he hasn't come back yet?"

The woman shrugged, quite a feat in her position. "We were busy until five minutes ago, with no time for looking out windows to spy on our neighbors." Her thoughts made it clear it was the kind of busy that required both humans to be naked. Lamprophyre quickly blocked the woman's thoughts despite her curiosity about human sexuality, feeling it was the wrong time to pry about that subject. Someday she really needed to find a human who didn't get as embarrassed as Rokshan did to explain how sex worked for humans.

She released them both. "Thank you for your cooperation," she said. "Rokshan, I think we should check that house."

"Did he do something wrong?" the woman asked.

"We don't know," Rokshan said, "or, rather, we're not sure he's the man we're looking for."

"I hope he is, your highness," the man said, his fear subsiding. "Because then you might get rid of him. He really isn't our sort at all."

"What is—"

"Thank you again," Rokshan said, overriding Lamprophyre's query. Instead of mounting, he walked away down the street. Lamprophyre caught up with him in a few long strides.

"What does he mean, our sort?" she asked.

"He's just a snob, that's all," Rokshan said. "Interested in keeping his neighborhood pure and free from people who aren't as wealthy as he is. I despise that kind of person, but it doesn't matter now." He came to a halt in front of the house the two had indicated. To Lamprophyre, it looked the same as all the other houses along the street, though without the curves and lines and dots painted on its neighbors. Its roof was tiled the same blue as the embassy, with a rain gutter angled toward the rear of the house. Lamprophyre hadn't seen any rain barrels on this street and guessed rich people might consider them an eyesore.

Small windows cut into the brown brick of the façade indicated the house's height represented at least two stories inside as opposed to a single tall room. That also meant Lamprophyre wouldn't fit inside. Irritated at this hint that she would not be able to smash through the door and drag Jagen into the street, she said, "So what are we supposed to do now? We don't know if this is the right house."

"I have a feeling it is," Rokshan said. He put his hands on his hips and tilted his head back to regard the roof. Lamprophyre followed his gaze. The roof ridge was wide enough Rokshan could easily stand on it, and the roof itself was more gently sloped than the embassy. It overhung the house by only a little bit, not enough to provide decent shade at this hour of the afternoon.

Rokshan lowered his head. "Can you perch on the roof ridge?"

"If it's sturdy enough. It doesn't look any weaker than the embassy."

"Fly up there and listen to my thoughts. If I shout for you, verbally or mentally, take the house apart."

Lamprophyre blinked. "But this isn't Jagen's house! Should we really destroy someone else's property?"

"We'll make Jagen pay for the damage. At worst, well, it means a few more mining trips for us. But if Bhakriya is in there, she could be in serious danger, and I think it's a risk worth taking."

Lamprophyre had temporarily forgotten about Bhakriya. "You're right. Are you just going to knock on that door?"

"I am." Rokshan wiped his palms on his trousers. "If it's not Jagen, we move on. If it is..."

Lamprophyre flexed her right hand and let her claws extend. "Take the house apart."

She flew up to the roof ridge and settled on it cautiously, not putting her full weight down until she was sure the ridge would support her. It occurred to her that with all those windows, someone might have seen her and Rokshan, since they hadn't bothered to conceal themselves. Well, it wasn't as if this plan depended on secrecy. Rokshan would introduce himself by name, if they didn't recognize him outright. She shifted her weight, heard the beam creak, and froze.

Rokshan was knocking on the door thinking *hope they aren't stupid enough to attack a prince*. That possibility hadn't occurred to Lamprophyre, and it made her more tense than she already was. It didn't disturb Rokshan, who'd started whistling an unfamiliar tune as calmly as if he were visiting an old friend.

Beats passed. No one came to the door. Maybe they were wrong, and no one was home. Rokshan thought *could be wrong* and *where to next* as if he could hear her thoughts and not the other way around. She heard him knock again, more forcefully. The street was filling up with people staring at the roof—Stones, she hadn't concealed herself. Dragon concealment didn't last long, but it would have been long enough if she'd remembered to do it before landing on the roof. Now it was too late, and the street had started to look like a carnival town, and she and Rokshan were running out of options.

She heard music, and looked to see a different kind of movement at the far left end of the street, people being nudged by their whispering neighbors to turn and look up the street. She squinted into the bright afternoon light and saw a litter approaching, surrounded by the musicians and reverends of an ecclesiast's entourage. Its red curtains, bright as Porphyry, fluttered in the light breeze; unlike most of the ecclesiasts' litters she'd seen recently, the curtains were not tied back, and the litter's occupant was obscured. It must be hot behind those curtains, not that Lamprophyre cared about the comfort of ecclesiasts.

Then the strangeness hit her. Red curtains, not yellow. This was no ordinary ecclesiast. This was one of the High Ecclesiasts. And there was only one reason a High Ecclesiast might be on this street at this time, unless the world was more ruled by coincidence than Lamprophyre was willing to allow.

"Rokshan!" she shouted, just as she heard him think *finally*. The sound of the door opening came to her ears, and Rokshan said, "I'm looking for Jagen, is he—"

Then everything happened at once. Rokshan thought *Lamprophyre, now!* She heard him cry out in pain, heard fists striking human flesh. A woman screamed nearby. Lamprophyre leaped down from the roof, roaring a wordless challenge, and smashed the door as it began to close with Rokshan inside. And a powerful voice from behind Lamprophyre cried out, "Stand down, godless creature, or face Jiwanyil's wrath!"

CHAPTER TWENTY-EIGHT

L amprophyre ignored the voice and struck another blow to the door. It shattered under her fist. Lamprophyre reached inside and grabbed a fistful of cloth and the arm inside it and pulled. A screaming man flew through the doorway and hit the ground in a boneless heap. Snarling, Lamprophyre stuck her head and one arm inside and searched for Rokshan. He was fighting two other men, punching and kicking in a controlled but violent manner that suggested he knew what he was doing. Lamprophyre decided to inter-vene anyway.

She stretched her arm to the limit imposed by the door frame and grabbed one of Rokshan's assailants by the leg. She dragged him away from Rokshan and pinned him against the wall. "Jagen," she said. "Are you Jagen? Answer quickly."

"No!" the man screamed, shoving ineffectually at her hand with his one free one. The other was pinned to his side. Not-quite-fresh bruises on his chin and cheeks, dark purple, suggested Depik had gotten in some solid blows before he was overcome. "Let me go!"

Lamprophyre hooked her fingers into the back of his waistband and hoisted him into the air. She blew a hot cloud of smoke into his face, making him choke, then dragged him through the doorway and deposited him next to his unconscious friend.

A blow to her hindquarters startled her into turning away from the house. "How dare you ignore the Third Ecclesiast?" a reverend said. He held his giant book like a weapon and raised it as if to strike her again. Lamprophyre lowered her head and growled at him. He flinched, but didn't back away. His courage would have impressed her if she weren't so worried for Rokshan, alone and facing Stones knew how many more of Jagen's men.

"The Third Ecclesiast can wait," she said. But when she turned around again, Rokshan stood in the doorway. His hair and clothes were in disarray, but he looked unhurt. He had a heavyset man by the back of his shirt and shoved the man ahead of him out the door. To Lamprophyre's relief, Bhakriya followed.

The relief was short-lived. As soon as Bhakriya emerged fully into the light, Lamprophyre snarled again. The woman had been severely beaten, with one of her eyes swollen shut and her jaw puffy, and bruises covered both her arms. Furious, Lamprophyre dove for Rokshan's captive, who had to be Jagen, but Rokshan interposed his body between her and the heavyset man.

"Don't," he warned Lamprophyre. "I know it looks bad—"

"Bad? It looks like a nightmare!"

"Trust me, Lamprophyre, it will be all right." Rokshan glanced past her and swore. "Maybe not. The last thing we needed was the Third Ecclesiast wading in with both her giant feet."

The reverend threatening Lamprophyre had backed away gracefully, again not at all as if he were afraid, though Lamprophyre could hear his thoughts and he was not certain how this would end. "You are in violation of the laws of God and man," he said, making the watching crowd shift nervously. "Someone send for the guard to take these two into custody for destruction of property. And stand aside. We are here for the ecclesiast Preyanka."

Bhakriya gasped. "No. You can't have her."

"Bhakriya—" Rokshan said.

She shook her head and glanced over her shoulder. Lamprophyre could just see someone standing inside the house, someone whose agitated thoughts were those of Preyanka.

Rokshan shoved Jagen in Lamprophyre's direction. She caught him by the shoulders and squeezed just hard enough to make the man gasp in pain. Rokshan turned to face Bhakriya. "You have to have faith," he said in a voice low enough that only Bhakriya and Lamprophyre could hear. "This is the right decision. It's Preyanka's life at stake."

"An ecclesiast's destiny is clear," the reverend said. Lamprophyre had begun to hate the smug smoothness of his voice. "She belongs to Jiwanyil and to the people. Do not attempt to thwart Jiwanyil's will."

"I won't allow it!" Bhakriya screamed.

"You don't have that power, woman," Jagen shouted. "I'm her father and the decision is mine by law."

Lamprophyre held Jagen more tightly and leaned down so her hot breath that smelled of fire blew over him. "I can make you disappear so thoroughly your own parents will forget your name," she whispered. "You had better stop talking about what's yours before I forget I'm civilized."

"That's enough," a new voice said. The red curtains parted, and a woman stepped out of the litter. She was small even for a human female, with dark hair cut short to frame her face, which had delicate, well-shaped features and lines creasing her forehead and the corners of her eyes and mouth. The red silk robe she wore over black shirt and trousers bore stitched designs of animals, all of them predators. Golden tiger faces adorned the front of her robe, over the lumps on her chest.

As she walked toward Lamprophyre, the reverend and his companion knelt and bowed, and then like a spreading wave everyone in the street did the same until Lamprophyre, Rokshan, Bhakriya, Preyanka, and Jagen were the only ones still standing before the Third Ecclesiast.

The Third Ecclesiast's thoughts were placid, neither angry nor afraid nor curious. She seemed utterly unimpressed by Lamprophyre, as if meeting dragons was an everyday occurrence for her. "This seems an unnaturally dramatic way for me to greet a new ecclesiast," she said. "Preyanka. Please come forward."

"I won't let you take her from me," Bhakriya said, stepping in front of Preyanka, who hadn't moved.

"No one will take her from her parents," the Third Ecclesiast said. "We're not monsters. But Preyanka's gift must not be ignored or denied. She needs training and treatment to be able to use that gift to its fullest without suffering injury." She held out a hand to Preyanka. "I'd like to see you, child. I promise I won't take you anywhere you don't choose to go."

Preyanka hesitated a few beats longer. Then she walked past her mother, prompting her to let out a small cry and begin weeping. She stood before the Third Ecclesiast, who was no taller than she was. "You'll stop me having these attacks?" she said.

The Third Ecclesiast shook her head. "Those attacks, as you call them, are the gift of Jiwanyil, and may not be denied. But we can ease the toll they take on you."

"I don't want to leave Mama."

"You will see her as often as you like, but for your safety you must live in the Archprelate's palace for the next five years, until you are capable of enduring the prophecies that possess you." The Third Ecclesiast looked past her at Rokshan, still standing between Bhakriya and the street, and at Lamprophyre, still holding Jagen in place. "But your mother and father must stop consorting with outcasts and dragons. Jiwanyil's decree must not be disregarded."

"It's a false decree!" Lamprophyre exclaimed, just as Jagen said, "These two attacked me, unprovoked!" and Bhakriya said, "They saved me and my children, which is more than Jiwanyil ever did for us!"

The Third Ecclesiast appeared unmoved by the outbursts. When silence fell again, she said, "Prince Rokshan. You, of all people, should know better than to ignore a prophecy. Your faith has always been remarkable. And you choose to throw it away for a heretic creature?"

"I'm not going to argue with you, Ayusha," Rokshan said. "Preyanka was possessed of a prophecy while she was under Lamprophyre's protection. Jiwanyil can't be that angry with humanity if he's willing to speak to her under those circumstances."

The Third Ecclesiast's delicate eyebrows raised, deepening the wrinkles on her forehead. "That's a subject for another time," she said. "At the moment, I want to know—"

A disturbance at the edge of the crowd drew Lamprophyre's attention. Five men in the sky blue tunics of the city guard approached, short sticks in hand, their thoughts a mixture of fear and apprehension and awe. They moved through the kneeling people carefully until they reached the open area surrounding the litter and the house. "Who is responsible for this destruction?" the first guard asked. His voice was gruff, as if he were trying to sound assertive, but there was no power behind it.

"I broke the door down," Lamprophyre said. "This man's servants were attacking Rokshan, and I was defending him."

The guards exchanged glances. All of them were suddenly thinking variations on *can't take a dragon into custody* and *that's Prince Rokshan, how can we arrest a prince?* Lamprophyre pressed on with, "This man beat his mate—look, you can see how badly she's hurt—and you should take him into custody before he tries to hurt Preyanka as well."

The guard straightened. "Sirrah, did you attack this woman?" he asked. By his thoughts, he felt himself on firmer ground.

Jagen tried to stand up straight, but Lamprophyre's hands on his shoulders weighed him down too heavily. "She fell," he said. "Ask her. She's very clumsy."

Bhakriya's shoulders heaved with her heavy breathing. "I did not fall," she said, her voice low and furious. "Jagen beat me to punish me for running away from an abusive marriage. I refuse to be ashamed any longer. I intend to divorce him and see him in prison for what he's done."

Jagen's astonishment cheered Lamprophyre. She leaned on him a little more heavily and enjoyed the whimper of pain he made.

"Did anyone else see the attack?" the guard asked.

"Her word isn't good enough for you?" Lamprophyre snarled.

The guard took an involuntary step back. "More witnesses are always better," he said, his voice shaking.

"I think you'll find these men," Rokshan said, pointing at Lamprophyre's victims, "saw what Jagen did. I'm sure they'll want to testify so they aren't charged along with him."

The conscious man glanced at Rokshan, then at Lamprophyre, and nodded vigorously.

"Then we'll take them all into custody," the guard said, "and, your highness, you and the dragon will—it's procedure that you come with us."

"We'll be happy to bear witness against Jagen as well," Rokshan said cheerfully. Lamprophyre could tell that wasn't what the guard had in mind, but he didn't want to fight royalty.

"What a pleasant solution," the Third Ecclesiast said. Lamprophyre had almost forgotten she was there. "Preyanka, please join me, and—I beg your pardon, but what's your name?"

"It's Bhakriya, your Holiness," Bhakriya said. She stood stiffly, and Lamprophyre heard the sadness in her thoughts.

"Bhakriya, when your marital difficulties are resolved, come to the Archprelate's palace and ask to see Preyanka. You'll be admitted at any time." The Third Ecclesiast looked at Jagen. "I believe your compensation has already been paid. I hope that doesn't make things difficult for you."

"I don't care about the money, your Holiness. I just want Preyanka to be well."

"She will be." The Third Ecclesiast turned to Lamprophyre as Lamprophyre passed off Jagen to one of the guards. "So. You believe Jiwanyil's word is false. Take care, dragon. I was the one possessed of that prophecy. Challenge it, and you challenge me."

Lamprophyre gazed back at her fearlessly. "I don't know any more about your religion than you know about mine. But I think it's very suspicious that you received a prophecy that coincidentally tells you to do exactly what you already wanted to do."

"Lamprophyre," Rokshan said quietly, "this isn't the time."

"Isn't it, Rokshan? When *would* be the time? Your Holiness, that decree has hurt so many people. Just a thousand beats ago I spoke to a woman who almost refused to help an injured man because she feared being outcast. How is that right? How can a just and loving God force that kind of moral decision on anyone?"

The Third Ecclesiast returned Lamprophyre's gaze. "I will not explain my faith to a creature who deliberately stands outside God's grace," she said. "A prophecy is a prophecy, and we humans know that obeying prophecy, following the will of Jiwanyil, brings us lasting happiness. I don't expect you to understand." She turned her back on Lamprophyre and walked to the litter, holding out a hand for Preyanka to join her.

"At least you can call off your search now," Lamprophyre said. "That ought to make everyone happy."

The Third Ecclesiast stopped. Her placid thoughts turned confused. "Excuse me?" she said, turning around.

"Your search for Preyanka. Or did you think people loved seeing all those ecclesiasts in the streets?"

The Third Ecclesiast's thoughts became sharp and wary all at once. Lamprophyre heard her think *can't possibly know almost a disaster must find*, and then the woman said, "You're mistaken. We weren't searching for Preyanka. The ecclesiasts are here to bring order and peace in these troubled times and to counsel people who have been contaminated by inadvertent contact with your kind."

"That's enough, Ayusha, we get the point," Rokshan said. "Give my regards to Khadar."

The Third Ecclesiast turned around without acknowledging Rokshan. She helped Preyanka climb into the litter, then climbed in herself, and her little procession moved off down the street as kneeling people stood and bowed her past.

Bhakriya's face was wet with tears, but her thoughts were calmer now. "I feel so lost," she said. "Is Abhit safe? And Depik—" The tears flowed faster. "I wasn't fast enough. He fought to give us a chance to get away, but I was too slow. Is he—?"

"He's receiving treatment and will be fine," Rokshan said.

"We should get a healer for you, too," Lamprophyre said.

Bhakriya shook her head. "I need these marks to speak on my behalf. Jagen can't be allowed to get away with his evil behavior anymore. Will you go with me to the judiciary? I want to see justice done."

"We'll stand by you," Rokshan said. "But we should go now. That poor guard shouldn't get in trouble just because he didn't know how to take a dragon and a prince into custody."

253

~

Justice, it turned out, moved slowly. Lamprophyre had hoped, with Bhakriya as injured as she was, that a judge would take one look at her and declare her marriage to Jagen over. But instead, Lamprophyre had to tell the story of what she and Rokshan had done to several different people, and she never saw Jagen at all. Rokshan told her he was in the custody cells, which was where people waiting for trial were kept. Then he had to explain about trials, which took a while.

After that, a fussy little woman wearing a black gown that hung only to the middle of her shins came in to the courtyard where Lamprophyre waited, the judiciary not being built to hold dragons, and tried to get Lamprophyre to admit to destroying the entire house Jagen had rented. She had a list of damages she wanted Lamprophyre to confess to causing. Finally, Lamprophyre became annoyed enough to say, "You know full well I didn't do anything but smash the door, and I've offered to pay for that. If you persist in trying to cheat me, I'll tell the judge that this isn't the first time you've tried this and see what she does. Now, get out of here, and live an honest life from now on." The woman ran.

It was nearly sunset when Rokshan entered the courtyard and said, "We're free to go."

"Thank the Stones," Lamprophyre breathed. "Is that all? They don't want us back?"

"We'll need to come back with Bhakriya in a few days, but that's for her divorce. And we'll bring Dharan along, in case there's any problems with custody. That means we have to make sure they don't say Abhit has to return to his father," Rokshan explained when she looked blank.

"They wouldn't do that, would they?"

"The courts don't award custody to an abusive parent, and we've already proved Jagen is that, but no sense taking chances." Rokshan hauled himself up. "Bhakriya already left. I told her we—you—would give her a ride, but she said she needed to be alone for a bit."

"I understand. She was thinking such a jumble of thoughts, and worries about Preyanka, it's not surprising she wanted some time to herself." Lamprophyre leaped into the sky and flew almost straight up until the air became cool and the light of the setting sun shone clear and unimpeded along the western horizon.

"I never get tired of this view," Rokshan said. "Tanajital an anthill below us, the ground stretching out as far as we can see. If we flew higher, we might see the ocean."

"If we flew higher, you'd start to freeze." Lamprophyre turned to face north. Her distant mountain home was a charcoal blur on that horizon, but she imagined she could see Mother Stone, her peaks dusted with white year-round. "*I'd* start to freeze. It's not the way I want to go, freezing solid and dropping out of the sky like a stone."

"So when dragons near death, they fly up the slopes of Mother Stone and do what?"

Lamprophyre craned her neck so she could see his right leg. "Nobody knows. The tradition is that Mother Stone opens, and the dragon flies inside to a realm where there's no more death or pain, just flying endlessly with all the dragons who have ever lived. But even if it's just that the dragon finds a place to land, high on the slopes, and freezes peacefully to death, that's an acceptable answer. Either way, we're part of Mother Stone."

"And the High Ecclesiasts want to turn you to the complicated worship of Katayan. How frustrating."

Lamprophyre started a slow, shallow spiral that would bring her back to Tanajital eventually. "Is it complicated? How so?"

"I suppose in absolute terms it's not complicated. Just by comparison to what you believe. There are rituals, and holy days, and codes of behavior...huh."

"What?"

"It just occurred to me that dragons are never possessed of a prophecy. At least, I assume not."

Lamprophyre shook her head. The air was growing warmer, but wasn't yet uncomfortable, and she spread her wings wider to take advantage of the air currents. "If they are, it doesn't look anything like when humans are. So I'm going to say, definitely not."

"Well, wouldn't it make sense that if Jiwanyil speaks to humans, Katayan would speak to dragons?" Rokshan leaned forward and then sat back quickly before he could put more than a slight pressure on the sensitive spot at the back of her head. "Sorry. I suppose what I mean is, it's more proof that Katayan as we know him isn't real."

"I wish we'd realized that when the Third Ecclesiast was near. Her eyes might have popped right out of their sockets. Is that the right expression?"

Rokshan laughed. "Why are you suddenly so obsessed with human idiom?"

"I don't know. I guess because it's versatile and clever."

"Well, Ayusha is hard to rattle. She's been a High Ecclesiast for longer than any of the others and her faith is rock solid. Though knowing that she's responsible for that false decree, I don't know what to think."

"I did rattle her, though," Lamprophyre mused. "When I asked about them calling off their search?"

Rokshan straightened. "What do you mean?"

"Wasn't it obvious? I asked if she intended to stop searching now that they'd found Preyanka, and she was startled and said something about how they hadn't been searching for her. But she was thinking how it was impossible I knew about the search, and they still had to find whatever or whoever it was." Lamprophyre considered her words. "I suppose you couldn't have known her thoughts, but I thought her surprise was clear."

"I remember she said they weren't searching, and I didn't know what to make of that," Rokshan said. "Because I'm certain of what we deduced from Dolomite's observations. But if it wasn't Preyanka they were looking for, what is it?"

"I don't know," Lamprophyre said, "but if the Third Ecclesiast lied about it, it might be time for a more direct approach."

CHAPTER TWENTY-NINE

L amprophyre smelled soup just before the embassy came into view, and the aroma heartened her. It meant Depik was well. She remembered what he'd looked like when they left and wished she hadn't agreed to let Jagen go without a well-deserved beating.

"You're tense. Is something wrong?" Rokshan asked.

"Just regretting giving up my own form of justice." She slowed her speed until she could alight neatly on the roof ridge. The courtyard, while still not as full as it used to be, was still busier than it had been the night before. Bromargyrite's arms and head extended from the doorway of the embassy, and he was watching Abhit read to Rassika and Kavari. Coquina was barely visible in the depths of the dining pavilion. A few humans were serving themselves from the soup caul-dron, casting wary glances at the dragons, but the mood was remark-ably placid considering what had happened just a couple of thousand beats before.

Lamprophyre climbed down from the roof carefully beside the dining pavilion and let Rokshan hop down. Coquina glanced over at her, then returned her attention to the cow she was eating. "Depik said he could cook two as easily as one," she said, "so I feel no guilt at eating your supper."

Depik looked up from the trolley, where lay a perfectly butchered and cooked half-eaten cow. He didn't look as if he'd ever been injured. "My lady!" he exclaimed. He looked past her, then out the front of the pavilion. "Where's Bhakriya?"

"She wanted to walk back from the judiciary building alone," Lamprophyre said. "Everything will be all right, except Preyanka had to go to the ecclesiasts."

"That was necessary, Lamprophyre," Rokshan said. "Can I have some soup? I'm starving."

Depik was holding his knife like a weapon. "But they took her. I couldn't stop them." He looked away. "He hurt her, didn't he?"

"He did. She's a survivor, Depik. She denounced Jagen and he's in the holding cells pending trial. In a few days she'll stand before a judge and receive a divorce." Rokshan gripped Depik's shoulder and made the man look at him. "You need to honor that."

Lamprophyre didn't know what that meant, but Depik seemed to. "I do," he said. "I will."

"And if you two were pair-bonded, that would be wonderful," Lamprophyre said impulsively.

Depik smiled and shook his head. "Too soon, my lady," he said. "I'm not interested in burdening her more, and I'm not as reliable as I'd like yet. She knows what I'd do for her and hers, and that's enough."

"And no suggesting it to Bhakriya, Lamprophyre," Rokshan said. "Let things happen as they will."

Disappointed, Lamprophyre said, "I know, but you humans are so short-lived, you shouldn't waste any of the years you have."

Both men laughed. "I'll bring out your food in a bit, my lady, it just needs to finish cooking," Depik said.

"And I'll watch over the soup pot until Bhakriya gets here," Rokshan said.

"I take it no one attacked?" Lamprophyre asked Coquina.

"It's been this quiet for a thousand beats." Coquina tore off another mouthful. "The healers came to help Depik, and once he was well, the other humans lost interest. Bromargyrite played with the children for a while, and I took a couple of short flights to observe anyone who might try an attack. Everything's fine."

Lamprophyre stepped into the courtyard and surveyed the people waiting there. For a change, none of them were afraid of her, though the strangers never got too close. Rassika, supervising Kavari from the entrance to the embassy, nodded at her in a gesture far older than her years. The nod drew Abhit's attention, and he dropped his book, leaped to his feet, and sped toward Lamprophyre. "Where's Mama?" he demanded.

"She'll be here soon—actually, she's here now," Lamprophyre said, gesturing toward the street. Bhakriya's bruises looked worse than before, but she moved easily, and Lamprophyre reflected on how fortunate it was that Jagen hadn't broken any of her bones. Abhit ran to embrace his mother, who bent to hug him tightly. With as many people as were in the courtyard, Lamprophyre couldn't hear either of their thoughts, but that wasn't necessary. Bhakriya's smile said everything she was thinking.

"But he hit you, Mama, I should have stopped him!" Abhit was saying as the two returned to the courtyard.

"You did the right thing," Bhakriya said. "And it truly doesn't hurt much."

The smell of roasted cow became stronger, and Lamprophyre turned toward where Depik had rolled the trolley into the dining pavilion. "Suppertime, my lady," he said. He saw Bhakriya and stood perfectly still. His thoughts were both close enough and clear enough that they cut through the background noise despite how they ran together in his rage: *should have killed how dare she looks* and a sweeping red haze of fury that dizzied Lamprophyre so much she had to block everything.

Lamprophyre heard Bhakriya approaching, and she stepped back to allow her to pass. Bhakriya stood before Depik, whose expression was impassive and whose only movement was a convulsive clenching of his fist. "You tried to stop them," she said. "Thanks to you, Abhit got away. I'm so sorry I wasted your sacrifice."

"It was nothing." Depik's hand twitched as if he wanted to touch the side of her jaw, which was still puffy. "I wish I'd done more. God's breath, Bhakriya, what kind of man could do this?"

Bhakriya rather self-consciously touched her swollen eye. "An evil man, and one I'm well rid of," she said. "And I'd welcome another thousand bruises if they were evidence of his evil. I chose not to be healed so I'd have an even better chance with a judge. Don't pity me."

"I would never," Depik said. "You're braver than me."

Bhakriya laughed. "We both took a beating today," she said. "I'm not sure we should compete for which of us was braver. I'm so glad you were healed." She hesitated for half a beat, then put her arms around Depik. Startled, Depik returned her gesture, his eyes wide and fixed on Lamprophyre. She risked listening in briefly and was cheered at what she heard: Depik astonished but pleased, and Bhakriya filled with contentment. That was the next best thing to love, at least to Lamprophyre's mind. She looked away and pretended not to notice.

After a few beats, the two humans released each other, and Depik cleared his throat. "Dishes," he said. "Unless you want to serve?"

"I know I look terrible, and I'd rather not be stared at," Bhakriya said, and touched her swollen eye gingerly again. "Besides, I'd welcome something so normal as washing up."

Lamprophyre settled herself beside the trolley and tore into her cow. Depik had used a different seasoning this time, and she liked the change. The dining pavilion was crowded with both her and Coquina in it, but it was nice to share that closeness with a friend. "Did Bromargyrite eat?" she asked.

"He said he'd wait until I finished. Stones, but this is delicious." Coquina let out a cheerful belch she didn't bother to control or conceal.

Rokshan returned with his bowl of soup and settled next to Lamprophyre. "I'm having trouble relaxing," he said. "So much has happened, it's hard to think Bhakriya's troubles are over. Mostly over. The ones involving the possibility of someone finding her family and taking them away."

"But we have a different problem now, which is we still don't know what the ecclesiasts are looking for and they're still committed to calling dragons evil," Lamprophyre said.

Coquina shifted her weight and burped again. "We don't? I thought the ecclesiasts wanted Preyanka."

Lamprophyre explained what she'd learned from the Third Ecclesiast's thoughts. "I wish I'd heard more," she concluded. "I'm certain the Third Ecclesiast knows what they're searching for. Or who."

"If we could find Khadar, that might be as helpful," Rokshan said. "*I* wish I knew why he's hiding in the Archprelate's palace. It's not as if he knows his thoughts are vulnerable to being overheard."

"And the Third Ecclesiast was agitated enough by my questions I'm sure it will benefit us to beat them to finding whatever it is." Lamprophyre chewed slowly, thinking hard. "Maybe we need to approach another of the ecclesiasts in the street. Though...no, that would be pointless. There are so many other people surrounding them I can't hear their thoughts over the noise of the crowd."

"How are you not exhausted, Lamprophyre?" Rokshan asked. "I'm too weary to make plans. Let's just enjoy a good night's sleep, and figure out the next step in the morning."

Now that he mentioned it, Lamprophyre did feel rather tired. "I suppose I feel it's become a race. The Third Ecclesiast isn't stupid, is she?"

"She's extremely intelligent. Far smarter than Khadar."

"So she knows *we* know they're searching for something, even though they kept that search secret. And if she's intelligent, she'll want to step up their search in case our knowledge means we're looking for whatever it is, too. Which we are."

"Even so, Rokshan's right that there's nothing we can do about it tonight," Coquina said. She stretched and picked up the remains of the cow carcass. "I'm taking this to Bromargyrite, and then I'm heading for my warehouse, unless you still need me?"

"I think the danger is over. Thank you for helping."

Coquina shrugged. "I find I'm more attached to these humans than I first expected when I came to Tanajital." Her expression stilled. "Though maybe that was a mistake, since it got Melika hurt."

"Humans aren't forced to serve dragons," Rokshan said. "Melika chose to help because you're her friend, and that's what friends do for each other. Don't diminish her choice by blaming yourself for what happened."

Coquina's expression became thoughtful. "That makes sense," she said. "Good night, and I'll see you both in the morning."

Lamprophyre watched her walk over to the embassy and sighed. "I never thought we'd be friends again. Never thought I *wanted* to be friends again. Life is so strange sometimes." She watched as the old man stood, leaving his empty bowl on the ground as he always did, and walked away down the street, his bent body looking frail and yet determined on the unswerving path he took.

Rokshan drained the last drops of soup and leaned against her flank. "I should go before I fall asleep here." Despite his words, he made no move to rise.

"You could sleep in one of the servants' houses," Lamprophyre said.

"I like that plan."

"It means you have to get up, Rokshan."

Groaning, Rokshan pushed himself to his feet. He moved rather stiffly, and Lamprophyre, suddenly remembering, said, "You're hurt! Why didn't you say anything?"

"I'm not hurt badly. Just stiff." Rokshan stretched until his joints popped. Lamprophyre shuddered, and he grinned at her. "Sometimes I do that just to see the look on your face."

"Really?" Lamprophyre shifted so her face was close to his. "Well, sometimes I ask questions I know will embarrass you. Like, why was Depik thinking about how warm his body got when Bhakriya—"

"Don't ask," Rokshan said, blushing. "I give up. You win."

"Dragons always win," Lamprophyre said smugly.

CHAPTER THIRTY

Lamprophyre rose late the next morning. She still felt tired, as if nothing about her sleep had been restful even though she had had some very pleasant dreams about flying with Rokshan through the mountain heights. In the dream, the air had been warm, not hot and sticky like the lowlands or bitter cold like the real heights, and they had flown until Rokshan had leaped from her shoulders and flown away under his own power. At the time, it had seemed the most natural thing in the world, but now Lamprophyre reflected on it and wondered why she hadn't imagined Rokshan with wings.

Everyone seemed dull that morning. Depik wasn't there when Lamprophyre entered the dining pavilion; only Bhakriya and Rassika were in the kitchen, which smelled of porridge and not delicious broiled cow. "I tried to rouse Depik, my lady, but he groaned and wouldn't look at me," Bhakriya said.

"He's just ill. It will pass by afternoon," Lamprophyre said, trying to sound patient, though she was actually a little resentful of having to cook her own meal on a day like this when she didn't want to exert herself to do anything.

Gradually, the rest of her...what could she call it, this strange collection of humans she'd acquired? Not a family, because she had a family and the humans were, except for Rokshan, too humble in their speaking to her to be considered true equals. Household? She'd heard Anamika's mother refer to her family that way—not just the people, but their property and responsibilities. That sounded right. Her household.

That reminded her that she hadn't seen Anamika, or any of the neighborhood children who usually visited her, since the ecclesiasts' decree had driven everyone away. She'd tried to talk to Anamika's father and been shooed off, politely but firmly. That ought to be reassuring, that at least they didn't hate her, but the memory just made her angrier at the ecclesiasts.

At any rate, her household gradually arose and gathered in the kitchen for breakfast. Rokshan appeared last, moving more stiffly than he had the night before, his eyes bleary and his hair in disarray. "You look awful," Lamprophyre said. "And I think you lied to me about how badly hurt you were."

"It wasn't a lie," Rokshan said, "and it wasn't so bad until my muscles stiffened up. I just need food and a chance to move around. There's really only a few bruises." He smiled. "I'm sure the men Depik and I thrashed can't say the same."

"You're sure Depik will be all right?" Bhakriya asked. Though the swelling in her eye and jaw had gone down, her bruises were even more startlingly vivid than before.

"This happens sometimes," Lamprophyre said. "Less than it used to, but he's still always embarrassed about it. So don't draw attention to it when he finally gets up."

"I understand." Bhakriya's thoughts said she didn't actually understand, but Lamprophyre knew enough about humans to recognize when they meant they accepted something even though they didn't understand it.

She flew the short distance to the butcher's where Depik usually bought her meat and paid for a cow, which she then roasted in the courtyard because the dining pavilion was full of humans. Kavari watched her in childish awe, her thoughts full of fiery butterflies, and the child's peaceful thoughts soothed Lamprophyre's irritation. She ate, set the carcass aside for Depik to dispose of when he recovered, and washed her face and hands at the rain barrel.

"I feel better," she told Rokshan as he climbed up to the notch behind her shoulders.

"I wish I did," Rokshan said with a grunt. "Don't worry, it will pass."

The flight to the warehouses seemed to take longer than usual, and not just because Lamprophyre flew slowly. She watched a couple of yellow litters pass below them and thought once more about accosting them. "Pointless," she muttered.

"What was that?" Rokshan said.

"I was just saying it would be pointless to try to get an ecclesiast to talk."

"We need a new approach," Rokshan said. "And...huh. It occurs to me I haven't seen Dharan in several days. I hope he's all right."

"Why wouldn't he be all right?"

"He's more or less an unbeliever. Some people might think that makes him fair game, if the ecclesiasts are stirring everyone up to think in terms of being worthy of Jiwanyil's love."

That worried Lamprophyre. "Should we look for him?"

"I think maybe we should," Rokshan said. "Let's talk to the others first, maybe make a plan, and then—"

Lamprophyre peered ahead at the warehouses. "Actually, it looks like he found us."

Dharan was, in fact, at the warehouses when they arrived, talking to Porphyry. Porphyry's excited thoughts were audible from several dragonlengths away. "Lamprophyre, the book of poetry," he said before she'd fully touched earth. "Dharan says it's going to be printed!"

"But who would do that, if we're outcast?" Lamprophyre said.

"Not everyone believes the ecclesiasts are right," Dharan said. "Among them is a printer I know. She's agreed to print the book and have it bound. We just have to decide how to distribute it."

"That's remarkable," Rokshan said. "Is that what you've been doing all this time?"

"That, and researching your prophecy." Dharan's smile fell away.

"It's been difficult, and not in the fun way. I think the Hall of Visions is close to banning me."

Puzzled, Lamprophyre said, "Did you do too many heathenish things? Because I can imagine they wouldn't like that."

"No, it's that they've started to deduce what I'm after, and I get the feeling they don't want anyone looking into that prophecy." Dharan turned to Rokshan. "Will it disturb you if I say that my printer friend is not the only person questioning the ecclesiasts?"

"Not the way you probably think," Rokshan said. "We think the ecclesiasts lied about that decree coming from Jiwanyil. I'd like to believe people can feel the truth of God's prophecies, so it makes sense that some people would feel the inherent wrongness of a false one."

Dharan's eyes were wide. "God's breath," he said. "I never thought I'd hear you say anything like that. What brought you to that conclusion?"

"A lot of little things, plus Khadar being uncharacteristically uncertain on the subject. We want to find a way to prove that prophecy false, or to force the High Ecclesiasts to recant."

Dharan was utterly silent. Lamprophyre didn't need to break her rule about not listening to her close friends' thoughts to know what he was thinking, because his face was utterly astonished. "I don't think I can call myself a heathen ever again, now that I know what it really looks like," he finally said. "How can I help?"

"First, I want to know what you learned in the Hall of Visions," Rokshan said. "It worries me that the ecclesiasts might want to prevent people knowing of a prophecy."

"And we've heard a prophecy about that subject that won't be in the Hall of Visions," Lamprophyre said. "I forgot to tell you because everything was so chaotic, Rokshan, but Preyanka was possessed of a prophecy that ended with 'the skies will burn.'"

"Do you remember the rest of it?"

"I'm a dragon, Rokshan, of course I remember." Lamprophyre sat back and cleared her throat. "*Find the lost. That which is spoken by the old stone is true and false, and the hearers wander like lambs. Faith is not enough. The skies will burn.*"

Flint and Coquina poked their heads out of their warehouses as she spoke, probably because the cadence of her voice was the one she used when reciting poetry. They came to join the little group outside Porphyry's warehouse, listening closely. When Lamprophyre finished, Flint said, "Was that a prophecy? Are they all so oblique?"

"It's less oblique than some, at least to me," Rokshan said. "The ecclesiasts are looking for something or someone who's lost. And then there's 'faith is not enough.' We've already decided that unquestioning faith about the ecclesiasts' decree isn't enough for a real believer."

"Wandering like lambs—how do lambs wander?" Coquina asked.

"I don't know. It's outside my experience. Dharan?" Rokshan said.

"I'm a city boy, too, so I have no idea," Dharan said. "But infant creatures in general follow whoever looks like an authority figure. A parent, or a spiritual leader. So it might mean people wandering without clear direction."

"Which is sort of what's happening now," Lamprophyre said. "Some people following the ecclesiasts, some not knowing who to listen to."

"It's 'old stone' that makes me curious," Flint said. "If this were a prophecy for dragons, it might mean an old dragon. An old dragon giving advice. Remember when Gabbro was in the first stage of his decline? He would talk about things that never happened and refused to believe us when we repeated what he'd said. That's like an old stone speaking true and false."

"But it's a human prophecy. What could an old stone that speaks mean to humans?" Lamprophyre asked.

"It could mean someone well-respected, someone with experience," Dharan said.

Rokshan opened his mouth, then closed it again rapidly. "No," he said. "It—suppose it means the Archprelate?"

"That makes sense," Lamprophyre said.

Rokshan was shaking his head. "But the prophecy says the old stone speaks true and false. The Archprelate is without question the human closest to Jiwanyil, and his prophecies have always been true ones."

"There's the current decree, though," Dharan said.

"Ayusha claimed responsibility for that one. If anyone's lying, she is." Rokshan squeezed his eyes tight shut and let out a deep breath. "I can't believe I just suggested the Third Ecclesiast lied about a prophecy. Regardless, I refuse to believe the Archprelate is anything but faithful to God."

"Well, what if the 'old stone' isn't a person?" Porphyry said. "What if it's your religion? You already know some of the ecclesiasts are faithful, and their prophecies are true, and you know that at least one prophecy is false—that could be the old stone speaking true and false."

"I actually like that interpretation," Dharan said. "For what my opinion's worth."

"It does make sense," Rokshan said. "So, as far as we can tell, Preyanka was possessed of a prophecy that instructs the hearers to find what is lost. It contains a warning that some authority is speaking both truth and falsehood, and probably that's causing the people to wander without clear direction. It says that faith is not enough. And that the skies will burn."

Everyone was silent for several beats. Finally, Lamprophyre said, "None of that seems related to the final sentence. Unless it means that we have to resolve the puzzle or the result is the skies will burn."

"Wait," Dharan said. "Every time that phrase occurs in a prophecy, it's the final sentence."

"Is that significant?" Rokshan asked.

Dharan shrugged. "I don't know. But it's always the final sentence. It's possible each of those prophecies is like this one—a puzzle to solve. And the reason 'the skies will burn' makes no sense in most of them is that it's a promise, maybe. Or a result. Something the prophecy either points toward, or is intended to thwart." He patted his chest a few times. "Damn. I left my blank book at home. It has all the prophecies I copied down. I should add Preyanka's prophecy to the list, and look at all of them in this new light."

"Not to be critical, but is this important right now?" Coquina asked. "It doesn't have any direct bearing on the problem at hand. We need to find a way to thwart the ecclesiasts."

"No, you're right," Dharan said, "but it is something concrete I can deal with."

A few dragonlengths away, Dolomite emerged from his warehouse.

"What time is it? Midmorning?" He groaned. "I hate oversleeping. It makes me feel like I weigh as much as a mountain, all day long." He stretched, spreading his wings wide. "Did I tell you what I saw yesterday? I can't remember."

"We haven't seen you since yesterday morning," Flint said.

"Oh, right." Dolomite ambled toward them. "The ecclesiasts are doubling up on their patterns. There are two ecclesiasts walking each one."

"That's odd," Flint said.

"Not if they were afraid one set of eyes wasn't enough," Coquina said. "Dolomite, you really need to take a break from watching the ecclesiasts. You're going to exhaust yourself."

"That's probably why I slept so late," Dolomite agreed. "But I do like flying, and it's fun to watch the ecclesiasts and know they know I'm up there and they can't do anything about it."

"That may be the nastiest thing I've ever heard you say, Dolomite," Lamprophyre said.

Dolomite laughed. "I don't like them. They're rude and they've frightened people. And they leave papers cluttering up the streets."

"Them and every would-be tangal performer and civic improver in Tanajital," Rokshan said sourly. "It's such a waste of paper, all those handbills."

"I thought the ecclesiasts put their handbills on the sides of buildings, not threw them around the streets," Lamprophyre said.

Dolomite shrugged. "I don't know whether it's usual, but they were throwing out papers by the handful yesterday evening. It was just before I came back for the night, when they were all headed for the Archprelate's palace. Wait a moment." He walked back to his warehouse and returned with a large, by human standards, sheet of paper held between two claws. Rokshan took it from him and scanned its contents. Lamprophyre could only tell that it had JIWANYIL'S BELOVED! printed across the top in big, bold letters and smaller printing in two columns below that, filling the page.

"Interesting," Rokshan said. "The ecclesiasts have declared this coming Jiwanyisan—that's two days from now—a day of holiness and peaceful gathering. They're going to hold a special meeting of prayer and contemplation in the coliseum that evening. The intent is to pray for the souls of the outcasts in the city, human and dragon."

Coquina snorted, sending up a puff of smoke. "How generous of them."

"Oh, but this is perfect," Rokshan said, handing the paper to Dharan to read. "All those High Ecclesiasts and the Archprelate in one place, all of them potentially thinking about what they're searching for...it's ideal."

"I thought you said the Archprelate lives in seclusion," Lamprophyre said.

"Lives in, yes, but he always leads these special ceremonies." Rokshan looked as satisfied as if he had arranged for the day of prayer himself. "It's the perfect time to discover what we need to know."

"That assumes we'll be welcome, as outcasts," Lamprophyre said.

"We don't have to attend." Rokshan gripped her shoulder. "Trust me, I've attended many of these before. We just have to fly close enough to the ecclesiasts."

"That's true," Lamprophyre said, brightening. "And if the ecclesiasts don't think the right thoughts, we can get Khadar alone and worm it out of him."

"You sound like that would be your preferred outcome," Coquina said with a smile.

"It almost is. Khadar annoys me."

"He annoys everyone," Rokshan said. "And I think we have a plan."

CHAPTER THIRTY-ONE

Two days later, Lamprophyre circled high above the coliseum and watched it fill with humans. At that distance, the humans weren't distinguishable as individuals, but instead resembled flowing, bubbling black oil, streaming through the largest streets. When the oil reached the wide thoroughfare surrounding the coliseum, its movement slowed as thousands of people all tried to enter at once through the tiny doorways leading to the stands.

"My parents aren't here yet," Rokshan said.

"How can you possibly tell from up here?"

"When a member of the royal family is in attendance, they fly the banner of our family. It's green and yellow and hideous, but it's also instantly recognizable. I'm betting on them not making a spectacle of their entrance, given that this is a religious ceremony."

Lamprophyre flew in a slightly wider circle that passed the palace. "I think that's the king's litter down there."

She felt Rokshan shift to look over her shoulder. "It is. Let's see if the High Ecclesiasts have arrived."

Someone had erected a platform like the one the king used halfway between the royal box and the center of the coliseum floor. This left a great open space, fully half of the coliseum grounds, as empty as if the

High Ecclesiasts wanted dragons to attend. Well, maybe they did want that. Lamprophyre didn't care.

She swooped lower, down to where individual humans were visible like bustling black and brown ants. She couldn't tell if any of them were looking up, and their thoughts were a seething mass of curiosity and fear and anxiety, but she felt certain that even the ones who knew she and her clutchmates were there didn't want to look at them, in case that violated the ecclesiasts' decree. Stupid ecclesiasts.

She looked off toward the palace. The litter—two litters now, so probably the king and queen—drove an open path right down the middle of the widest street leading to the coliseum. Ants stopped to bow as the litters passed by, backing away to the sides of the street and then following slowly in the litters' wake.

Lamprophyre saw the banner Rokshan had described, waving limply in the heavy, still air Lamprophyre wished meant a nice storm was coming. Though it was probably just as well there was no storm due until evening, because what the dragons didn't need was an interruption that might mean the High Ecclesiasts would cancel their prayer ceremony. She didn't think green and yellow were ugly; they reminded her of the dragon Sapphire, who'd taught her so many poems and stories before he rejoined Mother Stone.

She flew another couple of circles while she waited for the litters to reach the coliseum and for the king and queen to ascend to the stairs. But finally the green and yellow banner flew atop the royal box, and Lamprophyre dove for the open space of the coliseum grounds.

She'd flown high enough not to be able to hear the noise of the crowds, but as she descended, she heard a dull murmur, much quieter than she'd expected. It reminded her of the sound the city made late at night, when almost everyone was abed and the city's voice rumbled, low and peaceful. "Why is it so quiet?" she asked Rokshan.

"It's a day of peaceful, prayerful contemplation," Rokshan reminded her. "Everyone is trying to maintain a spirit of holiness by not chattering to their neighbors or shouting to get someone's attention."

"It's nice. I hate to admit that."

Rokshan put a hand flat on her shoulder. "Remember that almost everyone here believes they're in harmony with Jiwanyil, and has good intentions in wanting dragons to embrace Katayan. That's what makes me angry, that they've all been lied to and are turning their spiritual energies toward a false prophecy."

Lamprophyre nodded. "We'll change that. I know we will."

As she descended, the noise diminished further until Lamprophyre could hear the quiet, united breathing of thousands of humans, all staring at her. She looked out across the sea of brown faces, all of them too distant for her to easily make out expressions. Their thoughts were still too chaotic to understand, but the crowd lacked the restless movement that would indicate anger or an incipient riot. She'd been afraid of being shouted at or assaulted—not frightened of those things, neither of which could hurt her, but afraid that the humans' anger and fear of dragons and what they represented might make it impossible for her to learn what she'd come here to learn.

The platform looked a lot more permanent and a lot more gaudy than the king's. Five colored banners hung along its front, green, red, black, white, and blue, each of them bearing an embroidered picture. Lamprophyre recognized the willow tree on the green banner; it reminded her of Khadar's robe. And there was a tiger's face stitched on the red banner that looked just like the ones on the Third Ecclesiast's robe. It was easy to guess that each banner represented one of the High Ecclesiasts, or maybe the god each of the High Ecclesiasts spoke for. Though that didn't tell Lamprophyre where the Archprelate's banner was, or what it might look like.

Stairs at the back led up to the top of the platform. Lined up down its center were five chairs, all of them gilded with real gold whose scent made Lamprophyre wish she'd eaten more at breakfast. Five chairs. That made no sense. There should be six. "Rokshan," she murmured, not wanting to disturb the silence, "why—"

Trumpets blared to the right and left. The sudden noise startled Lamprophyre into an upward jerk she straightened out of immediately, not wanting to look like she was afraid. A litter shrouded in green silk entered through a door beneath the royal box. Lamprophyre heard a sigh as of thousands of voices breathing out in unison. The litter circled the coliseum floor once, and then its bearers headed for the platform and the stairs at its rear.

The litter made a neat turn next to the stairs so its long side faced them, and the bearers set down their burden. Khadar stepped out. He tilted his head to look at Lamprophyre circling above, shielding his eyes from the late afternoon sunlight. Lamprophyre tried to listen to his thoughts, but couldn't pick them out from the background noise. If that would be the case for all the High Ecclesiasts, this plan might fail before it had even started.

Lamprophyre chose to ignore her pessimistic thought. Watching Khadar closely, she perched on one of the red stone arches and furled her wings. Rokshan gripped her ruff more tightly as her position tilted him backward sharply, but he felt secure to her. She would see if Khadar would denounce her, or get back into his litter and leave, cancelling the ceremony.

Khadar continued to watch her. Lamprophyre listened to the crowd's thoughts briefly before the cacophony deafened her; they were wary and angry, and fragments of words like *dare* and *monster* and *get rid* floated through them like bits of sharp ice in a wintry stream. But they remained mostly silent. She thought they, too, were waiting to see what Khadar did.

After a dozen beats, Khadar's gaze fell away. He lifted his robe a few inches and began ascending the stairs, taking slow, measured steps. When he reached the top, he walked to the left end of the row of chairs and stood before the last one with his hands clasped behind his back. Lamprophyre once more tried to hear his thoughts and once more failed to hear anything but noise.

As soon as Khadar had stopped moving, the bearers carried the litter away, and another litter, this one with fluttering sapphire-blue curtains, emerged from the same door Khadar's had. It, too, made a circle around the coliseum before stopping at the foot of the stairs. A woman with very dark brown skin wearing a bright blue robe matching the curtains stepped out. She didn't pay any attention to Lamprophyre, just climbed to the platform and took up a position in front of the rightmost chair. Her black hair was cropped close to her head the way the Third Ecclesiast's had been, but Lamprophyre was too far away to make out the details of her features, or determine whether she was old or young.

She had been staring at the woman, so she'd missed the entrance of the Third Ecclesiast's litter and her ascent of the stairs. The woman strode more confidently than either of the other two, and stopped in front of the chair next to Khadar's with a brisk turn that made her red robe swirl out around her. She was a lot shorter than Khadar, but her presence was so powerful it made her seem to tower over him. Khadar shifted slightly, bowing his head toward her, and Lamprophyre thought he might have been speaking to her. If he was, she didn't respond in any way, and finally Khadar straightened again and stared out over the crowds.

The next litter was draped in white, and the man who climbed out of it was enormous by human standards, very fat and, as Lamprophyre discovered when he stood next to the blue-clad woman, very tall. His white robe and the banner hanging in front of his chair were embroidered with a dragon's head, sketched out roughly the way Dolomite might begin a portrait. It was only the suggestion of a dragon, but its lines contained so much pent-up power Lamprophyre felt moved by it. Katayan might not be real, but humans definitely respected him.

Finally, a black-draped litter that looked like a moving ink blot circled the coliseum, and a black-clad man stepped out to climb the stairs and take the central position. Unlike the other four, whose robes were embroidered with recognizable pictures, the black robe and its matching banner bore a complex sigil in copper and gold embroidery. If this one represented Jiwanyil, God of humans, maybe nobody wanted to see representations of human figures as his symbol. Or maybe they'd tried, and the pictures looked stupid.

Lamprophyre regarded the last man closely. His skin was a lighter, more coppery brown than the other four, and he wore his black hair long for a human male, swept back from his face and clasped at the nape of his neck in a way that reminded Lamprophyre unpleasantly of Nevrita. He regarded the crowd for a moment, turning his head for his gaze to sweep the stands as far as possible without turning around. There might be some symbolism in the way the High Ecclesiasts had their backs to the royal box, but Lamprophyre felt tense and on edge and didn't want to ask irrelevant questions of Rokshan, not when she was still curious about the missing sixth seat.

As one, the High Ecclesiasts took their seats, and another sigh rose up from the watching crowd. Lamprophyre saw the central figure—the First Ecclesiast, perhaps?—tilt his head toward the Third Ecclesiast, who didn't look at him. For several beats, the entire coliseum was as still as if it were empty. A breeze brushed Lamprophyre's furled wings, bringing temporary relief from the heat. She didn't want to speak, and break the heavy, oppressive silence.

Finally, the First Ecclesiast nodded. He rose from his seat and walked to the front of the platform. "This gathering is a place of holiness and peaceful worship," he said. His voice carried throughout the coliseum, as loud and clear as if he and Lamprophyre were in a small room together. Lamprophyre caught the glint of a stone hanging around his neck, distant enough she couldn't smell it. Another glance showed that all the High Ecclesiasts wore similar stones. Voice amplifying artifacts. How useful.

"It is also intended for Jiwanyil's faithful, and not for those who reject his word," the First Ecclesiast was saying. "But Jiwanyil's forgiveness extends to all who reject their evil ways and embrace his light. We invite all such to attend." He looked directly at Lamprophyre. "Join us, if you are here in peace and honor."

"Stones. What do we do?" Lamprophyre asked Rokshan.

"Go down there, of course."

"But we aren't here in peace and honor!"

"Lamprophyre," Rokshan said with some amusement, "neither are they, really."

Lamprophyre blushed. She'd forgotten why they were there. The First Ecclesiast had sounded so very reasonable. She opened her wings and stepped off the arch to glide neatly to the big open space. Getting closer to the High Ecclesiasts was good. Close enough, it wouldn't matter what the crowd was thinking. "Stay there," she told Rokshan. "If this goes bad, we'll want to be able to leave in a hurry."

"O ye who are faithful, pray with me," the First Ecclesiast said. He held his arms out wide above his head so he looked like the letter Y.

"May Jiwanyil's grace overflow upon us. His light shines in dark places, bringing us to his presence. Let us be one."

The crowd responded as one, possibly repeating his last four words; with all of them speaking, the words weren't more than a jumbled din that would have been a roar if the people hadn't spoken so quietly. Lamprophyre, caught off guard, said nothing. Then she remembered she didn't really want to take part in this ceremony.

The First Ecclesiast was looking at her with a disappointed expression. "Let us remember God's blessing of creation," he said, addressing the crowd though he was still staring at her. "From the Immanence arose the Five Gods."

On the word "arose" the other High Ecclesiasts stood and walked to the front of the platform. Khadar raised his hands as the First Ecclesiast had. "The Immanence gathered, and life arose," he said, his voice sounding unnaturally nasal through the effect of his voice-amplifying artifact. "Thus came Meyari, God of the Living World."

"Meyari," the crowd echoed. This time, Lamprophyre could make out the word.

The blue-clad woman at the opposite end raised her arms. "Life needed a foundation, and the mountains arose," she said. Her voice was high-pitched and pleasant, like birdsong. "Thus came Nirinatan, God of the Living Stone."

"Nirinatan," the crowd repeated.

The Third Ecclesiast raised her arms. It didn't make her look any larger. "The mountains cried out for children, and animals arose," she said in a resonant voice Lamprophyre could almost believe could fill the coliseum unaided. "Thus came Vrelok, God of the Living Creatures."

Lamprophyre glanced around as the crowd said, "Vrelok." Many of the humans had their eyes closed. Some were swaying as if to music only they could hear. This part of the ceremony struck her as a formality, something to invoke the gods. If it were a dragon ceremony, it would be over already. She would have been bored if she weren't so anxious about the possibility of learning the truth about the ecclesiasts' search. If only they would move on!

The large man in white said, "The creatures of the world needed to be kept in check. Thus came Katayan, God of the Living Fire."

That was different. The sound of the name "Katayan" echoed off the walls. Why humans had landed on a characteristic of only female dragons to identify their made-up male dragon god, she didn't know, though fire was definitely more dramatic visually than acid.

The First Ecclesiast, who hadn't lowered his hands the whole time, said, "The dragons needed someone who could control their baser desires. Thus came Jiwanyil, God of the Living Man."

Lamprophyre shifted, feeling uncomfortable and irritated all at once. Baser desires? If she hadn't already believed that at least some of the human religion was false, that would certainly prove it.

The High Ecclesiasts lowered their arms, and all of them but the Third Ecclesiast returned to their seats. The Third Ecclesiast took a few steps until she was opposite Lamprophyre. "You don't like hearing the truth," she said.

"I don't like being told I'm inferior to any species as a whole," Lamprophyre retorted. "And I certainly don't believe I have any baser desires for humans to control. That doesn't make any sense." She sounded much louder than she was used to, and guessed she was close enough to the Third Ecclesiast's artifact for it to amplify her voice, too.

The Third Ecclesiast tilted her head to one side. "You challenge our faith on this holy day?"

Lamprophyre felt the conversation slipping away from her. "I don't mean to. I just want to know what you intend. Your decree has hurt so many people. I don't know why you wanted that."

"We will not argue with the faithless, especially not on this day. Participate in silence, or show the respect you claim you have and leave."

Lamprophyre stood, prompting a murmur from the crowd. "Yet you don't respect us," she said, and listened for the Third Ecclesiast's thoughts. She heard mostly the massed din of the watching worshippers, but over that, closer words: *respect nothing why listen they must be stopped.*

"We respect those who repent of their mistaken ways to serve their true God," the Third Ecclesiast was saying. Lamprophyre barely heard her audible words because she was listening hard to their thoughts. She'd begun to hear other mental voices as the rest of the High Ecclesiasts leaned forward to pay attention to this conversation. *Don't know,* one thought, and another thought *bring to truth.*

She focused briefly on Khadar and heard, to her surprise, uncertainty and fear. Why those emotions? They weren't shared by his fellows. *Can't believe, find the lost, not what I thought* came to her mind.

"Can I ask a question? Not a rude question," she said, cutting off the Third Ecclesiast without hearing her words at all. "Why isn't the Archprelate here to lead this ceremony?"

"The Archprelate chooses to remain in isolation that his prayers on behalf of the people of Gonjiri will remain pure," the Third Ecclesiast said.

Khadar's thoughts became more agitated. *Find the lost.*

Lamprophyre almost let out a cry of surprise. Swallowing her own agitation, she said, "I'm afraid I don't understand how that's possible. Surely he should go among the people, to know their needs?"

"Jiwanyil tells him everything he needs to know," the Third Ecclesiast snapped. "Do not blaspheme."

"It's a fair question, Ayusha," Rokshan said. "Lamprophyre means no disrespect."

"I think you should leave," the Third Ecclesiast said. "You have disrupted the peace and holiness of this meeting."

"I think we should, too," Lamprophyre said quickly. Her guess filled her with excitement and fear, and she wanted to discuss it with Rokshan as soon as possible. "I'm sorry we disturbed you." It was only a tiny lie. She needed to be careful not to fall into the habit.

She backed away so she wouldn't knock anyone off the platform with the wind from her wings, and took to the sky. Her mind whirled. If she was right—but it had to be impossible. And why would Khadar, of all people, be the only one feeling uncertain and worried?

"I think that tiger woman is the real leader," she said. "The Third Ecclesiast."

"I told you she's got more experience than the others," Rokshan said. "But the First Ecclesiast has never been so overtly deferential to her before. He looked very uncertain of what to do about us." He leaned forward so she could hear him more clearly. "And Khadar was afraid of something, but I couldn't tell what."

"That's what I thought, too." It had to be the right answer, but it still didn't make sense. "He definitely knows who they're looking for. And I—but it's impossible."

"What is?" Rokshan asked.

"Let's land and discuss it. I'm tired of shouting."

The embassy courtyard hadn't yet filled up with people looking for a free meal. The aroma of soup had begun to fill the air, along with the scent of fresh raw meat. Lamprophyre gave the soup pot an idle stir and inhaled the delicious smell that wafted from it.

"So, talk," Rokshan said, sitting cross-legged beside Lamprophyre. "What's so impossible?"

Lamprophyre glanced at Depik, who'd retreated into the kitchen and wasn't paying them any attention. "When I asked where the Archprelate was, Khadar's thoughts became very worried, and he thought, 'Find the lost.' I know it sounds impossible, but..." She let out a deep breath. "I think it's the Archprelate they're looking for."

CHAPTER THIRTY-TWO

"That *is* impossible," Rokshan said. "In the first place, why would the Archprelate leave his palace, and in the second place, how could he get lost in Tanajital? Or, rather, why would he get lost, because even if he left, it's not like he can't find his way back."

"I don't know, Rokshan, I just know what I heard." Lamprophyre scooted to where she could look him in the eye. "It would explain why there are so many ecclesiasts in the streets, because the Archprelate is more important to them than anyone else in the city. Would the Archprelate have a reason to become lost? I mean lost as far as the other ecclesiasts are concerned. Like, if he's hiding."

"That makes no sense either. Why would the Archprelate hide?"

"Maybe he wants to get to know the people better," Lamprophyre said, "and he knows the High Ecclesiasts would be upset about that. Maybe he had a prophecy that told him to leave the Archprelate's palace. Maybe his life was threatened."

Rokshan shook his head. "No one would dream of hurting the Archprelate."

"Are you sure?" Lamprophyre shot back. "You know at least one High Ecclesiast is corrupt. What if she's corrupt enough to want to take his position? How is the Archprelate chosen, anyway? One of the High Ecclesiasts?"

"No, it's simpler than that." Rokshan stood and began pacing the stone floor of the pavilion. "The ecclesiasts come together after the death of the last Archprelate, and Jiwanyil's light shines on the one who's intended to become the new Archprelate."

"Actual light?"

"Actual light." Rokshan stopped pacing and rubbed the bridge of his nose with one hand. "Anyway, even if Ayusha were that corrupt, killing the Archprelate—I can't believe I just said those words—wouldn't guarantee her the position."

"Killing the Archprelate?" Depik exclaimed as he came out of the kitchen with a stack of bowls and a handful of spoons. "What are you talking about?"

"It's a long story," Lamprophyre said. "Is the soup ready? I'll carry it out."

She set the cauldron outside the pavilion and returned to her place. "I don't know if it matters why," she said, "but I'm very certain it's the right answer."

"I have to say I agree with you, impossible as it seems," Rokshan said. He helped himself to a bowl of soup and returned to his seat.

Lamprophyre inhaled the smell of cooking cow and wished it would cook faster. "So, what do we do? We can't find the Archprelate any better than the ecclesiasts. Worse, because we don't know what he looks like. Unless you've seen him."

"I know he's very old, but that's it," Rokshan said.

"And Tanajital may be small by dragon standards, but there are thousands of humans living here, and there are plenty of places we can't fit into. I don't know that we're any better off than we were a thousand beats ago." Lamprophyre shifted her weight and propped her elbows on the floor, resting her chin in her hands.

"We're better off because we know what we're looking for," Rokshan said, "even if we don't know where the Archprelate is."

"But we know where he isn't," Lamprophyre said, "thanks to Dolomite's exhaustive work. If he were in any of those streets, they'd have found him by now, especially now they've got multiple ecclesiasts searching each pattern. The only places they don't go are the academy, the slums, and here—"

She stopped as a memory caught her up, something she hadn't thought about at the time. "They don't come here, ever," she murmured. Rising, she stepped to the front of the pavilion and surveyed the courtyard. Beggars with soup bowls stood or sat, eating placidly despite her sudden appearance. There still weren't many of them by comparison to before the decree. She ignored the Sister of the Red, who pretended not to notice her in turn, and crossed the courtyard to the embassy, where the white-haired old man sat with his bowl.

She crouched low and searched her memory for something Khadar had told her, back when she'd first arrived in Tanajital. "Excuse me," she said to the old man, "Most Holy One?"

The old man stared vacantly at her, his eyes unfocused as if he didn't see her. His fractured thoughts were even less coherent than usual, a roiling soup of fragments of syllables and placidity. Lamprophyre sat on her haunches. It had been so obvious. Maybe that's why it was wrong, because life was never that perfect.

"Lamprophyre?" Rokshan said from behind her. "You didn't think *he*... Lamprophyre, the Archprelate isn't a decrepit madman!"

"It made so much sense," Lamprophyre said. "The ecclesiasts are looking for the Archprelate, and why couldn't that be because the Archprelate is helpless? What if that's why no one ever sees him?"

"That's blasphemy," Rokshan said, his voice cold. "There's no way Jiwanyil would allow his representative on earth to fall into such a state. It would mean Gonjiri couldn't receive God's word. Maybe you're right that the Archprelate is what the ecclesiasts are searching for, but it has to be because the Archprelate wants to be hidden."

"You're right," Lamprophyre said, feeling chastened. "I'm sorry. I didn't mean any insult."

"I know." Rokshan clapped her on the shoulder, as high as he could reach. "Look. Let's eat, and we can think about what to do next."

Lamprophyre nodded. She rose to her feet, but didn't move right away, instead looking down at the old man. His gaze was now fixed on a point in the distance, the way it did before he had one of his keening episodes. Lamprophyre gently took the bowl from his hands so he wouldn't drop it just half a beat before he grabbed the sides of his head and let out a thin, pained whine. Rocking in place, he closed his eyes and whimpered. It was such a helpless sound Lamprophyre's heart went out to him.

On impulse, she picked him up and carried him to the pavilion, where she set him down near the kitchen. The old man curled into a ball, holding his head and breathing in short, weeping gasps. Lamprophyre put her large hand beneath the old man's head, cushioning it from the hard stone. After a few beats, his restless motion stilled, and he lay quietly on the floor, his hands still cradling his head and his breathing still erratic. With his eyes still closed, he looked as if he'd fallen into a shallow, dreaming sleep.

"I wonder if we should take him to a healer," Lamprophyre said. "I don't know if they can do anything for a broken mind, though. And maybe it's been going on too long for them to help. But it might be worth the attempt."

"I'd say something about how you can't save everyone," Rokshan said, "but I know that won't stop you trying."

"I don't like watching people suffer." Lamprophyre gently withdrew her hand, hoping not to disturb the old man if he really was sleeping. But it wasn't gentle enough. He stirred and sat up, blinking. For the first time since she'd seen him, he focused on her, taking in her height and the spread of her wings as if they meant something to him. He moistened his dry lips with his tongue, which flicked in and out like a lizard's. Lamprophyre held very still. She didn't know what she was waiting for, but it felt like the world had stopped moving and was waiting, too, for what would happen next.

The old man closed his eyes and shuddered once, like a deer shaking off a fly. His breathing slowed into regularity. He shuddered once more, and opened his eyes.

They blazed with a vivid green light.

Lamprophyre gasped and stepped back, her eyes never leaving the old man's. Beside her, Rokshan let out a hiss of surprise. She stretched out her hand, feeling for his shoulder to steady herself. It was a mad impulse, because she was far more likely to knock him down, but in her amazement she felt the need for physical contact to remind her the world hadn't gone crazy.

The old man's eyes seemed to focus on her, though without pupil or iris it was impossible to be sure. There was just so much intent in his countenance she felt the weight of his gaze regardless. He licked his lips once more, working his mouth as if it had been a twelveday since he'd spoken. "*The voice speaks from darkness,*" a strange voice neither male nor female said. "*The faithful wander, lost despite familiar paths. Seek the chosen and destroy the link. Restore the lost.*" He took a deep breath and let it out in a long, thin stream. "*Man and dragon, listen and obey.*"

Lamprophyre's mouth fell open in astonishment. The old man closed his eyes and shuddered once more, then sagged as if exhausted. When he opened his eyes, they were their normal dark brown.

"God's breath," Rokshan said. Lamprophyre glanced his way, because he'd sounded like he might pass out. But he was staring at the old man, as stunned as she felt. "What am I saying?" he continued. "Literally God's breath. I don't understand. He's clearly senile, and yet he was possessed of a prophecy—one more comprehensible than any I've heard before."

"And it didn't hurt him the way it did Preyanka," Lamprophyre said. "What does it mean? Rokshan, it's your faith. What do we do now?"

Rokshan squatted next to the old man and tilted his head gently so he could look into the Archprelate's eyes. The Archprelate gazed back at him with his familiar vacant smile. Rokshan shook his head. "Clearly his mental state doesn't prevent him receiving Jiwanyil's word. But I can see why the ecclesiasts wouldn't want this getting out. People might question why Jiwanyil hasn't replaced him."

"Well, why *hasn't* Jiwanyil replaced him?" Lamprophyre asked. "I apologize if this is rude, Rokshan, but it feels almost like keeping a corpse moving, having him in this condition but still having prophecies."

"I don't know. I've never heard of a living Archprelate replaced. They always hold the position until they die." Rokshan rocked back on his heels, suddenly looking ill. "God's breath," he said. "They couldn't —but what if the High Ecclesiasts have prevented him being replaced because they want control?"

"I don't understand," Lamprophyre said. "If he's alive, he's the Archprelate, and we just saw him have a prophecy, so he's still in charge, right?"

"Unless the High Ecclesiasts are pretending to deliver instructions in his name," Rokshan said. "Instructions that benefit them. Like wanting all the dragons out of Tanajital." He shook his head. "No," he said, "no, Ayusha claimed responsibility for the prophecy making dragons outcast. And there haven't been any prophecies from the Archprelate for weeks. Whatever's going on, it's not that the High Ecclesiasts are using this frail old man to deceive the people."

"Except they are doing something," Lamprophyre said. "A voice speaking from darkness, a chosen someone who should be destroyed, leading the people astray...there's corruption somewhere, and I'm sure it's among the High Ecclesiasts. And Jiwanyil wants us to do something about it. Human and dragon working together."

"Well, we can't return him to the Archprelate's palace," Rokshan said. "He must have left for a reason, and it's almost certainly that he was in danger."

"Or that he was looking for help," Lamprophyre said. "What was that about 'man and dragon obey'? That prophecy was aimed at us as surely as if he'd spoken our names."

"It doesn't have to be us. It could mean it's for humans and dragons generally," Rokshan said, but he sounded as uncertain as she felt. That gaze, so intent and so piercing. The Archprelate had seen her somehow through those green eyes, and had addressed his prophecy to her. The thought made her extremely uncomfortable. She didn't want to be the focus of another religion's prophecy.

"All right," she said, seeing Rokshan's gaze turn on her, "he meant us. So what are we supposed to do?"

"Let's look at the prophecy one phrase at a time," Rokshan said. "The most obvious one is that the faithful wander. The ecclesiasts, maybe just the High Ecclesiasts, are giving them false guidance."

"So even though they're following as they always do—down familiar paths—they're lost," Lamprophyre said. "We already guessed this."

"But combined with 'seek the chosen', that suggests there's one person in particular doing it," Rokshan went on. "But I don't know what 'the link' might be."

"I think a voice speaking from darkness is important," Lamprophyre said. "That sounds like someone giving bad or evil instructions, and maybe that's why the faithful wander. Destroy the link between the chosen and something else?"

Rokshan blew out his breath impatiently. "We could go on guessing all day," he said. "It's time we gained more information."

"How are we going to do that?" Lamprophyre asked. She felt weary at the thought of following the ecclesiasts again, or talking to people who didn't want to reveal what they knew.

Rokshan smiled. "By doing what you've longed to do ever since this started."

CHAPTER THIRTY-THREE

"Suppose someone comes while we're gone?" Lamprophyre said as she winged her way toward the coliseum. "This would be the worst possible time for the ecclesiasts to decide to bring Jiwanyil's light to the heathen dragon ambassador."

"They're all at the prayer ceremony," Rokshan pointed out, "and if Rassika is fast, Coquina will be at the embassy before we return. And we can't afford to wait for her. The ceremony could already be over."

"That's logical, but I still worry." Lamprophyre flew faster. Rokshan was right; it was unlikely the Archprelate would be snatched at exactly this time just because they'd finally found him.

The prayer ceremony was still going strong when Lamprophyre and Rokshan returned to the coliseum. "I can't perch on the arches to wait," Lamprophyre said.

"We need a tower we can watch from," Rokshan replied. "Maybe that one over there?"

The tower Rokshan indicated had a pointed cone for a top, highly impractical as far as Lamprophyre was concerned, and was gilded so brightly that on a clear day it might blind anyone passing near it. It was too steeply inclined for her to land on it, but near its top a stone balcony circled it, doubling the tower's diameter with how wide and deep it was. Lamprophyre descended slowly, flapping hard to keep from overshooting the mark, and landed with one foot on the balcony and the other on the rail. It was an awkward position, but Rokshan had been right: it gave her a perfect view of the coliseum, including the back half of the platform.

From that distance, she could hear the gentle noise of human speech in a rhythm that suggested they were chanting. "Do you know what they're saying?" she asked Rokshan.

"I think it's a prayer of praise to Jiwanyil," Rokshan replied. He hadn't climbed down from her shoulders, and now he leaned forward as if that would bring the sounds better into resolution. "It could also be the hymn to Katayan, but that would be louder, so maybe not."

"You humans have so many religious rituals. It's fascinating."

"Dragons don't?"

"No. Our invocations are very short and amount to reminding those present of Mother Stone's love." She wondered for the first time if that meant something about dragon religion, that dragons didn't spend a lot of time on worship. If it meant anything, it was probably that dragons felt a kinship to Mother Stone that didn't require much pageantry, the way nobody composed hymns of praise to their feet for carrying them across the land.

Rokshan shifted his weight again. "It's stopped." Sure enough, the rhythmic hum had ceased, and the air was once more still and tranquil. Lamprophyre peered into the distance. It looked like the people atop the platform were moving.

"Time to go," Rokshan said. "We'll wait until they've all five left the coliseum, and then…"

Lamprophyre nodded. She let go of the rail and dropped, snapping her wings open before she fell too far, and flew in the direction of the coliseum. This time, she flew high enough that no one below could take offense or feel she was intruding. She didn't care about not offending anyone, but their plan depended upon a certain amount of surprise, and she needed to look like a dragon idling across the sky.

Far below, splotches of color that were the High Ecclesiasts' litters left the coliseum, spaced very far apart. Exactly as Rokshan had predicted. One, two, three, four, and *dive*. For once, Rokshan didn't shout with excitement as she plummeted toward the ground, suggesting he was as tense with nervous excitement as she was. After all, if this went wrong, they might have the entire city after them.

She landed heavily in the street and dropped to one knee to keep her balance. It wasn't a very wide street, and people scattered when she landed, her wings spread wide to take up even more space. Amid screams and the rush of running feet, she said in her deepest voice, "I want a word with you, ecclesiast."

Khadar's green-draped litter had come to a halt half a dragonlength away. The bearers looked as if they wanted to back up, but the fleeing pedestrians had taken shelter behind the litter, and there was nowhere to go. For once, there were no reverends or musicians in Khadar's entourage, making his litter look small and naked by comparison. The green curtains fluttered, but Khadar didn't emerge. Lamprophyre tried to listen to his thoughts, but heard only the fearful and anxious thoughts of the bystanders. Whatever Khadar was thinking, it was more of the same.

Rokshan hopped down and took a few steps toward the litter. "We just want to talk, Khadar," he said in a voice that carried over the hum of the crowd. "You know Lamprophyre won't hurt a human. You're in no danger."

Still nothing from the litter. Rokshan took another step forward. "It won't—"

The curtains parted, and Khadar climbed out of the litter. His dark hair was sweaty around the hairline and the nape of his neck, and his green robe was rumpled, with a crease across one of the willow tree embroideries. "If you think there's nothing worse we can do than cast you out," he said, "you're mistaken."

"Find the lost," Rokshan said. "We know what it means. How did you manage to lose him?"

Khadar didn't move, but he swallowed hard once. "You're bluffing." Lamprophyre heard a flash of focused thought, *can't know*, that had to have come from him.

She leaned down so her head was level with Khadar's. "White hair like dandelion fluff," she said. "Dark brown eyes. Walks a little hunched over—"

Terror struck her so hard it felt like a weapon. She gasped and flinched before regaining her composure. Khadar looked like his best friend had just struck him. "How did you," he said, blinked, and wiped sweat from his forehead. "Where is he?"

"Safe," Rokshan said. "Now tell me why he needs protection, him of all people."

Khadar glanced quickly to either side. People lined the street, watching this interaction with curiosity and fear, though Lamprophyre judged it was fear for themselves rather than fear for Khadar. That struck her as odd, but she didn't have time to pursue it, because Khadar had stepped closer, close enough for Lamprophyre to touch.

"We can't discuss this in public," he said in a low voice even Lamprophyre's draconic hearing had to strain to understand. "Come to the Archprelate's palace."

"Not a chance," Rokshan said. "The danger is there, whatever it is. We talk here and we take our chances. Though I'm sure you're capable of concealing your meaning from these bystanders."

Khadar flinched. "You think so little of me?"

"I think you're complicit," Lamprophyre said, "and you'd better start talking if you want to redeem yourself. When all of this comes out, which side do you want to be on?" She didn't have any idea what she was talking about, knew only that her words were prompting Khadar to think indecisive thoughts and, she hoped, were pushing him toward revealing everything.

Khadar once more glanced from side to side. "He disappeared three weeks ago," he said. "We keep a close eye on him because, well, you know why. But one morning he was just gone. We started searching, but it was as if every white-haired old man in Tanajital had just vanished. How did you find him?"

"You don't search thoroughly enough," Lamprophyre said, then hoped she hadn't given away the secret of the Archprelate's location.

Khadar drew himself up. "I insist you take me to him."

Despite his defiant posture, his thoughts were frightened, filled with phrases like *must get him back* and *if anyone finds out*. Lamprophyre stood taller and loomed over him. "You don't get to insist," she said. "Keep talking. Why is he still the Archprelate?"

"Because he is still possessed of prophecies," Khadar said. "And he is still Most Holy One and deserving of reverence. God does not desert his creations just because their minds are broken."

"That's the most honest thing I've ever heard you say," Rokshan said. "But you aren't being completely forthcoming. Why did you run away from me when we last spoke? About the decree naming dragons outcast?"

Khadar looked away. "Because I didn't want to argue with you over a prophecy."

"That's not true," Lamprophyre said, not caring how she was risking revealing her secret. "Tell us about that prophecy. It's false, isn't it?"

Khadar's mouth fell open. "Blasphemer," he said in a hoarse voice.

"That's rich, coming from you," Rokshan said. "You supported that prophecy even though you knew the truth. Why did Ayusha lie, Khadar?"

Lamprophyre held her breath, listening to Khadar mentally wrestle with himself. She would have known the moment he gave in even if she hadn't heard his thoughts, because his whole body sagged. "I don't know if she's lying," he said. "We just haven't seen her possessed of a prophecy in the last three weeks, and yet she tells us things she claims are prophecy and attacks us verbally if we challenge her. It was her idea not to let anyone know the Ar—he was missing, because we can't afford for anyone to find out his condition. But I thought..." He drew in a deep breath. "I thought it mattered more that we find him, even if it means having to answer some hard questions."

Lamprophyre would have sworn Khadar was a lying hypocrite who didn't believe in his own religion, and she'd never expected to hear his thoughts ring with truth. By his expression, Rokshan felt the same. "Then you don't think he's in danger," he said, watching Khadar closely.

Khadar shook his head. "I think we need him," he said, lifting his head so he could meet Rokshan's eyes. His own eyes glittered with unshed tears. "I don't think we can stop Ayusha without him. I don't like the way she's been going. I don't like dragons, but she's afraid of what they might do. She thinks they'll destroy our faith. I don't think that's possible, but she has control now, and I know she's planning to reveal some new decree soon. She has to be stopped, and the Archprelate is the only one who can do it."

"But he's—not himself," Lamprophyre exclaimed, realizing in time that they still had an audience. "He can't stop anyone."

Khadar turned his gaze on her. "That's how I used to think," he said. "That religion was all about temporal power and doing things to benefit myself with my influence over worldly matters. When I was actually possessed of a prophecy..." He shook his head. "I can't explain it well. I realized all those things I'd thought were nonsense, faith and prophecy and even God, were more powerful than anything I could do of my own abilities. Now I know faith is about acting on belief, doing God's will even when you can't see how it could possibly work out for the best."

"I don't believe you," Rokshan said. "You've never been anything but selfish and immature, and now you expect us to believe you've had a major change of heart that just happens to coincide with what we want to hear?"

"I don't care what you believe, Rokshan," Khadar said, sounding more like himself. "I know what *I* believe. If you won't bring him back, I'll send people for him. If you found him, I can guess where he is, and you can only defend him for so long. But it would be better if you brought him yourselves."

"Why is that?" Lamprophyre asked.

Khadar turned away. "Because even faith can use some help," he said. "And Jiwanyil teaches that only a fool fails to make use of the gifts God gives him." He walked back to his litter and paused with his hand on the frame. "Now, let me pass."

Lamprophyre and Rokshan stared at each other in bewilderment. Rokshan recovered first and climbed into the notch behind Lamprophyre's shoulders. "But—" she began.

"Later," Rokshan said. "Let's go."

Lamprophyre pushed off with her powerful legs and beat her wings until she was once more high above Tanajital. She flew for a few dozen beats, not conscious of a direction until she realized she'd crossed the wall and was heading north toward Mother Stone. Maybe she'd unconsciously sought out a familiar source of comfort and stability, something she could hold onto when the world came unraveled as it was now. "What do we do?" she asked, hearing an unexpected note of pleading in her voice.

"I don't know," Rokshan replied. "I think Khadar is wrong, because the Archprelate clearly is in no condition to help himself, let alone rein in a powerful ecclesiast who has the support of every other religious person in Tanajital. But if Ayusha plans to take more action against dragons, we have to stop her. Not just for us, but for the sake of the city. That prophecy demanded as much."

Lamprophyre wheeled and headed back south. "Let's at least see what we can do for the Archprelate. We have to protect him. Khadar might follow through on his threat to come after him sooner rather than later."

"And then we'll consider what to do about Ayusha." Rokshan leaned forward so he was lying along her neck, his forehead pressed against her scales. "Damn Khadar for his cowardice. He and the other High Ecclesiasts would stand a far better chance of denouncing her than we do."

"I thought it was pretty brave of him to admit to what he knew."

"Admitting it to us is a lot easier than proclaiming it to the city. He'd like us to do the dirty work." Rokshan sighed. "Though it is true that was more than I ever believed I'd hear from him."

Lamprophyre swooped down toward the embassy. "How did he ever become an ecclesiast if he never was possessed of a prophecy until a dozen twelvedays ago?"

"I didn't witness the first one, the one that declared his status. I always thought he'd pretended to one and was accepted for political reasons, or because Father gave money to the ecclesiasts to accept him. But now that I've seen a prophecy, I realize faking one is impossible. So he must have been possessed of one and then no others for years, for him to be so overwhelmed by the one we saw together." Rokshan sat up straight as she descended into the courtyard. "I don't know how they choose the High Ecclesiasts. That might have been political. But it doesn't matter, does it? If Ayusha is corrupt, Khadar's inadequacies seem minor by comparison."

He hopped down and headed for the dining pavilion. Lamprophyre followed, ducking into its shelter. She stopped only a few steps in. The pavilion was empty.

CHAPTER THIRTY-FOUR

Lamprophyre and Rokshan stared at each other in growing horror. "Where—?" Lamprophyre began. She rapidly walked to the kitchen and looked over the wall. Depik was in the final stages of preparing that evening's cow. He was alone. "Depik, where is the old man?"

Depik looked up. "Who, my lady?"

"The old man I brought in here. Where did he go?"

"I'm sorry, I didn't notice anyone in the pavilion. Maybe Bhakriya saw him?"

Rokshan had already run to where Bhakriya stood next to the soup cauldron, ladling out rich beefy broth. "I remember seeing him walk past me," she told him. "I noticed because normally the people who eat here don't venture into the pavilion. But I didn't watch him after he left the courtyard for the street. Is it important?"

"I'll go on foot," Rokshan said to Lamprophyre. "You take to the skies. How long ago was this?" he demanded.

Bhakriya looked worried. "I don't know. Twenty minutes, maybe half an hour? I'm sorry, if you'd said you wanted him watched—"

"It's not your fault, it's ours," Lamprophyre said. She could kick herself for assuming the Archprelate wouldn't leave so long as there was food. "If he comes back, steer him into the pavilion and make him stay there, all right?" Without another word, she took two running steps into the courtyard and launched herself skyward.

Cries of surprise and fear followed her, but she left them behind almost immediately, banking to follow the street where it curved west toward the river. The streets were as crowded as they always were at this time, a surging tide of humanity sweeping toward home and supper. Lamprophyre flew as slowly as she dared, scanning the crowds for a smudge of white hair standing out against all the black-haired people. The warm scent of human bodies all crammed together, slightly sour and tinged with the sweeter odor of the river, made her empty stomachs feel sick—or maybe that was the knowledge that the ultimate spiritual leader of the country was wandering alone and unprotected through the city, and she felt partly at fault.

She couldn't remember how many days he'd been coming to the embassy for food. He'd been on his own all that time, and no one had hurt him. Maybe God was watching out for him, in which case she didn't need to worry. Jiwanyil might not be her God, but she was certain he had the power to protect his most beloved servant. It still felt like failure. And it felt like defeat, as well, because she had the suspicion that the Archprelate might be the key to defeating the Third Ecclesiast, even if she had no idea how to do that.

In the distance, she saw a blotch of green and rose that resolved into Coquina. Lamprophyre flew to meet her clutchmate. "Thank you for coming," she said.

"Rassika wasn't very clear on what you wanted. You need me to watch the embassy?" Coquina said.

"I did, but—" Lamprophyre suddenly didn't feel equal to explaining everything to Coquina. "It's nothing. I'll tell you all about it tomorrow."

Coquina looked skeptical, but she nodded. "All right. Get some rest. You look tired."

Lamprophyre was sure she looked more than tired. She felt exhausted, stricken by all the revelations, all the secrets coming to light. But she still had a duty.

She coursed over all the streets the Archprelate might have

conceivably taken, remembering Rokshan's point about counting the beats since he'd disappeared and calculating how far he could have gotten in that time. Traffic had thinned, and lamplighters had begun lighting lanterns along the streets, before she had to give up the search as a lost cause. Dejected, she flew back to the embassy and crouched in the middle of the courtyard, feeling weary enough that even the smell of hot cooked cow couldn't tempt her from her position.

"Lamprophyre," Rokshan said from behind her. She turned to see him approaching from the street, unaccompanied. Her heart sank further. Rokshan looked her over as if expecting to see the Archprelate appear from beneath her wing. "It's all right," he continued. "He'll come back tomorrow night."

"Maybe," Lamprophyre said. "He doesn't always show up."

"Let's just stay optimistic, all right?" Rokshan clapped her on the shoulder. "I'm hungry. Let's eat, and maybe we can work out a plan."

Lamprophyre nodded. She settled into the pavilion, but discovered she'd lost her appetite. Rather than hurt Depik's feelings, she carved off a piece of meat with her claws and nibbled it. It was delicious as always, but it sat like rock in her stomach, not the nice digestible kind of rock, but a heavy, leaden lump even her robust digestive system couldn't manage.

She tore off another bite and chewed slowly, savoring the juices. "If we confront the Third Ecclesiast directly with our knowledge," she said around her mouthful, "maybe she'll break down and admit to lying."

Rokshan had his knife out and was cutting off morsels of cow for himself rather than eating soup. "I doubt it," he said. "Ayusha is tough. She's been in power for years and she's withstood any number of challenges to her authority. Us accusing her with no proof won't so much as rattle her."

"What challenges to her authority? I thought humans respected their religious leaders."

"They do. It's other ecclesiasts who make those challenges. Mostly they're challenges to interpretation of prophecy. Ayusha's understanding of prophecy has always been on the edge of what's reasonable. Like, well, you and I interpreted the Archprelate's prophecy a few hours ago, right? Ayusha would have looked for meaning that wasn't so literal. She might have said 'voice in darkness' meant...I don't know, I'm not her. Maybe that it was a blind person speaking."

"Isn't it more likely the true meaning is the obvious one?"

"Sometimes. But Ayusha is right often enough that she's well-respected for her interpretations. And she's good at defending those interpretations."

"You must know her well to use her given name instead of her title."

Rokshan shrugged. "All the High Ecclesiasts are in and out of the palace, all the time. I grew up hearing my father refer to them by their names, and it was natural for me and my siblings to do the same. It means I'm not as overawed by them as I otherwise would be."

Lamprophyre's attention was drawn by a flurry of movement at the mouth of the street. She sat up to look past Bhakriya, who had gone very still. People entering the courtyard moved very quickly to either side to allow a line of muscular men, dressed in knee-length trousers with their chests bare, to march past them. The men ignored the scuttling people and came to a halt in the center of the courtyard, taking up watchful positions with their legs in a wide stance and their bulging-muscled arms folded over their chests.

Behind them, borne by four more men like the others, came a red-draped litter. Lamprophyre got to her feet and walked slowly to the edge of the dining pavilion, following Rokshan. She felt superstitiously as if their conversation had summoned the Third Ecclesiast, and for a moment wondered if the woman had the ability to hear her thoughts. Then she shook off her ridiculous thoughts. It couldn't mean anything good, the Third Ecclesiast being here, and Lamprophyre needed not to be distracted by irrational fancies.

She hadn't been this close to the Third Ecclesiast's litter before, and was struck by how good it smelled, a tangy-sweet odor like a blend of pyrite and kyanite. It blended with the smell of the soup and the cow meat to overcome the ranker, sweaty odor of the muscular men. Lamprophyre looked at them more closely. Six men, plus the four bearers. She remembered what had happened to Coquina's friends in the coliseum, and took another step forward so she fully emerged from the dining pavilion and could loom over the Third Ecclesiast's companions. If the woman intended to start a fight, she would find that not so easy a prospect.

Rokshan had stepped to the side to give Lamprophyre room and gestured to Bhakriya to go to the kitchen. Bhakriya gave one wary look at the litter, dropped the ladle into the pot, and retreated. It relieved Lamprophyre's mind to have Depik and Bhakriya safe, but it also worried her that she didn't know where the children were. In the embassy, hopefully, and with luck they'd think to stay there. The rest of the people—Lamprophyre didn't know how she could protect all of them, but she'd think of something.

No one moved. The earlier breeze had died down, and the air was heavy and tense with the oncoming storm. The lanterns ringing the courtyard, and the ones hanging from the embassy buildings, seemed to be working harder than usual to push back the oncoming dark. Gray clouds bulging with rain moved ponderously slow across the sky. If the rain came, it might send the Third Ecclesiast running. That was probably too much to hope for.

The litter's curtains fluttered. The Third Ecclesiast emerged, putting one small foot delicately on the ground as if testing the waters of an unfamiliar pool. Satisfied, her other foot joined the first, and she brushed the curtains aside and stood before them, one hand resting lightly on the litter's frame. She said nothing, merely regarded Lamprophyre with the expression of someone who'd seen an unfamiliar insect and was working out whether or not to squash it. Lamprophyre stared back at her, wishing she could speak thoughts to a mind as easily as hear them. The Third Ecclesiast's thoughts were placid, though what Lamprophyre heard made no sense: *almost done* and *nothing left* and *perfect solution should have thought before.*

"Dragon," the Third Ecclesiast finally said. "You have gone too far."

Startled, Lamprophyre said, "What? I don't understand. I haven't done anything to you."

"To me, no." The Third Ecclesiast stepped away from her litter and approached Lamprophyre, passing between her muscular men as if they were so many pillars and not people. "To Gonjiri, most certainly. Or did you think we would not find out?"

Lamprophyre glanced at Rokshan, who looked as bewildered as she felt. "I—find out what?"

"Your crime," the Third Ecclesiast said. She stopped half a drag-onlength from Lamprophyre and looked up at her fearlessly. "You abducted the Archprelate. Return him, or face our wrath."

CHAPTER THIRTY-FIVE

"*W*hat?" Lamprophyre exclaimed.

"You're out of your mind, Ayusha," Rokshan said.

The Third Ecclesiast didn't move, but her thoughts became triumphant. "Witnesses place you at the Archprelate's palace at midnight several days ago," she said. "Did you think you could force him to stop prophesying of your wickedness?"

"I didn't kidnap the Archprelate!" Lamprophyre shouted. A flash of light and a crack of thunder shattered the stillness as she said *kidnap*, as if the sky were emphasizing her words. "You know very well I didn't!"

"Rokshan, how could you lend yourself to this?" the Third Ecclesiast said, ignoring Lamprophyre. "I expect no better from a beast, but you? You should have known better."

"Ayusha," Rokshan said, then appeared to be struck mute, groping for something to say to answer this unexpected and bizarre challenge.

"I am here to demand his return," the Third Ecclesiast said. "And to take you both into custody for kidnapping."

"You can't prove—" Lamprophyre realized that sentence made her sound guilty and changed her words to, "You lost the Archprelate and you want to blame it on us. Why are you so desperate to get rid of dragons? Are we such a threat to you?"

"I have been possessed of many prophecies, and my instructions are clear." The Third Ecclesiast hadn't moved and seemed not at all afraid of Lamprophyre's looming presence. "Jiwanyil has spoken, and it is my honor to obey."

"Ayusha," Rokshan said again, "you have to stop. We know the truth. The Archprelate ran away from the palace and you've been searching for him ever since. We didn't kidnap him, and you know it. And we won't help restore him to you."

The Third Ecclesiast took another couple of steps to put herself next to Rokshan. "Whose story is Tanajital more likely to believe?" she said in a low voice, pitched to carry no farther than Rokshan's and Lamprophyre's ears. "I am giving you this chance to hand him over. Refuse, and the city learns of your crime. They will tear this place apart and will do their best to kill you both."

"They can try," Lamprophyre said, just as Rokshan said, "You'd start a riot just to get your way?"

The Third Ecclesiast shrugged. "Give him to me now, and we'll never have to find out."

"What makes you think he's here?" Rokshan said.

"Don't play that game with me, Rokshan," the Third Ecclesiast said. "I realized the searchers had deliberately avoided this place in their investigations, and after the questions you asked today, I deduced where he had to be."

So it was a guess, and a very lucky one. Rokshan and Lamprophyre looked at each other. Rokshan had the expression she rarely saw, the one where his eyebrows came together in the middle like he was thinking hard, and she listened to his thoughts and heard *He's not here, and there's no point concealing that.* She nodded once.

Rokshan turned to the Third Ecclesiast. "He's not here," he said. "He left before we returned."

"I think you're lying," the Third Ecclesiast said.

"Liars always assume they're being lied to," Rokshan shot back. "It's true. He comes for soup and then he leaves again. We don't know where he goes during the day."

The Third Ecclesiast regarded him narrowly. "He comes here every evening?"

"Most evenings," Lamprophyre said, feeling like a traitor for helping the Third Ecclesiast in any way.

"You had better hope that means tomorrow night," the Third Ecclesiast said. "I will return then."

Rokshan suddenly grabbed Lamprophyre's wrist. "What, you won't leave your men here to watch us?" he said. His voice sounded tense, and his brows looked like thunder. Lamprophyre, baffled, again listened to his thoughts and heard only the word *LOOK* repeated over and over.

She looked past the Third Ecclesiast and saw the Archprelate standing at the end of the street, just inside the courtyard.

She swiftly turned her gaze back on the Third Ecclesiast and cast about for anything she might say to keep the woman's attention on her, all the time willing the old man to turn and run, to vanish into the crowds before the Third Ecclesiast saw him. "Yes, aren't you afraid we'll make him disappear again if we aren't closely observed?" she said.

The Third Ecclesiast didn't notice their agitation; her thoughts were again triumphant with her victory. "What, and put him beyond your protection? I don't think so."

"Being free in Tanajital has to be better than whatever you have planned for him," Lamprophyre said.

A frown touched the Third Ecclesiast's lips and then fell away as quickly. "Planned for him? I want him restored to his position, to guide Gonjiri."

"Except he's not sane," Rokshan said. The Archprelate hadn't moved from his position, his familiar vacant smile driving Lamprophyre mad with frustration. "And now we know the truth. What's to stop us telling everyone?"

"You won't tell anyone," the Third Ecclesiast said. "You know what that would do to the worship of Jiwanyil if people believed the Archprelate was incompetent. Which, of course, he's not. Sane or no, he still is possessed of prophecies, and you really are a heretic if you deny that."

"If that's the case, then he must have seen something to make him run," Rokshan said. "A danger posed to him by other ecclesiasts. Which means if we hand him over to you, we could be complicit in his death. I'd rather face whatever you have in mind for me than be party to that."

"Still defiant? We'll see if you still feel the same when the mob attacks. Even your dragon friend can't save you from that." The Third Ecclesiast began to turn away. Lamprophyre grabbed her shoulder and let her go immediately when the woman turned on her with an unexpected snarl.

"You're counting on me being unwilling to defend Rokshan from other humans regardless of the situation," she said. "I don't want to hurt humans, but I won't let him suffer for your evil."

"You say evil, I say obedience to Jiwanyil's word." The Third Ecclesiast took a step closer. "If you'd only been willing to obey yourself, this could all have been avoided."

The Archprelate blinked and licked his lips as if suddenly aware there was food available. He began walking toward them with his slightly hunched gait, ignoring the muscular men filling the courtyard. Lamprophyre realized if he continued on his straight line to the soup cauldron, he would pass right beside the Third Ecclesiast. She took a step to the other side, hoping the woman would turn with her, putting her back to the cauldron. "If you hadn't been so demanding and offensive, none of this would have happened either," she said.

"I am God's chosen, and I obey his words," the Third Ecclesiast said. Her attention was fully on Lamprophyre and she didn't notice the Archprelate had nearly reached them. "I don't expect you to understand."

Lamprophyre held her breath as the Archprelate, only paces from the Third Ecclesiast, picked up a bowl and stepped over to the soup cauldron. But he didn't serve himself. He waited there with his bowl outstretched just the way all of them did for Bhakriya or Preyanka or Depik to fill it.

The Third Ecclesiast's eyes narrowed. "What are you—" she began.

"Chosen?" Rokshan said, slowly.

The Third Ecclesiast ignored him and turned around. Lamprophyre heard the sharp surprise of her thoughts as she recognized the Archprelate. Rokshan swore in a low voice. The Third Ecclesiast reached for the Archprelate's arm, saying, "Jiwanyil be praised."

The Archprelate stepped back before she could touch him, and the bowl fell from his hands. The staccato crackling of his broken thoughts surged loud enough that Lamprophyre couldn't help hearing, fragments of words like *not her* and *time past later* and *speaks like thunder*. On that last thought, thunder boomed as if the storm, too, could hear thoughts and agreed with the Archprelate.

Rokshan pushed past the Third Ecclesiast and put himself protectively between the Archprelate and her. "Don't touch him," he warned. "I'm already a heretic and I'll have no trouble defending him from you and your men."

"Try defending against all of Tanajital," the Third Ecclesiast murmured. In a louder voice, she said, "This man is ill and needs healing. I have seen it in prophecy. These two heretics stand in the way of prophecy. O faithful of Jiwanyil, do not allow them to prevail!"

Rokshan cursed again. Lamprophyre got behind the Archprelate and crouched low, spreading her wings to protect him, though no one had moved yet. "Take him away, Lamprophyre," Rokshan said. "I'll deal with this."

"Are you insane?" Lamprophyre said. "And where would I take him?"

"People of Tanajital, to me!" the Third Ecclesiast shouted.

The Archprelate suddenly staggered and fell against Lamprophyre's leg. She put a hand out to steady him and felt a shudder run through him. "Everybody listen!" she screamed over the rising wind and the murmurs of the crowd. "Listen to this!" She hoped she was right and that the Archprelate was about to be possessed of a prophecy, and hoped even more it would be something that would turn the tide in their favor.

The Archprelate stood unassisted and took a step away from her. He blinked his eyes, once, twice, and when he opened them a final time, they blazed with leaf-green light. "*O faithful of Jiwanyil,*" he began.

The Third Ecclesiast grabbed him by the shoulders and shook him into silence. Rokshan moved to intervene, and she shoved him aside. "It's not true, it's a lie," she shouted. "I am the one who receives true prophecy. I am the chosen of God!" She let go of the Archprelate and clutched herself, wrapping her arms around her stomach as if it pained her. Rokshan once more put himself between her and the Archprelate, then stood still, his hands half-raised as if he wanted to take hold of her but was afraid to.

The Third Ecclesiast shuddered much as the Archprelate had. Then she stood upright with her hands at her sides and tilted her head back the way a bird might before bursting into song. With her eyes closed, she said, *"Listen to her, dragon. She tells the truth."*

Lamprophyre shivered. The voice was not the Third Ecclesiast's. It was low and throaty, like deep water running over stone, like thunder rolling over the mountaintops, and it sent a chill up her spine. It sounded nothing like what Lamprophyre had come to think of as the Voice of Jiwanyil, the strange voice neither male nor female she'd now heard from three different people possessed of prophecies. And yet it had a similar quality, resonant and certain and impossible to forget.

"She is my chosen," the voice said. *"You should have listened when you were commanded. Now the city will burn, and it will take you and yours with it."*

Lamprophyre looked down at the Archprelate, whose eyes were still vivid green. He was listening to this with great interest, for the first time appearing to be conscious of his surroundings. "Dragons worship Mother Stone, not Katayan," she said. "And I don't think—"

The Third Ecclesiast laughed. It was a horrible, mocking sound that made Lamprophyre cringe inside. *"Mother Stone? You dragons have no idea what waits for you there. Your God is dead, and you have nowhere to turn but to me. Leave this city or be destroyed."*

Lamprophyre's heart was beating so hard it hurt her ribs. "You're lying," she whispered, wishing she could summon a louder voice.

Another laugh, louder and more menacing than before, issued from the Third Ecclesiast's lips. *"Am I? I have more power than you have ever dreamed. You know nothing, fallen child of a fallen race. I am your doom."*

Rokshan grabbed the Third Ecclesiast's shoulder and swung her around to face him. She didn't resist. "Who are you?" he demanded.

The Third Ecclesiast opened her eyes. Instead of bright green light, they were filled with a dark smoke that roiled within their depths like the heavy clouds lowering above. Blood tricked from their corners. *"I am Jiwanyil, foolish boy,"* she said.

"You absolutely are not," Rokshan said. "I would bet my eternal soul on it."

"Your eternal soul is already lost for consorting with this creature. Step back—"

A hand reached past Rokshan to grip the Third Ecclesiast by the wrist. *"Listen and obey,"* the Archprelate said a clear voice that rang through Lamprophyre like a bell. *"The old stone speaks lies through the chosen. There is no more time for the faithful to wander. Give the tiger her desire and let it scour her clean."*

The Third Ecclesiast tried to wrench free, but the Archprelate's grip only tightened. "What are you doing?" she demanded in her own voice. Then, in that cold, horrible voice, she said, *"The old man speaks lies. He is senile and knows nothing. God's grace has passed from him."*

"I don't think so," Rokshan said. "Whoever or whatever you are, we know you're not God."

Lamprophyre was thinking hard. The muscular men hadn't moved. The people surrounding the courtyard were shifting uncomfortably, as if they weren't sure what voice to listen to. Hearing their thoughts, Lamprophyre knew she and Rokshan only had a few beats before they attacked, uncertain of anything but that the Third Ecclesiast was their spiritual leader and knowing the Archprelate only as the senile old man who had fits. Give the tiger her desire. The Third Ecclesiast was the tiger. What was her desire?

"Jiwanyil!" she shouted, startling everyone. Another crack of thunder split the sky, followed almost immediately by a spike of white lightning. "Ayusha believes she is the Archprelate. Give her her heart's desire!"

CHAPTER THIRTY-SIX

The Third Ecclesiast jerked onto her toes as if someone had grabbed her hair and pulled straight up. Deep within the murk of her eyes, glints of green light shone, dimming and fading and then brightening again until the smoke burned away. "*I am your God!*" the dark voice said, sounding less resonant and farther away. "*You will worship—*"

The voice cut off sharply. The Third Ecclesiast's body arched like a bow, and a hiss of pain emerged from her clenched teeth. Rokshan stepped back. The Archprelate took the opportunity to move into the space where he had been, taking the Third Ecclesiast's other wrist and holding her as if tethering her to the ground. Though he said nothing, his eyes were still the same vivid green as hers now were.

The Third Ecclesiast threw her head back and opened her mouth. "*That which comes cannot be stopped,*" she said, and this time her voice was the ringing music of the real Jiwanyil. "*Fear nothing except the enemy you do not know. God and man, dragon and God, no one is to say where truth lies, or where lies are truth. Ward against the voice in darkness. The skies will burn.*"

Lamprophyre realized she was holding her breath and let it out slowly. Rokshan, beside her, stood as still and tense as if he were the one possessed of a prophecy. The Archprelate continued to hold the Third Ecclesiast's wrists, his head tilted to look at her; Lamprophyre hadn't understood how short he was until she saw him next to the Third Ecclesiast, who was a tiny woman and only barely shorter than he. She reached out to free the Third Ecclesiast from his grip, and he twitched the woman out of Lamprophyre's reach. "Don't," he said in a normal if very elderly voice. "It's not over."

The Third Ecclesiast jerked and fell to her knees. Then she was thrashing madly, held upright only by the Archprelate's hands. Blood trickled from her nose and the corners of her eyes, foam bubbled from her lips, and her head moved so rapidly Lamprophyre could hear her joints popping. Through it all, the Archprelate held firm, anchoring the woman so she couldn't fall and hit her head against the hard earth of the courtyard.

Eventually, the Third Ecclesiast's seizure passed, and she hung limp in the Archprelate's grasp. He gently lowered her to the ground and stood over her, looking down as intently as if he understood who she was and what had happened to her. Lamprophyre bent to arrange her in a more comfortable position, and froze. "No," she said, leaning closer to rest her cheek near the woman's mouth, which lay slack in death. "I don't understand. Why—"

"The thing that possessed her altered her brain," the Archprelate said, "made it incompatible with true prophecy. I don't know why Jiwanyil didn't act sooner, but there is much I do not understand about divinity."

Lamprophyre stared at him. "You...aren't you—"

"Mad?" The Archprelate turned to look up at her. "I am, or will be again." He held out a hand to let a few raindrops spatter his palm. "What terrible timing the heavens have."

Lamprophyre became aware of the murmuring crowds beginning to press forward. She couldn't tell from their agitated thoughts what they believed had just happened, but even if all they thought was that two ecclesiasts had been possessed of prophecies at the same time, and that one of them had been overtaken by it, that was enough to overwhelm the embassy. "Please stand back," she said, walking toward the center of the courtyard. "Rokshan, would you—"

"Already thought of it," Rokshan said. He had the Third Ecclesiast's body in his arms and was moving through the muscular men toward the litter. All of them had turned to watch him. They weren't as stolid as Lamprophyre had thought. Lamprophyre walked around the courtyard, saying things she barely remembered speaking, her whole mind focused on the Archprelate, who stood by the soup cauldron with no apparent concern for the rain now falling on him.

"Go home—the Third Ecclesiast needs rest—the ecclesiasts will explain everything tomorrow—really, just *go home*," she said, and with those words and some well-timed flaps of her enormous wings, she got the courtyard cleared of everything but the litter and the Third Ecclesiast's entourage. The bearers and the other men had gathered together in a huddle, alternating glances at the litter whose silken draperies were spattered dark red with rain with glances at Rokshan and Lamprophyre. One of the men moved as if to lift the curtain, and another slapped the first man's hand away.

"We can't send them back," she told Rokshan when she returned to his side. "A litter shows up with a dead Third Ecclesiast, and who knows what they'll think?"

"She can wait," Rokshan said. "I have questions."

They turned to face the Archprelate, who smiled sadly at them and turned to enter the pavilion. Following him, Lamprophyre settled on the stone floor and tucked her tail around herself. Outside, the rain continued to patter lightly, and she glanced over her shoulder at the bearers in their huddle, who seemed not to notice or care about the weather. Well, they hadn't noticed the Third Ecclesiast was dead, because they were unlikely to remain so calm if they had. Maybe that sort of unobservant behavior was something the ecclesiasts looked for in bearers. The rain wasn't falling heavily, and Lamprophyre found she didn't much care if the men got wet.

"I don't believe I have much time," the Archprelate said, drawing her attention. "But I remember how kind you were, and I saw your faith, and I think that's deserving of answers."

"You weren't pretending to be mad, were you?" Rokshan said.

"Unfortunately, no. When I knew a great danger was coming, I pleaded with Jiwanyil to spare my life until it had passed, so I would not leave my people unprotected from it. In his grace, he chose to grant my request, but he apparently believed I would be capable of acting even if my mind was gone." The Archprelate closed his eyes and let out a deep sigh. "I can feel the fog coming on again, so I need you to listen and not interrupt."

"But—" Lamprophyre began. Rokshan shushed her.

"Months ago, I had a terrible dream," the Archprelate said. "A voice spoke to me, claiming to be Jiwanyil. It said my worthiness allowed it to speak to me directly, with no need for the obscurity of prophecy. It told me many flattering things and assured me I was destined for greatness. When I woke, I realized it was no dream.

"My mind was already going by then, and I believed the 'dream' to be just another manifestation of madness. But a second, similar dream convinced me it was an entity speaking to me, and—well, I have been an ecclesiast most of my life, and I know Jiwanyil's voice. This was not Jiwanyil. When it spoke to me again, I fought back. It told me if I resisted, it would raise up another Archprelate in my place. Fearing for my life and in the grip of delirium, I fled the Archprelate's palace.

"Since then, I have roamed the city in a fog, only coming briefly to myself on some occasions when I was possessed of a prophecy. I do not know what led me to this place—probably it was just hunger. But this evening, the first prophecy I spoke left me aware that here was where I needed to be. And I returned. You know the rest."

"So Ayusha was the entity's second target," Rokshan said. "Do you think she would have killed you?"

"Almost certainly," the Archprelate said. He swayed and sank to his knees in one sudden movement, but waved Rokshan off when he moved closer to help. "No, I'm well, or at least as well as I can be. Ayusha has always been determined and ambitious. I don't know if the entity put the idea of becoming Archprelate into her head, or if it was something she aspired to despite the impossibility of controlling Jiwanyil's choice, but I suppose it hardly matters now." He put a hand to his head. "Questions, now, while I can still answer."

"You said you saw our faith. What faith?" Lamprophyre asked.

The Archprelate tilted his head to regard her closely. "You called upon a God not your own to break the entity's hold on Ayusha. Why?"

Taken aback, Lamprophyre said, "I don't know. It was the prophecy that told me what needed to happen. I'm sorry if that was presumptuous."

"Not presumptuous. You spoke as one with the certainty of faith, and God responded. I honor that."

"But I don't worship Jiwanyil."

"I've found, in my long life, that Gods care more that their instructions are heeded than that people mouth platitudes in their direction," the Archprelate said wryly. "Don't worry. Jiwanyil knows your heart, and I'm sure your Mother Stone does too."

Lamprophyre still felt uncomfortable with the idea of her faith being enlisted in the cause of a religion not her own, and cast about for a change of subject. "Why are you sane now?"

The Archprelate nodded slowly, as if he knew what she'd done. "As I said, I have moments of clarity, and I think the power of that last prophecy left me clear for longer than usual." He grimaced. "Or possibly Jiwanyil wants you to know the truth, since no one else does. It will be up to you to decide who to share it with. Though I believe you could do worse than confide in Khadar. The boy is more faithful than he realizes, though I wish he would abjure whorehouses. It's so undignified."

"So, what was that entity?" Rokshan asked.

"That, I don't know. Something very old and very evil. Something that intends to bring about our destruction if it can. There are prophecies referring to the skies burning that I believe have something to do with it."

"We know some of those prophecies," Lamprophyre said. "We know they speak of a calamity like the Great Cataclysm so many hundreds of years ago."

The Archprelate looked at her without comprehension for a moment, then shook his head as if clearing away fog. "Calamity. Yes. We are almost certainly facing something as terrible." He pressed a hand to his head, and fear flickered in his eyes. "What else? Oh. I believe the entity wanted dragons out of Gonjiri because dragons and humans working together, fighting together, spells disaster for its plans. Don't let anyone drive you out, dragon...God's breath, I can't remember your name. I can't—"

"It's all right," Lamprophyre said. "You'll correct the prophecy."

He looked up at her, his face stricken. "I can't," he said. "My memories...I feel them dissolving. I'm going—I can't stop it."

"What do we do?" Lamprophyre said. "Can't we—Rokshan, Jiwanyil can't want this!"

Rokshan knelt beside the Archprelate, looking as torn as she felt. "I don't know, Lamprophyre. But—"

The Archprelate grabbed Lamprophyre's arm, groping as if he were blind. "Everything's fading," he cried out, sounding terrified. "My mind —dear God help me, I can't bear losing myself again!"

Impulsively, Lamprophyre put her arm around the Archprelate and held him close. "Don't be afraid," she said. "We'll remember for you. You'll be safe, I promise."

The Archprelate closed his eyes and nodded, shuddering and then growing calm. His breathing steadied. "I'm ready," he said, and bowed his head.

Lamprophyre didn't move. Rokshan knelt beside them both, his eyes fixed on the Archprelate. She heard movement from the kitchen as Depik and Bhakriya emerged, hand in hand, but with their attention on Lamprophyre in a way that suggested they didn't realize they were touching. "Most Holy One?" Lamprophyre whispered.

The Archprelate looked up at her and smiled. His vacant gaze struck her to the heart.

"Is that—?" Depik asked, his voice low and uncertain.

"It is," Rokshan said, "but I think you had both better forget what you saw. If Jiwanyil loves him, he will take this old man back to him soon." He rose and extended a hand to help the Archprelate to his feet. "I'll go back with Ayusha," he said. "Do you think you can fly with him? I know it's uncomfortable to fly with anyone but me."

Lamprophyre regarded the old man, who looked about him as if he'd never seen the dining pavilion before. "It will be an honor," she said.

CHAPTER THIRTY-SEVEN

The news that the Archprelate had died in his sleep spread throughout Tanajital five days later, carried by reverends in wide yellow drapes whose paths took them through every part of the city, including the slums and the dragon embassy. Lamprophyre took to the skies when she heard the news, feeling an ache in her heart that only flying could soothe. She watched the ecclesiasts' litters travel the streets and wondered what prayers their progress defined.

Tentatively, feeling vaguely heretical, she spoke to Jiwanyil in her heart the way she was accustomed to address Mother Stone on the rare occasions she felt justified in praying: *He served you until the end, in ways he never thought would be expected of him. I don't know anything about what you do with the souls of your followers, but I hope you give him rest.*

Nothing happened. She wasn't sure what she'd expected, whether a voice in her head or a feeling in her bones, but Jiwanyil remained silent. Relieved, because being touched by a foreign God was not something she wanted to have happen, she headed back to the embassy.

The courtyard was silent when she landed, without the laughter and pattering footsteps of children that had rung through it when the reverend had delivered his announcement. Lamprophyre ducked inside the hall and found Abhit there, looking at books. "Where did Anamika and Varnak go?" she asked.

Abhit closed the book on his finger to mark his place. "Their papa called them home because of the Archprelate's death," he said. "Mama said I was to be quiet out of respect."

Lamprophyre only partly understood that. Dragons honored death by participating in the things the deceased had loved in life, and were only quiet during a dragon's flight to Mother Stone, but she could respect human traditions. And it wasn't as if she'd known the Archprelate as he truly was except for those few last minutes before his madness claimed him again. Still, remembering the sharp, intelligent look in his brown eyes, his clear voice, she wished she could have flown with him while he had the wits to appreciate it.

That flight returning him to the Archprelate's palace had been terrifying, with the rain dampening her wings and her not sure he'd remember to hold on, and she'd nearly started a riot by landing on their very doorstep. But Khadar had taken things in hand, immediately helping the Archprelate down as if he'd been waiting for her arrival. She never thought she'd be grateful to Khadar for anything. She doubted his change of heart was complete enough to make him permanently less of an arrogant ass, but for now, at least, she could behave as if she believed it.

She hadn't seen Rokshan since he'd left to escort the Third Ecclesiast's body to the Archprelate's palace. On her flight there with the Archprelate, she'd considered waiting at the palace until he arrived, but the agitation of all the ecclesiasts at her arrival made her decide that was a bad idea. He'd sent word the next morning, hard on the heels of the official announcement of the Third Ecclesiast's death, that he would be occupied with royal duties for the next few days; it seemed a High Ecclesiast's passing was a state matter as well as a religious one. Lamprophyre tried not to feel impatient.

She settled on the stone and rested her head on her arms. "Why don't you read to me," she suggested. "If you don't mind. Dharan says practice is important, with reading."

"All right," Abhit said.

She'd already heard the book he'd chosen twice, so she let the words wash over her without paying them much attention. It was the sound of his high, childish voice that soothed her, a sound like birds chirping. For one so young, Abhit was remarkably good at reading. She idly made a mental note to ask Dharan to find more books for him.

Abhit finished the book and set it aside. "I'm bored," he said. "I know we're to be respectful of the Archprelate, but I don't think he cares anymore if we play games."

Lamprophyre privately agreed with him, but she felt she'd done enough to corrupt the youth of Tanajital recently and had no desire to be at odds with Bhakriya with respect to his religious education. "I think you're meant to reflect on...actually, I don't know what you believe happens after death."

"If you believe in the Gods, they take your soul to live with them when you die," Abhit said. "The reverend back home said you have to show you believe by following Jiwanyil's laws and commands. Or Katayan's, I guess. If you don't believe, then devils take your soul instead and tear it into pieces."

Lamprophyre shuddered. "Good thing the ecclesiasts declared dragons not outcast anymore, because I wouldn't want that happening to my friends just for being my friends." That had happened three days ago, and with the Third Ecclesiast's death and the announcement of the Archprelate's illness, it had felt like an afterthought even though to Lamprophyre it had been more important than anything else.

"I don't understand," Abhit said. "Were the ecclesiasts wrong in saying dragons were outcast for not worshipping Katayan?"

"They said not." It had been a masterpiece of human mendacity, really. The new decree had praised Tanajital for obeying the first one and had declared that it had been a test of faith. And with that, the old decree had been nullified, without a hint that the ecclesiasts had been wrong. All those formerly cut off were restored in Jiwanyil's sight. Lamprophyre hadn't even heard whispers that dragons should worship Katayan. All the thoughts she heard from people who came for food indicated relief that tensions had evaporated; no one harbored any secret doubts about the legitimacy of either decree.

"I guess Jiwanyil wanted to see if people still had faith in him when dragons' religion is counter to yours in some ways," she continued.

"Personally, I think if you've seen someone possessed of a prophecy, it's hard not to believe." As she said this, though, she thought of the Third Ecclesiast, who had believed a false voice claiming to be God. Suppose the voice everyone believed to be Jiwanyil was really just another creature like the false, evil one? Even if that voice was good, that didn't make it a God. Lamprophyre sighed. She wasn't fond of pondering religious matters, especially those of a religion not her own. She knew what she'd seen, and absent other evidence, she felt sure the voice she'd heard all those times was that of the actual Jiwanyil. He wasn't her God, but she could respect him.

"I have faith," Abhit said. "But you're right, some of that is because I've seen Preyanka be possessed of a prophecy. Do you suppose Jiwanyil likes it better when people believe even though they've never seen that?"

"I don't know." It was an interesting question, though another one she didn't have the knowledge to pursue.

Abhit put the book back in its pile and said, "I'm going to ask Mama if we can see Preyanka today. I wonder if she'll be busy preparing for the ceremony for choosing a new Archprelate. Wouldn't it be funny if Jiwanyil chose her?"

Lamprophyre thought it would be horrible to make a thirteen-year-old girl the religious leader of a nation. "Funny," she agreed.

She let the muggy warmth of the day soak into her bones and was falling asleep when the sound of running footsteps came to her ears. Rokshan was back.

She stepped halfway out of the hall to watch his approach. His pace slowed as he entered the courtyard, empty at this time of day. "I thought, with this announcement of the Archprelate's death, you'd be caught up in more ritual," she said.

"Not until tonight," Rokshan said. "Ayusha's death being so sudden and so violent meant the ecclesiasts enlisted our family in praying for her soul, in part because my father is king and in part because we knew her so well."

Lamprophyre grimaced. "I'm not sure I could have participated wholeheartedly, given all the evil things she did."

"All the more reason to pray to Jiwanyil for his grace in forgiving her sins." Rokshan walked into the embassy and sat against the wall with his eyes closed, breathing a little more heavily than usual. "I don't know what to think."

"Abhit says if you don't believe, devils rend your soul. What about people who believe, but do evil things?"

Rokshan opened his eyes. "Jiwanyil gives you the reward you deserve, based on his knowledge of your innermost heart. Sometimes that reward is torment until your heart changes. Some ecclesiasts like to speculate on how long that takes, and what happens after, and whether there's even any truth to the idea that we continue to grow and learn and change after death. I've always been more concerned about living an honorable life so it's not an issue."

"Don't be offended, but I like my religion better. So much less complicated."

"That's true."

Lamprophyre settled down near Rokshan. "When is the choosing ceremony?"

"For the new Archprelate? Tonight after sunset. They could do it any time, but it's tradition to do it after dark so the light of Jiwanyil is more dramatic."

"I'm sure they don't let outsiders watch."

Rokshan shook his head. "No, just royal outsiders. But they'll make the announcement immediately after it happens. The whole city waits for that."

Lamprophyre pictured everyone in Tanajital standing on their doorsteps or the flat roofs of their houses, watching the skies for a beam of light. "Well, if you're here for the day, I'll send for Dharan. He had some thoughts about the 'skies will burn' prophecy I told him I wanted to discuss when you were available." She turned and opened the back door. "Rassika?"

After a few beats, the child appeared. Lamprophyre still didn't know how old Rassika was, but she looked more mature now that she was clean and wore clothes that fit. "Will you take a message to Dharan?" she said. "Tell him Rokshan is here, and find out when he can visit."

Rassika nodded. "I'll run fast," she said, and darted away through the front doorway.

"You convinced her," Rokshan said.

"It took some talking, but it helped that she wanted to be convinced." Lamprophyre looked at the street into which Rassika had vanished. "She runs errands, and Dharan is teaching her to read so she can be even more efficient—"

"Not because you want to help her?"

Lamprophyre scowled. "Of course it's because I want to help her. But she won't take charity. Anyway, I pay Bhakriya to watch Kavari during the day, though I think Bhakriya would do it for free because she loves children, and I pay Rassika to be my messenger, and everything is perfect. Though wouldn't it be wonderful if Bhakriya took Rassika and Kavari as her own children, and married Depik? Then they would be a real family."

Rokshan laughed. "I hope you haven't told any of them this plan."

"I have self-control, Rokshan. Besides, you told me humans prefer to work things out for themselves. So I give them a home so they're close together and can see how wonderful it is to have each other."

"That is the most generous thing I've ever heard," Rokshan said. He'd stopped laughing and was regarding Lamprophyre with a curiously intent expression that made her feel uncomfortable. "This is what makes you happy, isn't it?" he continued. "Giving people what they need."

"I suppose," Lamprophyre said. "But I don't know that I ever did that with dragons. It's just that you humans are so fragile and short-lived, it feels like it means more when I can help you."

"That's an interesting perspective." Rokshan stretched out his legs, then folded them cross-legged beneath him. "The new Third Ecclesiast, by the way, is a man named Nitesh. I don't know him at all, but Khadar says he's famous among the ecclesiasts for his common sense in adjudicating religious disputes. Khadar sounded like he respects the man, for whatever that's worth."

"I'm still getting used to the idea that Khadar's opinion isn't completely self-serving. Do you think he'll go back to being selfish and self-centered?"

Rokshan ran his fingers over the smooth leather surface of the nearest book. "Oh, I think he's still that. But he's had experiences that have shaken him, and I really believe he's developed faith. What that means for the future, I don't know. I sincerely hope Jiwanyil doesn't pick him for the new Archprelate. I don't know that his new faith is strong enough to keep him from seeing that choice as proving how very special and superior to others he is."

"But you said it's entirely Jiwanyil's choice."

"It is. And, as I recall you pointing out, if I believe that, then I have to have faith that whoever Jiwanyil chooses is the right person for the job. Even if it's Khadar."

Lamprophyre shuddered. "I still hope it's not. I don't think your entire country should have to suffer while Khadar learns to be a good, unselfish person."

"I hope it's not, too."

Rassika ran through the doorway. Unlike Rokshan, she wasn't breathing heavily at all. "Dharan says he can come after noon," she said. "He also give me this to read." She waved a slim book at them. "Can I go read it, my lady, or do you need something else?"

"No, go and read, and I'll call you if I do," Lamprophyre said. She settled back down when Rassika was gone and said, "Isn't that nice? She really does love reading."

"It makes me wonder who she'll turn out to be," Rokshan said. "You saved her life, Lamprophyre. Children alone in the slums don't generally live to grow up."

"Well, that's two children who will," Lamprophyre said.

Dharan appeared closer to midafternoon than noon, carrying a stack of books atop which lay his blank book. "Sorry," he said. "I started buying books and forgot to stop."

"Are those for me?" Lamprophyre exclaimed. "What do I owe you?"

"Some of them are for you and your growing household, and some of them are mine. I'll settle up with Rokshan later." Dharan carefully deposited the stack on the protective sheet and wiped sweat off his forehead. "I hope there's a storm soon, because we could use the cooler weather."

Lamprophyre poked her head out the door and surveyed the sky, inhaling the moist air deeply. "Tomorrow before dawn," she declared. "Isn't that good, though? Because of the ceremony tonight?"

"Choosing the new Archprelate," Rokshan told Dharan, whose confused look vanished.

"As I understand it, the ceremony proceeds regardless of weather," Dharan said. "It might even be a bonus, having it in a rainstorm, because that makes it even more obvious what Jiwanyil's light is."

"I thought you were a heathen," Lamprophyre said.

"I had a very thorough religious education, Lamprophyre, and just because I'm not sure I believe it anymore doesn't mean I've forgotten it."

"But if Jiwanyil's light is so potent, even you have to admit it's real." Lamprophyre felt like she'd made a telling point, then wondered why she cared. It wasn't her religion.

"I've never seen it," Dharan said. "I'm sure there could be other explanations for it."

"I have," Rokshan said. "I thought it was obviously Jiwanyil's light. But if you want actual proof before you believe, I won't argue with you. I won't even be insulted that you won't take my word for it."

"Thanks," Dharan said with a grin. "Now, let me tell you what I've learned about our favorite prophecies."

Lamprophyre settled back on her haunches and furled her wings close to her side. "We told you what the Archprelate said, that he believed those prophecies were related to the evil entity that spoke to the Third Ecclesiast."

"Yes, and that gave me a direction for my research." Dharan picked up his blank book and leafed through the pages. "If 'the skies will burn' is a metaphor for an oncoming catastrophe, and the prophecies warn of that catastrophe or tell how to avert it, then it's an easy jump to assume that whatever this entity is, it wants the catastrophe to happen. Which means there should be references in some of these prophecies that will tell us more about the entity itself."

He picked up a piece of chalk and turned in a slow circle, looking around. "Where are the slates?"

"Still at the warehouses. We keep forgetting to bring them back," Lamprophyre said.

"Well, never mind. I can write on the wall." Dharan chose a different, storm-gray piece of chalk and turned to the wall. "There are ten references to a 'voice from darkness' in the collected prophecies. Two of them reference 'the old stone.' One mentions, in a general way, fearing the ally and welcoming the stranger. And Ayusha's prophecy said to 'fear no one except the enemy you do not know.'" He wrote all of that swiftly on the white wall of the embassy, large enough for Lamprophyre to read easily. "That all speaks to an unknown enemy, one that stays hidden, but one that on the surface appears to be good or supportive."

"Which is what Ayusha proved," Rokshan said. "What about 'old stone'?"

"I'm not sure." Dharan tapped the chalk against his lips. "Stone usually suggests strength and stability, a sure foundation. So in this case, it might well mean something you expect to be a support, but isn't. But all of that taken together definitely imply some non-human, non-dragon, single entity. It's not Fanishkor, for one."

"Which is a relief and a disappointment, because if it were Fanishkor, we'd know how to fight," Rokshan said.

"I don't like what the Third Ecclesiast said about this not being able to be stopped," Lamprophyre said. "That feels as if nothing we learn or do matters."

"Maybe it can't be stopped," Dharan said, "but if were impossible to overcome, there wouldn't be prophecies about it." He flipped pages. "This one says 'two become as one,' and *this* one—" He turned a few more pages. "This one is really long and flowery, but I'm pretty sure it refers to dragons and humans together. Doing what, it doesn't say. But definitely acting as one."

"So we're already doing something to defend against the entity by teaching humans and dragons to live in harmony," Lamprophyre said.

Dharan nodded. "Also, Ayusha's prophecy said to ward against the voice in darkness, which implies that such a warding is possible."

"I told Khadar that," Rokshan said. "Actually, I told him everything that happened in the courtyard. He didn't know what warding against such a voice might be, but he said the ecclesiasts would pray for a prophecy on the subject. And in the meantime, they're warning everyone not to be fooled by false voices."

"There are other hints to what the catastrophe will look like, or signs that it's coming," Dharan continued. "References to waking, either the world waking, which would mean spring, or something else waking, probably meaning the entity gaining power. Some prophecies talk about storms coming, which, if it's literal, might mean the rainy season, but I'm inclined to think it means the enemy's attack will be something we see coming from well off, or with time to prepare. But there are a few that make no sense. Yet."

"You sound like you're about to go into battle," Lamprophyre said, amused.

"I've never let an intellectual puzzle beat me, and this one is no exception." Dharan closed his blank book. "The more we learn, the easier these prophecies will be to understand."

"Convinced now that they're true prophecies?" Rokshan said with an arch smile. "Or is this really just an intellectual puzzle?"

Dharan shrugged. "Let's just say I'm willing to grant you the possibility they're real. We just disagree on the source. Besides—" His expression suddenly became very somber. "The consequences of not believing something like this that turns out to be true are greater than I'm willing to risk. If that means I have to revisit my stance on God, so be it."

Rokshan rose and clapped Dharan on the shoulder. "You know it doesn't matter to me whether you believe or not, right?"

"I do," Dharan said, "and that, more than anything, leads me to believe you're right."

CHAPTER THIRTY-EIGHT

Sunset came with no lessening of the punishing heat and humidity. Rokshan and Dharan left well before the evening meal, Dharan to a lecture, Rokshan to join his family for the Archprelate's ceremony. Lamprophyre dozed until the smells of good food cooking roused her. The courtyard still wasn't as full as it had been before the ecclesiasts' first, disastrous pronouncement, but there was still a line at the soup cauldron where Bhakriya stood. To Lamprophyre's surprise, Rassika had joined her and was handing bowls to beggars. Probably she was just looking for more ways to earn her keep, but how wonderful if she'd done it because she wanted to help!

Lamprophyre made her way past the line to the pavilion, where Depik had brought out the trolley—sheep this time, not something she loved for always, but a nice change from cow. He'd also served plates to Abhit and Kavari, and Abhit was supervising Kavari's meal. Just like a brother would. Lamprophyre stopped herself daydreaming along those lines and tore into the first sheep. The greasy meat satisfied her. Food now, and...no, flying with her clutch afterward wasn't a good idea, not on this night. If they passed too close to the Archprelate's palace while the ceremony was happening, and the ecclesiasts thought they were interfering—it was better not to take any chances on misunderstandings. They could fly another time.

She chewed, swiped her mouth with the large cloth Depik provided—he liked to joke about how messy an eater she was, but it was true as well—and took another bite. Delicious.

Kavari finished her meal and carried her plate carefully into the kitchen. Lamprophyre listened to Depik's amused thoughts at how grown-up the baby was becoming. He would have no trouble thinking of the children as his own, if it ever came to that. Lamprophyre scowled and stopped listening. She was a busybody, she thought the word was, and it didn't matter that she only wanted her friends to be happy, it was still interfering.

After finishing her meal, she crossed the courtyard to the embassy and settled in the doorway, watching the humans and idly listening to their thoughts. Another few nights, with more and more people coming for food, and the noise would be too great to hear any one person's thoughts. She saw one-legged Sumaan talking to an old woman whose thoughts flitted here and there like butterflies, not mad, but in the beginnings of a decline, and her heart ached. She should be glad of the Archprelate being free, finally, of his senility. If his religious tradition was true, he was happy now, safe with Jiwanyil and not lost to himself anymore. But she missed seeing him in her courtyard.

She glanced at the Sister of the Red, who crossed the courtyard toward her, holding her bowl of soup. The woman stopped near Lamprophyre and saluted her with the bowl. "Thank you for your generosity in feeding us all," she said. "I don't know if I said that before."

"It's no trouble, and you're welcome," Lamprophyre said.

The Sister of the Red raised the bowl to her very red lips, but didn't eat. "I'm sorry I missed the drama the other night. How exciting, to see the Archprelate. Is it true he was mad?"

The ecclesiasts had already told Lamprophyre what to say if anyone asked this question, and Lamprophyre, feeling loyalty to the old man if not to his compatriots, had decided to obey their wishes. "He was Jiwanyil's voice to the people, and perfectly coherent." That was even true.

The woman nodded slowly as if Lamprophyre had said something very wise. "And the decree has been rescinded. I suppose I'm grateful not to be excommunicated anymore—no, I tell a lie, I'm still not welcome among the good worshippers of Jiwanyil." She shrugged one shoulder, making the garnet on her arm flash in the low light. "It doesn't bother me, and I'm glad it didn't bother you."

"It's not my religion." Lamprophyre wondered what the point of this conversation was. She listened to the woman's thoughts and caught one that startled her so much she didn't hear the woman's next spoken words. "I beg your pardon?"

"I said, it seems dragons are more generous with each other's faults than humans are." The Sister of the Red took a delicate bite of soup. "I doubt a dragon would shun another dragon over a difference of religious opinion."

"We wouldn't, but it's not the same." Should she bring it up? Challenge the woman? "What's it like, doing what you do?" she asked.

The Sister of the Red smiled. "Interesting. I've always enjoyed sex, and I enjoy power, and this life lets me have some of both. You might be surprised at how some men can be manipulated through sex without their even knowing it. Though I know nothing of dragon sexuality, so perhaps it's not a surprise."

"I don't understand human sex. Rokshan won't talk about it. He says it's coarse to discuss it with someone of the opposite sex."

"I see." The Sister of the Red took another dainty bite of soup. "Well, I'd be happy to explain anything you like, if you're interested."

"I am, actually. Not tonight, but some time when there aren't so many people I might have to pay attention to. But that wasn't what I meant." Lamprophyre took a deep breath. "Were you spying on me from the start, or did Tekentriya take advantage of a coincidence?"

The spoon, halfway to the Sister of the Red's lips, halted. She lowered bowl and spoon and gazed intently at Lamprophyre. Then she laughed. "How long have you known?" she said.

"Long enough," Lamprophyre said. "Did Tekentriya think I was so dangerous? Or was it just curiosity?"

The Sister of the Red shook her head slowly, still chuckling. "The Princess Tekentriya is suspicious and clever, and I admire her for it.

She sees in dragons a new power in Tanajital, and she wants to understand that power, control it if she can. I told her that was impossible, but I don't think she believed me. Control is something she holds dear, and the possibility of being at the whim of something she can't control, well, you see how that might frustrate her."

"What did you tell her?"

"I'm a professional, Lamprophyre. I don't share my secrets with my marks, however much I might like them. But you needn't worry. I told her only what any observer might see—what she would see if she had the time to come here and watch."

Lamprophyre didn't know what to say. The revelation made her feel completely out of her depth. "And that satisfied her?" she managed.

"For now. I think if dragons were to take a more active role in Gonjirian politics, she would increase her scrutiny. Fortunate for everyone you don't intend that, yes?" Her red lips curved in a secretive smile.

"I don't—" Lamprophyre exhaled slowly, turning her head so her hot breath didn't touch the woman. "You'll stop now?"

"Why, because you know my secret?" The Sister of the Red leaned forward slightly. "Tekentriya will send someone else if I tell her I've been found out. Someone you won't know to suspect. I think we'll both be happier if I continue to make my reports—I'll go on eating here, and you'll know to put on a good face whenever I'm around."

Finding Tekentriya's next spy would be simple, now Lamprophyre knew such a thing was possible, but the idea of having to search every human who entered the embassy wearied her. And she liked the Sister of the Red, despite her continuing wariness of the woman. "I agree," she said. "But it would be a bad idea to try to deceive me again."

The Sister of the Red laughed. "I'll remember that." She turned away to face southwestward, setting her bowl on the ground. "It's getting dark. I wonder if it's dark enough for the ceremony?"

Lamprophyre followed her gaze, imagining a line extending all the way from the embassy to the Archprelate's palace. She didn't know where they held the ceremony. She'd only seen the narrow strip of white bricks—narrow by her standards—that ran in front of the Archprelate's palace when she'd arrived there days ago with the Archprelate perched behind her shoulders. That had been barely big enough to fit her, and certainly couldn't hold a host of ecclesiasts. But she'd seen an enormous field like the training grounds spread out behind the Archprelate's palace, and now she imagined it covered in bright green grass trampled flat by the feet of hundreds of ecclesiasts.

It occurred to her to wonder if there were ecclesiasts elsewhere in Gonjiri, if they felt left out because they couldn't attend the ceremony. Suppose one of them were the next Archprelate, and couldn't be named for that reason? But if that were a problem, surely the High Ecclesiasts would do something about it. It was fun to imagine those ecclesiasts drawn to Tanajital without knowing why, arriving just in time to participate in the ceremony, and then having that light fall upon them, declaring them Archprelate.

"How does it work?" she asked. "Is the light visible to outsiders, like a lantern shining through a gap in a wall?"

The Sister of the Red nodded. "Almost. The skies glow when the light appears. We won't see Jiwanyil's light, just its reflection."

Lamprophyre eyed the clouds, which had begun gathering shortly before sunset in preparation for the coming storm. They were still thin and gray, heavy enough only to dim the light of sunset and too high to reflect the lights of Tanajital, if there had been any; the city was remarkably dark tonight. Towers rising between the embassy and the Archprelate's palace were thin gray fingers reaching for the clouds, their gilded tops shining dully as they caught the last rays of light.

She and the Sister of the Red watched in silence as darkness fell. Depik didn't come to light the lanterns, but Lamprophyre didn't worry. It felt right that Tanajital should lie in darkness on this night, waiting to see what light Jiwanyil would send.

The courtyard was still. Lamprophyre heard Bhakriya putting the children to bed, though only Abhit and Kavari; Rassika had joined Lamprophyre at some point, standing next to her in silence and looking southwestward as well. The beggars had all either left or were sitting quietly here and there throughout the courtyard. Lamprophyre breathed shallowly, not wanting to disturb the stillness with even the smallest noise.

Then Rassika grabbed her hand. In the distance, faint light glowed, reflecting off the clouds as if someone had lit a lantern and was now trimming it to glow ever brighter. The light increased until the clouds were as white as if lit by the sun. A sigh ran through the courtyard, from the beggars to Depik and Bhakriya to Rassika and even to the Sister of the Red. Lamprophyre watched in awe as the light shifted with the movement of the clouds. It didn't look like anything special, if you didn't count how no lantern available to human or dragon could make a light that large. And yet it gave off an indefinable peace with its light, a sense of wonder even Lamprophyre could feel.

The light lasted for no more than ten beats, but no one moved in all that time. Then the light faded as steadily as it had appeared, and Tanajital was in darkness again—for half a beat. Lights, ordinary small lanterns, sparked into life throughout the city, marking the streets and the towers and the distant city wall. Lamprophyre made way for Depik to light the embassy lanterns. Rassika released her hand and walked away silently into the embassy, heading for the back door and her bed. Lamprophyre gave the distant clouds one last look, then nodded to the Sister of the Red and turned away. She pretended she didn't see the silvery marks of tears on the woman's face.

She settled in for the night, tail curled around her, wings covering her, head pillowed on her arms. Tomorrow she would learn who the new Archprelate was. It wouldn't be Preyanka. It might be Khadar, though she echoed Rokshan's hope that Jiwanyil wouldn't be so cruel—to Khadar, if not to Gonjiri. Probably it would be someone she'd never heard of. Someone who until a few beats ago had been nothing but an ordinary ecclesiast and was now responsible for an entire country's spiritual well-being. How had she or he felt when that light appeared? Lamprophyre couldn't imagine it.

Lamprophyre, someone whispered.

Lamprophyre sat up and looked around, dread rising within her. That had been no earthly voice, much as she wanted to believe some stranger had crept into the embassy to speak to her.

Lamprophyre, the voice said, *you have been chosen.*

"Stones," Lamprophyre cursed in a whisper. Ward against the voice in darkness, the prophecy had said, but how?

Listen to me well, the voice said. *I will*—

"No," Lamprophyre said. "You're not welcome. I will not listen."

The voice chuckled. *You have no choice but to hear me.*

Desperate, Lamprophyre did the only thing she could think of to block unwanted thoughts, something all dragons were taught to do as part of learning mental listening etiquette: she recited the first poem that came to mind. "Oh, the dragonet/Has never yet/Been taught to fly or warble;/But the dragon who/Flies straight and true/Will sing of slate and marble!"

She couldn't hear the voice anymore, but she had a feeling it was just biding its time. She went into the second verse, madly running through her options. She knew more poetry than anyone, and she could outlast the voice. But what if that was false? Suppose the voice had greater endurance, and could afford to wait for Lamprophyre to become exhausted? She needed a different plan.

Mother Stone, she pleaded silently, *protect me.*

The voice leaped on her moment of inattention. *Mother Stone cannot save you*, it said. *Listen to me. I will give you everything you ever desired.*

"I already have that," Lamprophyre exclaimed. The voice had given the Third Ecclesiast her every desire, and—but no. It hadn't. There had been one thing the voice couldn't give her, and Lamprophyre had known what that was.

"Jiwanyil!" she shouted. "This is your prophecy. Stop this creature, now!"

Green light blazed around her, surrounding her so she could see nothing beyond it. The voice shrieked, a high, shrill sound that pierced Lamprophyre's heart and made her ears ache. Then it was gone, and the light was gone, and Lamprophyre came to herself to find she was lying flat on her face in the embassy, breathing in the scent of the hard-packed, dead earth that was its floor.

Lamprophyre closed her eyes and took a few beats to appreciate the way her heart sent blood speeding through her body, how her lungs drew in and expelled air, how her mind was her own and not touched by the voice of some evil entity. Then she pushed herself upright and looked around. The embassy was dark and quiet and empty of anyone but herself. The voice, when she probed the corners of her mind, was gone.

She began shaking and curled in on herself to control it. That thing had spoken to her from Stones knew where, it had known her name, and nothing she could do could make it leave. It had taken divine intervention by a god not even her own to send it screaming away. Lamprophyre felt certain that intervention had been permanent. The voice wouldn't touch her again.

She felt sick. She'd called on Mother Stone and received no response. Was that because subconsciously, she hadn't expected to? Mother Stone had never spoken to her or to any dragon in Lamprophyre's whole life, and Lamprophyre knew no stories of that ever happening. It wasn't something Mother Stone did; she was a guardian and a refuge, but took no active role in her children's lives. It didn't mean Mother Stone wasn't real.

Unless it did.

Lamprophyre violently shook her head to dispel the awful thought. Mother Stone loved her, she was sure of it. And it was just that she'd seen Jiwanyil take action in exactly those circumstances that she'd thought to call on him. Knowing he was real wasn't the same as believing in him, in the sense of worshipping or giving him her allegiance. It wasn't a betrayal of her own faith that she'd called on Jiwanyil.

She made herself think of more practical matters. If this voice was going to keep trying to overwhelm people, they needed a more reliable defense than calling on Jiwanyil or reciting poetry. A better ward. That wasn't something she—

It came to her in an instant. The chlorite artifacts. Those made it impossible to hear thoughts; what if that extended to preventing someone from putting thoughts into your head? She was almost out the door before she remembered it was too late for any adepts to be reasonably burst in on, and she didn't know many adepts at any rate. Going to Manishi was out of the question. Lamprophyre settled back down and calmed herself. Time enough to do this in the morning.

Which left only the question of the entity itself. It had felt very old, and very clever, and very sure of itself. But that was all she knew. She didn't know what kind of creature it was, whether it was human or dragon—*please, Mother Stone, not dragon*—or something so alien they didn't have a name for it. She didn't even know if it had a body. Maybe she should have spoken with it long enough to learn what it wanted. No, that was a bad idea, because suppose a longer communication would have given it power over her?

If you can hear me, she thought, *and I hope you can't, but if you can hear me—I will stop you.*

Nothing replied. She closed her eyes and made herself relax by mentally reciting the longest and most boring poem she knew. At first, the idea of sleep seemed ridiculous, but as time passed, she found herself struggling to remember the lines, and gratefully drifted off.

The last thing she remembered, in a haze so profound she thought she'd imagined it, was a voice saying, *I am coming. And the skies will burn.*

SNEAK PEEK: EMBER IN SHADOW

Lamprophyre perched atop the highest tower in the city of Tanajital and surveyed the landscape below. The last rays of the sun tinted the stone and plaster of the buildings orange, warming the city despite the coolness in the air. Winter was coming, creeping over the lowlands so slowly Lamprophyre hadn't realized the weather was changing until it already had.

She gazed past the city wall, built of pinkish granite blocks even a dragon would have trouble lifting. The fields that had been golden with crops last spring and then turned verdant green with the rains of summer were dry and bare now, waiting for humans to lay in new crops. To the west, the Green River ran slow and shallow, its name even less appropriate than usual as winter drew near.

She'd rather be home in the mountains for winter, her favorite time of year. Snow covered the bare crags, softening their lines and giving the dragons something to roll around in. When storms raged, the flight took shelter in the many caves dotting the peaks, some of them natural, some hollowed out by dragons over centuries. The females heated stones with their fire and made the caves cozy and comfortable, and the dragons entertained each other with poetry recitation or drawing on the walls. Sometimes the oldest dragons told stories of what they remembered, taking the flight's imagination back in time almost to the Great Cataclysm. Lamprophyre always remembered her father Aegirine at this time, how he'd buried her laughing in snowdrifts when she was small and flung snowballs at her when she grew too large to be buried. She looked forward to winter every year.

This year, she wasn't so sure. She hadn't seen any of the signs of winter she was accustomed to, just changes that might have meant anything. First, the constant rains of summer had lessened and then disappeared, drying the air slightly. Then the sun had gradually shifted its position southward, and the brutal heat had diminished with it. Now, only three twelvedays from the shortest day of the year, the sun no longer beat down with such punishing heat, and the nights actually verged on chilly.

Even so, chilly wasn't the same as cold, and there was no way snow would fall on Tanajital. Lamprophyre looked at all the landmarks she was now so familiar with. The palace with its dozen gilded roofs, tawny in the light of the setting sun, surrounded by rich green parkland of trees and grass. The stone mountain of the city guard headquarters, a symmetrical pyramid of square segments that might have been cut from the granite by dragon claws, and the great plaza in front of it. The Archprelate's palace, low and squat except for the spire piercing its center, reaching for heaven. And, just north of where she clung, the dragon embassy, with its blue roof and matching painted decorations. She was too distant to smell supper cooking, but she imagined it anyway.

She let go of the tower and fell about a dragonlength before snapping her wings open to soar over the streets and houses of the human capital. Flying was wonderful no matter where she did it, but it was especially fun to listen to the amazed thoughts of the humans below, just within range of her mental hearing. It had been months—she prided herself on finally understanding human measurements of days and time—since dragons had come to Tanajital, and almost all the humans were used to them by now. Lamprophyre rarely heard fear from them anymore.

She coasted along above the wide street that ended at the embassy, which had once been a customs house for human trade, and landed neatly on the roof ridge beam to look down into the courtyard. There were more humans than usual, beggars come for a free meal, but Lamprophyre never knew what made the difference. So long as they had enough soup, it didn't matter.

She climbed down the rear of the embassy and entered the dining pavilion near the kitchen. Depik looked up when she loomed over him. "Five minutes, my lady," he said.

"It smells done now," Lamprophyre said, drawing in a big whiff of hot cooked cow, her favorite meal.

"It has to finish cooking outside the oven, you know I've told you that, my lady," Depik said with a smile.

Lamprophyre scowled, but half-heartedly. Depik's genius needed to be obeyed. "I know. I just hoped for once it would magically cook faster."

"I'm sure magic can't do better than me." Depik chuckled. "I'll bring it to you soon."

Lamprophyre proceeded to the main area of the dining pavilion and sat heavily in her accustomed place. Outside, Bhakriya was ladling soup into bowls, aided by young Rassika. "Good evening, my lady," Bhakriya said over her shoulder. "It's been a lovely day."

"If I were home, I'd be playing in the snow," Lamprophyre said. "It's so different here."

"What's snow?" Rassika asked.

"It's what happens when rain freezes. It's light and very cold, like frozen feathers."

Rassika's puzzlement deepened. "What's freezes?"

"I...it's hard to explain. It never gets cold enough in Tanajital for anything to freeze."

Rassika shrugged and picked up another wooden bowl. She'd changed so thoroughly since she and her baby sister Kavari had come to live with Lamprophyre it was hard to reconcile the clean, alert, helpful young woman with the dirty, frightened girl she'd once been.

Lamprophyre took a look around the courtyard. She didn't see any of her regulars, most of whom stood out in one way or another. Like Sumaan, the one-legged young man who'd been coming less often recently. Lamprophyre wasn't sure whether to worry about him or not.

Maybe it meant he'd found work and didn't need a free meal so often. Darsha, the Sister of the Red prostitute who spied on Lamprophyre for Crown Princess Tekentriya, wasn't here either. But Lamprophyre didn't worry about her at all. Darsha was clever and capable and was almost certainly busy with a client.

The idea of paying someone to have sex with you was still utterly foreign to Lamprophyre, and not just because dragons didn't use coin. She tried not to judge humans by dragon behavior. It seemed wrong and unfair to expect humans to do everything the way dragons did. But sex for dragons was tied so closely to mental communication, to the intimacy of knowing another's thoughts, Lamprophyre had trouble not being judgmental. She reminded herself again that her best friend Rokshan had had sex without being married and it didn't make him a bad person.

The thought of Rokshan made her wonder where he was. He'd left last night saying only that today was reserved for family matters, but she'd thought he meant the daylight hours and that he'd join her for supper as he usually did. Lamprophyre sat up straighter as the creak of trolley wheels signaled Depik's approach with her cow. It wasn't as if she wouldn't see him tomorrow. She'd just gotten used to eating with him in the evenings.

She tore into her cow with more alacrity than usual. Hot juices ran down her chin, and she licked up what she could manage and mopped the rest with a clean cloth Depik provided. He was more concerned about her dining manners than she was, saying frequently that ambassadors needed to set a good example. Lamprophyre had grumbled about her manners being perfectly acceptable among dragons, but she'd understood his point. So she used the cloth and pretended she was a dainty human eating soup in the palace dining hall.

She'd never actually seen the palace dining hall. It was deep within the palace, which wasn't built to accommodate dragons. But Rokshan had described it, filled with candles so it was lit bright as day regardless of the hour, the tables set in a U with the king and his family sitting at the base of the U and the guests spread out along the two long sides. The open space between was for entertainment, dancers or musicians or performing animals. Lamprophyre never wished she could be human

—the very thought made her scales tingle with disgust—but she did wish she could see the entertainments.

"Rokshan didn't send word he wasn't coming, did he?" she asked between mouthfuls.

"No, and we haven't seen him, my lady," Bhakriya said.

Lamprophyre grumbled to herself. Rokshan was a prince and the youngest of five royal children. His family had many duties associated with ruling Gonjiri. He might be her diplomatic liaison, but that didn't mean he could ignore all his other responsibilities. Even so, she looked forward to seeing him every day and it made her irritable when she didn't.

She tore off a somewhat larger mouthful of cow and chewed vigorously. "I suppose this ceremony has him preoccupied," she said when her mouth was mostly empty. "This pair-bonding thing...what did you call it?"

"The royal wedding," Bhakriya said. She released the ladle with a small splash and turned to face Lamprophyre. "It's so romantic. Princess Anchala and her betrothed from Sachetan...it's like a storybook romance, the way he swept her off her feet."

Rassika scowled. "I think it's silly. All that mush."

"You'll think differently when you're older, sweetheart," Bhakriya said fondly. Rassika scowled more deeply. "Falling in love is the most wonderful thing in the world."

Lamprophyre heard Depik's thoughts sharpen and realized he was listening carefully to this. She considered half a dozen leading questions before deciding there was no good way to approach what she wanted to know, which was whether Bhakriya's feelings for Depik were as deep as his for her. "For dragons too," she said instead. "My parents loved each other very much. I hope I fall in love like that someday."

"Aren't you in love with Porphyry?" Rassika asked. "He's here all the time."

"No, Porphyry and I are just good friends and clutchmates," Lamprophyre said. "I don't feel that way about any of the clutch." She listened to Bhakriya's thoughts, but heard nothing that might indicate she was thinking of Depik when she thought of love. Disappointed, she added, "But there are lots of dragons near my age. I'm sure someday one will be right for me."

"You just have to be patient," Bhakriya said. "I...it's not important. But love is sweeter when it comes slowly."

Asking Bhakriya to elaborate was probably a bad idea, given that her former husband had beaten her and tormented her, so whatever love they'd originally felt for each other hadn't lasted. Lamprophyre blocked out Depik's painfully clear thoughts and wondered, as she often did, whether it wasn't cruel to let him live in such close proximity to Bhakriya, if he loved her and she didn't feel the same. But it wasn't as if she could kick either of them out.

"I'll remember that," she said, and took a last bite of cow. "Rassika, would you fetch me a slab of mica? The courtyard is too full for me to safely cross."

Rassika nodded and darted away. Lamprophyre cracked a bone and sucked out the delicious marrow. Rokshan's absence aside, this was a beautiful evening.

She accepted the mica from Rassika and chewed the brittle, easily fractured mineral happily. It crunched like tiny bird bones in her teeth, but without the tickling sensation of feathers. Depik took the remains of the carcass away without comment and without looking at Bhakriya. Lamprophyre felt so bad for him. She'd been so sure Bhakriya would see Depik's wonderful qualities and fall in love with him. But now it seemed Bhakriya wasn't interested in falling in love with anyone. Lamprophyre wished she could pummel Bhakriya's former husband for hurting her so badly, emotionally as well as physically.

Movement at the mouth of the street caught her attention, and she sat up straight. "Rokshan!"

"Sorry about that," Rokshan said as he approached. "Lots of ceremonies today, all of them centered on the families meeting. It's important everyone receive attention according to their status, which means negotiations and politeness and I thought I might actually die of boredom."

"I thought your family outranked Lord Torannum's. Doesn't that make it easy?"

Rokshan lowered himself to sit beside her, his legs crossed under him. "You would think so, yes? But a woman who isn't heir to a title takes her husband's rank, and there's always dispute over when exactly that transfer of rank takes place. And Torannum, Jiwanyil bless him, has a very status-conscious mother and a father who defers to his wife in everything. So Lady Risha makes every ceremony longer with her 'are you sure that's how it should be' and her 'of course I don't know how you do it in Gonjiri, but in Sachetan...' and the way she clears her throat."

Lamprophyre settled back, amused, and took another bite of mica. "I didn't think there was more than one way to clear one's throat."

Rokshan rolled his eyes. "God's breath, Lamprophyre, the woman has turned throat-clearing into an art form." He stiffened his spine and put two fingers delicately over his mouth, and said, "A-*hem*," blurring the syllables so the word was barely intelligible. Lamprophyre laughed and wiped crumbs of mica from her lips.

"But Torannum is nice?" she asked.

"Very nice. He dotes on Anchala, but not in a servile way, and I think I like him best of all my brothers-in-law."

"I thought there was only one. Tekentriya's husband what's-his-name."

"Zekran, and you're not the only one who forgets about him. He's not a bad sort, just kind of a nonentity."

"I can easily understand how Tekentriya would overshadow anyone she's married to." Tekentriya, Crown Princess, was smart, powerful, domineering, and suspicious. It had been a surprise to learn she was pair-bonded at all, let alone that she had three children.

"Anyway, yes, he's the only living one. Manishi's husband Vorshan died of an illness years ago, and I disliked him intensely, if I can be allowed to speak ill of the dead—"

"You know that's not a dragon custom. Speak away."

"He was a braggart, and he and Manishi fought constantly, making everyone around them uncomfortable. They, of course, loved the fighting and didn't care what anyone else thought. I didn't wish Vorshan ill, naturally, but it was such a relief to have an end to the fighting."

Lamprophyre nodded. "I'm glad Torannum is a good man. I like Anchala."

Rokshan leaned against her flank. "And Dharan escapes his doom. Though just between us, I think Anchala was only interested in Dharan because he was a challenge. Torannum is a much better match for her."

"Will the...what did you call it? Will the wedding party come to the races tomorrow?"

"That's the plan, yes. Lady Risha demonstrated the first genuine emotion I've seen from her when my father told her about it. It seems she's fascinated by dragons. You might want to stay away from her, because she's the sort of person who would ask for a ride and not understand a refusal."

Lamprophyre shuddered. She swept the mica crumbs into a pile and pinched them into her mouth. "Thanks for the warning. What about Khadar? Will he deign to grace us with his presence?"

Rokshan tilted his head back. "He and the other High Ecclesiasts are performing purification rituals with the Archprelate, readying the training grounds to be a suitable location for a royal wedding. Though he did say the Archprelate was sorry to miss the races. She's fond of dragons, too."

Lamprophyre nodded. Shevaan, the new Archprelate, was only in her mid-thirties and much more active than her predecessor, who'd been very old when Lamprophyre had known him. Lamprophyre had met the new Archprelate a few days after the woman's appointment, if you could call being touched by Jiwanyil's light an appointment, and hadn't known what to expect. But the new Archprelate had a winning smile and a friendly, open demeanor, and had said, "Gonjiri is blessed indeed to receive such wonderful creatures. I hope you will feel welcome here." Lamprophyre, still smarting over several twelvedays' worth of insults and casual cruelties by ecclesiasts who'd felt themselves justified on religious grounds, smiled and bowed and said nothing. It wasn't this Archprelate's fault the former Third Ecclesiast had been corrupted by an evil entity into lying about prophecy, and Lamprophyre felt she could be generous.

"And Khadar's change of heart has lasted longer than I expected,"

Rokshan went on. "He and I had a civil conversation this morning, and he never took a single opportunity to lecture me on the evils of consorting with dragons."

"I thought all that was over."

"Over as far as official doctrine goes. There are still plenty of ecclesiasts who believe dragons should worship Katayan. And the truth is, that makes sense from a certain perspective. The Lonely God Katayan has dragons to worship him for the first time in nearly a millennium, so I can see how some humans might think the fact that dragons don't would be a problem."

"Just so they don't nag me, or threaten my friends again, they can think whatever they want."

Rokshan nodded. "Are you racing tomorrow?"

"Maybe once or twice. I'm out of practice. And no one's figured out a racing harness yet." Lamprophyre settled herself more comfortably, putting out a hand to keep from knocking Rokshan over. "Though none of us are sure we're comfortable with the idea. It's not as if we need riders when we race."

"I admit my interest is purely selfish. I like the idea of racing with you. I just don't want to worry about being knocked off." Rokshan yawned. "But I understand it might be undignified."

Lamprophyre laughed. "We're all too young to worry about our dignity. Except Chrysoprase, who is awfully stodgy for someone only twenty-seven years older than my clutch."

"I didn't know she was here. Will she race, too?"

"She and Massicot came down this morning to help build the obstacle course. It's going to be so much fun! Even if Chrysoprase is likely to win all the speed challenges."

Rokshan yawned again. "I should get back. I didn't realize how sleepy I was."

"You could sleep here," Lamprophyre pointed out.

"No, the ceremonies start at dawn. Much as I'd prefer to stay." He got heavily to his feet. "Give me a ride?"

"You must be tired if you're that lazy."

Rokshan made a perfunctory rude gesture in Lamprophyre's direction. "If you were in my place, you'd realize how exhausting all this social activity is."

Lamprophyre moved slowly into the courtyard, giving the remaining beggars time to get out of her way, and crouched to give Rokshan a leg up. It was almost full dark, and Depik had lit the lanterns illuminating the courtyard, but despite the dimness there were still plenty of men and women loitering. Lamprophyre flapped her wings a few times, hoping the humans would take the hint, then leaped into the sky, prompting a cry of exultation from Rokshan.

It had been a surprise to discover how much more she liked flying when she had a companion. It wasn't as if she were suddenly a more competent flyer, and as she'd said, dragons didn't need human direction to stay on course. But having someone to talk to was invigorating, and Rokshan loved flying so much it felt as if she'd discovered it all over again.

She dipped low over the palace, made a wide circle around the parkland as she descended, and alit neatly in front of the great front doors, closed now but still guarded by soldiers with halberds. Rokshan hopped down and said, "I'll see you tomorrow, all right? And let the others know Torannum and his family would like to meet them. I'll see if I can't impress upon Lady Risha the impropriety of asking to ride a dragon."

"We'll be all right," Lamprophyre said.

She watched until the great doors shut behind Rokshan before taking to the skies once more. With the light of the half-moon silvering the towers and rooftops, night flying wasn't very dangerous, not the way it was in the big open spaces between here and the mountains, but it still wasn't something Lamprophyre felt comfortable doing. And not because she felt unsafe; she had promised Hyaloclast, the dragon queen, that she wouldn't do it anymore, and keeping that promise felt important. Lamprophyre was sure that feeling didn't arise from her desire to please her mother, but instead came from a sense that the thrill of risking herself was...childish, perhaps?

In any case, she hurried back to the embassy and settled herself in the hall. The courtyard had cleared during her short flight, and no one moved throughout the embassy grounds. Lamprophyre closed her eyes and listened to the thoughts of her household. Depik and Bhakriya were in the kitchen, washing up. Rassika was behind the embassy where the servants' houses lay, putting Bhakriya's son Abhit and Rassika's sister Kavari to bed. They were just like a little family, and if only Bhakriya...but it was wrong to lay all of Lamprophyre's wishes on Bhakriya. If she didn't love Depik, that's all there was to it. And they'd all still care for each other regardless.

Lamprophyre sighed and lay down with her head pillowed on her arms. Time for her to stop wishing for the world to run her way and to accept the way it was.

She listened to the quiet sounds of washing and the idle thoughts of Bhakriya and Depik, both of whom weren't thinking anything more personal than how weary they were, but in a good way, the kind of weariness that comes from honest exertion and accomplishment. The courtyard dimmed further as the lights in the dining pavilion went out, and further still when Depik extinguished the lanterns flanking the embassy doorway. Then the night was still, with nothing but the distant hum of the living city to disturb the quiet.

Lamprophyre closed her eyes and made one last mental check of her human friends. Ever since the night, months ago, she'd been poisoned by someone who'd sneaked into the embassy grounds and tainted her food, she'd had worries about something like that happening again. Only her fears weren't for herself, but for the others in her household. So every night, she listened to their thoughts to assure herself they were well. The children were asleep. Depik was thinking of Bhakriya. Bhakriya was thinking of her daughter Preyanka, a young ecclesiast living in the Archprelate's palace while she learned to control her prophetic powers. Everything was fine. She let herself relax until she gradually drifted off to sleep.

She woke abruptly, disturbed by a sound she couldn't remember, something that in her dream had been two hands clapping once. Pitchy darkness surrounded her, far darker than night ever was, and she blinked as if that might clear her vision. In her confusion, she could tell only that she was surrounded by people—humans, they had to be humans because so many dragons wouldn't fit—whose wordless thoughts were sharp and intent on moving silently. "What—" she began.

Something grabbed her and *twisted,* making her scream in agony. All her bones grated against each other, muscles tore, and she tried to draw breath for another scream and found her lungs unresponsive. A high, keening whistle filled her ears, a shrill sound that felt like a needle drilling through her ears into her skull.

She felt as if she were falling, but the sensation went on and on without pause. Disoriented, she flung out her arms, desperate for balance. Her hands smacked the hard earth floor of the embassy. It felt strange, the surface grainier and rougher than before, and the smell of the dirt was distant, like the memory of a smell.

The hands wrung her again, and she smelled blood, faint as the smell of earth. She became aware that she was crouched on her hands and knees, and the floor still felt strange, as if she were suddenly aware of every particle on the clean-swept surface digging into her scales. The humans' thoughts intensified, and she heard *stop her screaming* and *wake the others* just as giant hands, far larger than any dragon's, took hold of her again. Someone shoved a large wad of cloth into her mouth, and when she reached up to remove it, those giant hands grabbed her wrists and hauled her to her feet.

She felt weak, so weak her legs wouldn't support her, and as off-balance as if her wings were frozen numb and unresponsive. She tried to break free of the giant, but then something struck her hard across the side of her head, and she saw sparks. *My eyes work fine,* she thought crazily, and then something smooth and cold touched the center of her forehead, and despite everything, she fell helplessly into sleep.

ABOUT THE AUTHOR

In addition to the Dragons of Mother Stone series, Melissa McShane is the author of many other fantasy novels, including the novels of Tremontane, the first of which is *Servant of the Crown;* the Extraordinaries series, beginning with *Burning Bright;* and *The Book of Secrets,* first book in The Last Oracle series.

She lives in the shelter of the mountains out West with her husband, three children and a niece, and three very needy cats. She wrote reviews and critical essays for many years before turning to fiction, which is much more fun than anyone ought to be allowed to have. You can visit her at her website **www.melissamc shanewrites.com** for more information on other books and upcoming releases.

For news on upcoming releases, bonus material, and other fun stuff, sign up for Melissa's newsletter **here**.

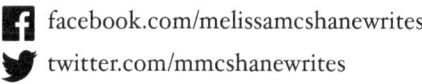

facebook.com/melissamcshanewrites

twitter.com/mmcshanewrites

ALSO BY MELISSA MCSHANE

THE DRAGONS OF MOTHER STONE
Spark the Fire

Faith in Flames

Ember in Shadow (forthcoming)

THE CROWN OF TREMONTANE
Servant of the Crown

Exile of the Crown

Rider of the Crown

Agent of the Crown

Voyager of the Crown

Tales of the Crown

THE SAGA OF WILLOW NORTH
Pretender to the Crown

Guardian of the Crown

Champion of the Crown

THE HEIRS OF WILLOW NORTH
Ally of the Crown

Stranger to the Crown

Scholar of the Crown

THE EXTRAORDINARIES
Burning Bright

Wondering Sight

Abounding Might

www.ingramcontent.com/pod-product-compliance
Lightning Source LLC
Chambersburg PA
CBHW051228260626
47162CB00002B/324